A BRIDE'S STORY

2

Kaoru Mori

TABLE OF
CONTENTS

Chapter Six
The Bread Oven

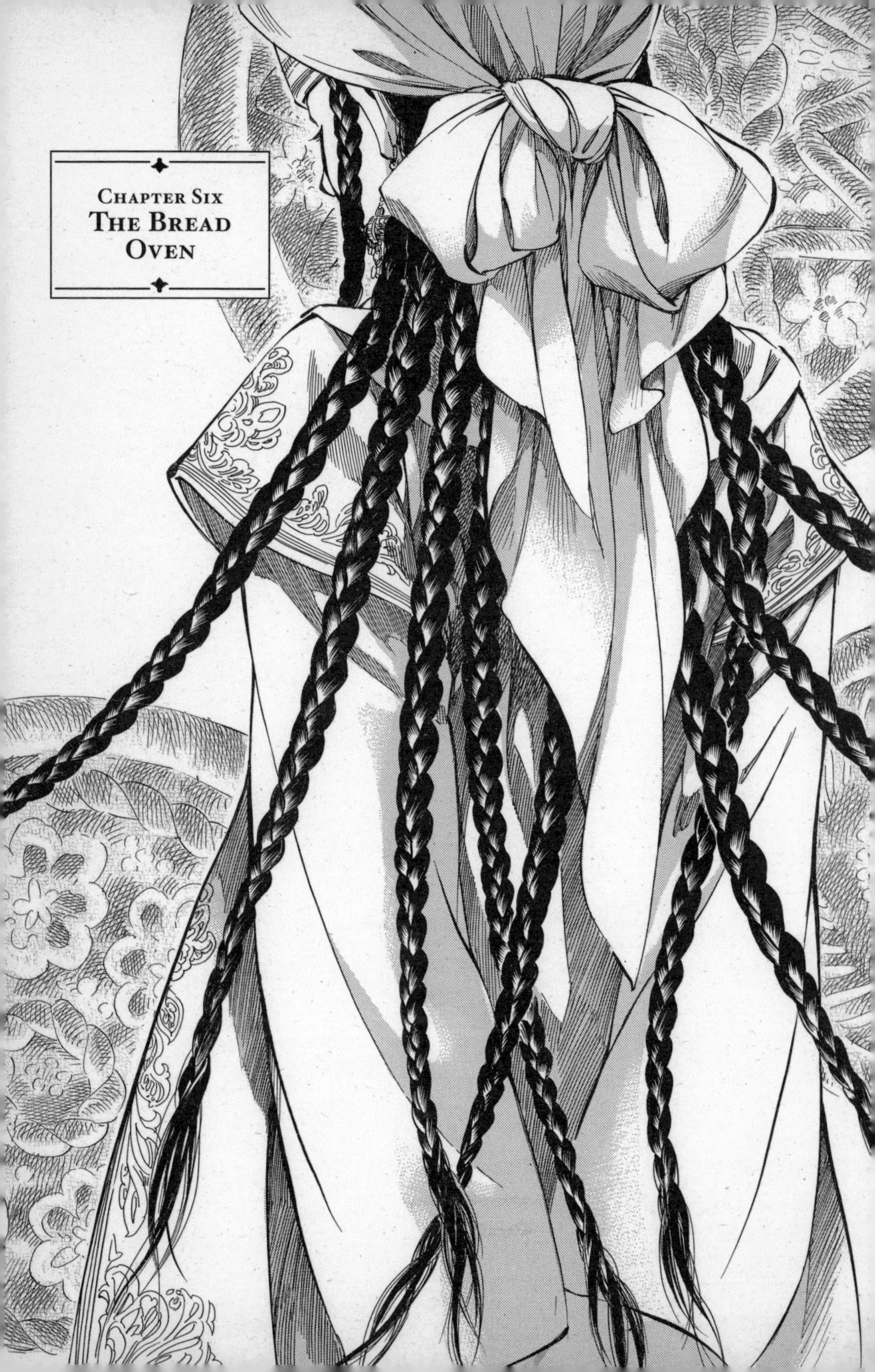

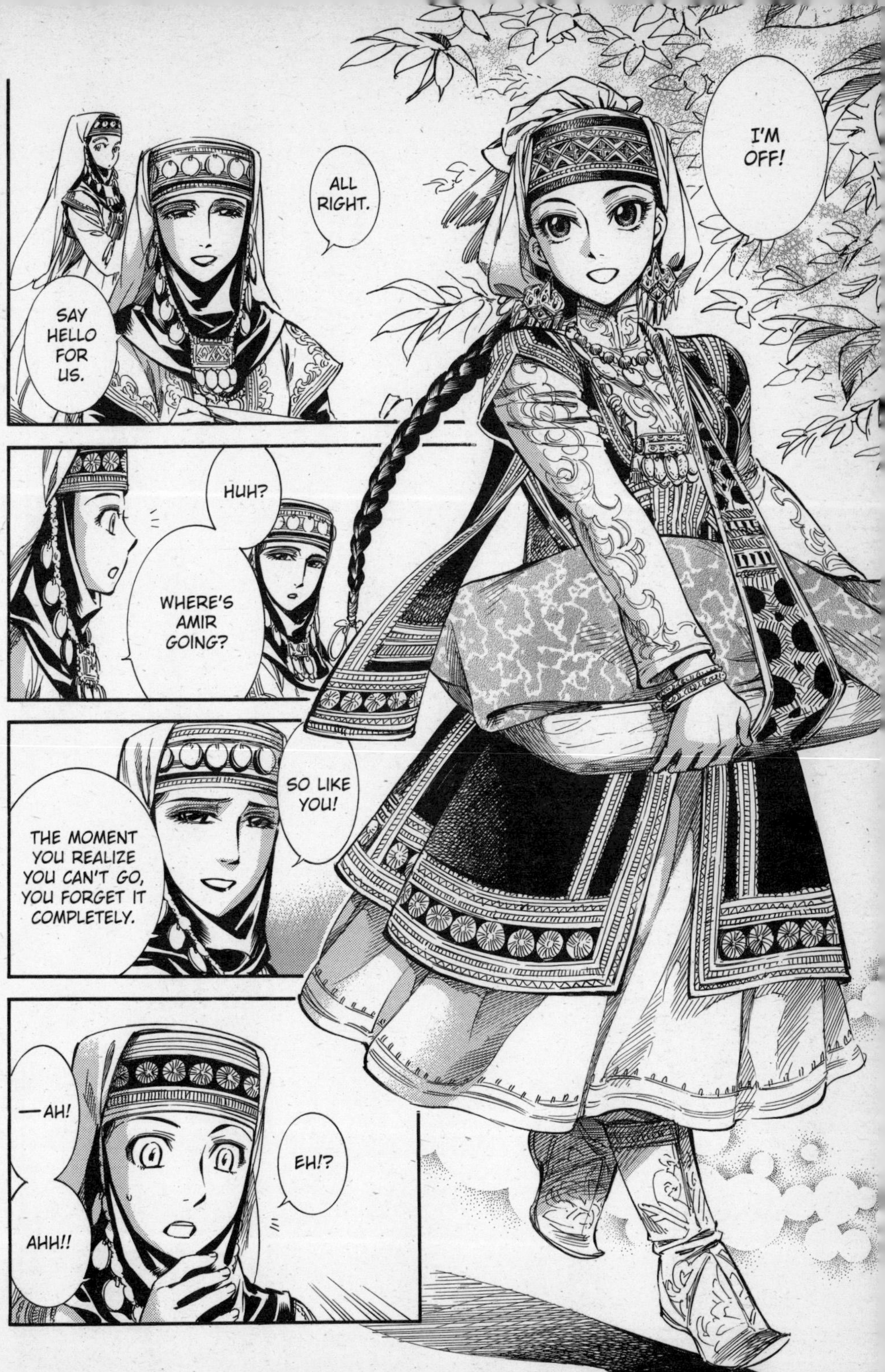
I'M OFF!
ALL RIGHT.
SAY HELLO FOR US.
HUH?
WHERE'S AMIR GOING?
SO LIKE YOU!
THE MOMENT YOU REALIZE YOU CAN'T GO, YOU FORGET IT COMPLETELY.
EH!?
—AH!
AHH!!

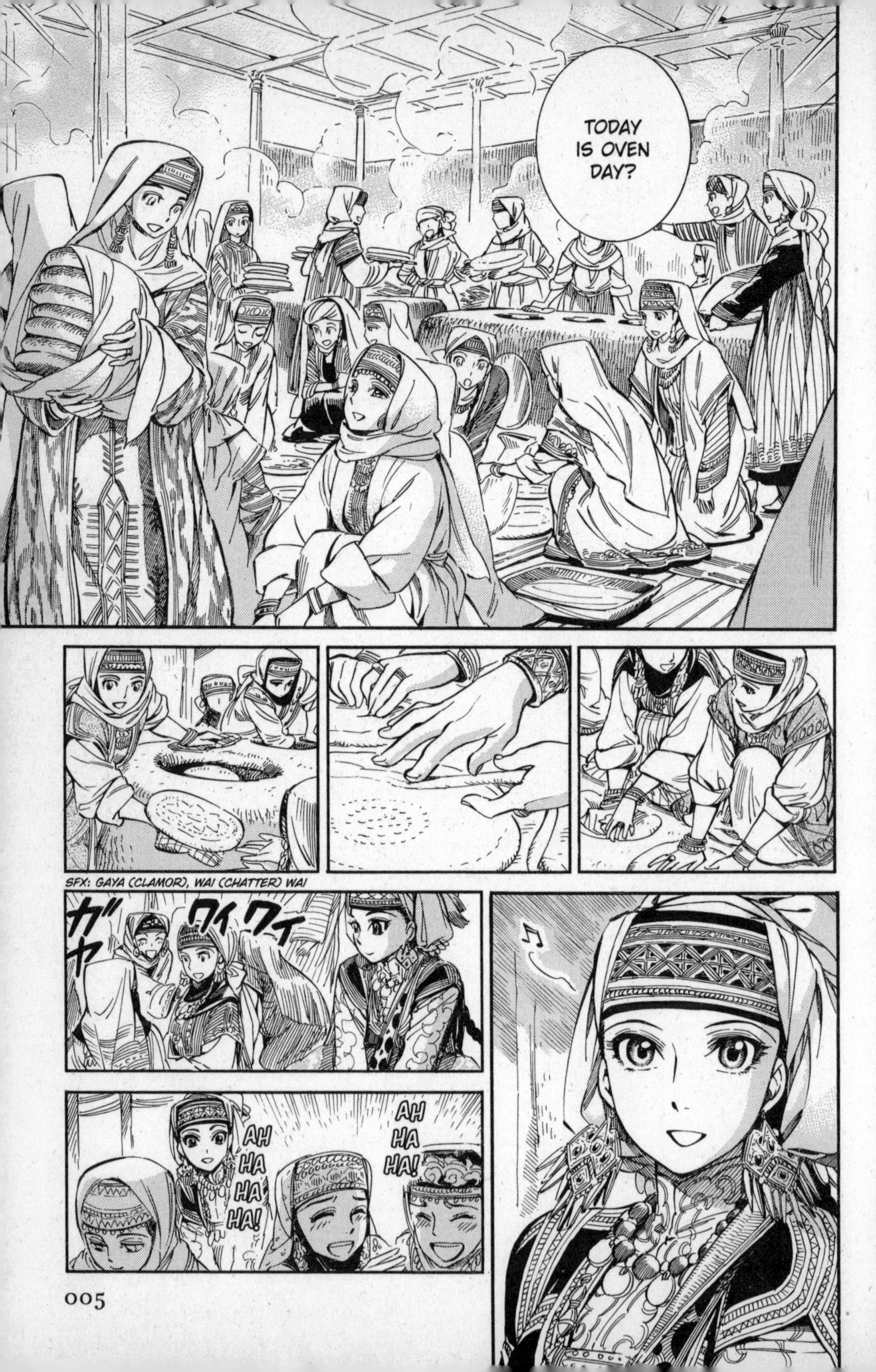
TODAY IS OVEN DAY?
SFX: GAYA (CLAMOR), WAI (CHATTER) WAI
♪
ガヤ
ワイワイ
AH HA HA!
AH HA HA HA!

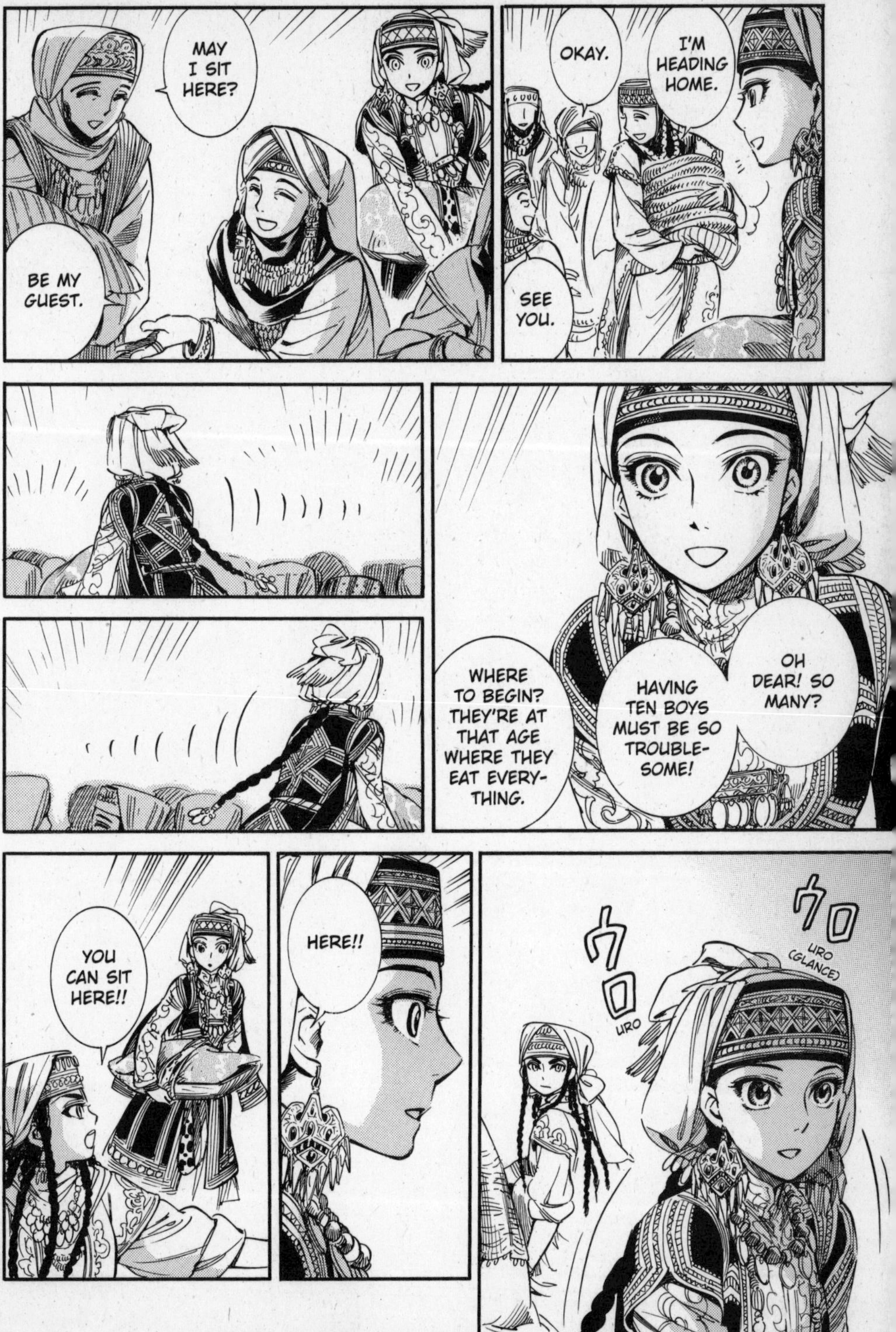
I'M HEADING HOME.
OKAY.
SEE YOU.
MAY I SIT HERE?
BE MY GUEST.
OH DEAR! SO MANY?
HAVING TEN BOYS MUST BE SO TROUBLE-SOME!
WHERE TO BEGIN? THEY'RE AT THAT AGE WHERE THEY EAT EVERY-THING.
ウロ
URO (GLANCE)
ウロ
URO
HERE!!
YOU CAN SIT HERE!!

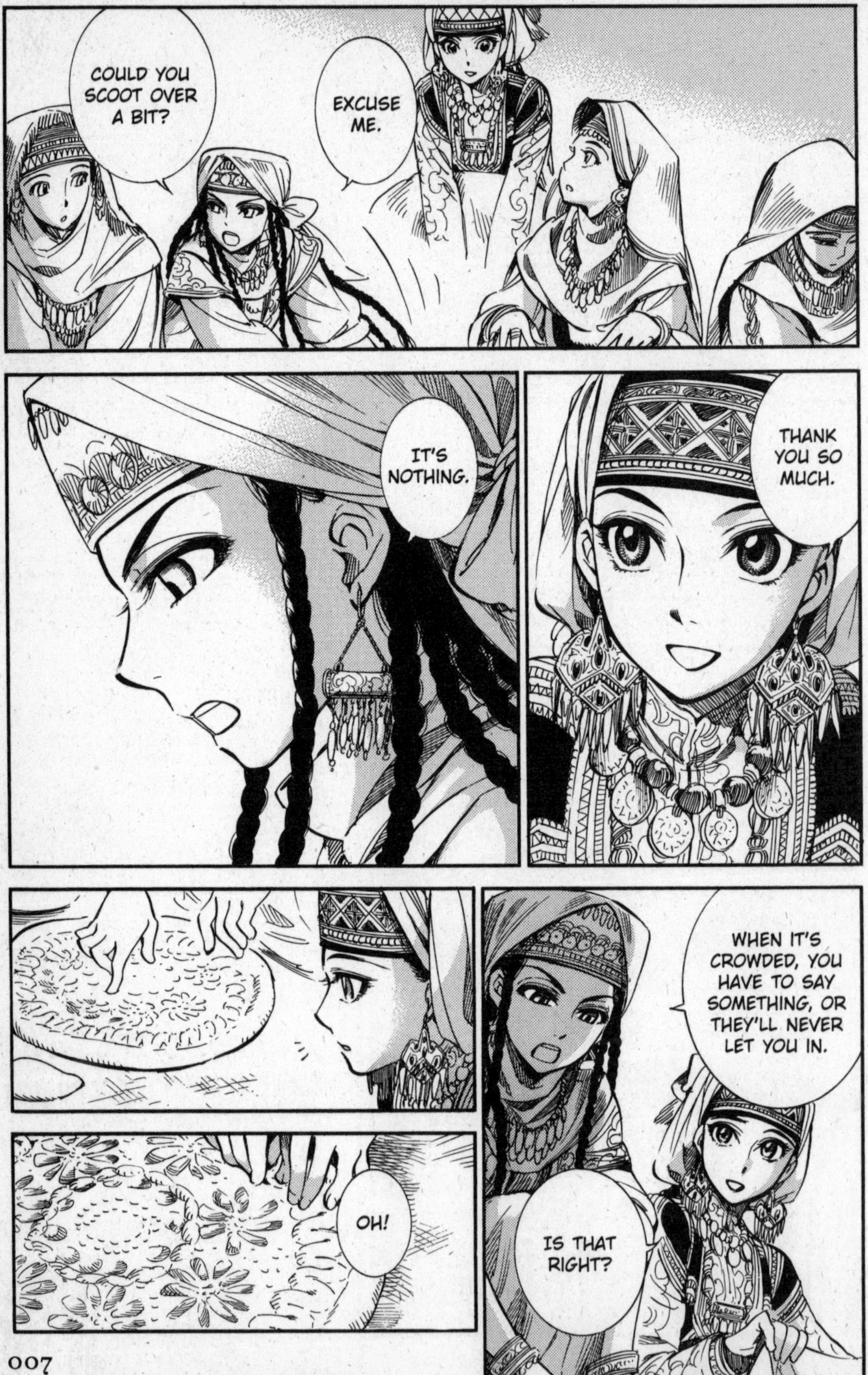
EXCUSE ME.
COULD YOU SCOOT OVER A BIT?
THANK YOU SO MUCH.
IT'S NOTHING.
WHEN IT'S CROWDED, YOU HAVE TO SAY SOMETHING, OR THEY'LL NEVER LET YOU IN.
IS THAT RIGHT?
OH!

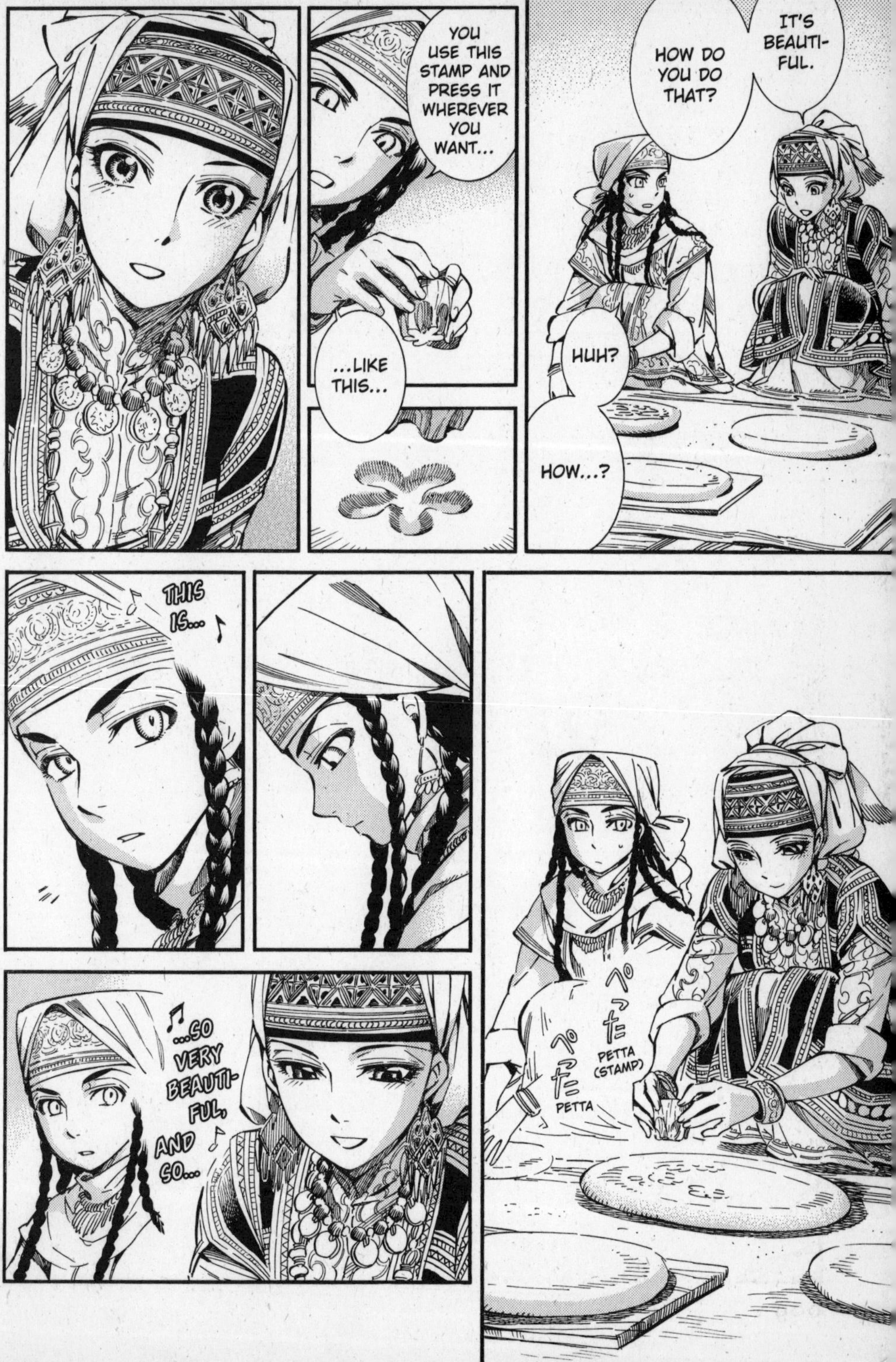
IT'S BEAUTIFUL.
HOW DO YOU DO THAT?
HUH?
HOW...?
YOU USE THIS STAMP AND PRESS IT WHEREVER YOU WANT...
...LIKE THIS...
ぺったPETTA (STAMP)
ぺったPETTA
THIS IS...
...SO VERY BEAUTIFUL, AND SO...

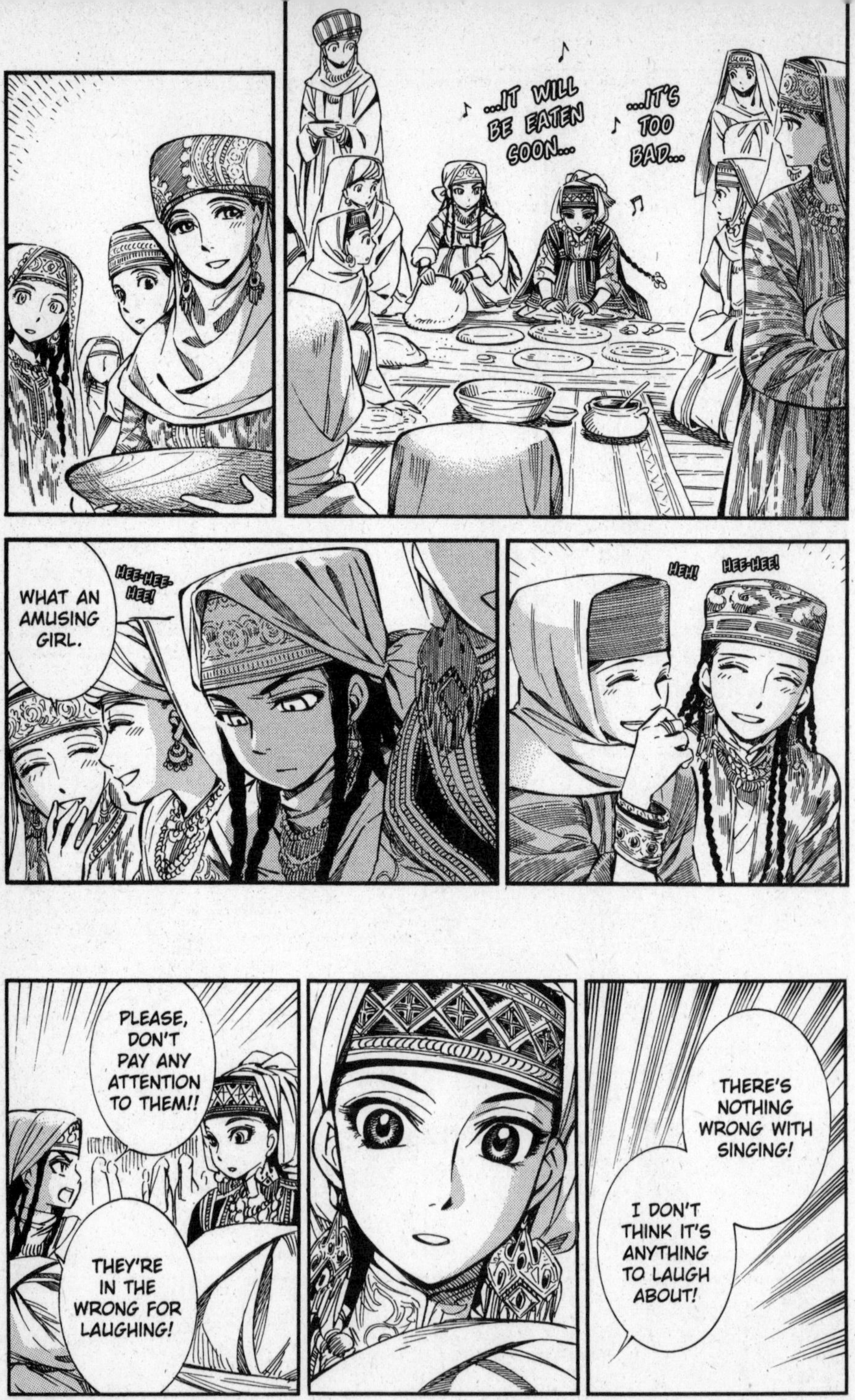
...IT'S TOO BAD...
...IT WILL BE EATEN SOON...
HEE-HEE!
HEH!
HEE-HEE-HEE!
WHAT AN AMUSING GIRL.
THERE'S NOTHING WRONG WITH SINGING!
I DON'T THINK IT'S ANYTHING TO LAUGH ABOUT!
PLEASE, DON'T PAY ANY ATTENTION TO THEM!!
THEY'RE IN THE WRONG FOR LAUGHING!

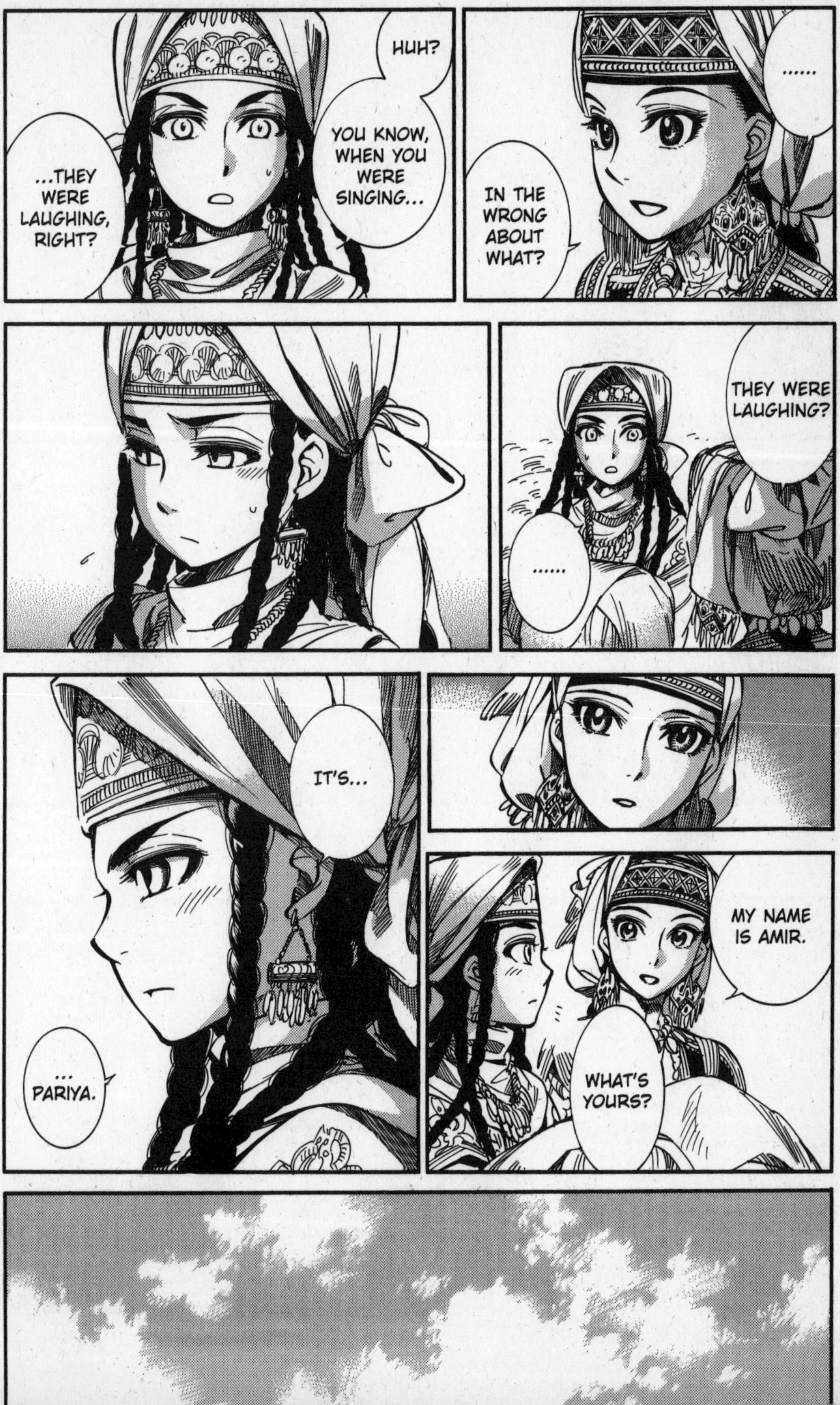
......
IN THE WRONG ABOUT WHAT?
HUH?
YOU KNOW, WHEN YOU WERE SINGING...
...THEY WERE LAUGHING, RIGHT?
THEY WERE LAUGHING?
......
MY NAME IS AMIR.
WHAT'S YOURS?
IT'S...
... PARIYA.

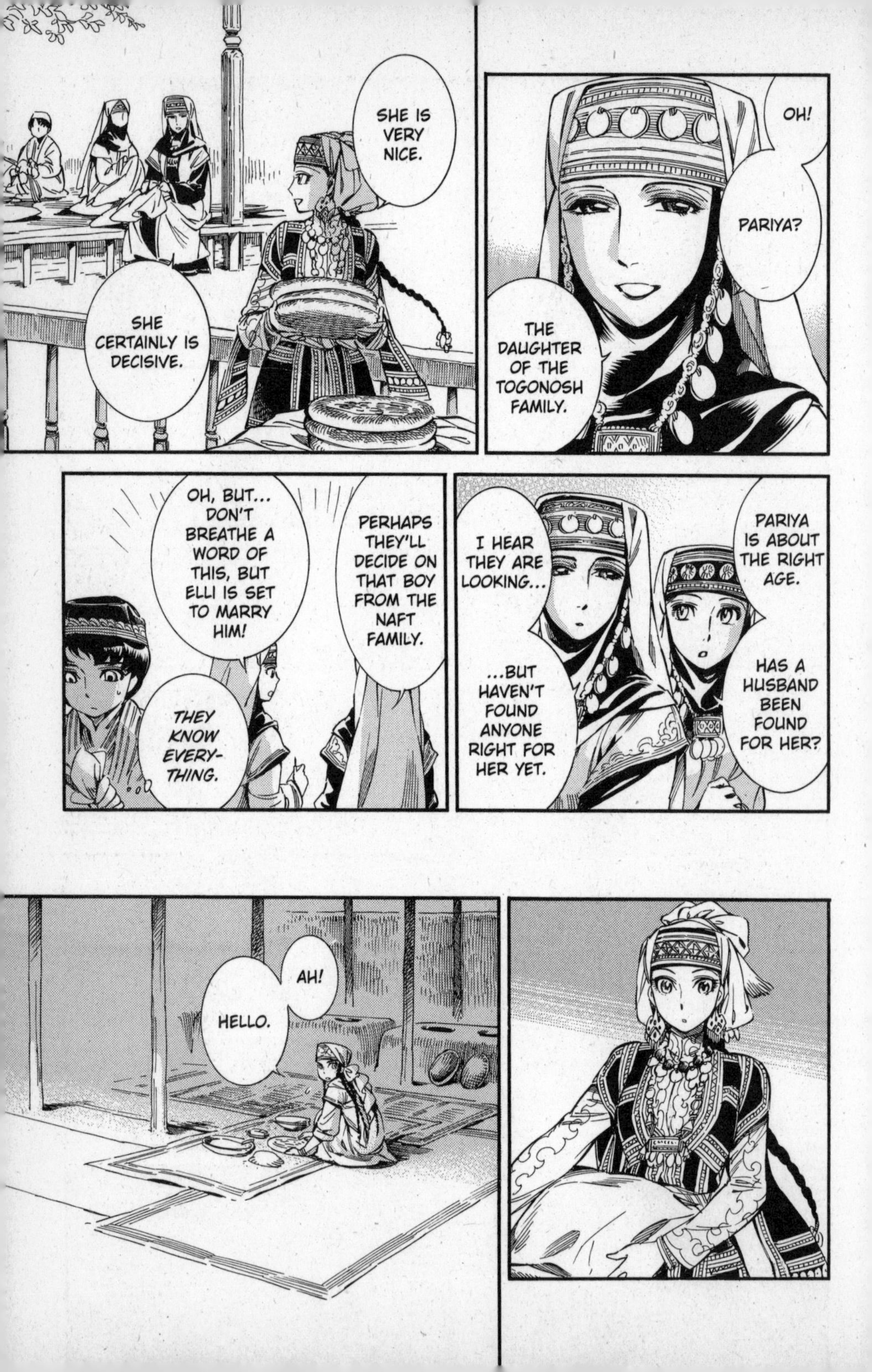
OH!
PARIYA?
THE DAUGHTER OF THE TOGONOSH FAMILY.
SHE IS VERY NICE.
SHE CERTAINLY IS DECISIVE.
PARIYA IS ABOUT THE RIGHT AGE.
HAS A HUSBAND BEEN FOUND FOR HER?
I HEAR THEY ARE LOOKING...
...BUT HAVEN'T FOUND ANYONE RIGHT FOR HER YET.
PERHAPS THEY'LL DECIDE ON THAT BOY FROM THE NAFT FAMILY.
OH, BUT... DON'T BREATHE A WORD OF THIS, BUT ELLI IS SET TO MARRY HIM!
THEY KNOW EVERY-THING.
AH!
HELLO.

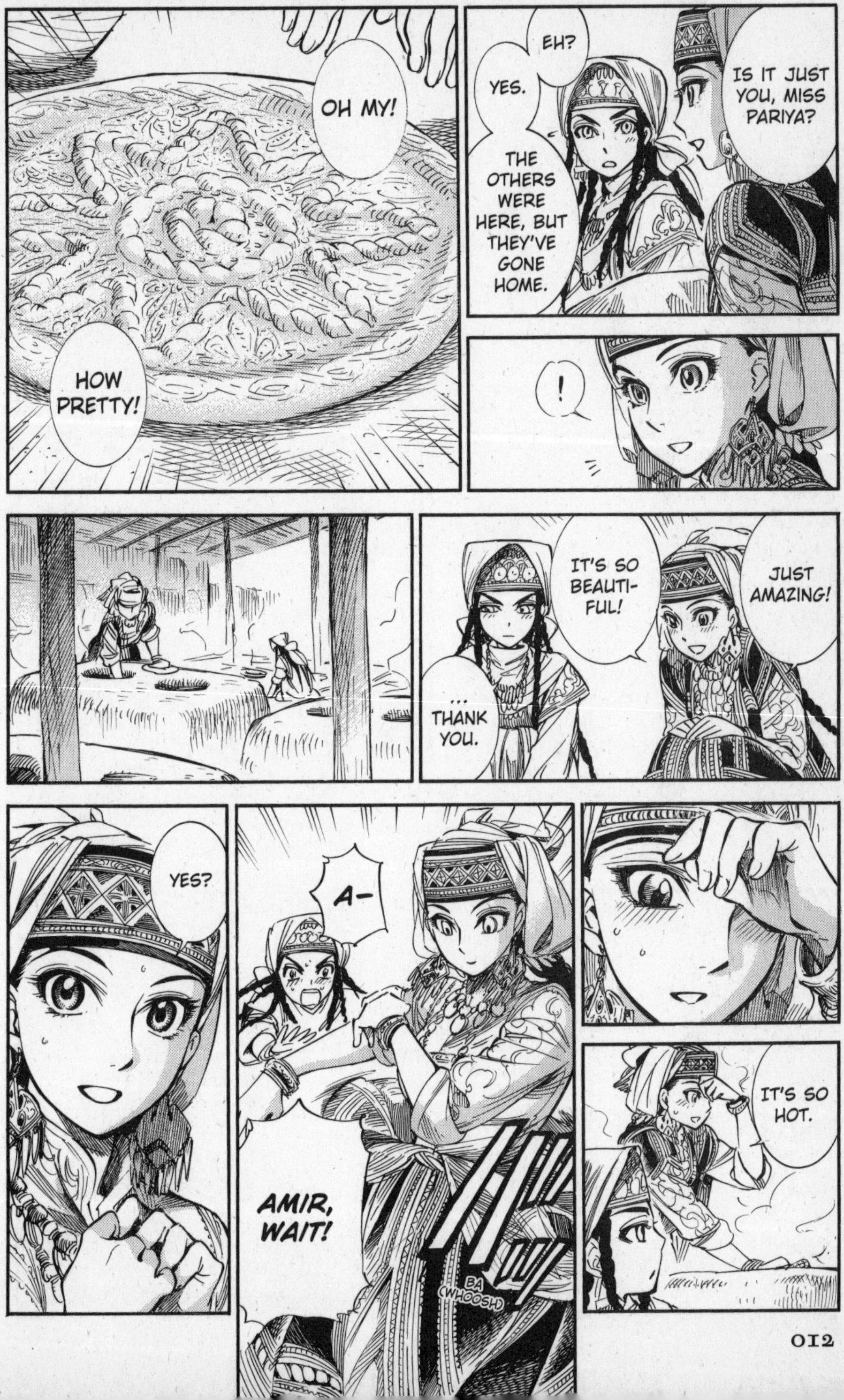
IS IT JUST YOU, MISS PARIYA?
EH?
YES.
THE OTHERS WERE HERE, BUT THEY'VE GONE HOME.
!
OH MY!
HOW PRETTY!
JUST AMAZING!
IT'S SO BEAUTIFUL!
... THANK YOU.
IT'S SO HOT.
A-
BA (WHOOSH)
AMIR, WAIT!
YES?

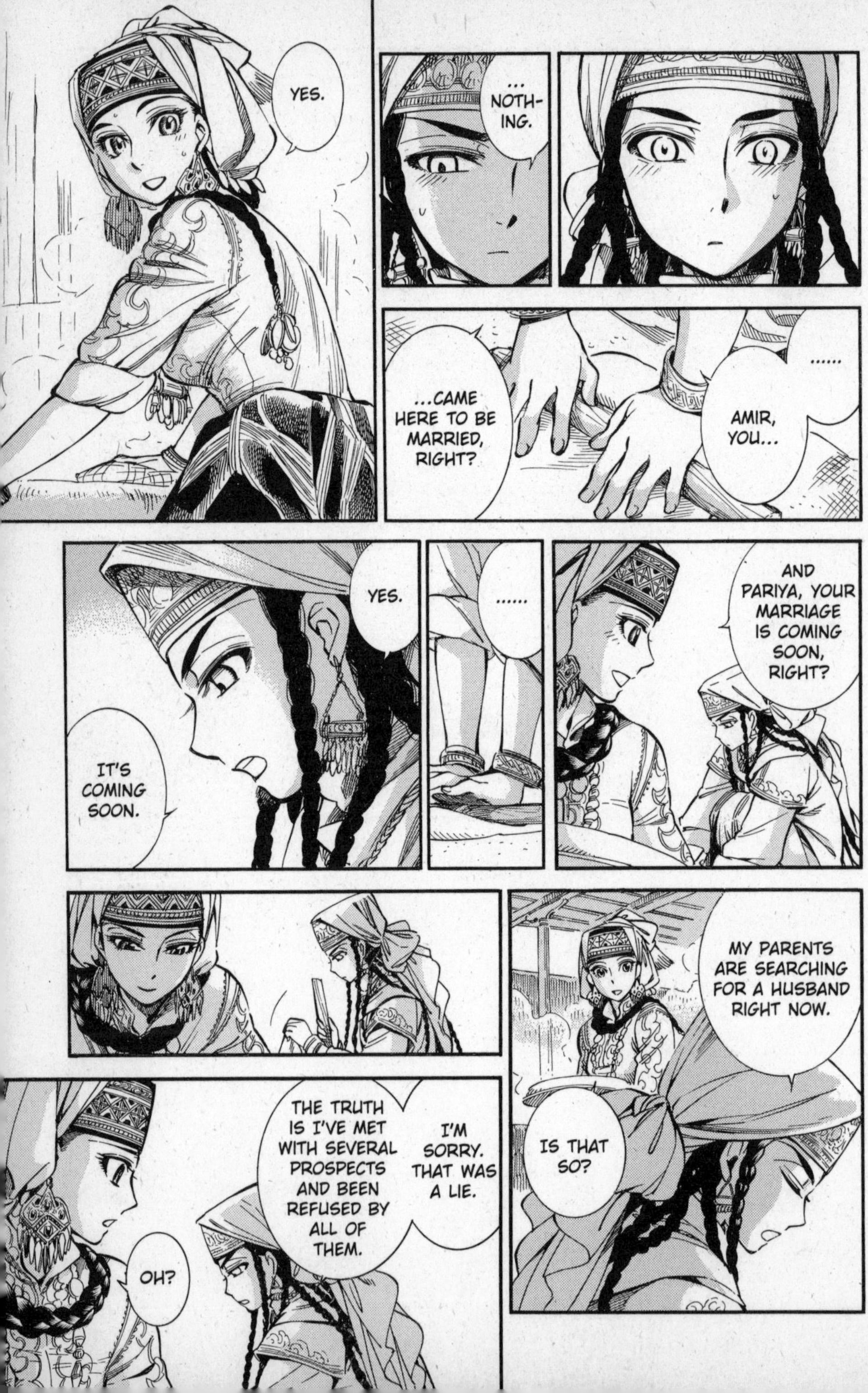

... NOTHING.
......
AMIR, YOU...
...CAME HERE TO BE MARRIED, RIGHT?
YES.
AND PARIYA, YOUR MARRIAGE IS COMING SOON, RIGHT?
......
YES.
IT'S COMING SOON.
MY PARENTS ARE SEARCHING FOR A HUSBAND RIGHT NOW.
IS THAT SO?
I'M SORRY. THAT WAS A LIE.
THE TRUTH IS I'VE MET WITH SEVERAL PROSPECTS AND BEEN REFUSED BY ALL OF THEM.
OH?

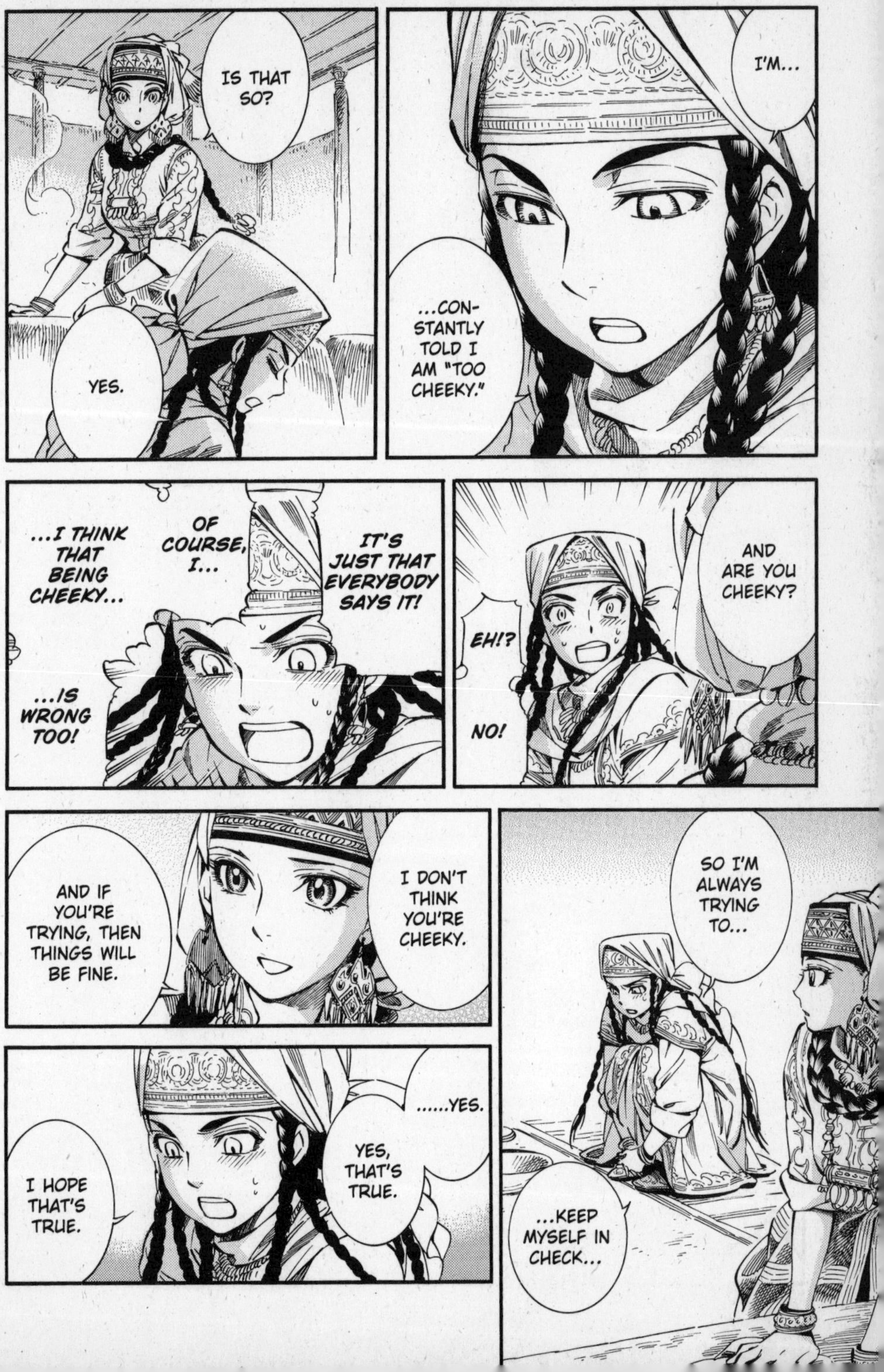
I'M...
...CON-STANTLY TOLD I AM "TOO CHEEKY."
IS THAT SO?
YES.
AND ARE YOU CHEEKY?
EH!?
NO!
IT'S JUST THAT EVERYBODY SAYS IT!
OF COURSE, I...
...I THINK THAT BEING CHEEKY...
...IS WRONG TOO!
SO I'M ALWAYS TRYING TO...
...KEEP MYSELF IN CHECK...
I DON'T THINK YOU'RE CHEEKY.
AND IF YOU'RE TRYING, THEN THINGS WILL BE FINE.
......YES.
YES, THAT'S TRUE.
I HOPE THAT'S TRUE.

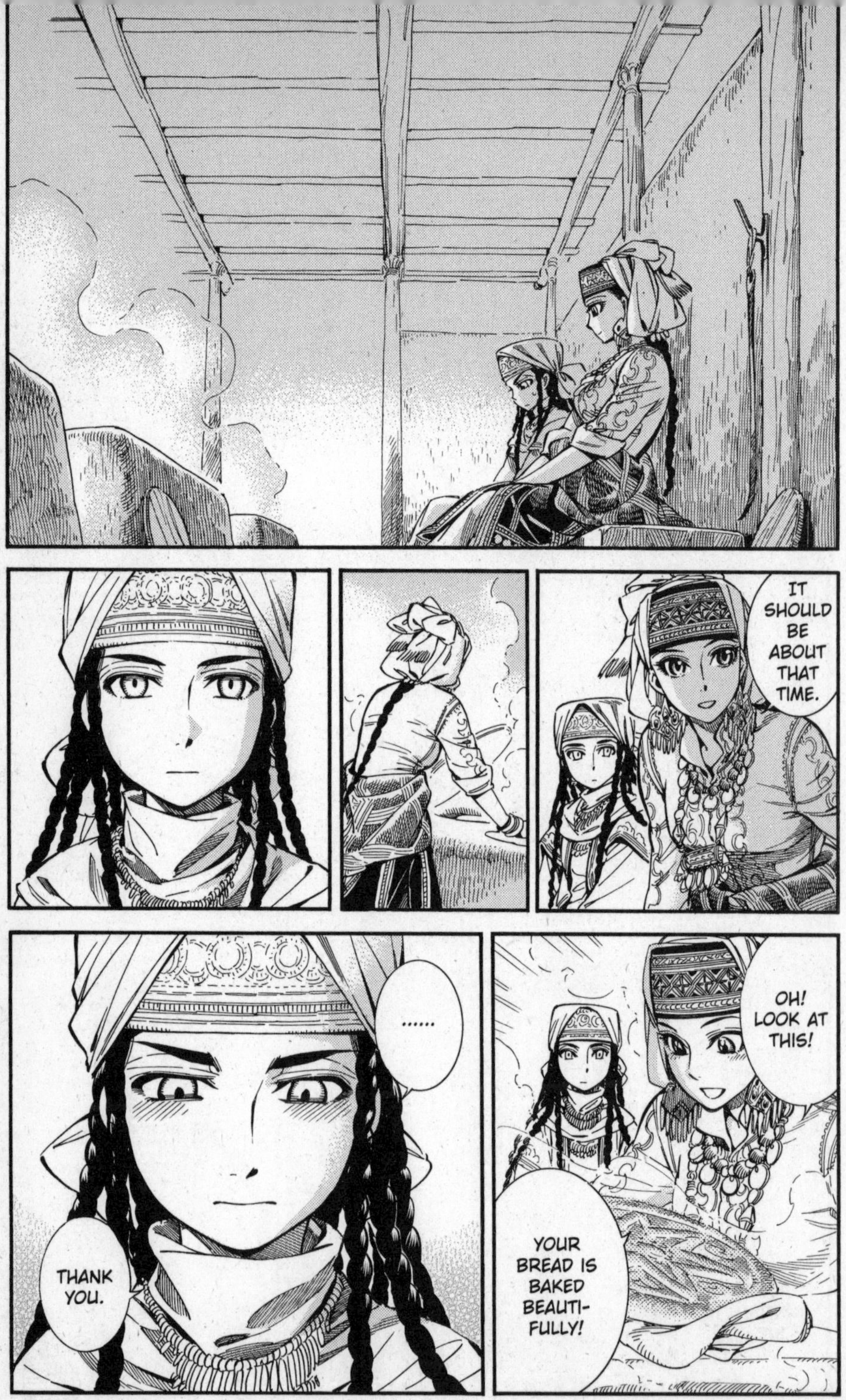
IT SHOULD BE ABOUT THAT TIME.
OH! LOOK AT THIS!
YOUR BREAD IS BAKED BEAUTI-FULLY!
......
THANK YOU.

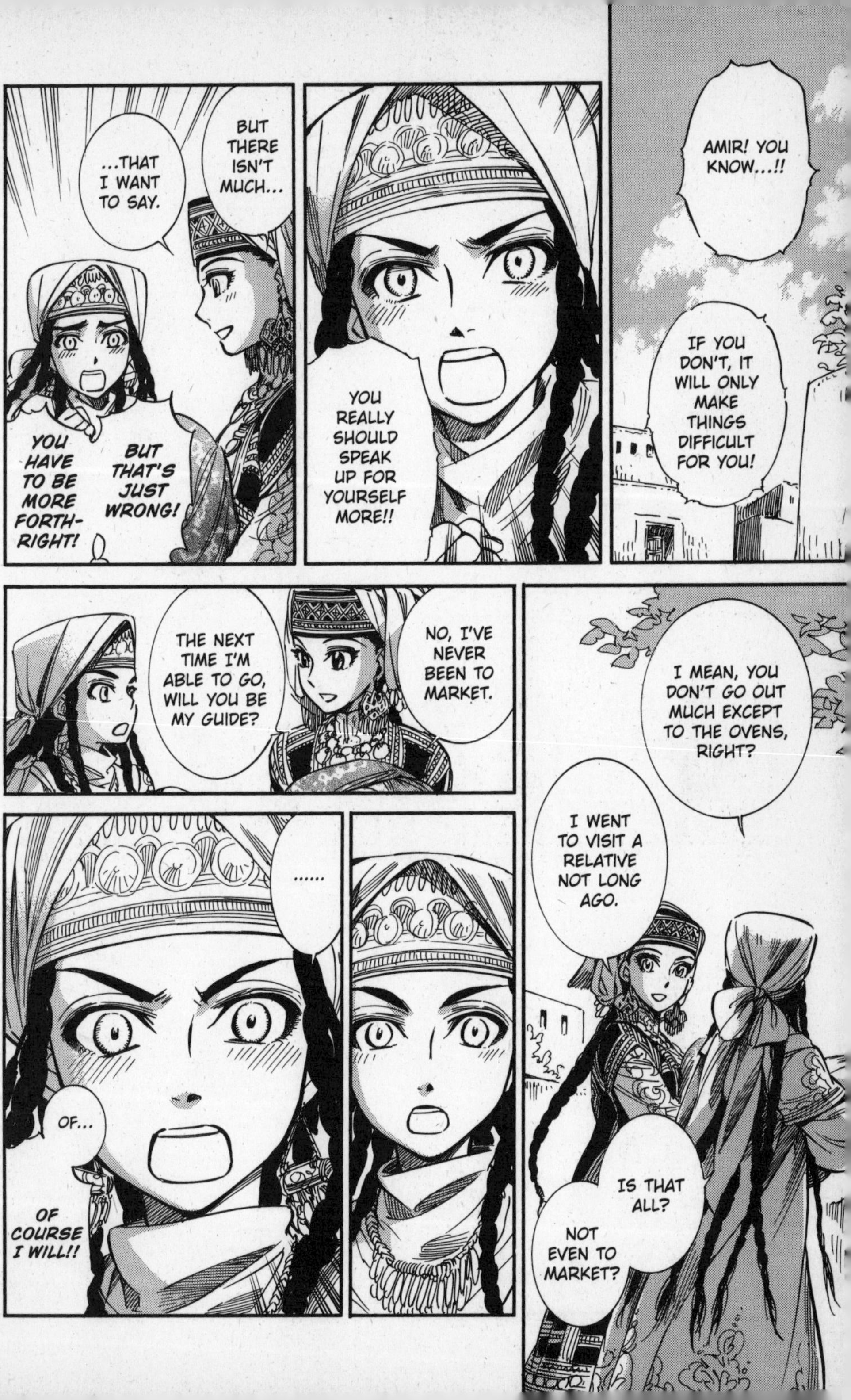
AMIR! YOU KNOW...!!
IF YOU DON'T, IT WILL ONLY MAKE THINGS DIFFICULT FOR YOU!
YOU REALLY SHOULD SPEAK UP FOR YOURSELF MORE!!
BUT THERE ISN'T MUCH...
...THAT I WANT TO SAY.
BUT THAT'S JUST WRONG!
YOU HAVE TO BE MORE FORTH-RIGHT!
I MEAN, YOU DON'T GO OUT MUCH EXCEPT TO THE OVENS, RIGHT?
I WENT TO VISIT A RELATIVE NOT LONG AGO.
IS THAT ALL?
NOT EVEN TO MARKET?
NO, I'VE NEVER BEEN TO MARKET.
THE NEXT TIME I'M ABLE TO GO, WILL YOU BE MY GUIDE?
......
OF...
OF COURSE I WILL!!

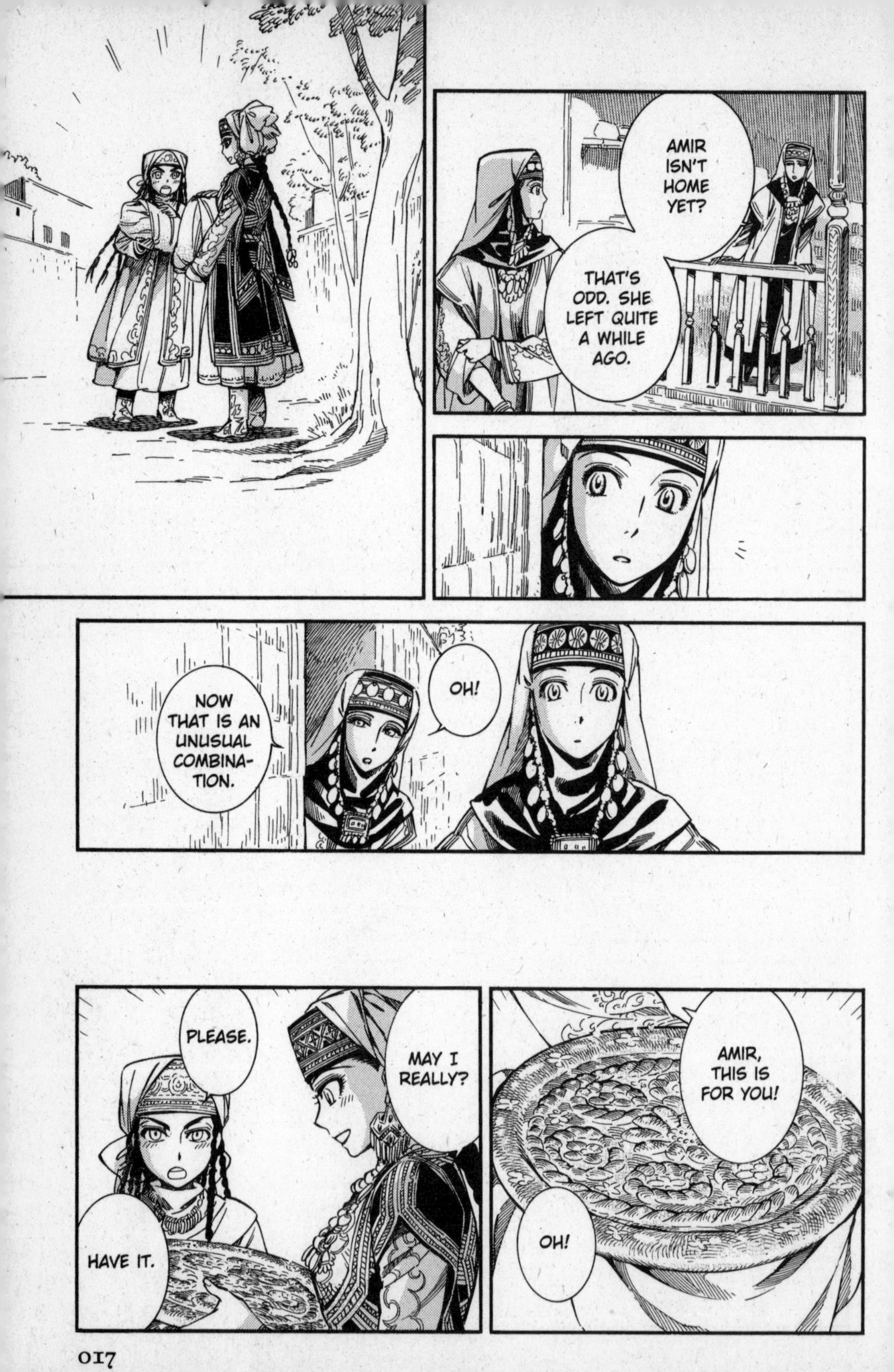
AMIR ISN'T HOME YET?
THAT'S ODD. SHE LEFT QUITE A WHILE AGO.
OH!
NOW THAT IS AN UNUSUAL COMBINA-TION.
AMIR, THIS IS FOR YOU!
OH!
MAY I REALLY?
PLEASE.
HAVE IT.

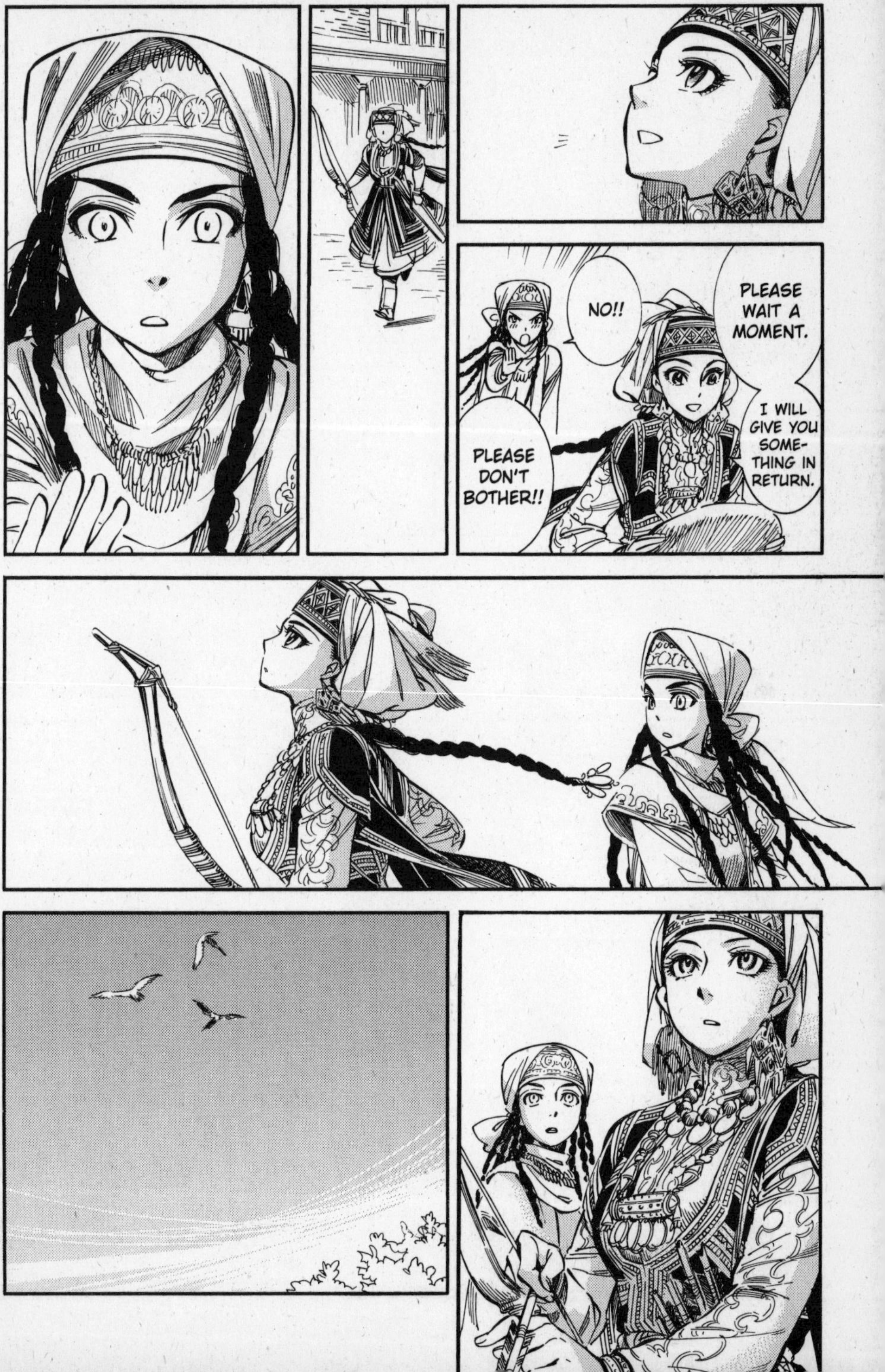
PLEASE WAIT A MOMENT.
I WILL GIVE YOU SOME-THING IN RETURN.
NO!!
PLEASE DON'T BOTHER!!

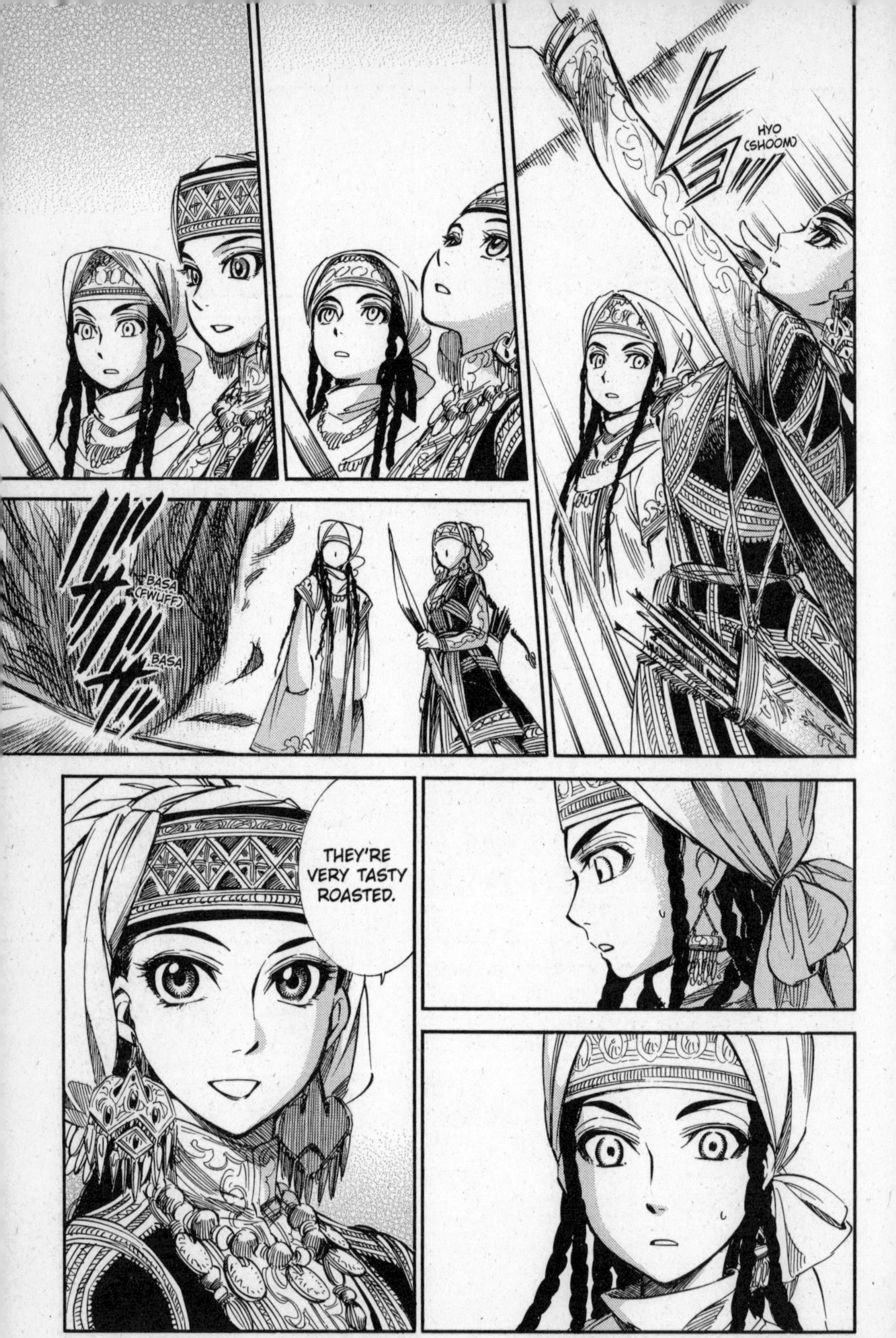
HYO (SHOOM)
BASA (FWUFF)
BASA
THEY'RE VERY TASTY ROASTED.

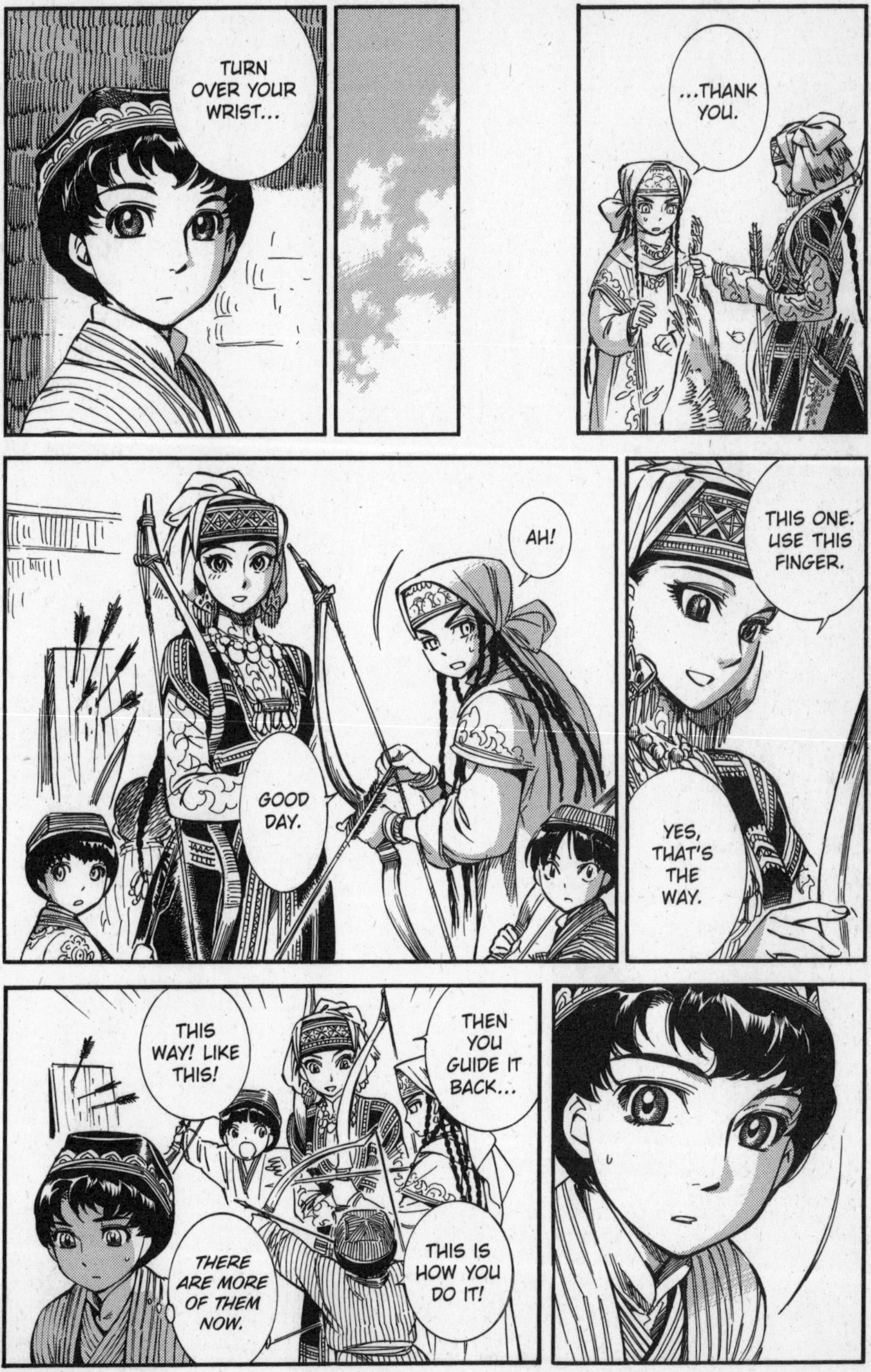
...THANK YOU.
TURN OVER YOUR WRIST...
THIS ONE. USE THIS FINGER.
YES, THAT'S THE WAY.
AH!
GOOD DAY.
THEN YOU GUIDE IT BACK...
THIS WAY! LIKE THIS!
THIS IS HOW YOU DO IT!
THERE ARE MORE OF THEM NOW.

✦ CHAPTER SIX END ✦

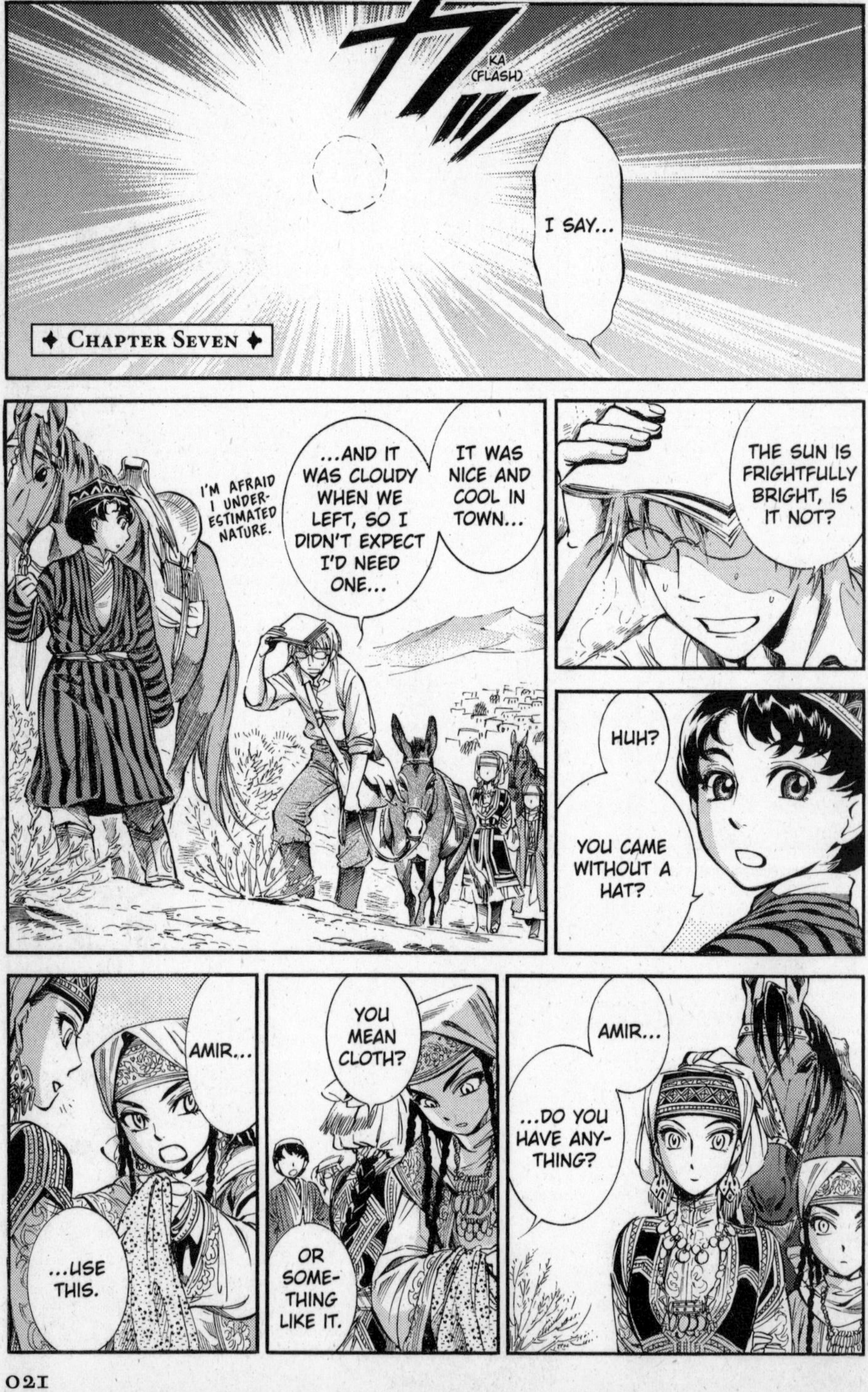
KA (FLASH)
I SAY...
CHAPTER SEVEN
THE SUN IS FRIGHTFULLY BRIGHT, IS IT NOT?
HUH?
YOU CAME WITHOUT A HAT?
IT WAS NICE AND COOL IN TOWN...
...AND IT WAS CLOUDY WHEN WE LEFT, SO I DIDN'T EXPECT I'D NEED ONE...
I'M AFRAID I UNDER-ESTIMATED NATURE.
AMIR...
...DO YOU HAVE ANYTHING?
YOU MEAN CLOTH?
OR SOME-THING LIKE IT.
AMIR...
...USE THIS.

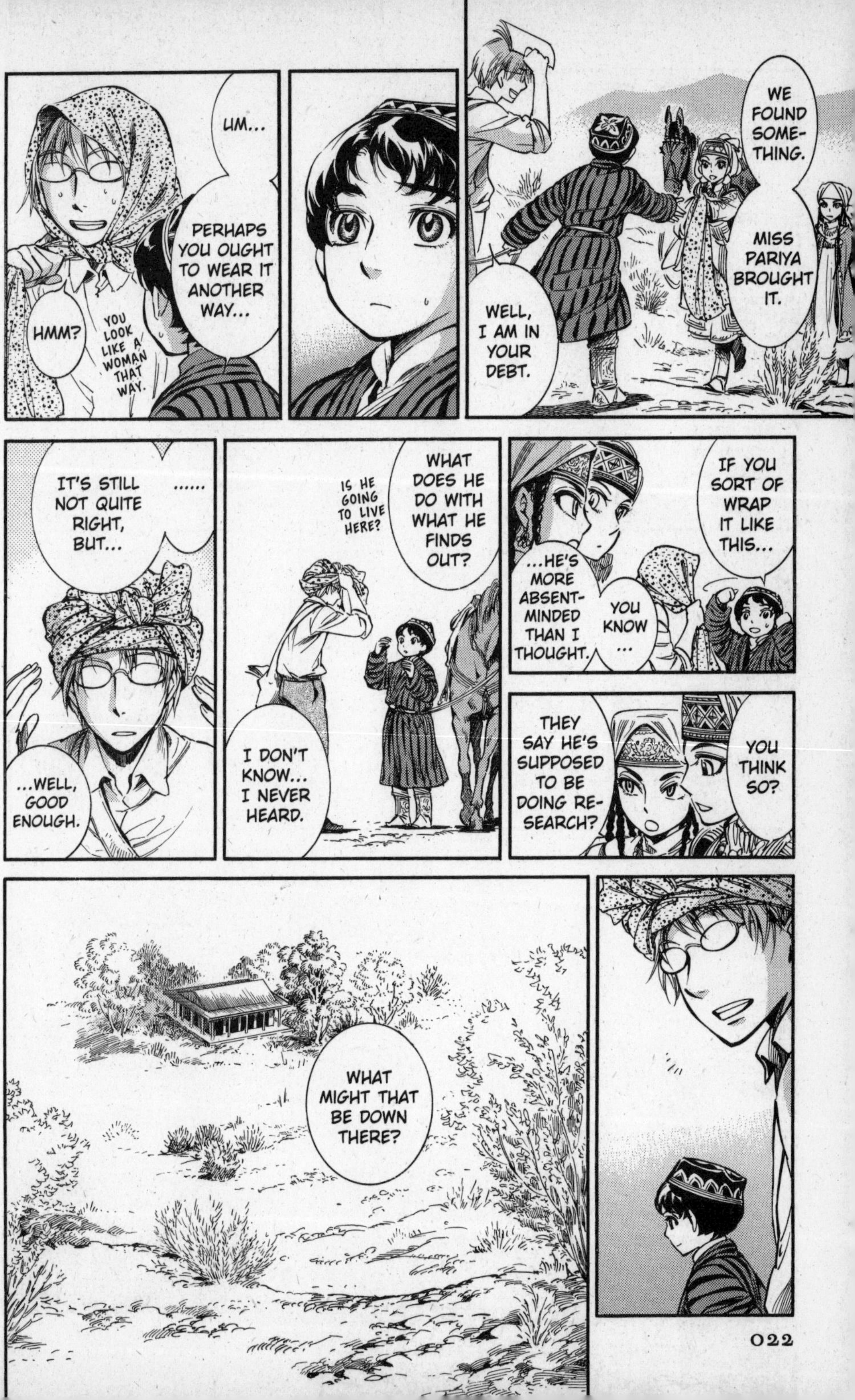
WE FOUND SOME-THING.
MISS PARIYA BROUGHT IT.
WELL, I AM IN YOUR DEBT.
UM...
PERHAPS YOU OUGHT TO WEAR IT ANOTHER WAY...
YOU LOOK LIKE A WOMAN THAT WAY.
HMM?
IF YOU SORT OF WRAP IT LIKE THIS...
YOU KNOW...
...HE'S MORE ABSENT-MINDED THAN I THOUGHT.
YOU THINK SO?
THEY SAY HE'S SUPPOSED TO BE DOING RE-SEARCH?
WHAT DOES HE DO WITH WHAT HE FINDS OUT?
IS HE GOING TO LIVE HERE?
I DON'T KNOW... I NEVER HEARD.
......
IT'S STILL NOT QUITE RIGHT, BUT...
...WELL, GOOD ENOUGH.
WHAT MIGHT THAT BE DOWN THERE?

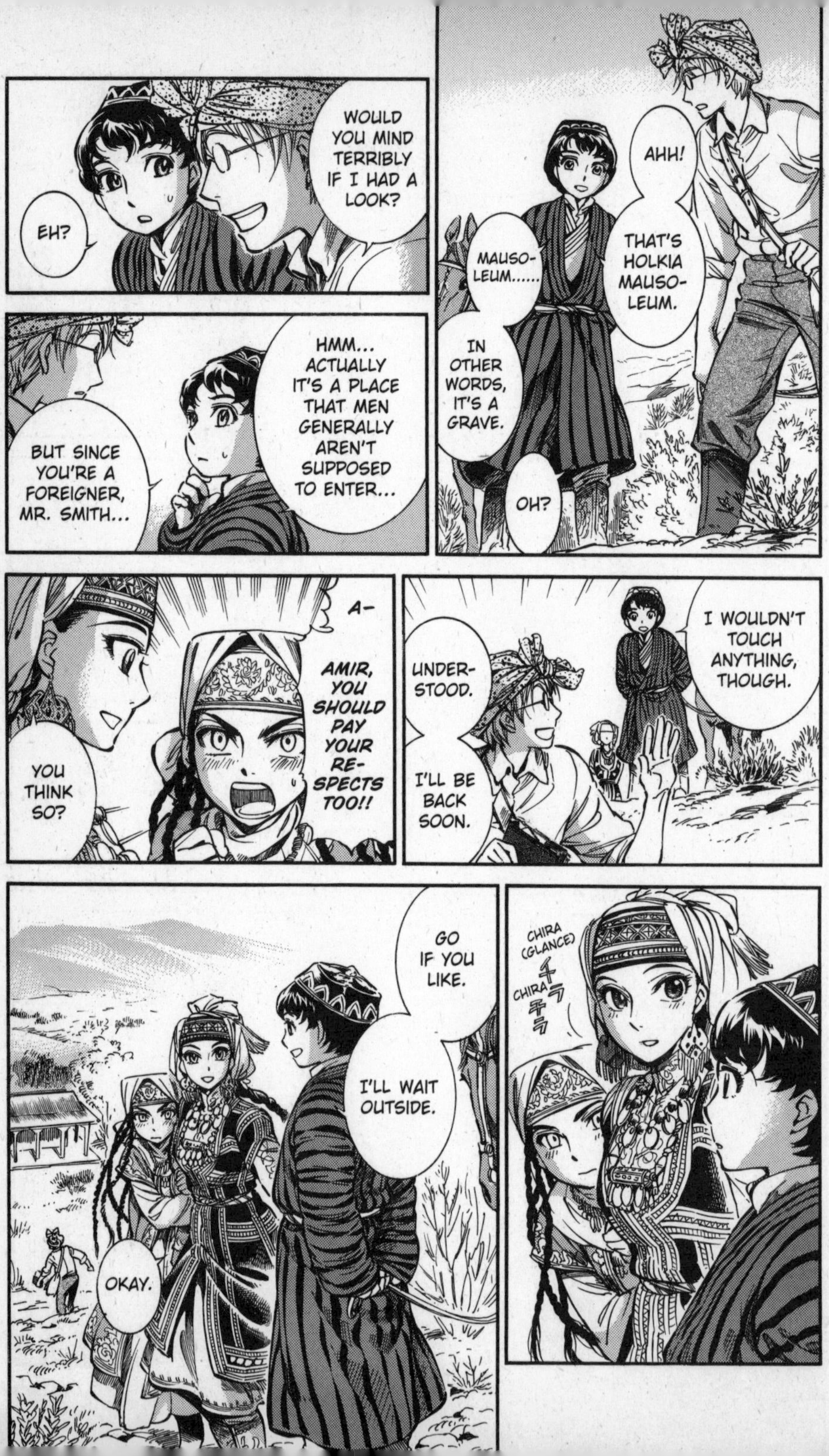
AHH!
THAT'S HOLKIA MAUSO-LEUM.
MAUSO-LEUM......
IN OTHER WORDS, IT'S A GRAVE.
OH?
WOULD YOU MIND TERRIBLY IF I HAD A LOOK?
EH?
HMM... ACTUALLY IT'S A PLACE THAT MEN GENERALLY AREN'T SUPPOSED TO ENTER...
BUT SINCE YOU'RE A FOREIGNER, MR. SMITH...
I WOULDN'T TOUCH ANYTHING, THOUGH.
UNDER-STOOD.
I'LL BE BACK SOON.
A-
AMIR, YOU SHOULD PAY YOUR RE-SPECTS TOO!!
YOU THINK SO?
CHIRA (GLANCE)
CHIRA
GO IF YOU LIKE.
I'LL WAIT OUTSIDE.
OKAY.

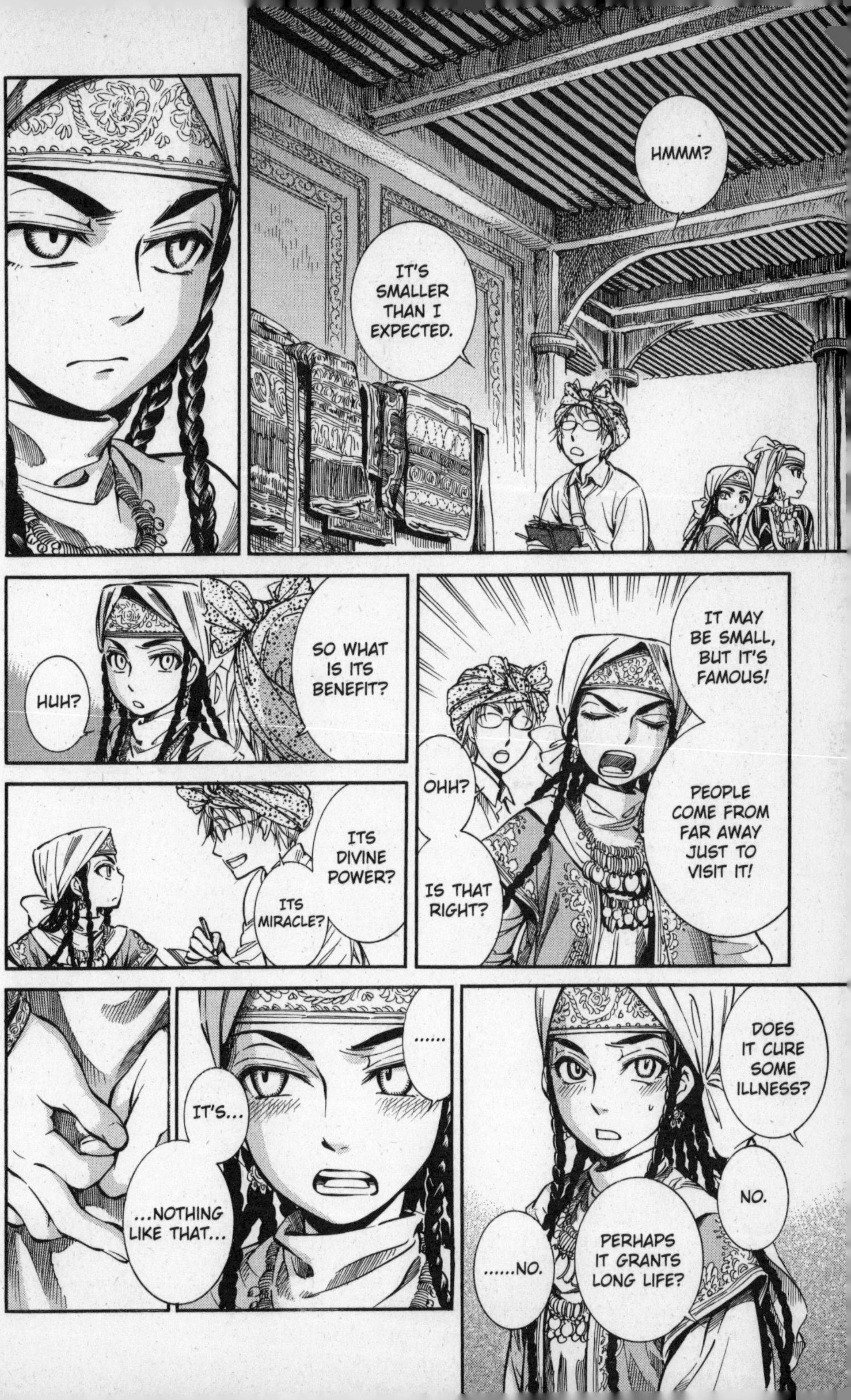
HMMM?
IT'S SMALLER THAN I EXPECTED.
IT MAY BE SMALL, BUT IT'S FAMOUS!
OHH?
PEOPLE COME FROM FAR AWAY JUST TO VISIT IT!
IS THAT RIGHT?
SO WHAT IS ITS BENEFIT?
HUH?
ITS DIVINE POWER?
ITS MIRACLE?
DOES IT CURE SOME ILLNESS?
NO.
PERHAPS IT GRANTS LONG LIFE?
......NO.
......
IT'S...
...NOTHING LIKE THAT...

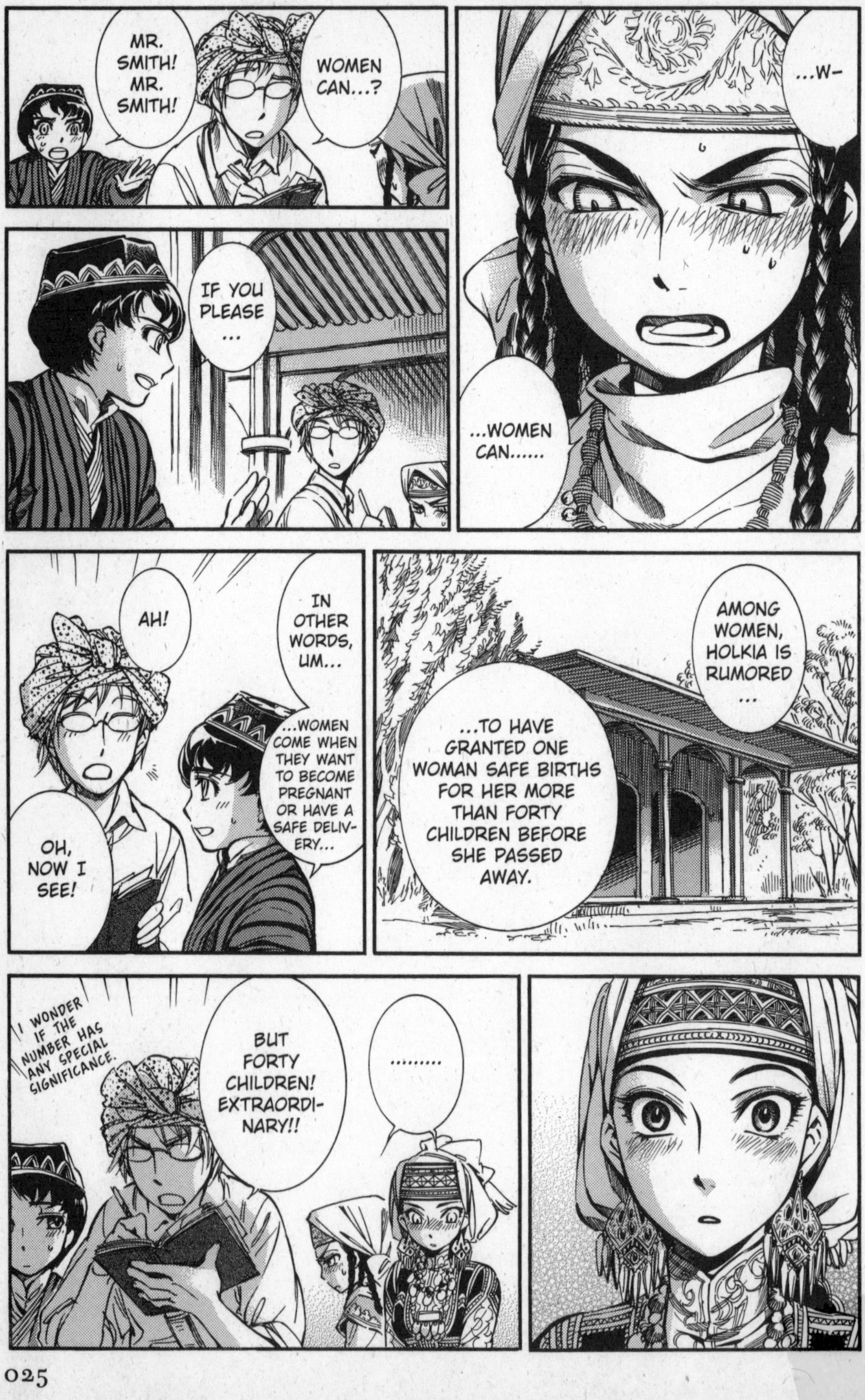
...W-
...WOMEN CAN......
WOMEN CAN...?
MR. SMITH! MR. SMITH!
IF YOU PLEASE ...
AMONG WOMEN, HOLKIA IS RUMORED ...
...TO HAVE GRANTED ONE WOMAN SAFE BIRTHS FOR HER MORE THAN FORTY CHILDREN BEFORE SHE PASSED AWAY.
IN OTHER WORDS, UM...
AH!
...WOMEN COME WHEN THEY WANT TO BECOME PREGNANT OR HAVE A SAFE DELIVERY...
OH, NOW I SEE!
....
BUT FORTY CHILDREN! EXTRAORDINARY!!
I WONDER IF THE NUMBER HAS ANY SPECIAL SIGNIFICANCE.

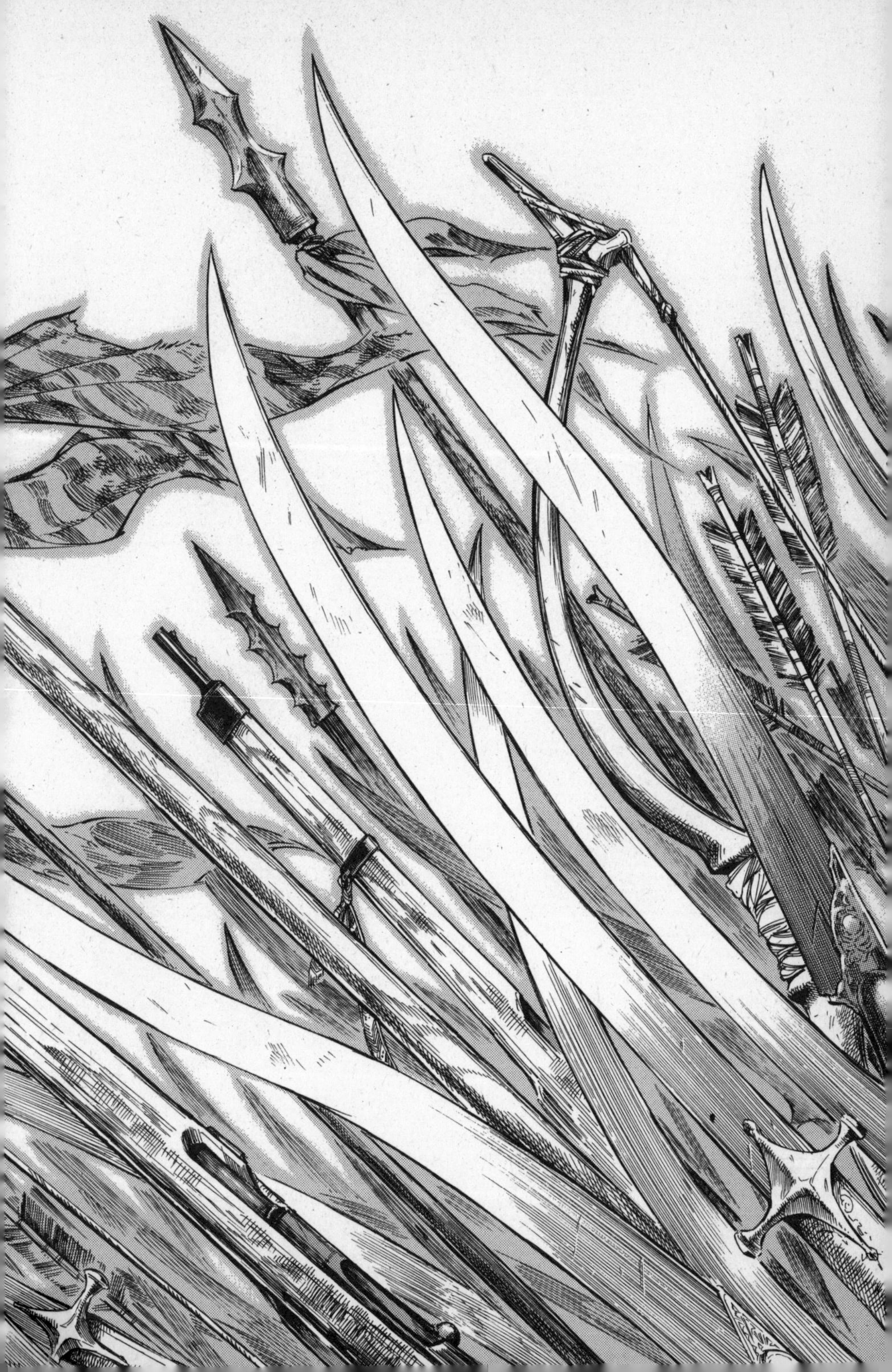

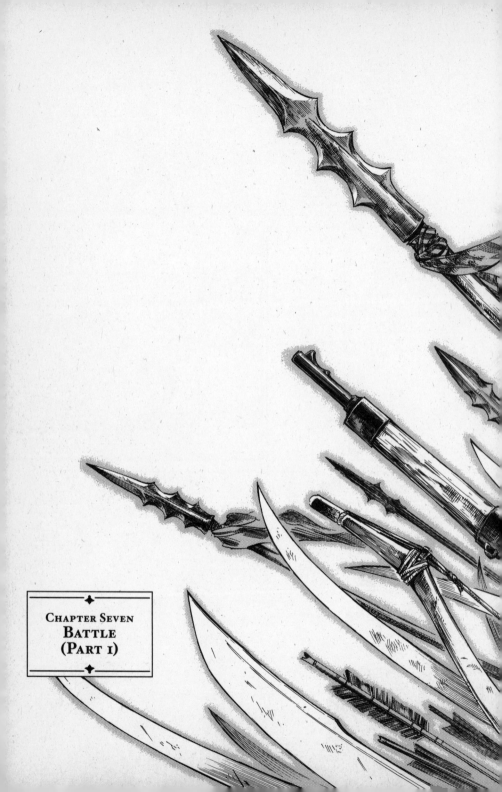

CHAPTER SEVEN
BATTLE
(PART 1)

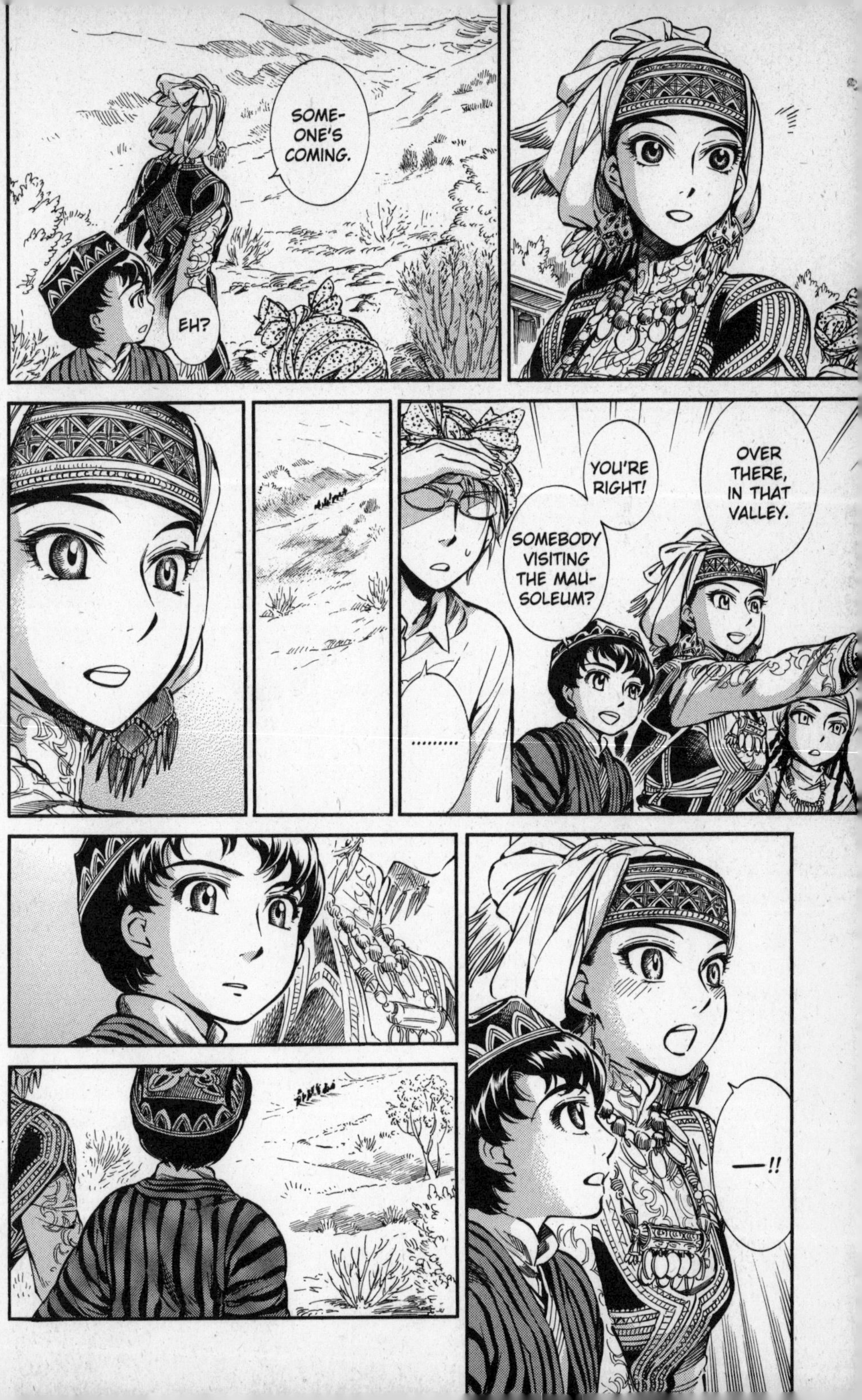
SOME-ONE'S COMING.
EH?
OVER THERE, IN THAT VALLEY.
YOU'RE RIGHT!
SOMEBODY VISITING THE MAU-SOLEUM?
....
—!!

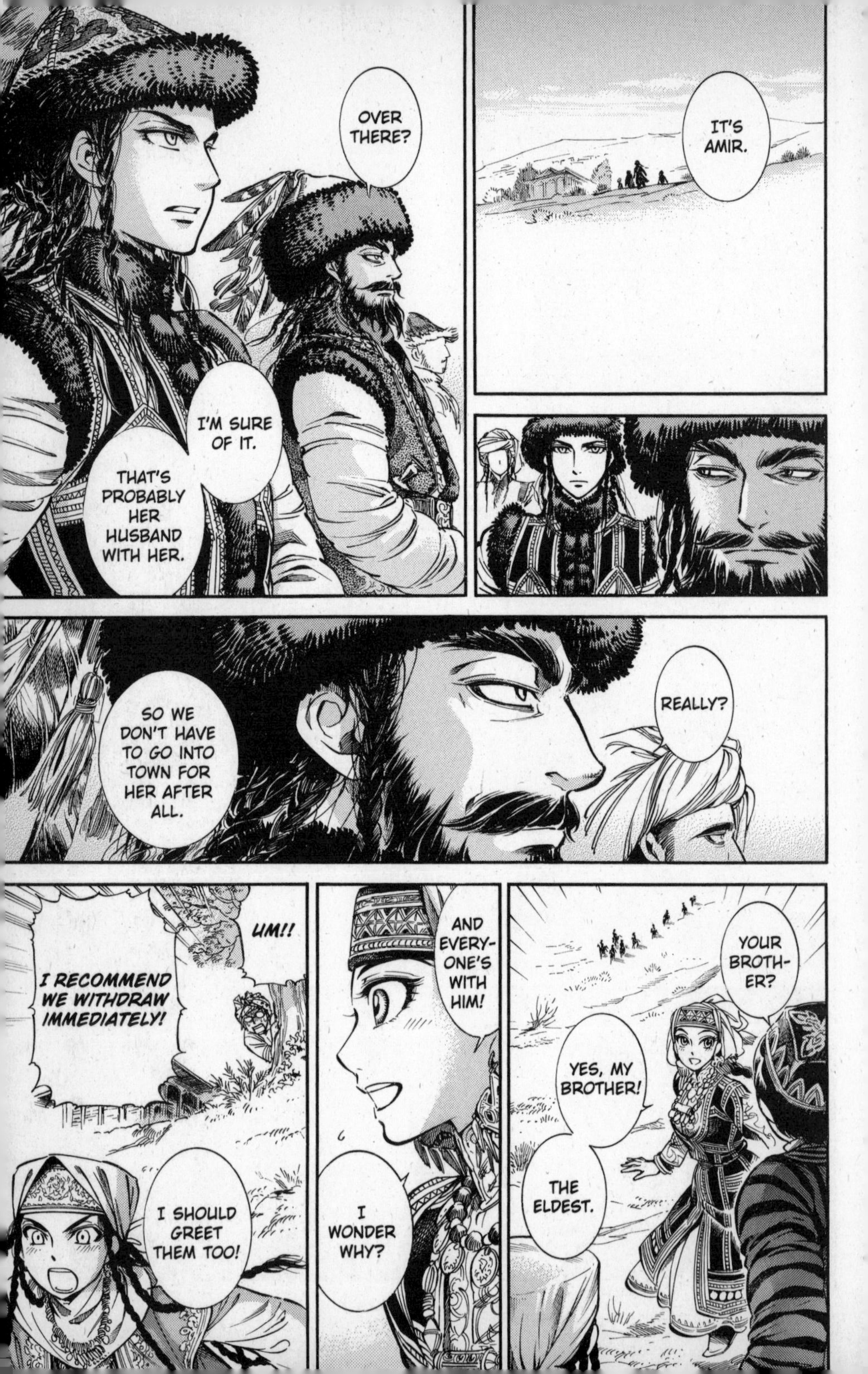
IT'S AMIR.
OVER THERE?
I'M SURE OF IT.
THAT'S PROBABLY HER HUSBAND WITH HER.
REALLY?
SO WE DON'T HAVE TO GO INTO TOWN FOR HER AFTER ALL.
YOUR BROTH-ER?
YES, MY BROTHER!
THE ELDEST.
AND EVERY-ONE'S WITH HIM!
I WONDER WHY?
UM!!
I RECOMMEND WE WITHDRAW IMMEDIATELY!
I SHOULD GREET THEM TOO!

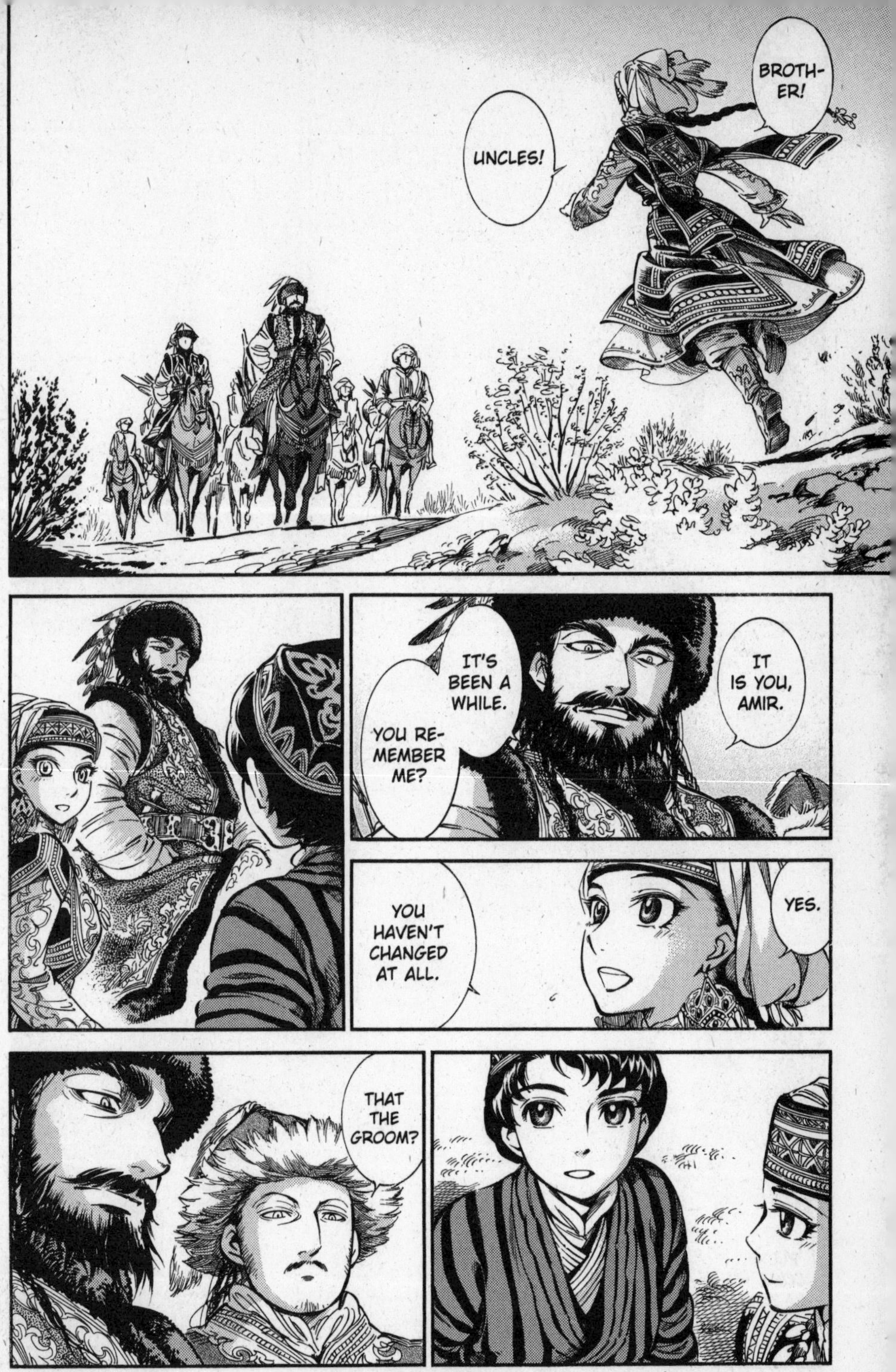
BROTH-ER!
UNCLES!
IT IS YOU, AMIR.
IT'S BEEN A WHILE.
YOU RE-MEMBER ME?
YES.
YOU HAVEN'T CHANGED AT ALL.
THAT THE GROOM?

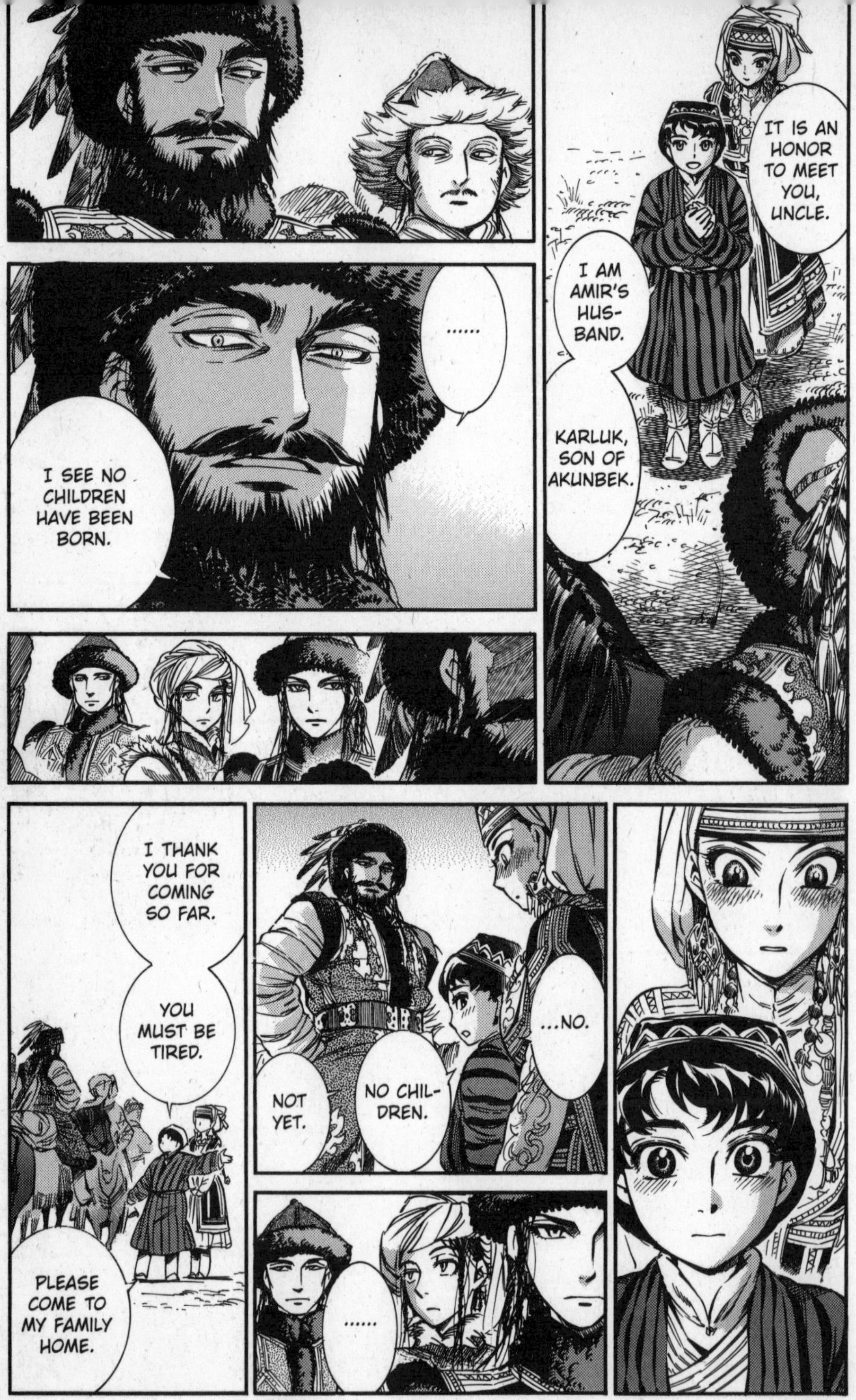
IT IS AN HONOR TO MEET YOU, UNCLE.
I AM AMIR'S HUS-BAND.
KARLUK, SON OF AKUNBEK.
......
I SEE NO CHILDREN HAVE BEEN BORN.
...NO.
NO CHIL-DREN.
NOT YET.
......
I THANK YOU FOR COMING SO FAR.
YOU MUST BE TIRED.
PLEASE COME TO MY FAMILY HOME.

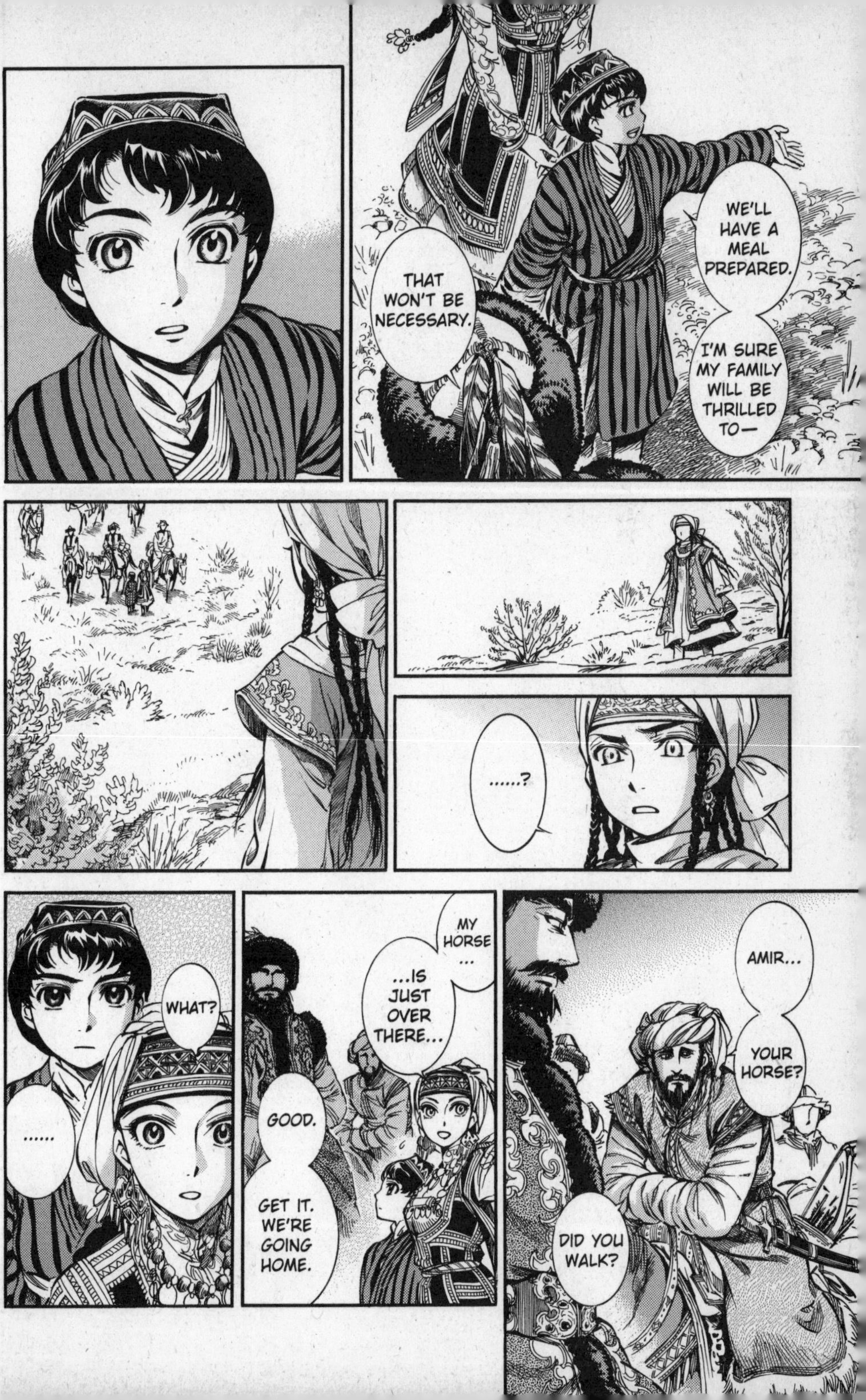
WE'LL HAVE A MEAL PREPARED.
I'M SURE MY FAMILY WILL BE THRILLED TO—
THAT WON'T BE NECESSARY.
......?
AMIR...
YOUR HORSE?
DID YOU WALK?
MY HORSE ...
...IS JUST OVER THERE...
GOOD.
GET IT. WE'RE GOING HOME.
WHAT?
......

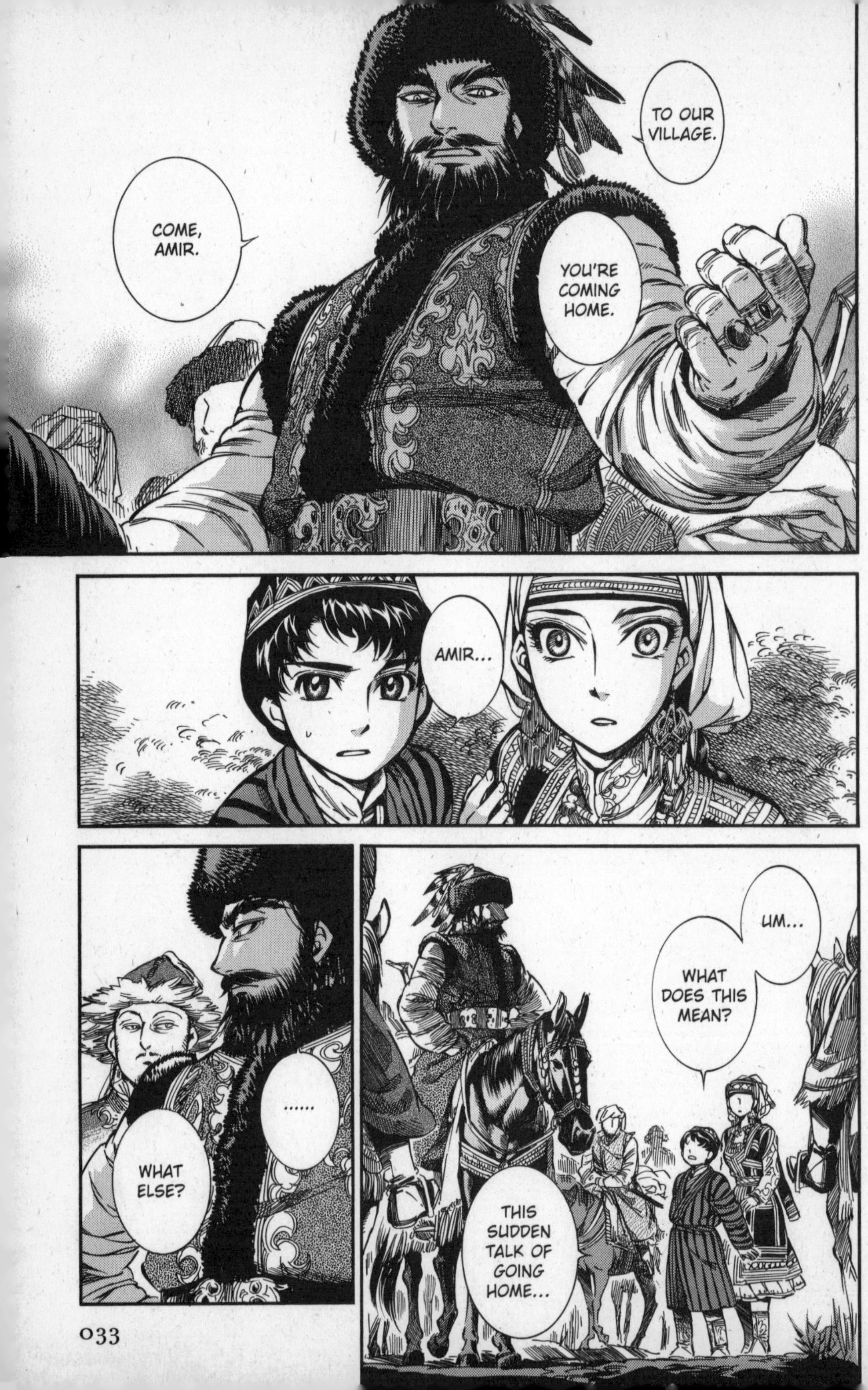
TO OUR VILLAGE.
YOU'RE COMING HOME.
COME, AMIR.
AMIR...
UM...
WHAT DOES THIS MEAN?
THIS SUDDEN TALK OF GOING HOME...
......
WHAT ELSE?

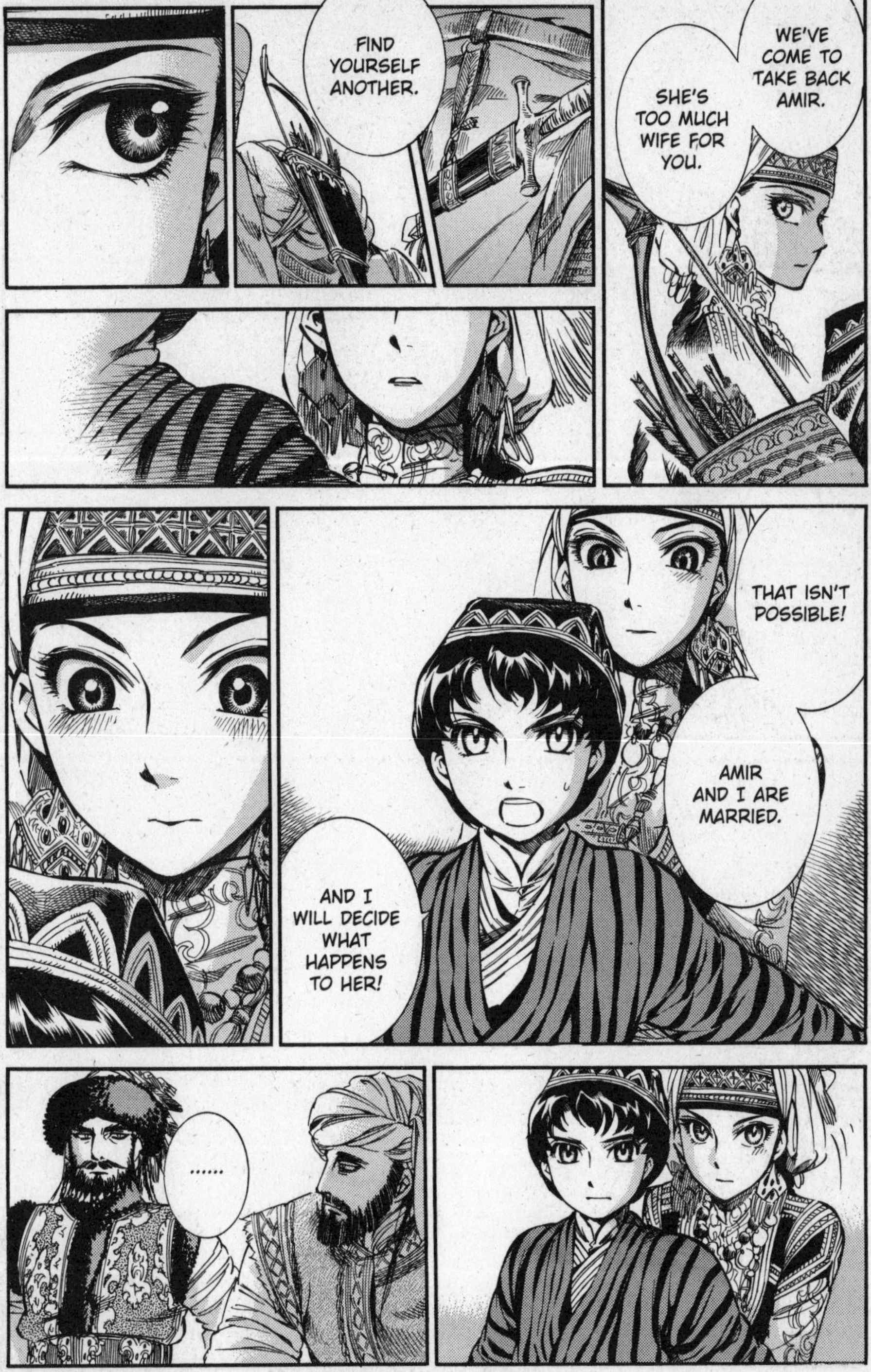
WE'VE COME TO TAKE BACK AMIR.
SHE'S TOO MUCH WIFE FOR YOU.
FIND YOURSELF ANOTHER.
THAT ISN'T POSSIBLE!
AMIR AND I ARE MARRIED.
AND I WILL DECIDE WHAT HAPPENS TO HER!
......

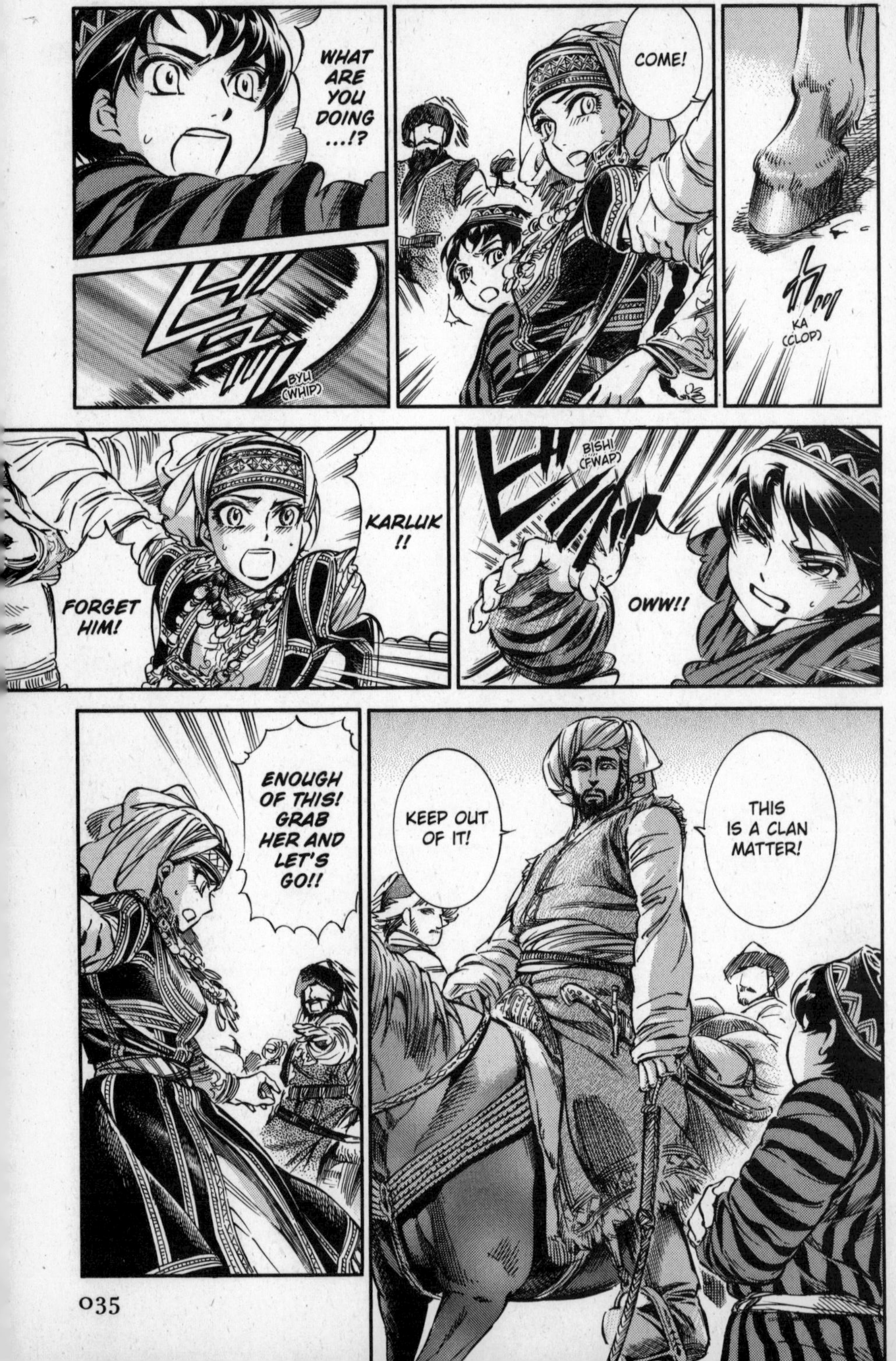
KA (CLOP)
COME!
WHAT ARE YOU DOING ...!?
BYU (WHIP)
BISHI (FWAP)
OWW!!
KARLUK !!
FORGET HIM!
THIS IS A CLAN MATTER!
KEEP OUT OF IT!
ENOUGH OF THIS! GRAB HER AND LET'S GO!!

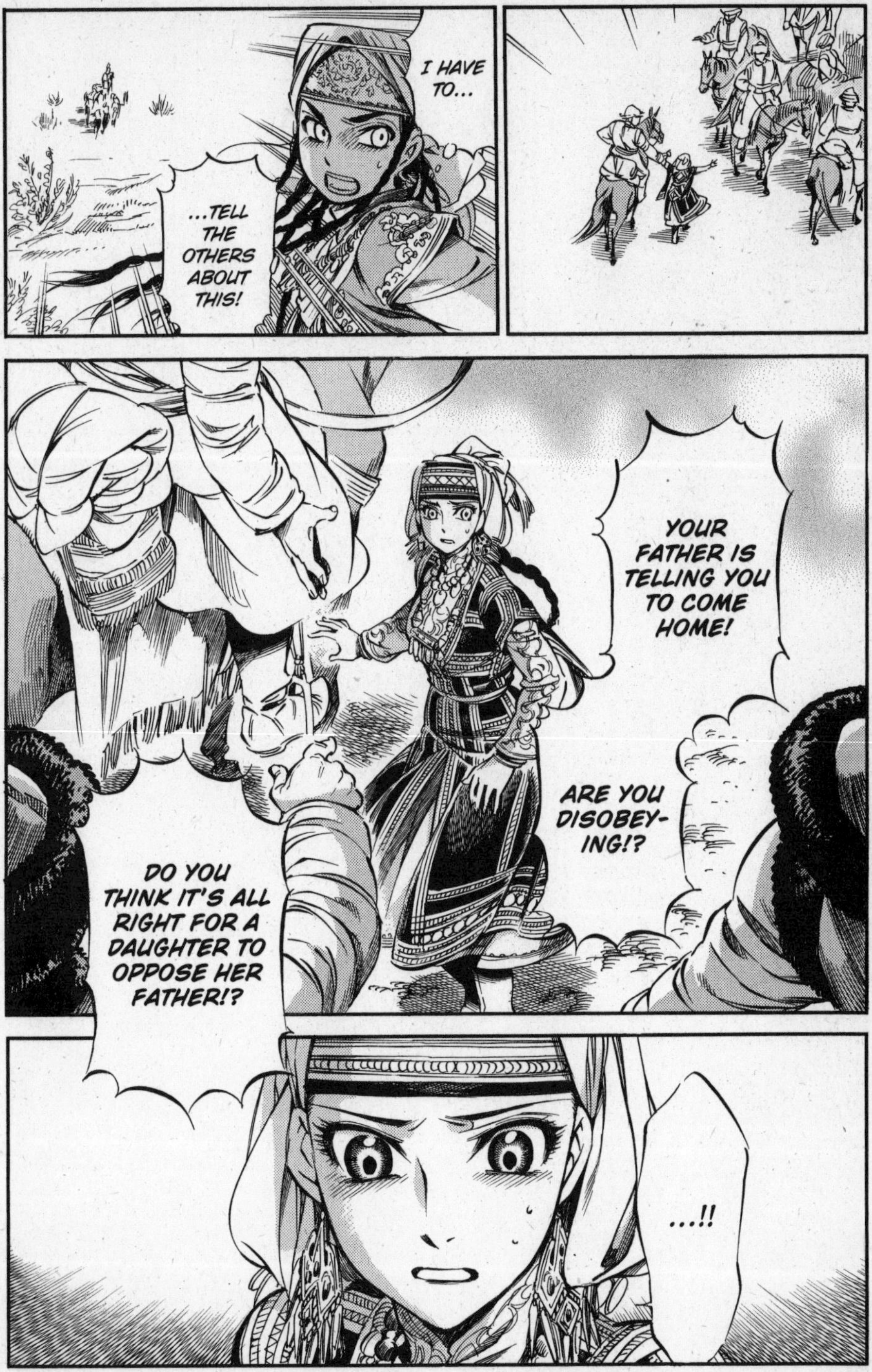
I HAVE TO...
...TELL THE OTHERS ABOUT THIS!
YOUR FATHER IS TELLING YOU TO COME HOME!
ARE YOU DISOBEY-ING!?
DO YOU THINK IT'S ALL RIGHT FOR A DAUGHTER TO OPPOSE HER FATHER!?
...!!

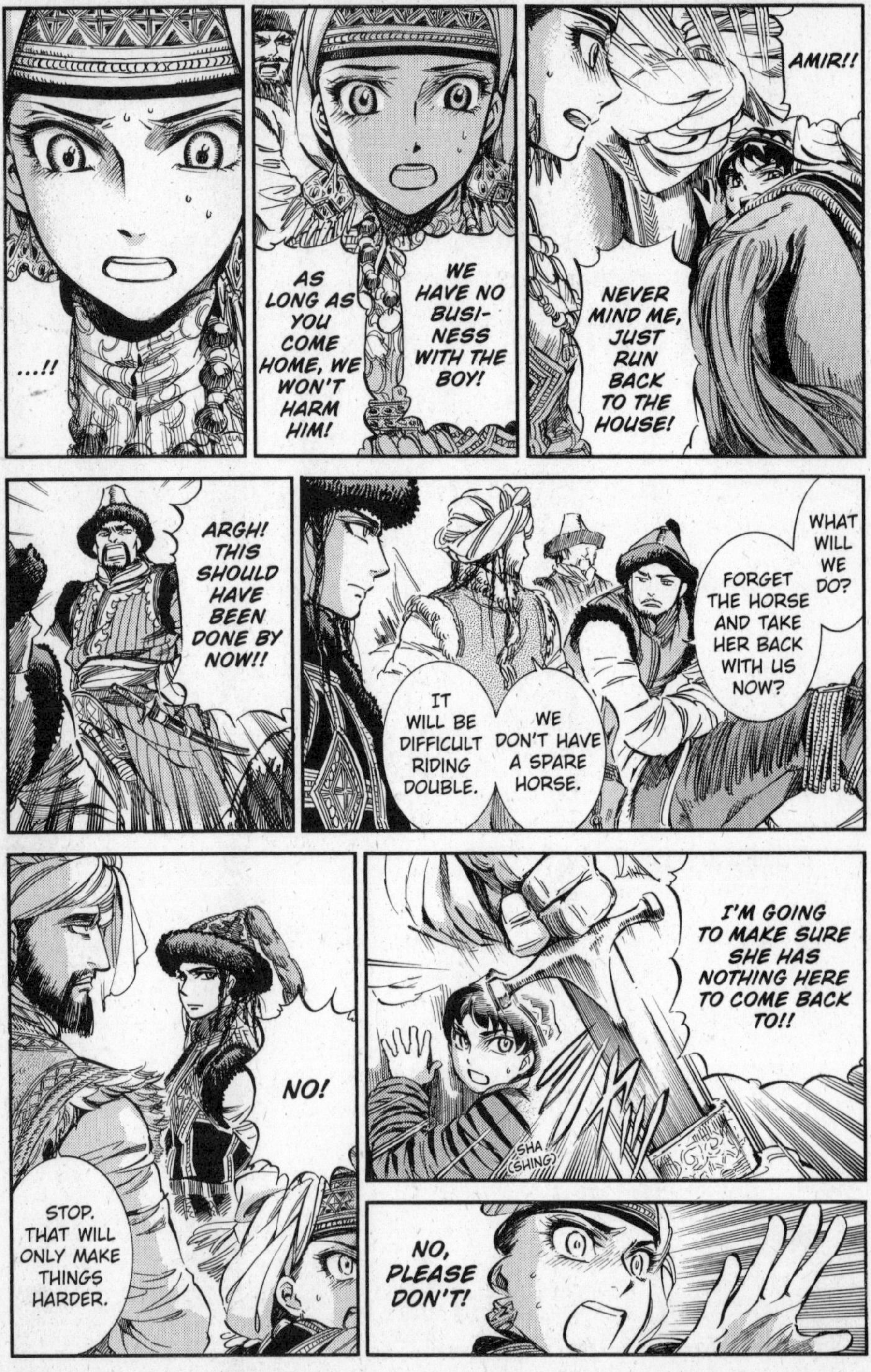
AMIR!!
NEVER MIND ME, JUST RUN BACK TO THE HOUSE!
WE HAVE NO BUSINESS WITH THE BOY!
AS LONG AS YOU COME HOME, WE WON'T HARM HIM!
...!!
WHAT WILL WE DO?
FORGET THE HORSE AND TAKE HER BACK WITH US NOW?
WE DON'T HAVE A SPARE HORSE.
IT WILL BE DIFFICULT RIDING DOUBLE.
ARGH! THIS SHOULD HAVE BEEN DONE BY NOW!!
I'M GOING TO MAKE SURE SHE HAS NOTHING HERE TO COME BACK TO!!
SHA (SHING)
NO, PLEASE DON'T!
NO!
STOP. THAT WILL ONLY MAKE THINGS HARDER.

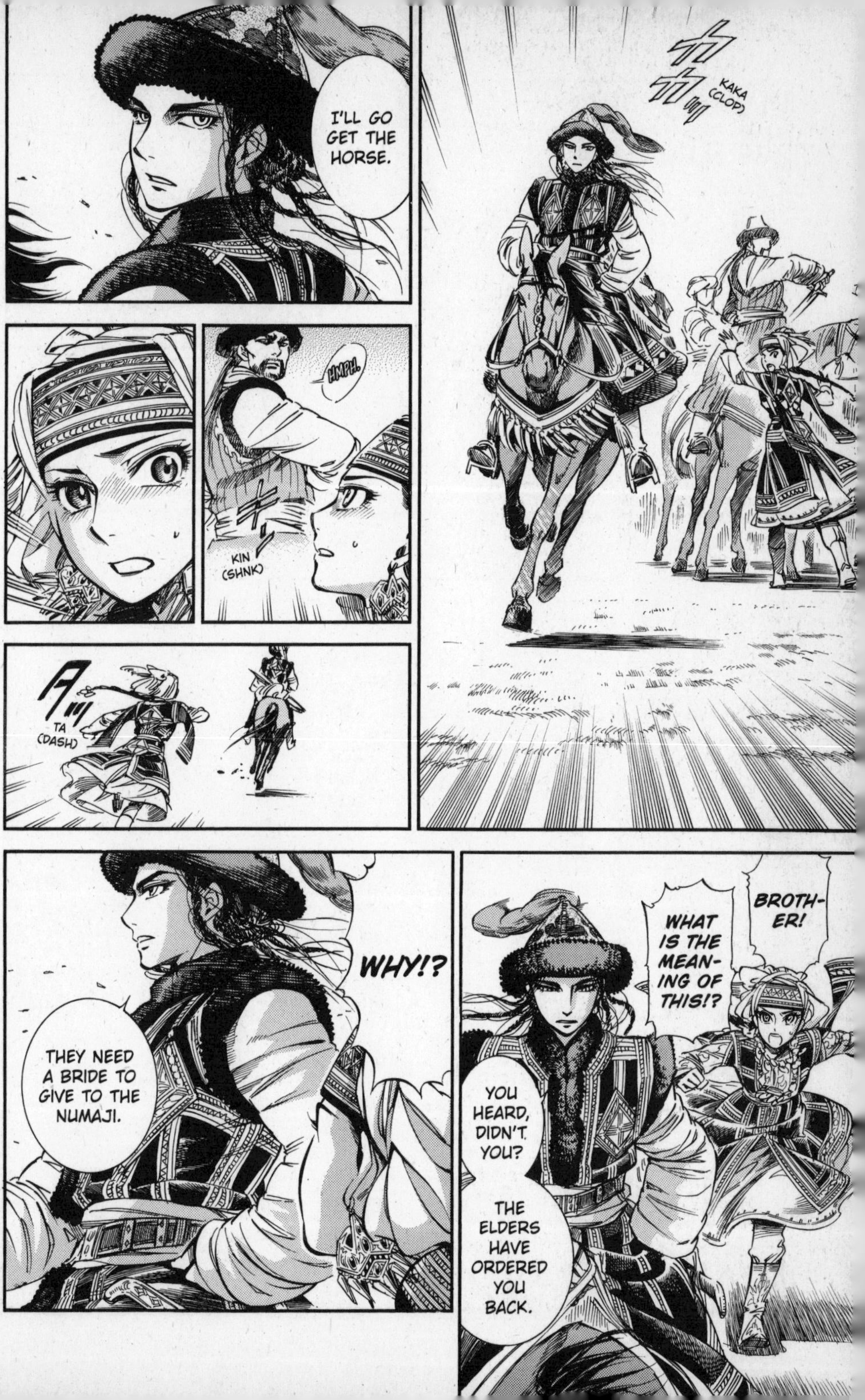

KAKA (CLOP)
I'LL GO GET THE HORSE.
HMPH.
KIN (SHNK)
TA (DASH)
BROTHER!
WHAT IS THE MEANING OF THIS!?
YOU HEARD, DIDN'T YOU?
THE ELDERS HAVE ORDERED YOU BACK.
WHY!?
THEY NEED A BRIDE TO GIVE TO THE NUMAJI.

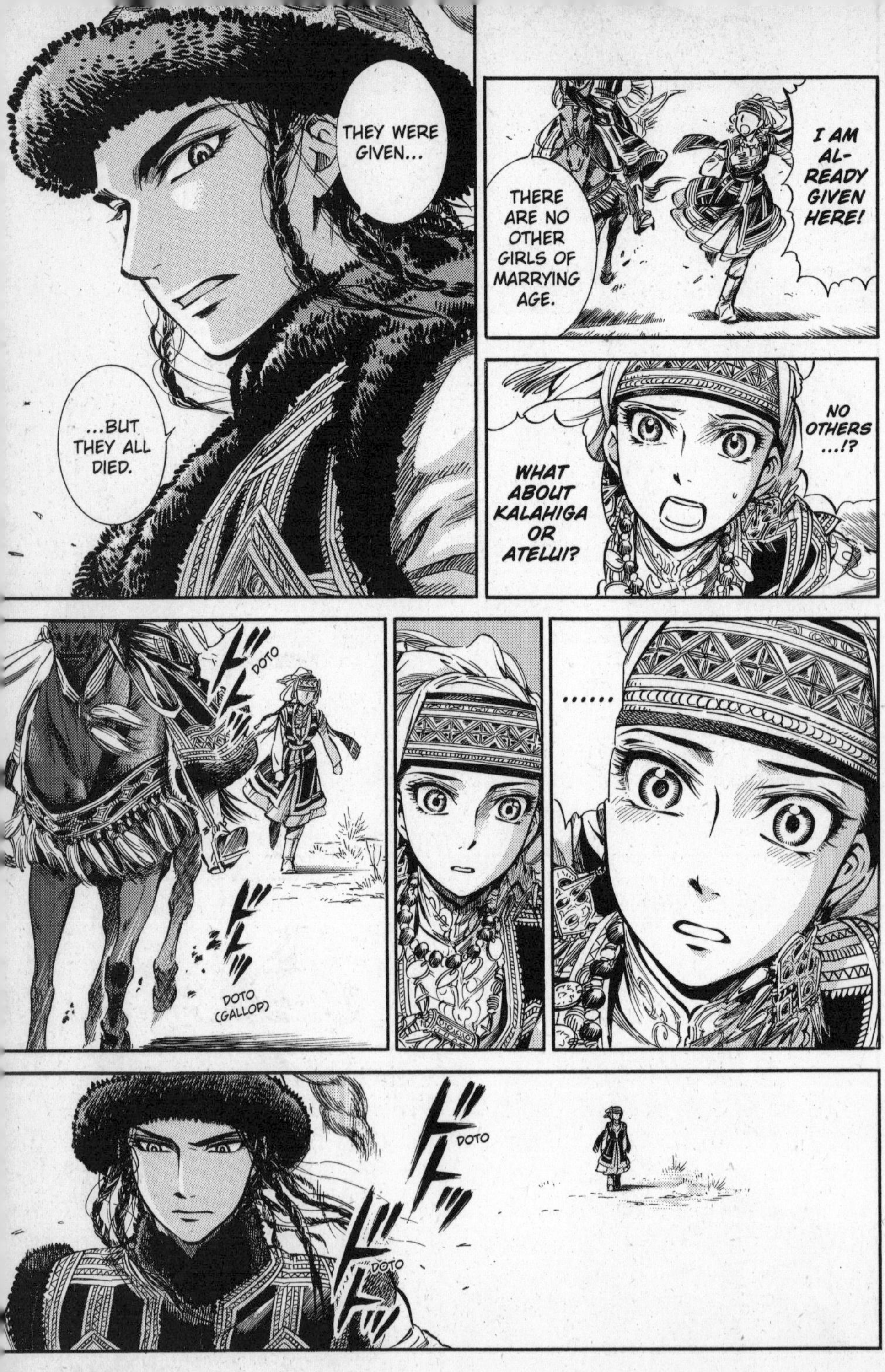
I AM AL-READY GIVEN HERE!
THERE ARE NO OTHER GIRLS OF MARRYING AGE.
NO OTHERS ...!?
WHAT ABOUT KALAHIGA OR ATELUI?
THEY WERE GIVEN...
...BUT THEY ALL DIED.
......
DOTO
DOTO (GALLOP)
DOTO
DOTO

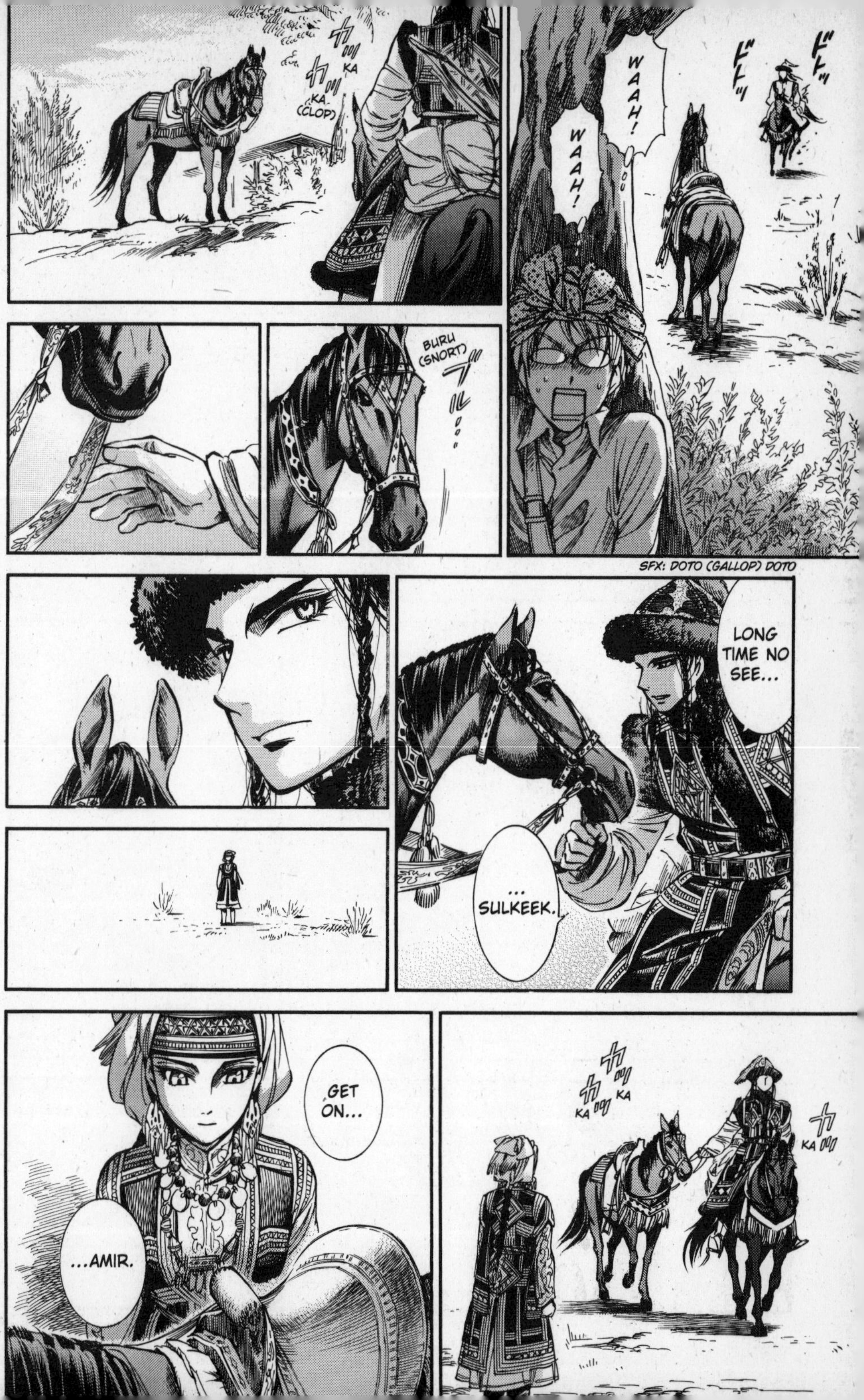
WAAAH!
WAAAH!
SFX: DOTO (GALLOP) DOTO
KA
KA (CLOP)
BURU (SNORT)
LONG TIME NO SEE...
...SULKEEK.
KA
KA
KA
GET ON...
...AMIR.

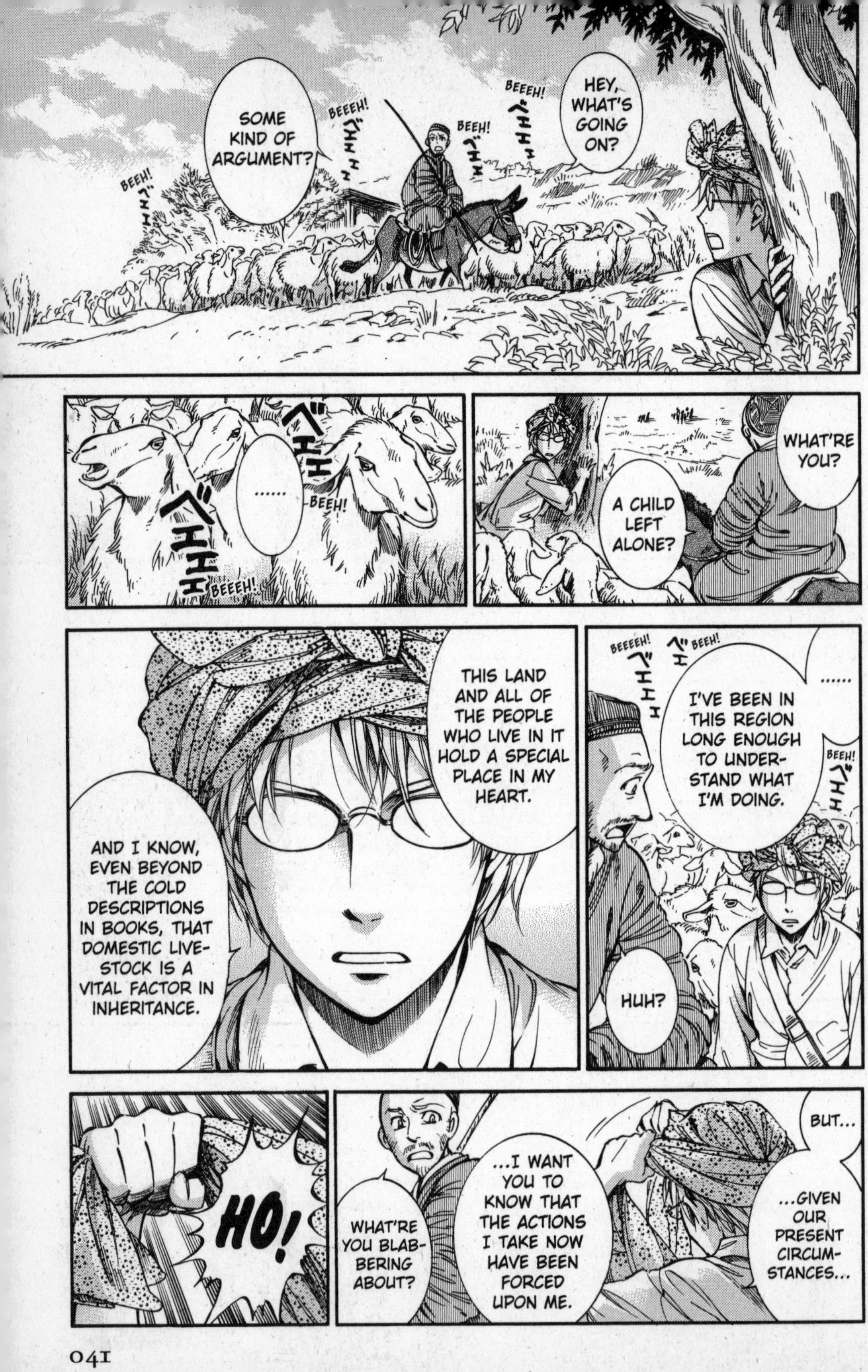
HEY, WHAT'S GOING ON?
BEEEH!
BEEH!
SOME KIND OF ARGUMENT?
BEEEH!
BEEH!
WHAT'RE YOU?
A CHILD LEFT ALONE?
......
BEEH!
BEEEH!
......
I'VE BEEN IN THIS REGION LONG ENOUGH TO UNDER-STAND WHAT I'M DOING.
BEEEEH!
BEEH!
BEEH!
HUH?
THIS LAND AND ALL OF THE PEOPLE WHO LIVE IN IT HOLD A SPECIAL PLACE IN MY HEART.
AND I KNOW, EVEN BEYOND THE COLD DESCRIPTIONS IN BOOKS, THAT DOMESTIC LIVE-STOCK IS A VITAL FACTOR IN INHERITANCE.
BUT...
...GIVEN OUR PRESENT CIRCUM-STANCES...
...I WANT YOU TO KNOW THAT THE ACTIONS I TAKE NOW HAVE BEEN FORCED UPON ME.
WHAT'RE YOU BLAB-BERING ABOUT?
HO!

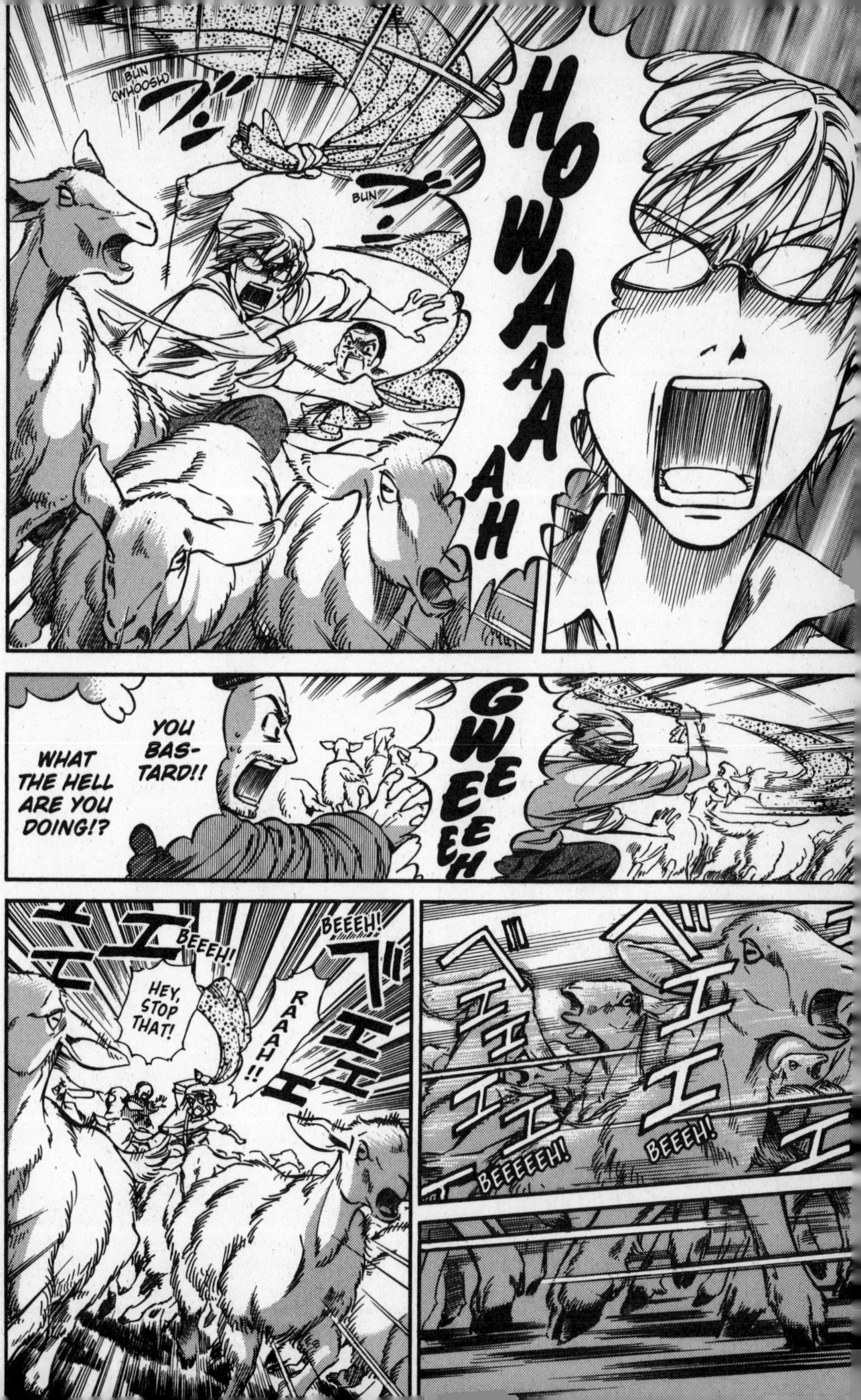
HOWAAAAH
BUN (WHOOSH)
BUN
GWEEEEEH
YOU BAS-TARD!!
WHAT THE HELL ARE YOU DOING!?
BEEEH!
BEEEEEH!
BEEEH!
RAAAAH!!
BEEEH!
HEY, STOP THAT!

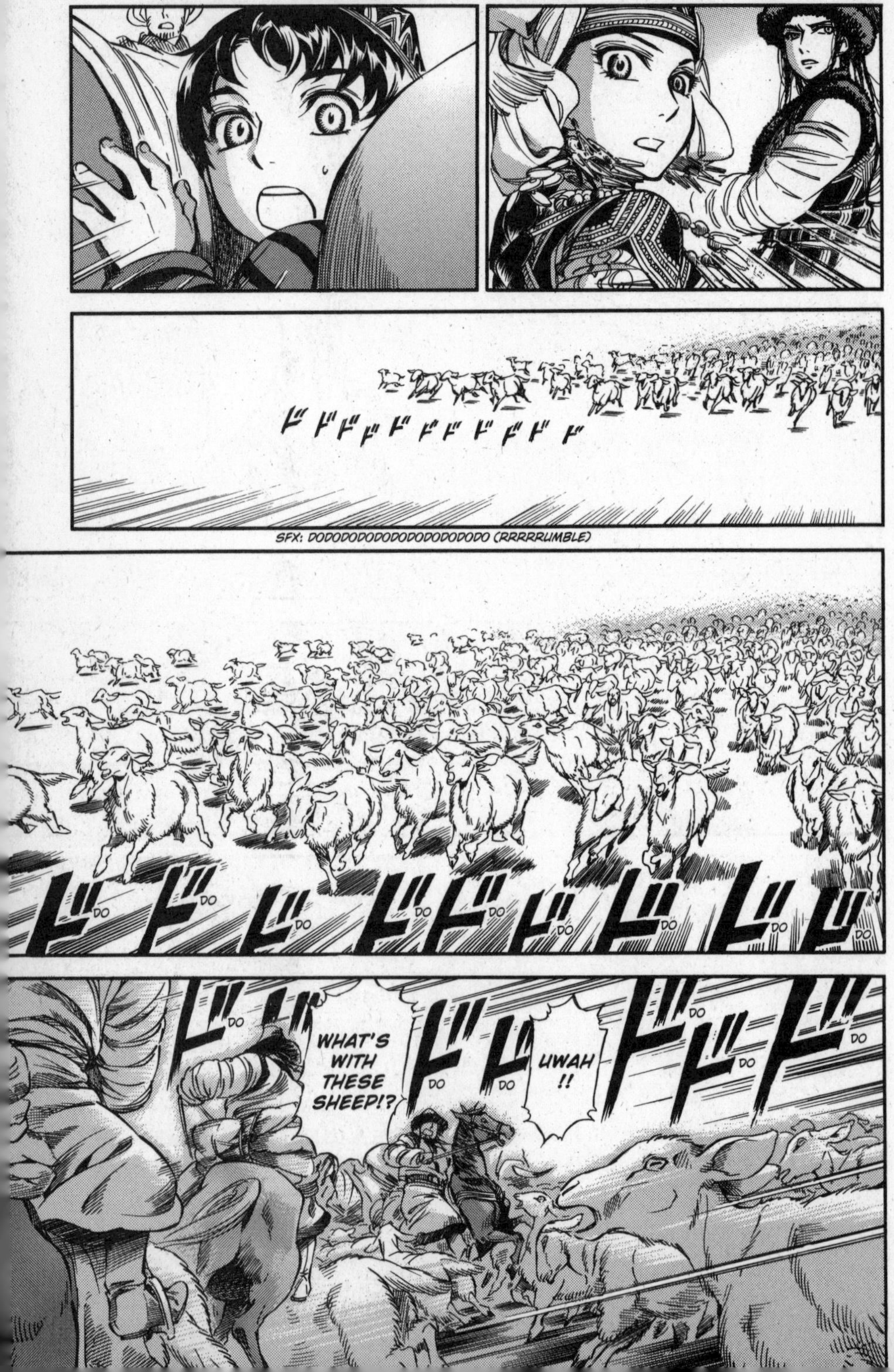
SFX: DODODODODODODODODODODO (RRRRRUMBLE)
UWAH!!
WHAT'S WITH THESE SHEEP!?

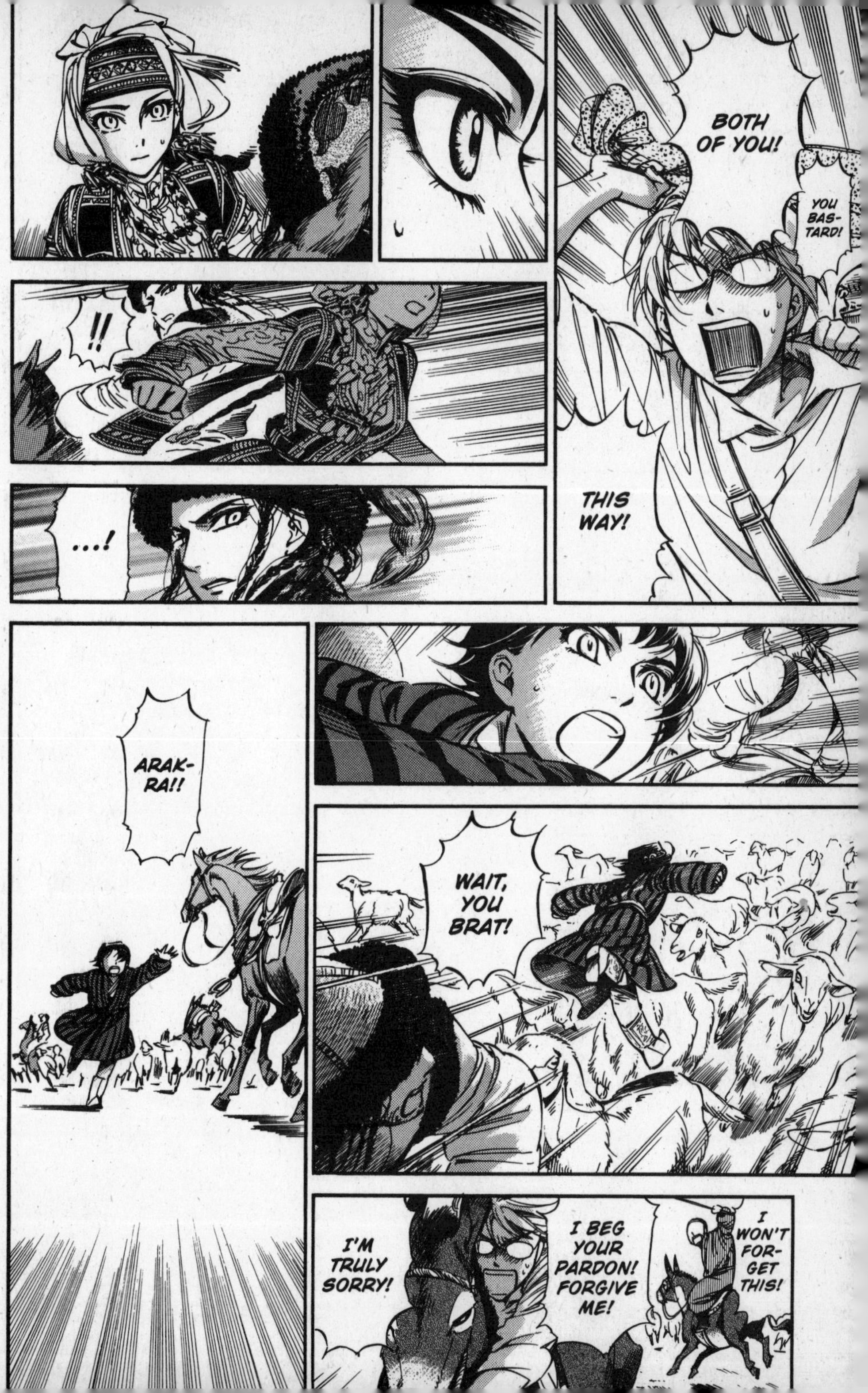
BOTH OF YOU!
YOU BASTARD!
THIS WAY!
!!
...!
WAIT, YOU BRAT!
I WON'T FORGET THIS!
I BEG YOUR PARDON! FORGIVE ME!
I'M TRULY SORRY!
ARAKRA!!

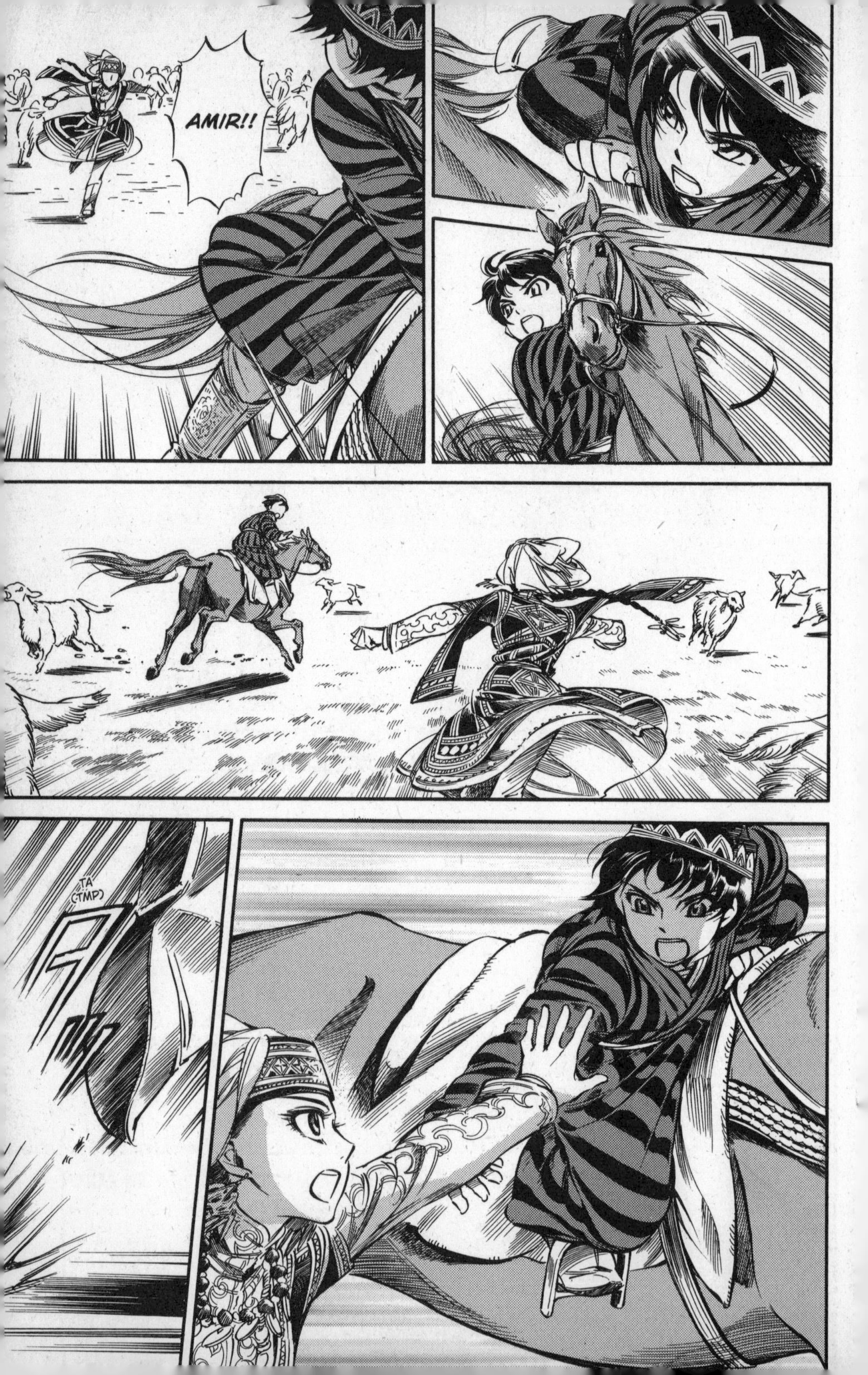
AMIR!!
TA
(TMP)

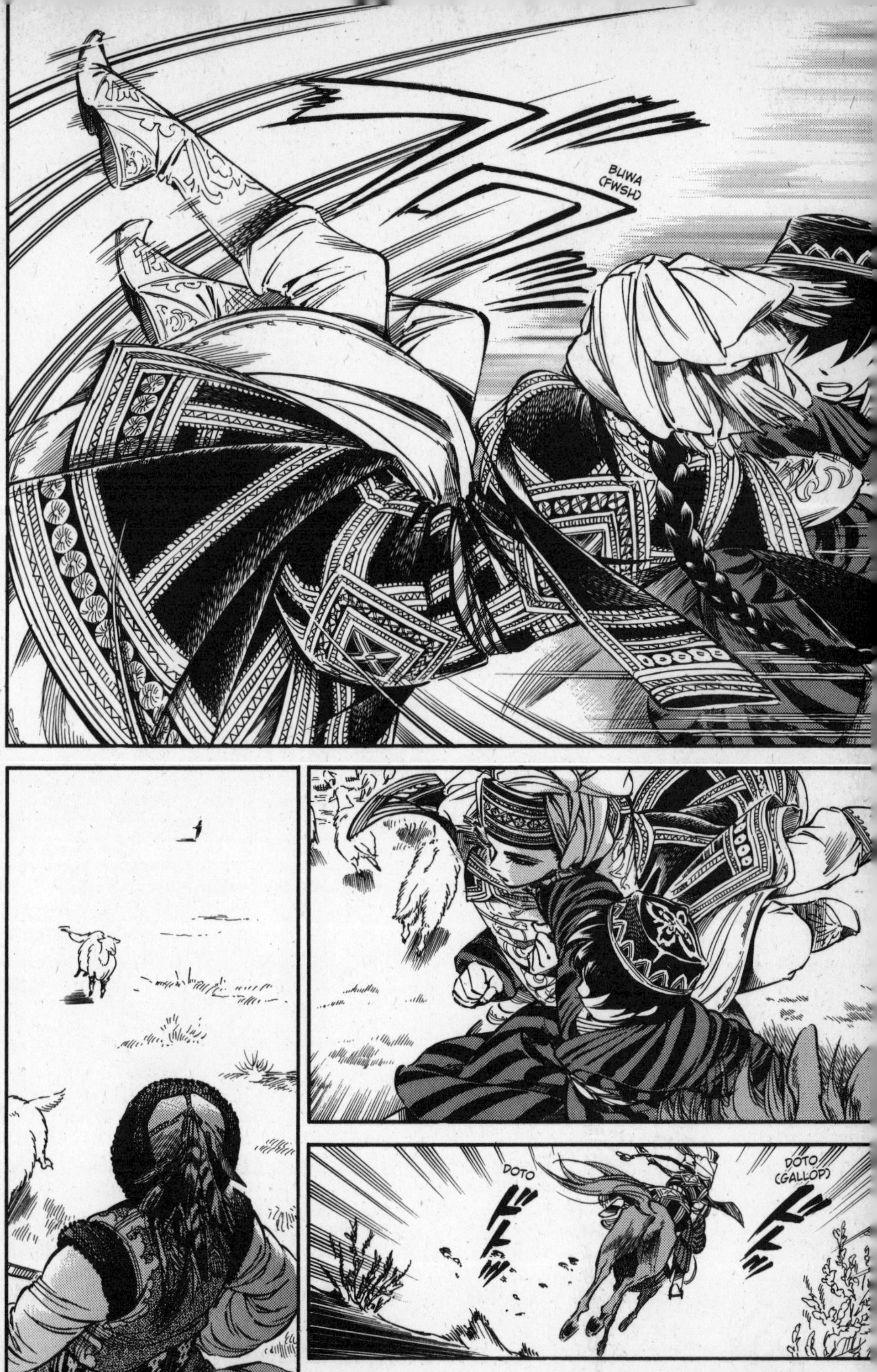
BUWA
(FWSH)
DOTO
(GALLOP)
DOTO

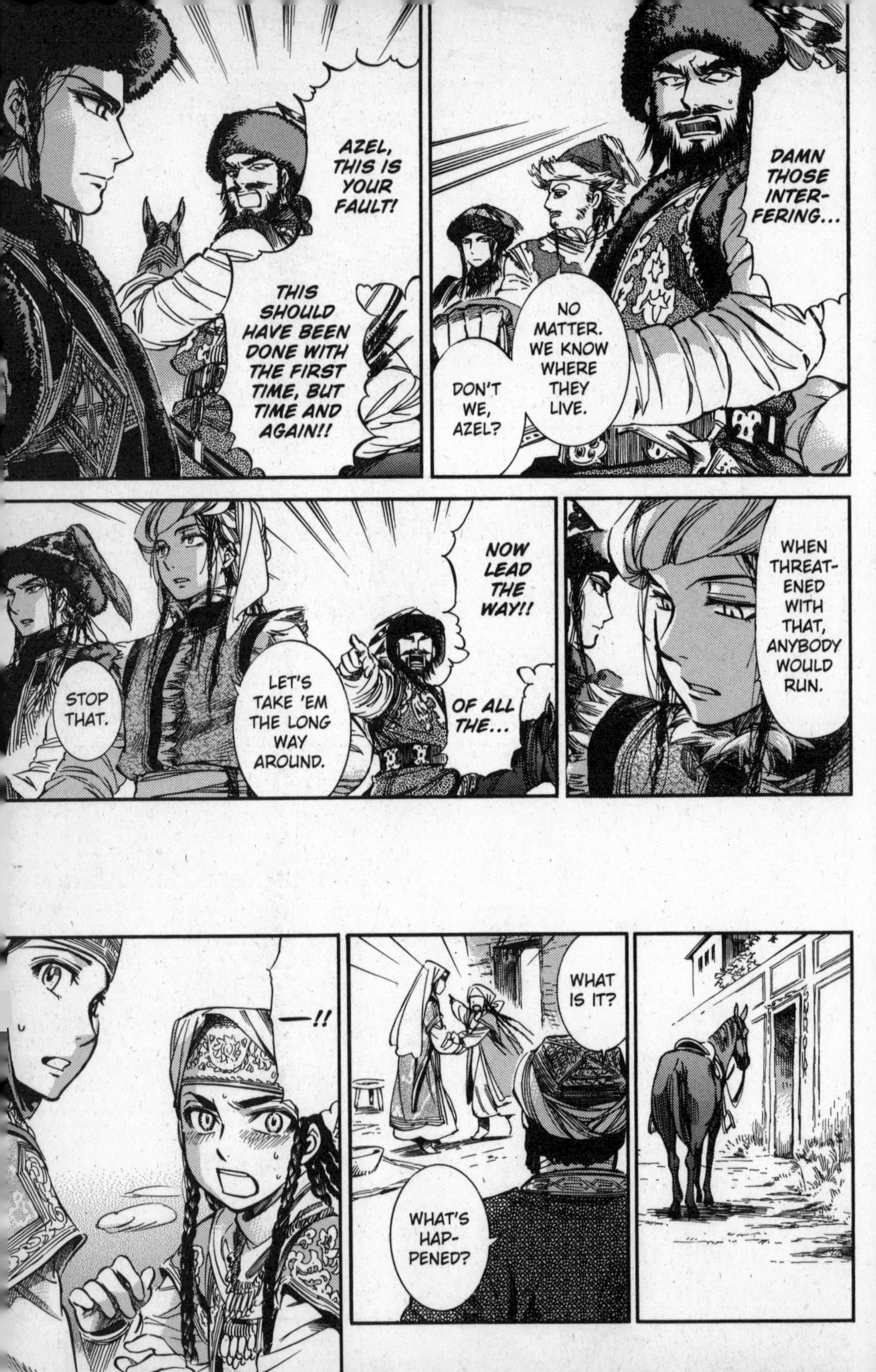
DAMN THOSE INTERFERING...
NO MATTER. WE KNOW WHERE THEY LIVE.
DON'T WE, AZEL?
AZEL, THIS IS YOUR FAULT!
THIS SHOULD HAVE BEEN DONE WITH THE FIRST TIME, BUT TIME AND AGAIN!!
WHEN THREATENED WITH THAT, ANYBODY WOULD RUN.
NOW LEAD THE WAY!!
OF ALL THE...
LET'S TAKE 'EM THE LONG WAY AROUND.
STOP THAT.
WHAT IS IT?
WHAT'S HAPPENED?
—!!

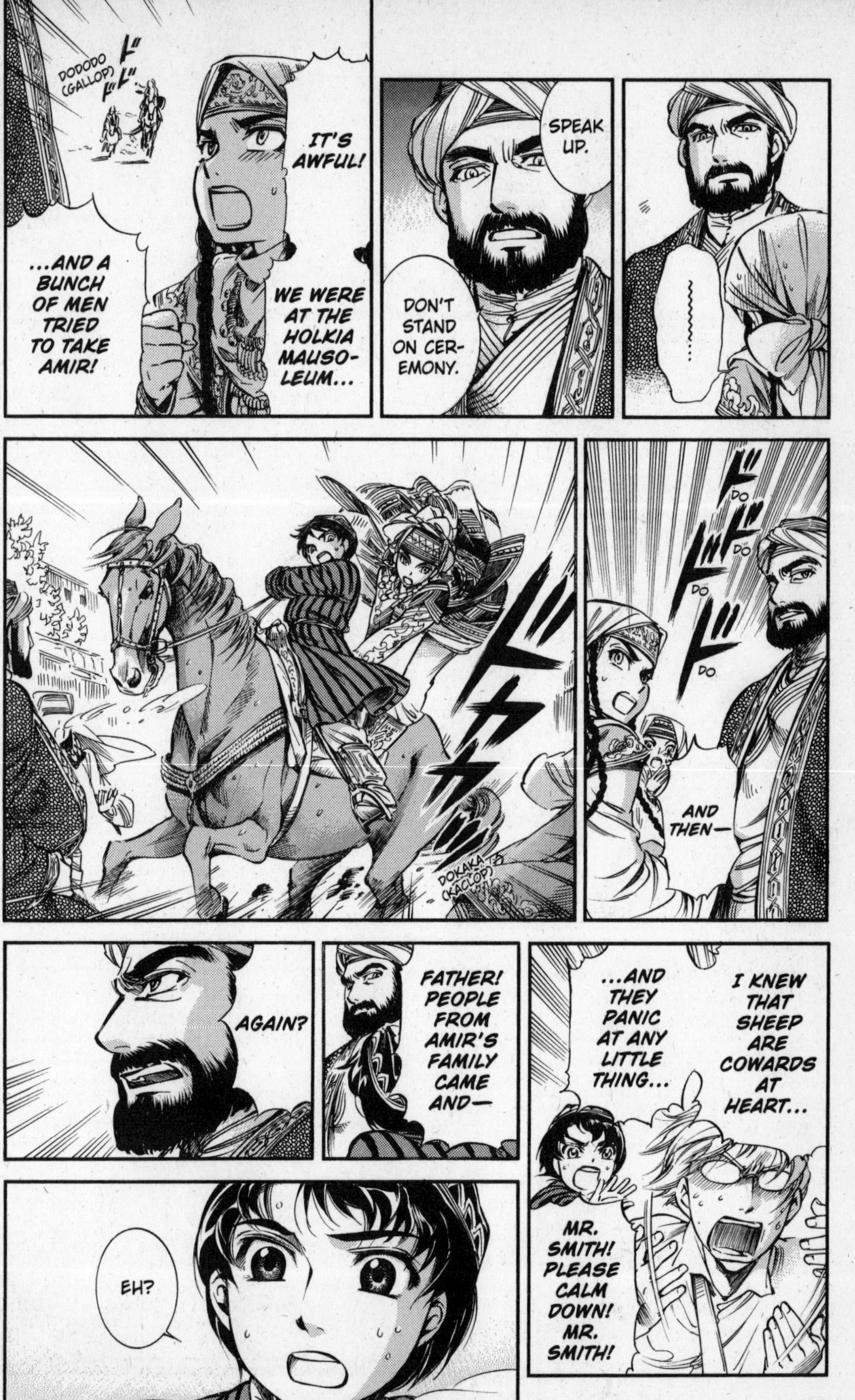

......
SPEAK UP.
DON'T STAND ON CEREMONY.
DODODO (GALLOP)
IT'S AWFUL!
WE WERE AT THE HOLKIA MAUSOLEUM...
...AND A BUNCH OF MEN TRIED TO TAKE AMIR!
DO DO DO DO
AND THEN—
DOKAKA (KACLOP)
I KNEW THAT SHEEP ARE COWARDS AT HEART...
...AND THEY PANIC AT ANY LITTLE THING...
MR. SMITH! PLEASE CALM DOWN! MR. SMITH!
FATHER! PEOPLE FROM AMIR'S FAMILY CAME AND—
AGAIN?
EH?

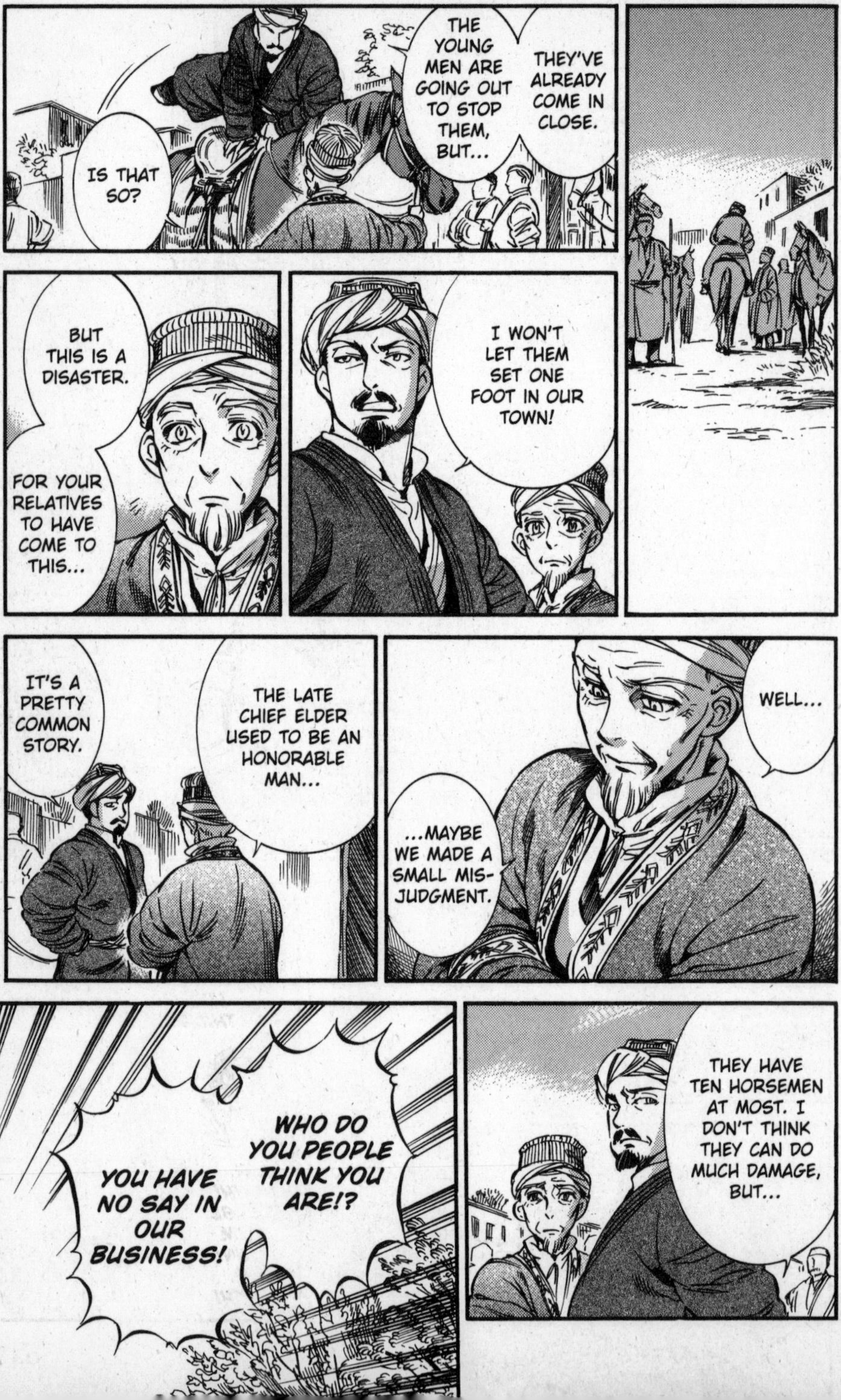
THEY'VE ALREADY COME IN CLOSE.
THE YOUNG MEN ARE GOING OUT TO STOP THEM, BUT...
IS THAT SO?
I WON'T LET THEM SET ONE FOOT IN OUR TOWN!
BUT THIS IS A DISASTER.
FOR YOUR RELATIVES TO HAVE COME TO THIS...
WELL...
...MAYBE WE MADE A SMALL MIS-JUDGMENT.
THE LATE CHIEF ELDER USED TO BE AN HONORABLE MAN...
IT'S A PRETTY COMMON STORY.
THEY HAVE TEN HORSEMEN AT MOST. I DON'T THINK THEY CAN DO MUCH DAMAGE, BUT...
WHO DO YOU PEOPLE THINK YOU ARE!?
YOU HAVE NO SAY IN OUR BUSINESS!

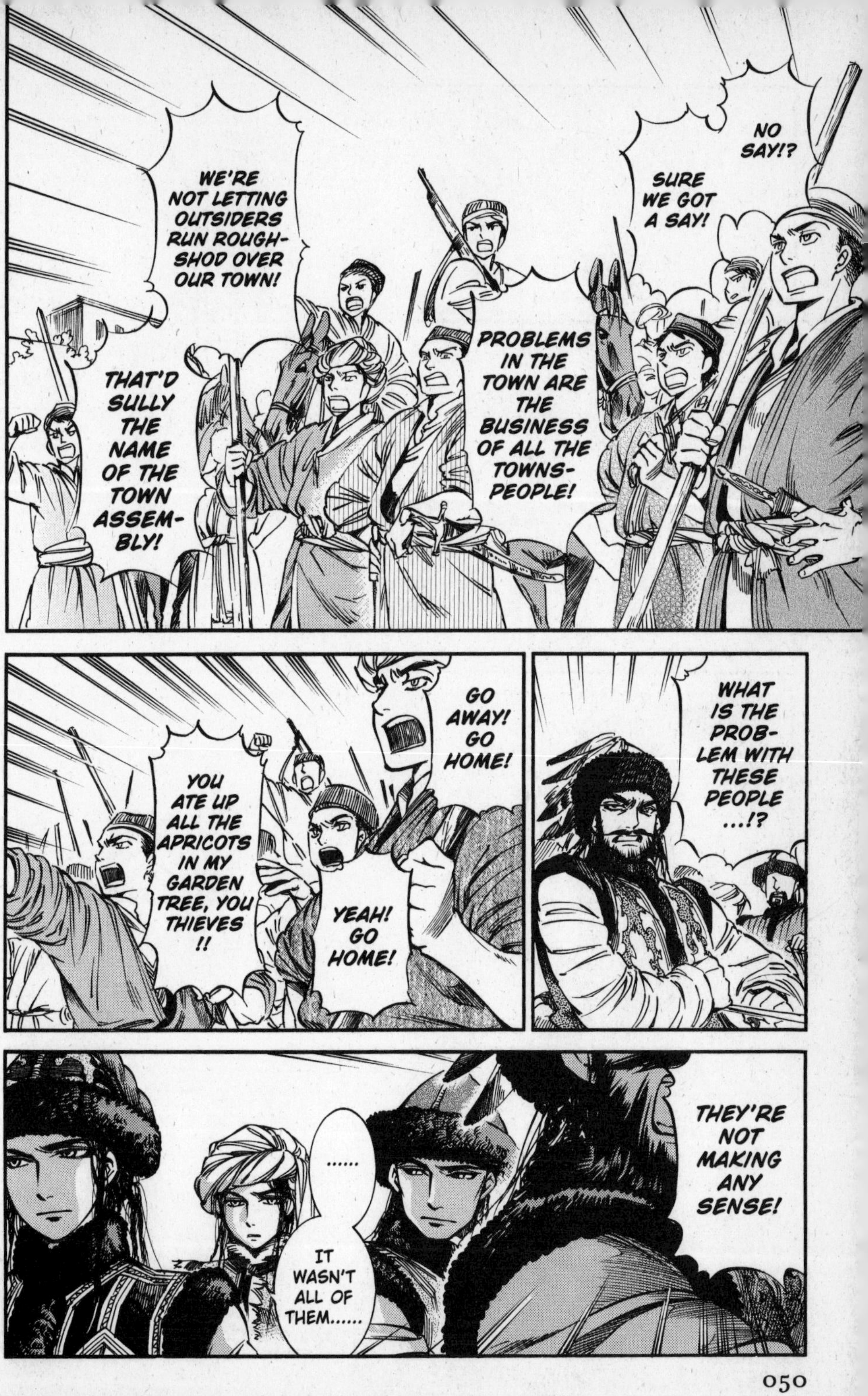
NO SAY!?
SURE WE GOT A SAY!
PROBLEMS IN THE TOWN ARE THE BUSINESS OF ALL THE TOWNS-PEOPLE!
WE'RE NOT LETTING OUTSIDERS RUN ROUGH-SHOD OVER OUR TOWN!
THAT'D SULLY THE NAME OF THE TOWN ASSEM-BLY!
WHAT IS THE PROB-LEM WITH THESE PEOPLE ...!?
GO AWAY! GO HOME!
YOU ATE UP ALL THE APRICOTS IN MY GARDEN TREE, YOU THIEVES !!
YEAH! GO HOME!
THEY'RE NOT MAKING ANY SENSE!
......
IT WASN'T ALL OF THEM......

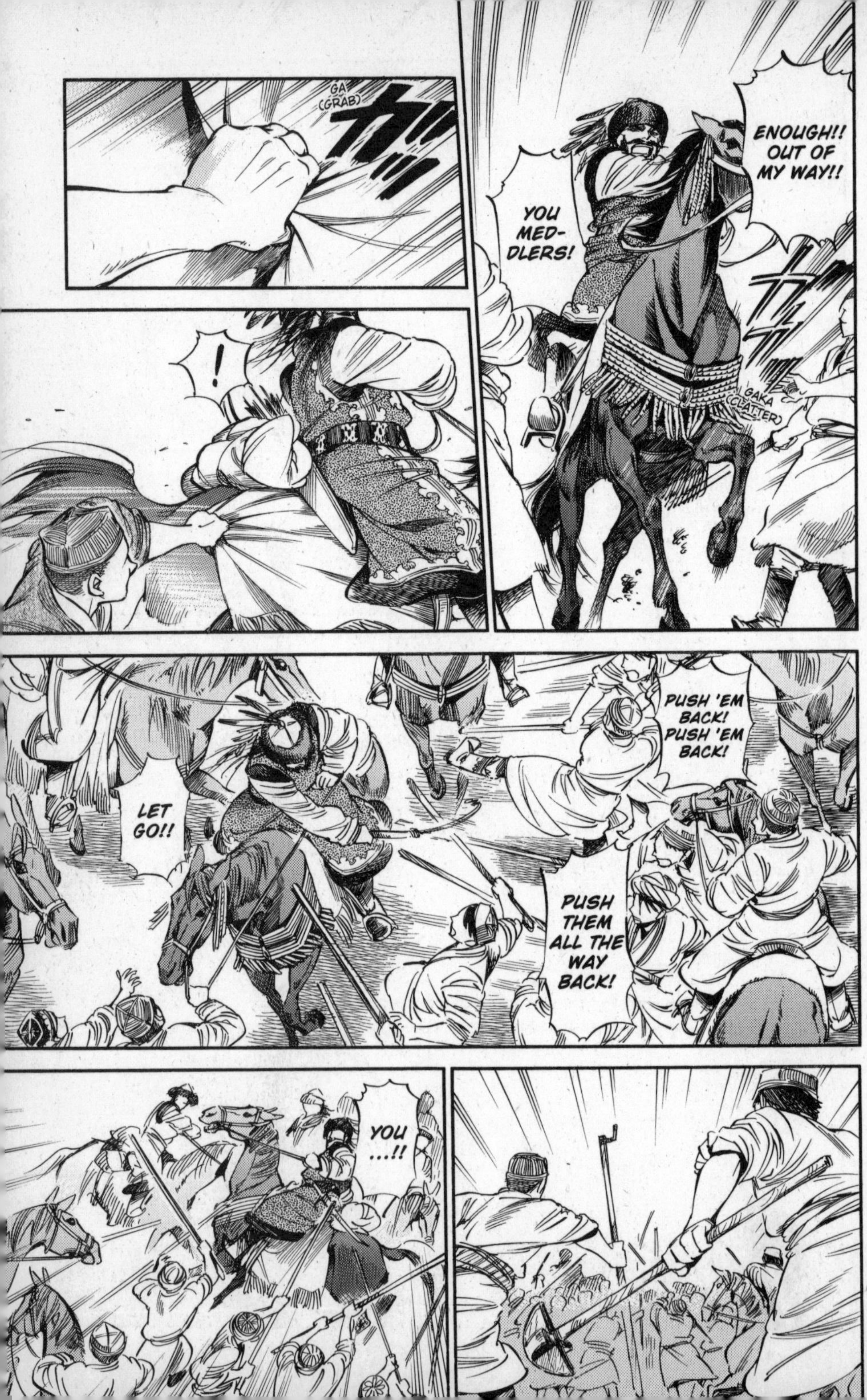
ENOUGH!! OUT OF MY WAY!!
YOU MED-DLERS!
GAKA (CLATTER)
GA (GRAB)
!
PUSH 'EM BACK! PUSH 'EM BACK!
PUSH THEM ALL THE WAY BACK!
LET GO!!
YOU ...!!

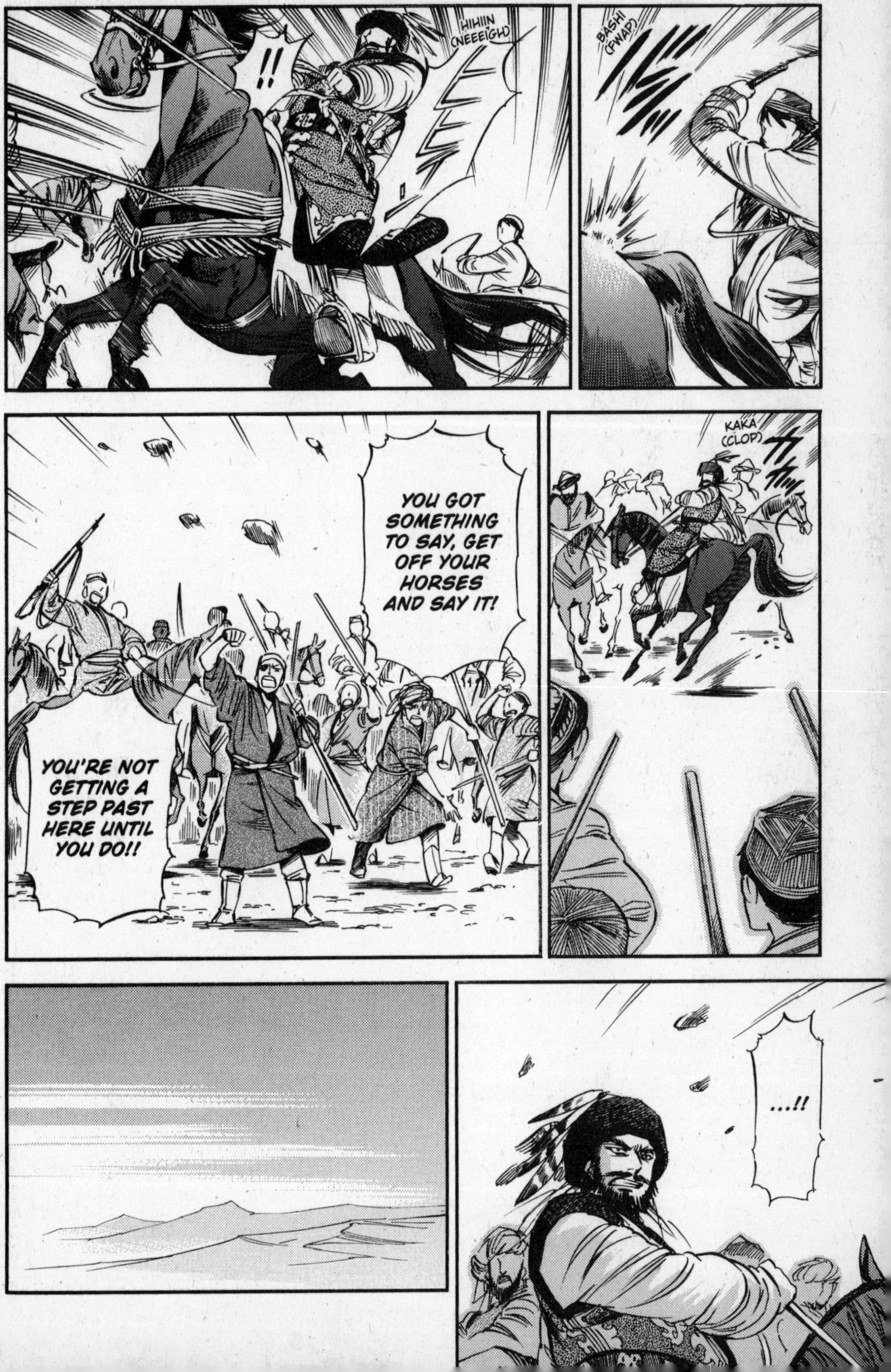
BASHI (FWAP)
HIHIIN (NEEEIGH)
!!
KAKA (CLOP)
YOU GOT SOMETHING TO SAY, GET OFF YOUR HORSES AND SAY IT!
YOU'RE NOT GETTING A STEP PAST HERE UNTIL YOU DO!!
...!!

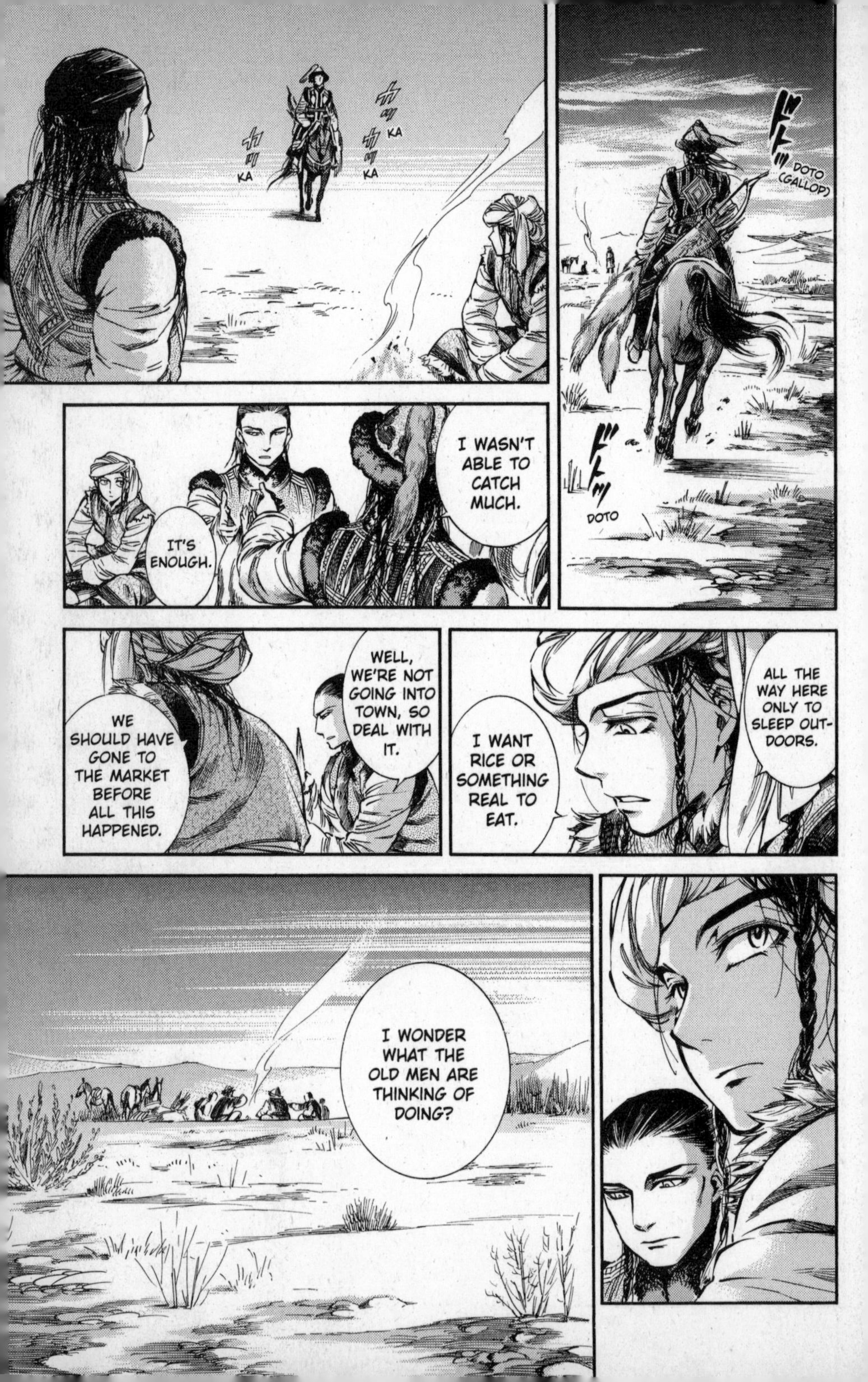
DOTO (GALLOP)
DOTO
KA
KA
KA
I WASN'T ABLE TO CATCH MUCH.
IT'S ENOUGH.
ALL THE WAY HERE ONLY TO SLEEP OUT-DOORS.
I WANT RICE OR SOMETHING REAL TO EAT.
WELL, WE'RE NOT GOING INTO TOWN, SO DEAL WITH IT.
WE SHOULD HAVE GONE TO THE MARKET BEFORE ALL THIS HAPPENED.
I WONDER WHAT THE OLD MEN ARE THINKING OF DOING?

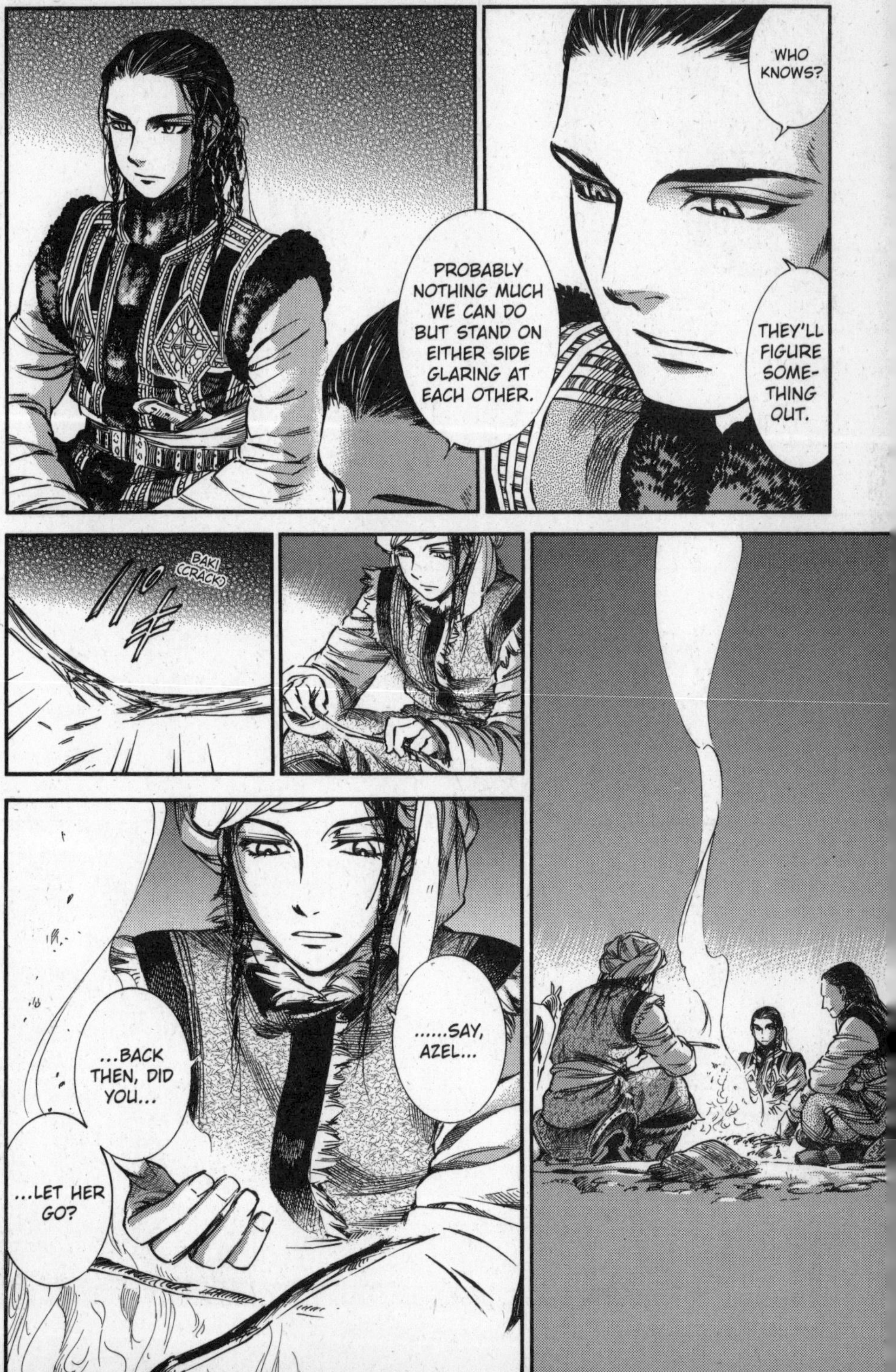
WHO KNOWS?
THEY'LL FIGURE SOME-THING OUT.
PROBABLY NOTHING MUCH WE CAN DO BUT STAND ON EITHER SIDE GLARING AT EACH OTHER.
BAKI (CRACK)
......SAY, AZEL...
...BACK THEN, DID YOU...
...LET HER GO?

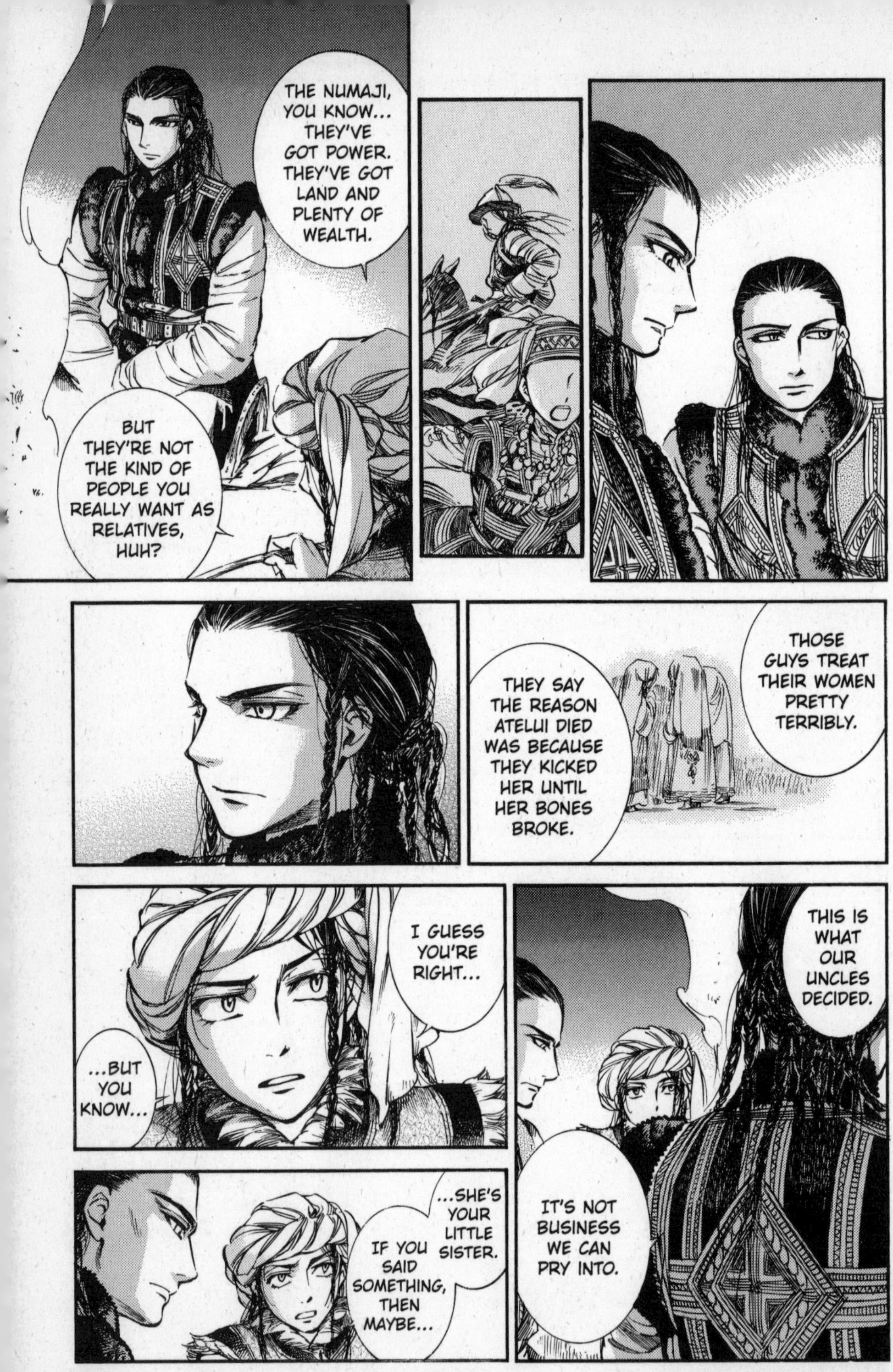

THE NUMAJI, YOU KNOW... THEY'VE GOT POWER. THEY'VE GOT LAND AND PLENTY OF WEALTH.
BUT THEY'RE NOT THE KIND OF PEOPLE YOU REALLY WANT AS RELATIVES, HUH?
THOSE GUYS TREAT THEIR WOMEN PRETTY TERRIBLY.
THEY SAY THE REASON ATELUI DIED WAS BECAUSE THEY KICKED HER UNTIL HER BONES BROKE.
THIS IS WHAT OUR UNCLES DECIDED.
IT'S NOT BUSINESS WE CAN PRY INTO.
I GUESS YOU'RE RIGHT...
...BUT YOU KNOW...
...SHE'S YOUR LITTLE SISTER.
IF YOU SAID SOMETHING, THEN MAYBE...

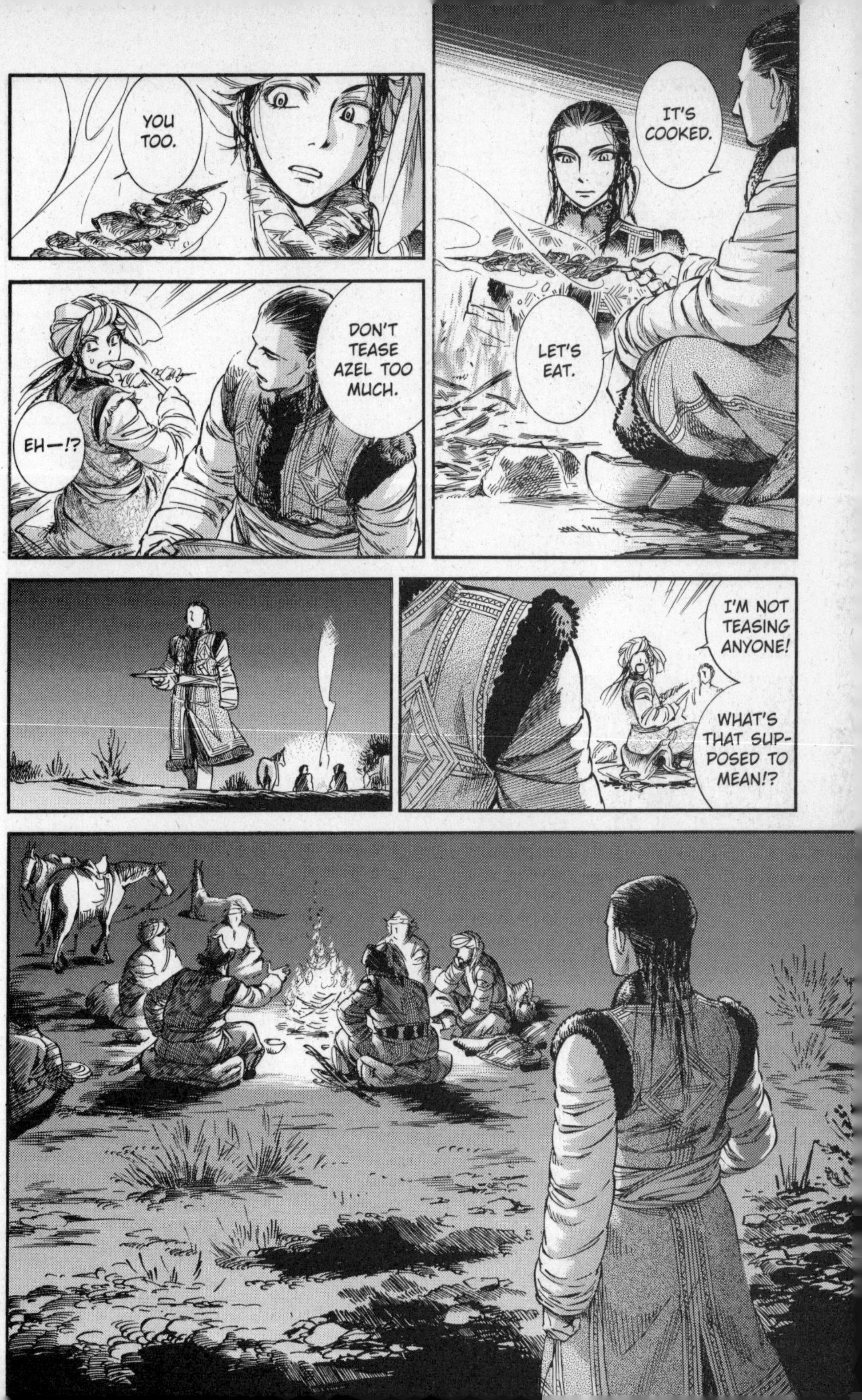
IT'S COOKED.
LET'S EAT.
YOU TOO.
DON'T TEASE AZEL TOO MUCH.
EH—!?
I'M NOT TEASING ANYONE!
WHAT'S THAT SUP-POSED TO MEAN!?

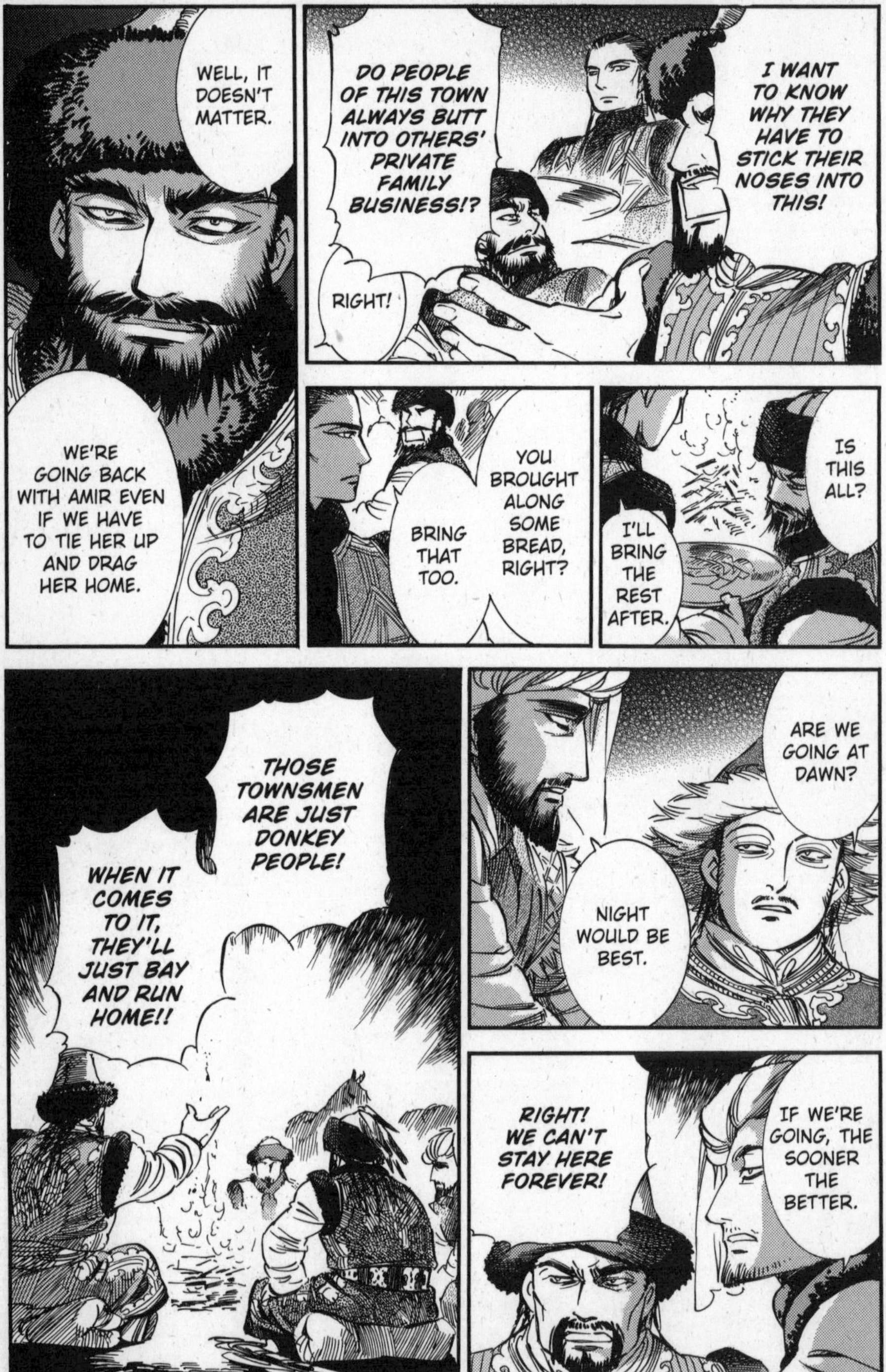
I WANT TO KNOW WHY THEY HAVE TO STICK THEIR NOSES INTO THIS!
DO PEOPLE OF THIS TOWN ALWAYS BUTT INTO OTHERS' PRIVATE FAMILY BUSINESS!?
RIGHT!
IS THIS ALL?
I'LL BRING THE REST AFTER.
YOU BROUGHT ALONG SOME BREAD, RIGHT?
BRING THAT TOO.
WELL, IT DOESN'T MATTER.
WE'RE GOING BACK WITH AMIR EVEN IF WE HAVE TO TIE HER UP AND DRAG HER HOME.
ARE WE GOING AT DAWN?
NIGHT WOULD BE BEST.
IF WE'RE GOING, THE SOONER THE BETTER.
RIGHT! WE CAN'T STAY HERE FOREVER!
THOSE TOWNSMEN ARE JUST DONKEY PEOPLE!
WHEN IT COMES TO IT, THEY'LL JUST BAY AND RUN HOME!!

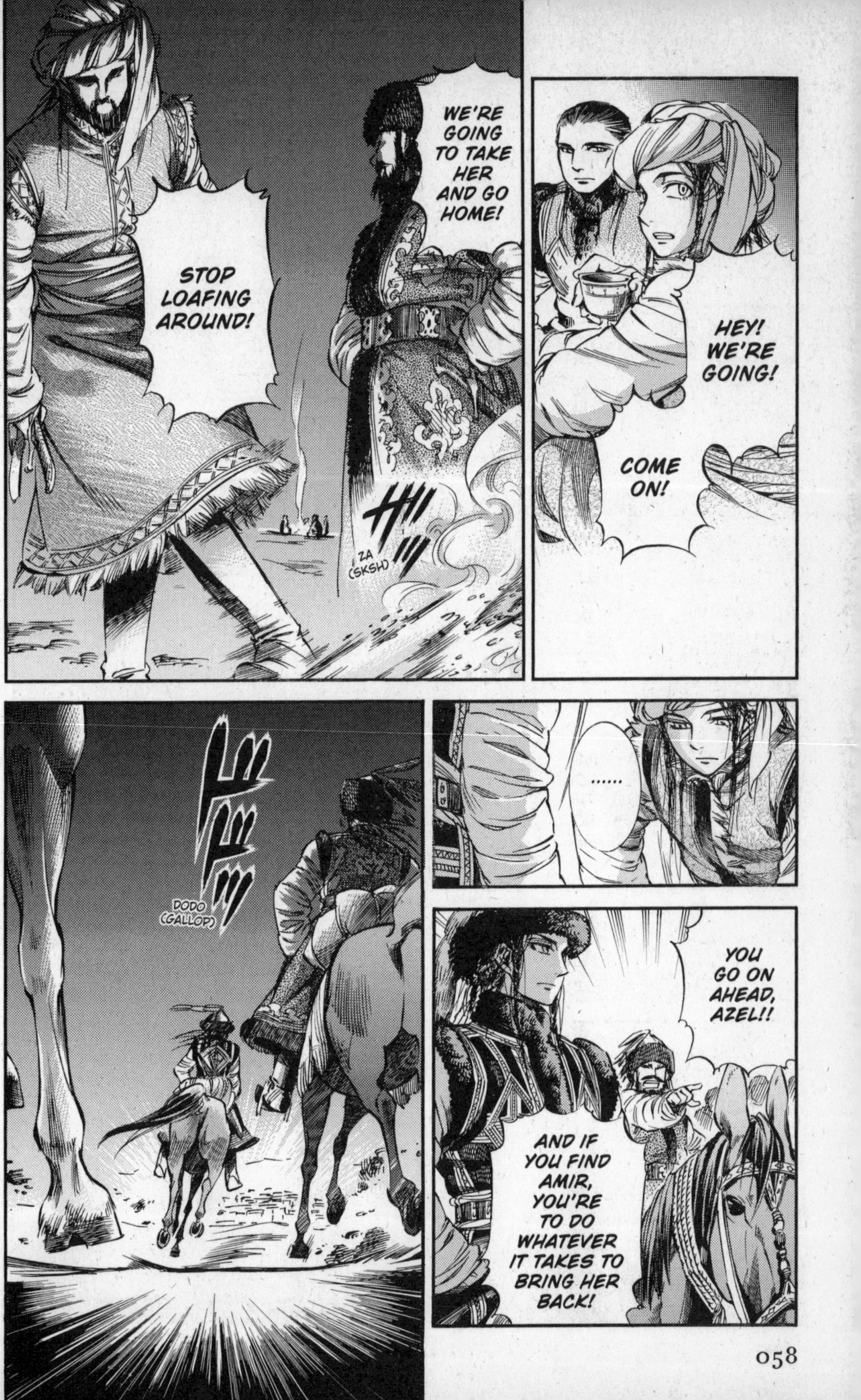
HEY! WE'RE GOING!
COME ON!
WE'RE GOING TO TAKE HER AND GO HOME!
STOP LOAFING AROUND!
ZA (SKSH)
......
YOU GO ON AHEAD, AZEL!!
AND IF YOU FIND AMIR, YOU'RE TO DO WHATEVER IT TAKES TO BRING HER BACK!
DODO (GALLOP)

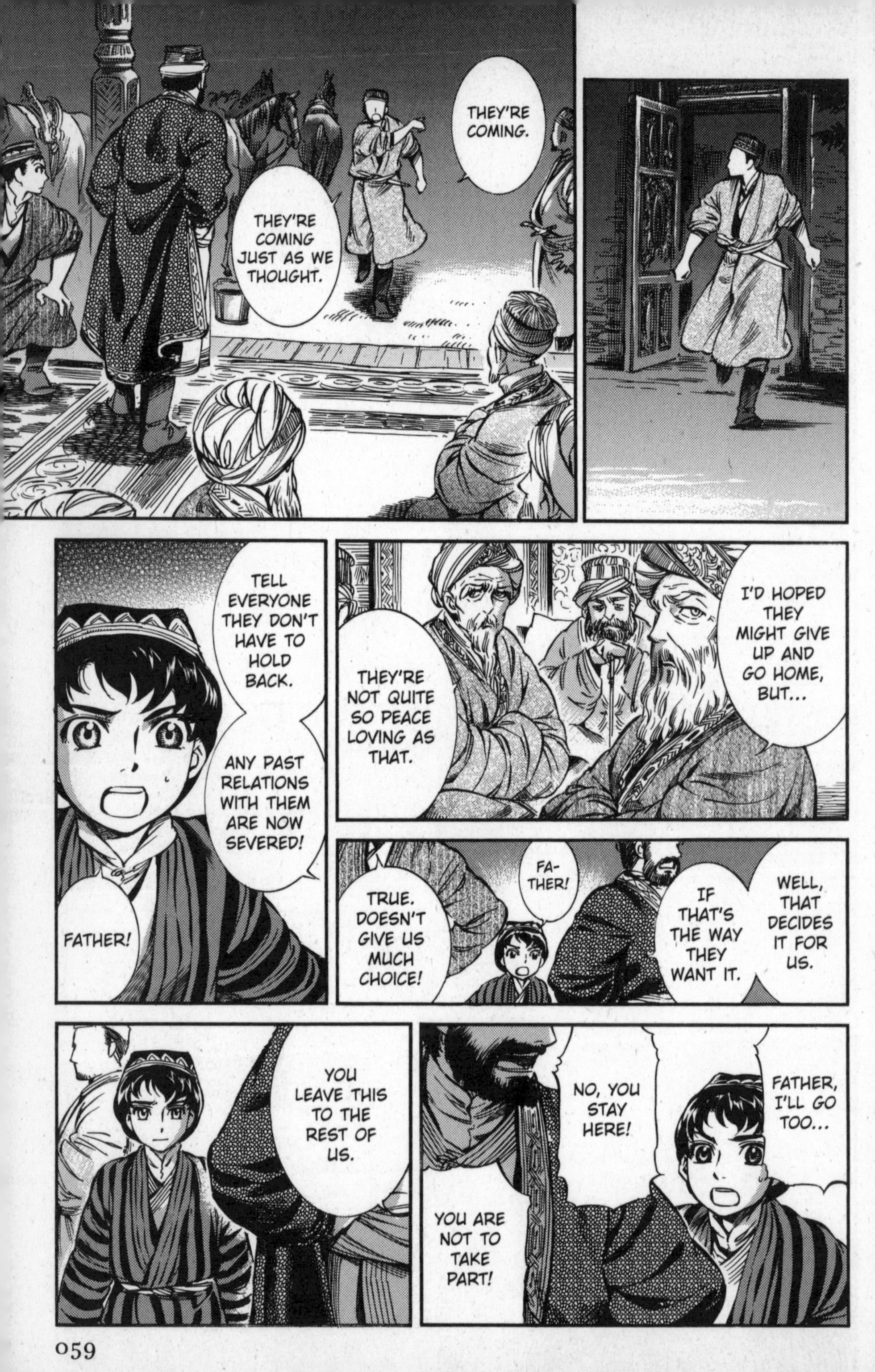
THEY'RE COMING.
THEY'RE COMING JUST AS WE THOUGHT.
I'D HOPED THEY MIGHT GIVE UP AND GO HOME, BUT...
THEY'RE NOT QUITE SO PEACE LOVING AS THAT.
WELL, THAT DECIDES IT FOR US.
IF THAT'S THE WAY THEY WANT IT.
FA-THER!
TRUE. DOESN'T GIVE US MUCH CHOICE!
TELL EVERYONE THEY DON'T HAVE TO HOLD BACK.
ANY PAST RELATIONS WITH THEM ARE NOW SEVERED!
FATHER!
FATHER, I'LL GO TOO...
NO, YOU STAY HERE!
YOU ARE NOT TO TAKE PART!
YOU LEAVE THIS TO THE REST OF US.

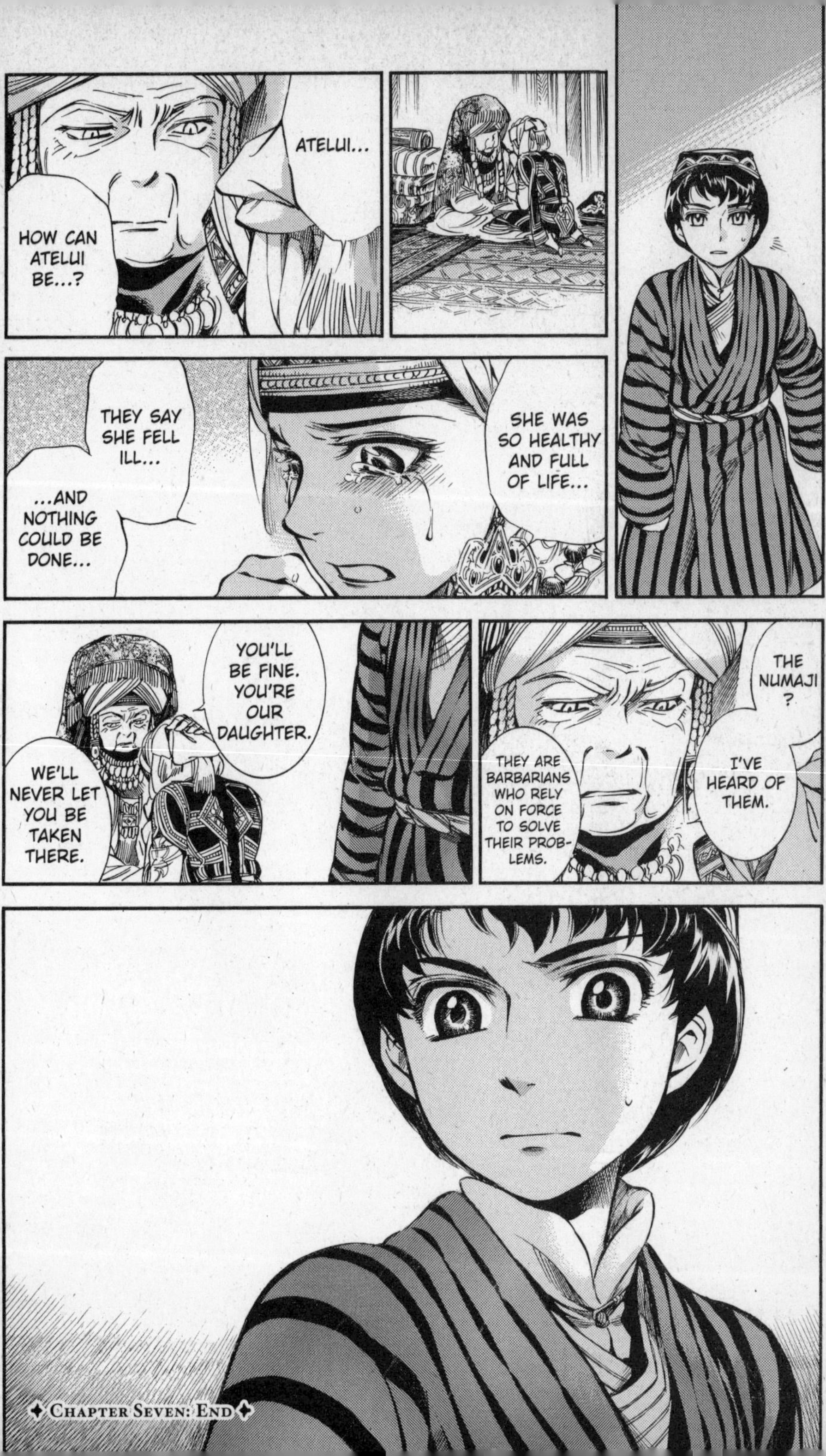
ATELUI...
HOW CAN ATELUI BE...?
SHE WAS SO HEALTHY AND FULL OF LIFE...
THEY SAY SHE FELL ILL...
...AND NOTHING COULD BE DONE...
THE NUMAJI?
I'VE HEARD OF THEM.
THEY ARE BARBARIANS WHO RELY ON FORCE TO SOLVE THEIR PROBLEMS.
YOU'LL BE FINE. YOU'RE OUR DAUGHTER.
WE'LL NEVER LET YOU BE TAKEN THERE.
✦CHAPTER SEVEN: END✦

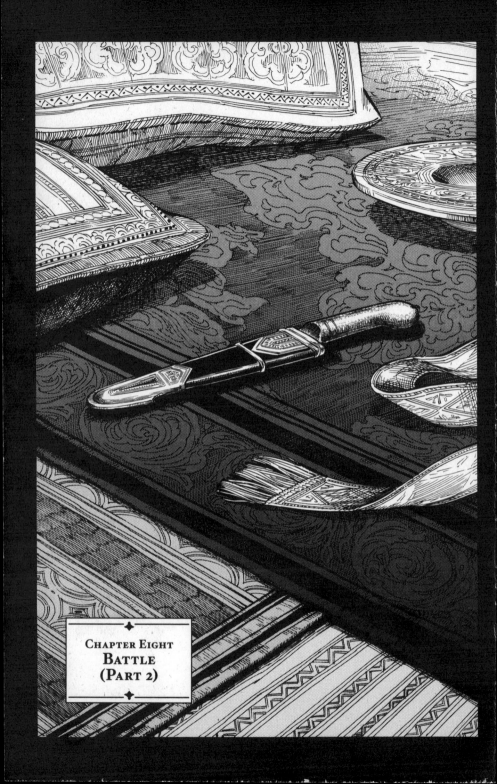

CHAPTER EIGHT
BATTLE
(PART 2)

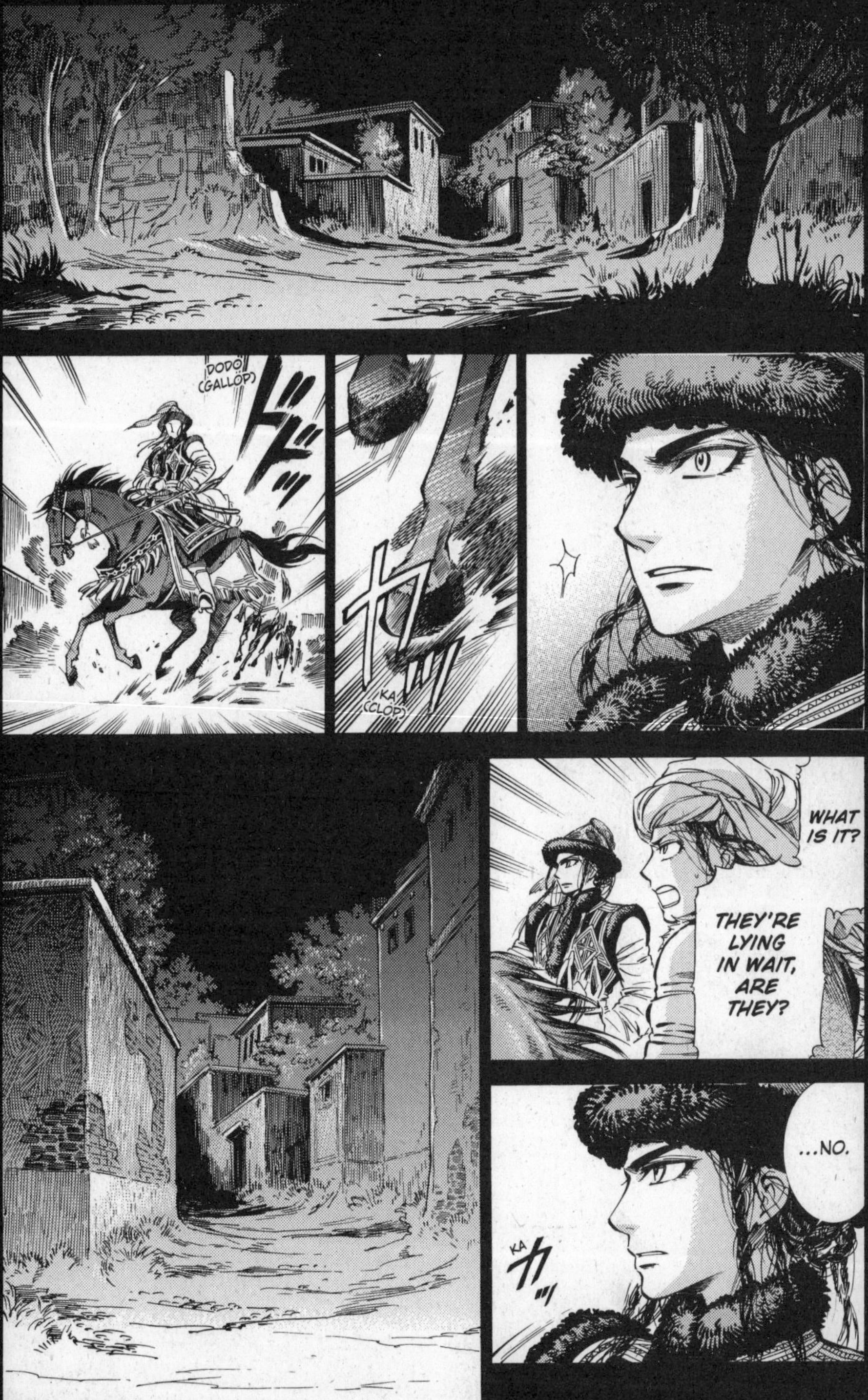

カッ
KA (CLOP)
ドドッ
DODO (GALLOP)
WHAT IS IT?
THEY'RE LYING IN WAIT, ARE THEY?
...NO.
カッ
KA

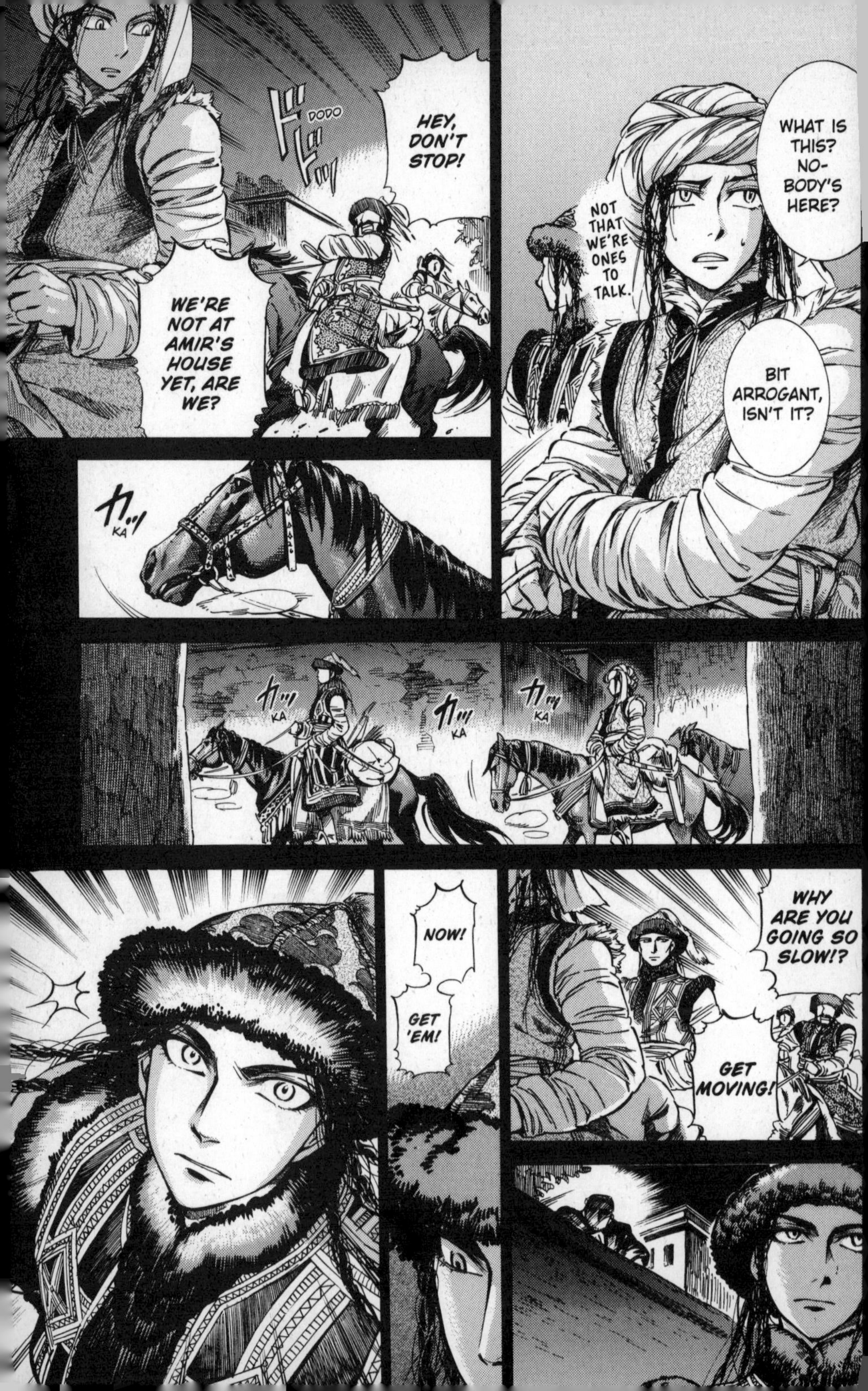
WHAT IS THIS? NO-BODY'S HERE?
NOT THAT WE'RE ONES TO TALK.
BIT ARROGANT, ISN'T IT?
HEY, DON'T STOP!
DODO
WE'RE NOT AT AMIR'S HOUSE YET, ARE WE?
KA
KA
KA
KA
WHY ARE YOU GOING SO SLOW!?
GET MOVING!
NOW!
GET 'EM!

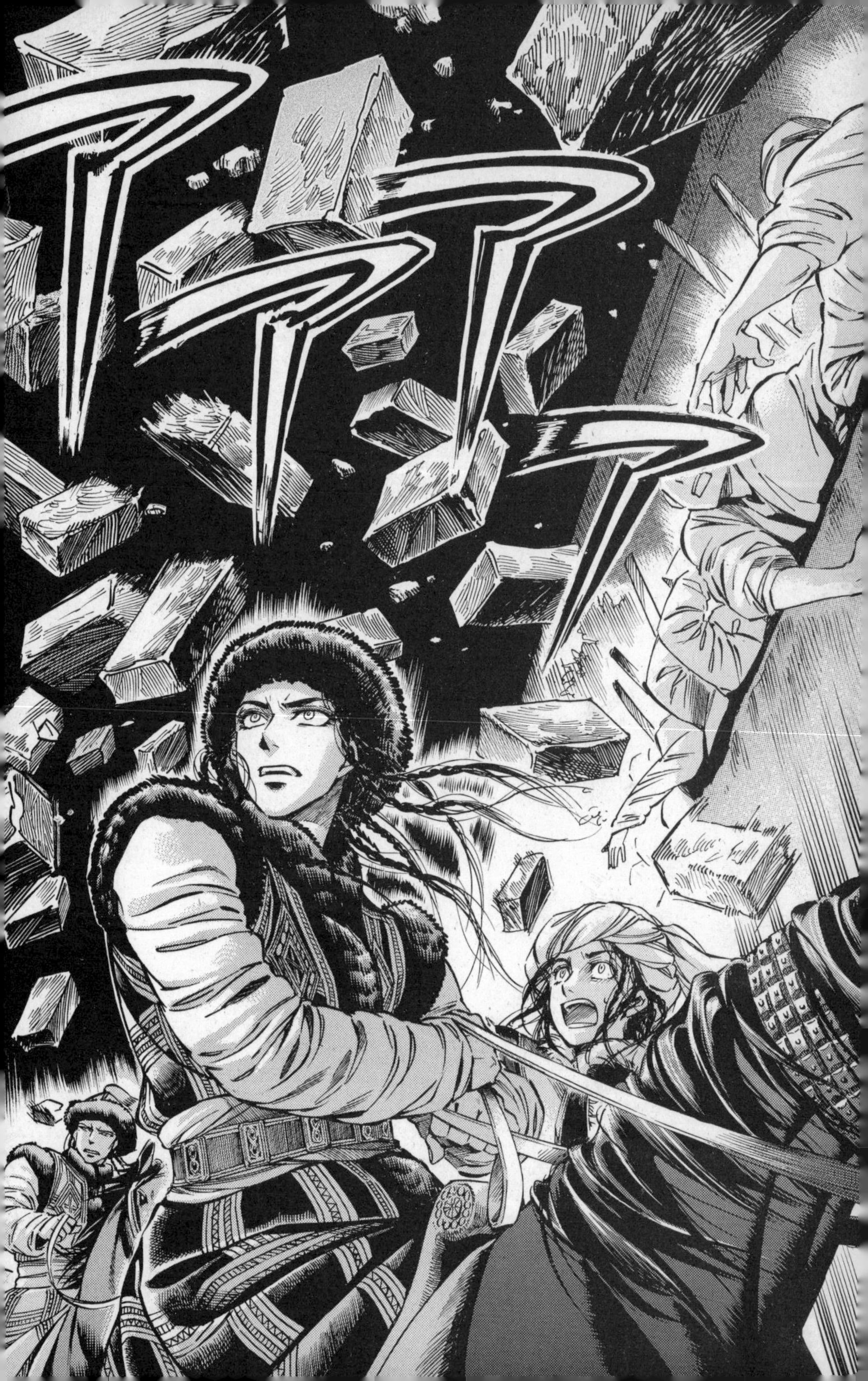

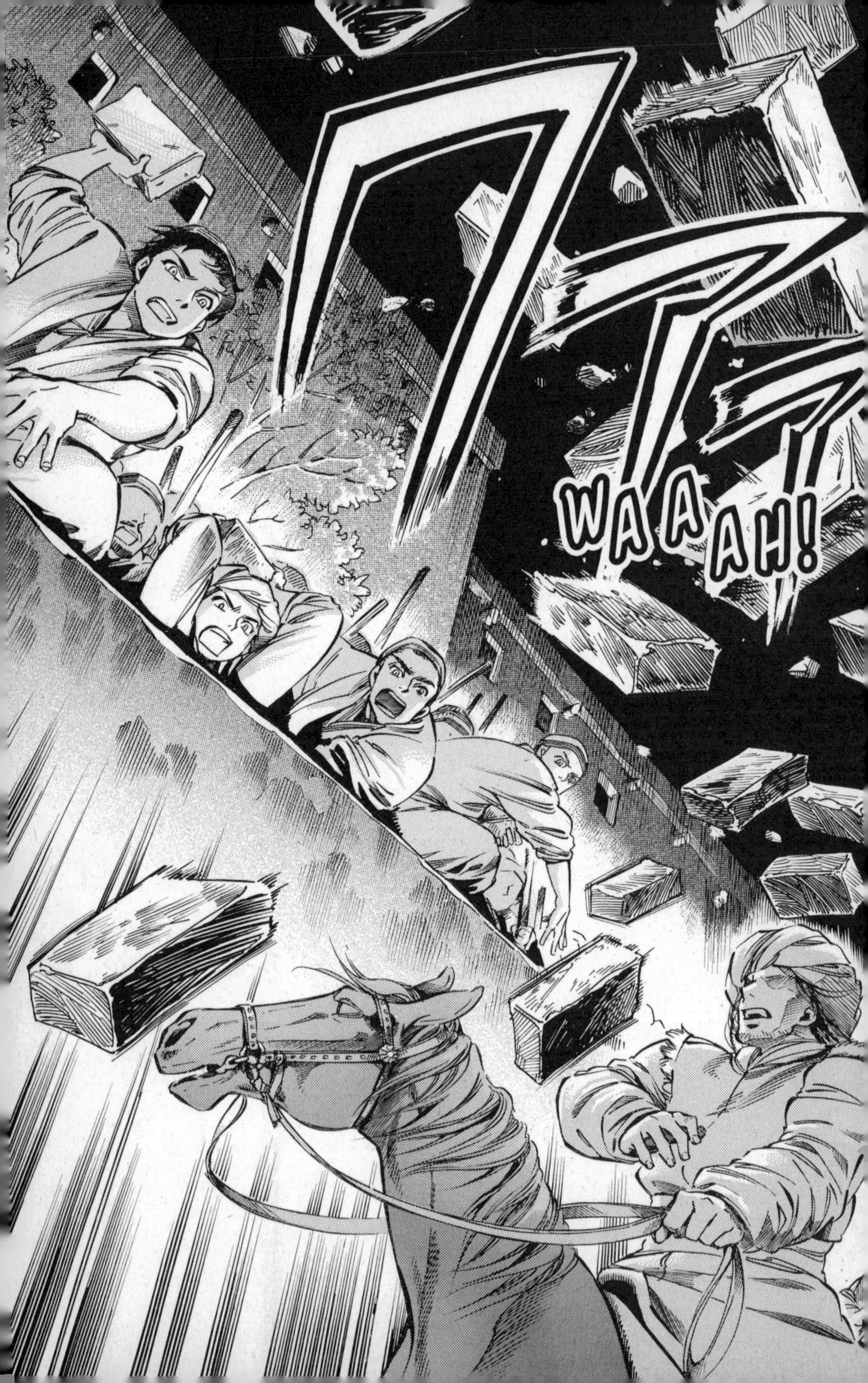
WAAAAH!

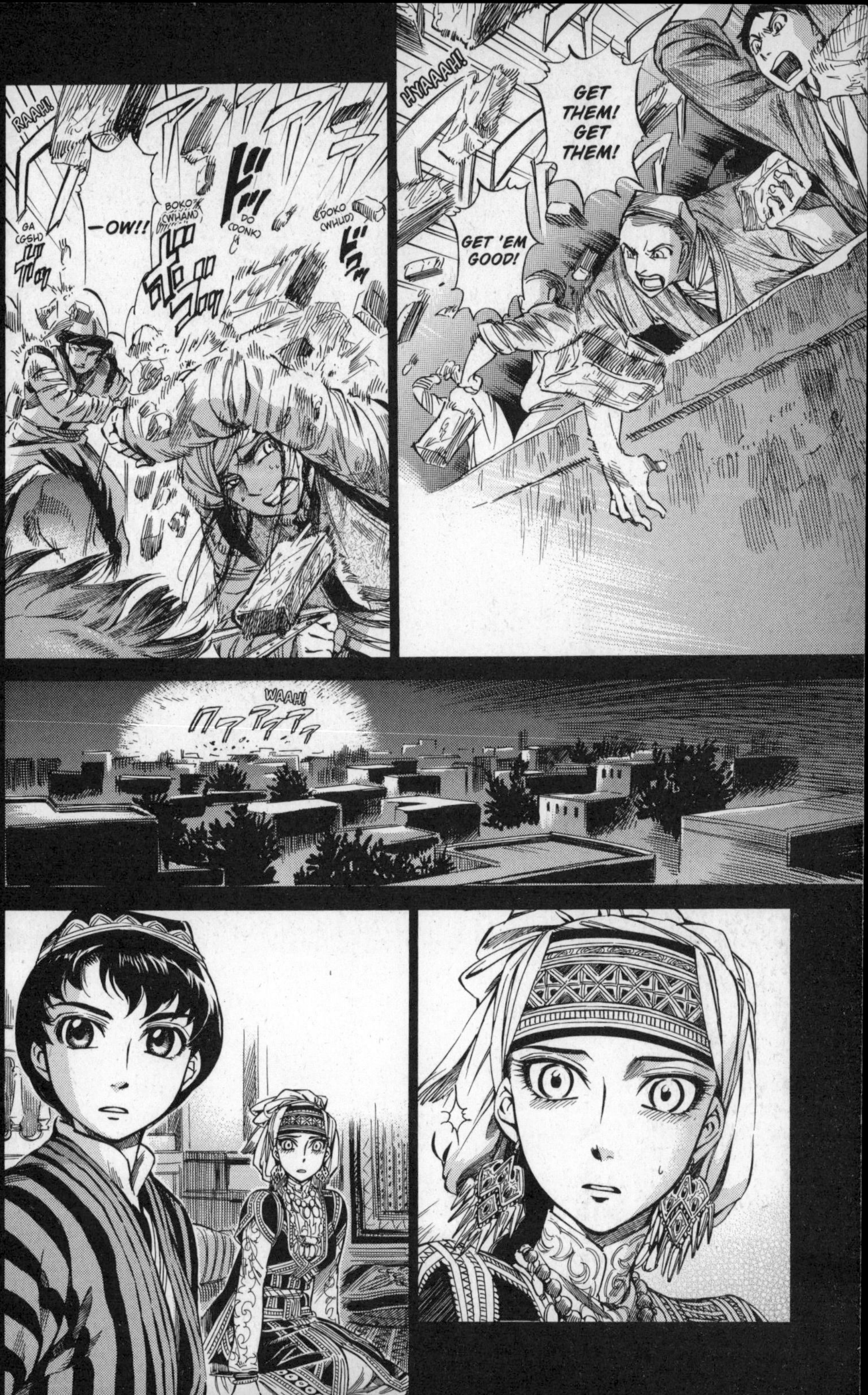
HYAAAH!!
GET THEM! GET THEM!
GET 'EM GOOD!
DOKO (WHUD)
DO (DONK)
BOKO (WHAM)
—OW!!
RAAH!
GA (GSH)
WAAH!

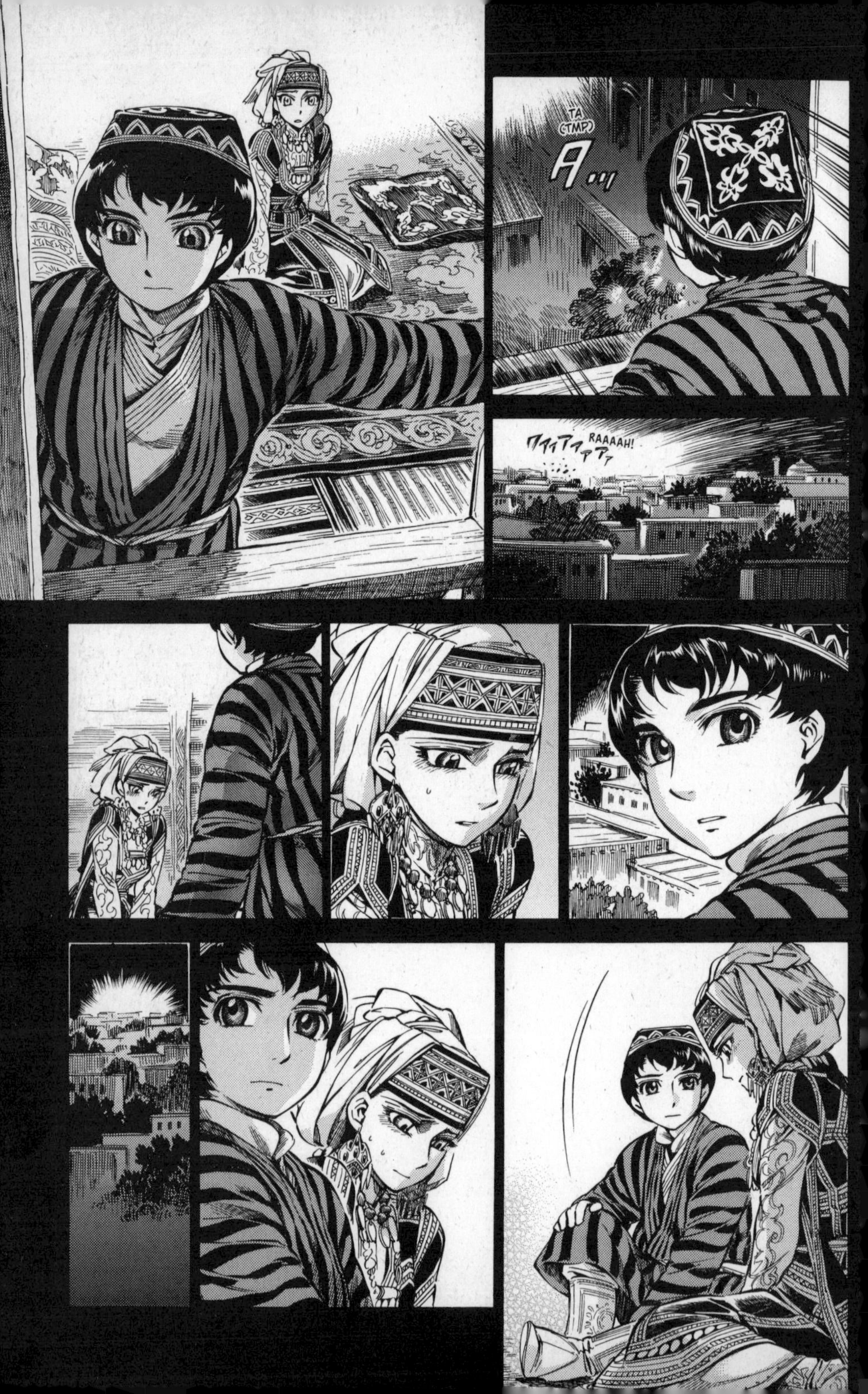
TA
(TMP)
RAAAAH!

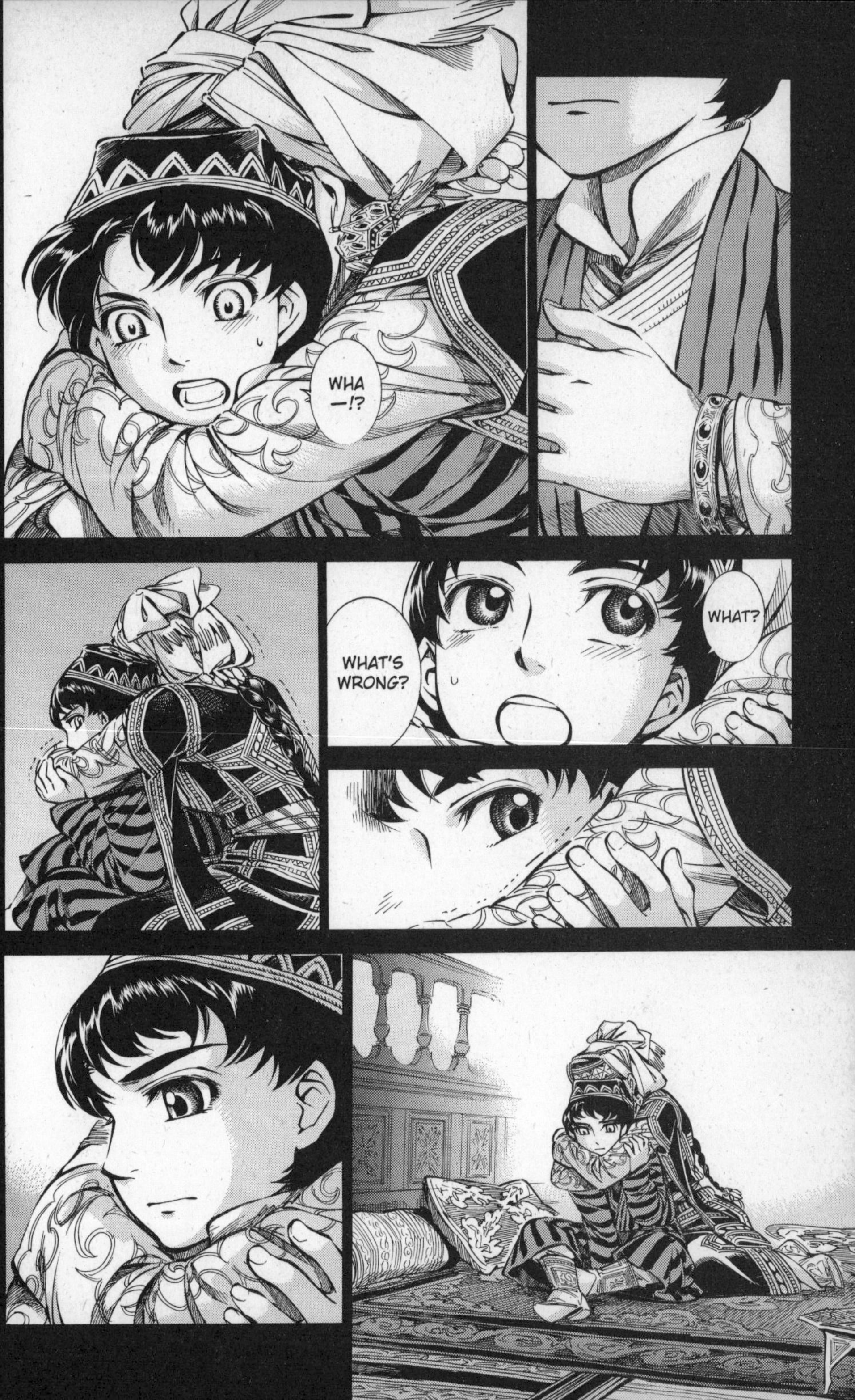
WHA—!?
WHAT?
WHAT'S WRONG?

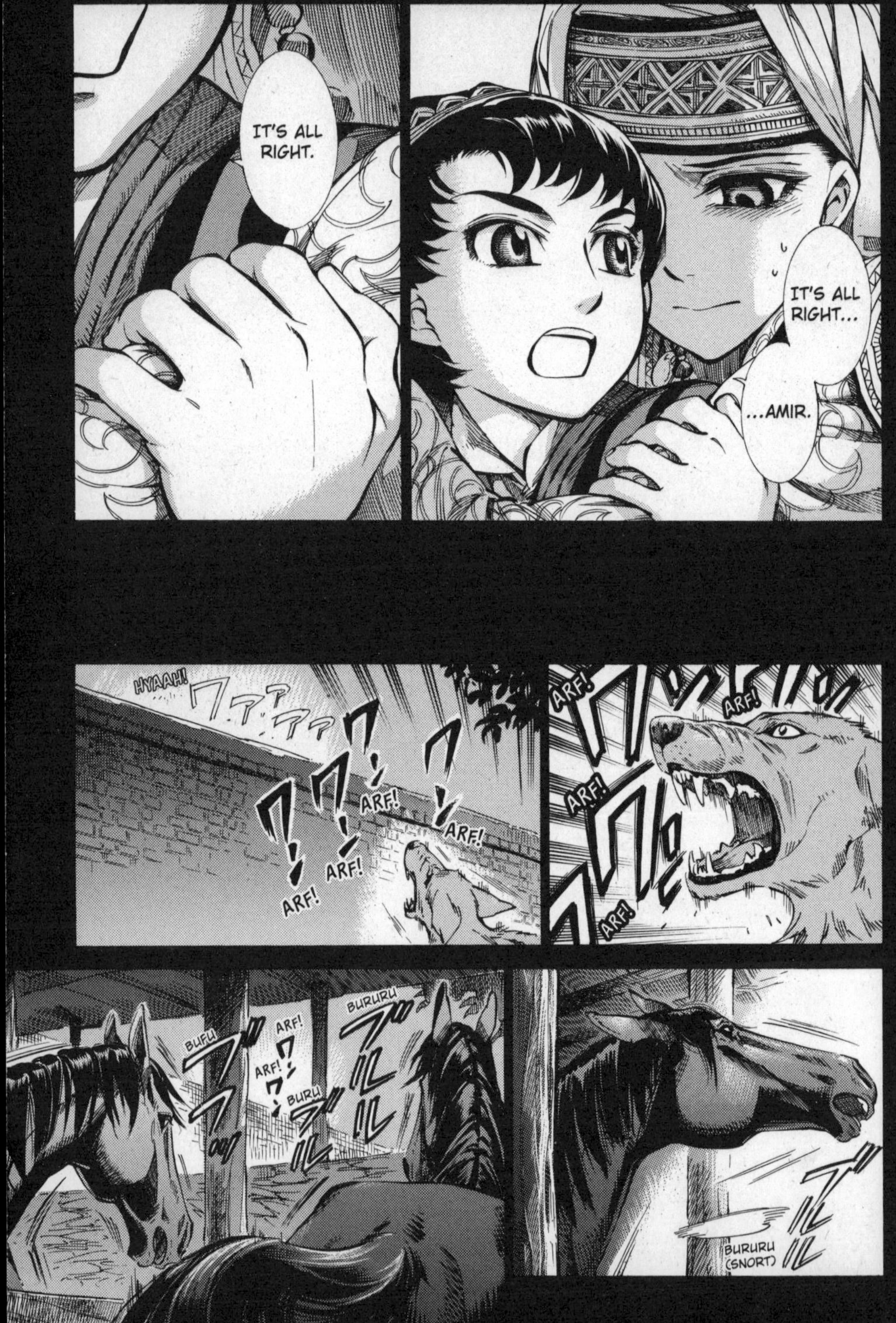
IT'S ALL RIGHT...
...AMIR.
IT'S ALL RIGHT.
ARF!
ARF!
ARF!
ARF!
HYAAH!
ARF!
ARF!
ARF!
ARF!
ARF!
BURURU (SNORT)
BURURU
ARF!
ARF!
BUFU
BURU

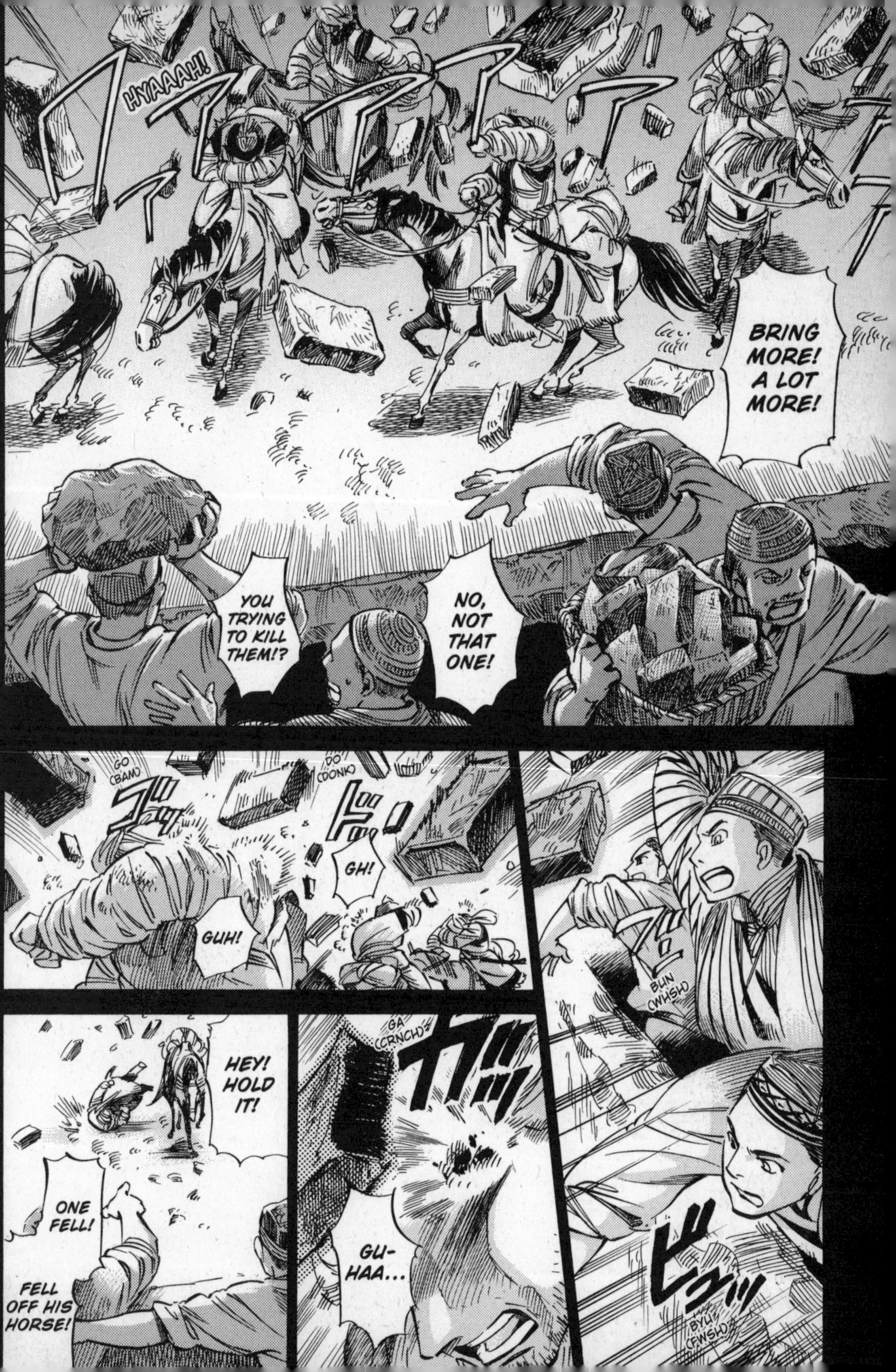
HYAAAH!
BRING MORE! A LOT MORE!
NO, NOT THAT ONE!
YOU TRYING TO KILL THEM!?
BUN (WHSH)
BYU (FWSH)
DO (DONK)
GH!
GO (BAM)
GUH!
GA (CRNCH)
GU-HAA...
HEY! HOLD IT!
ONE FELL!
FELL OFF HIS HORSE!

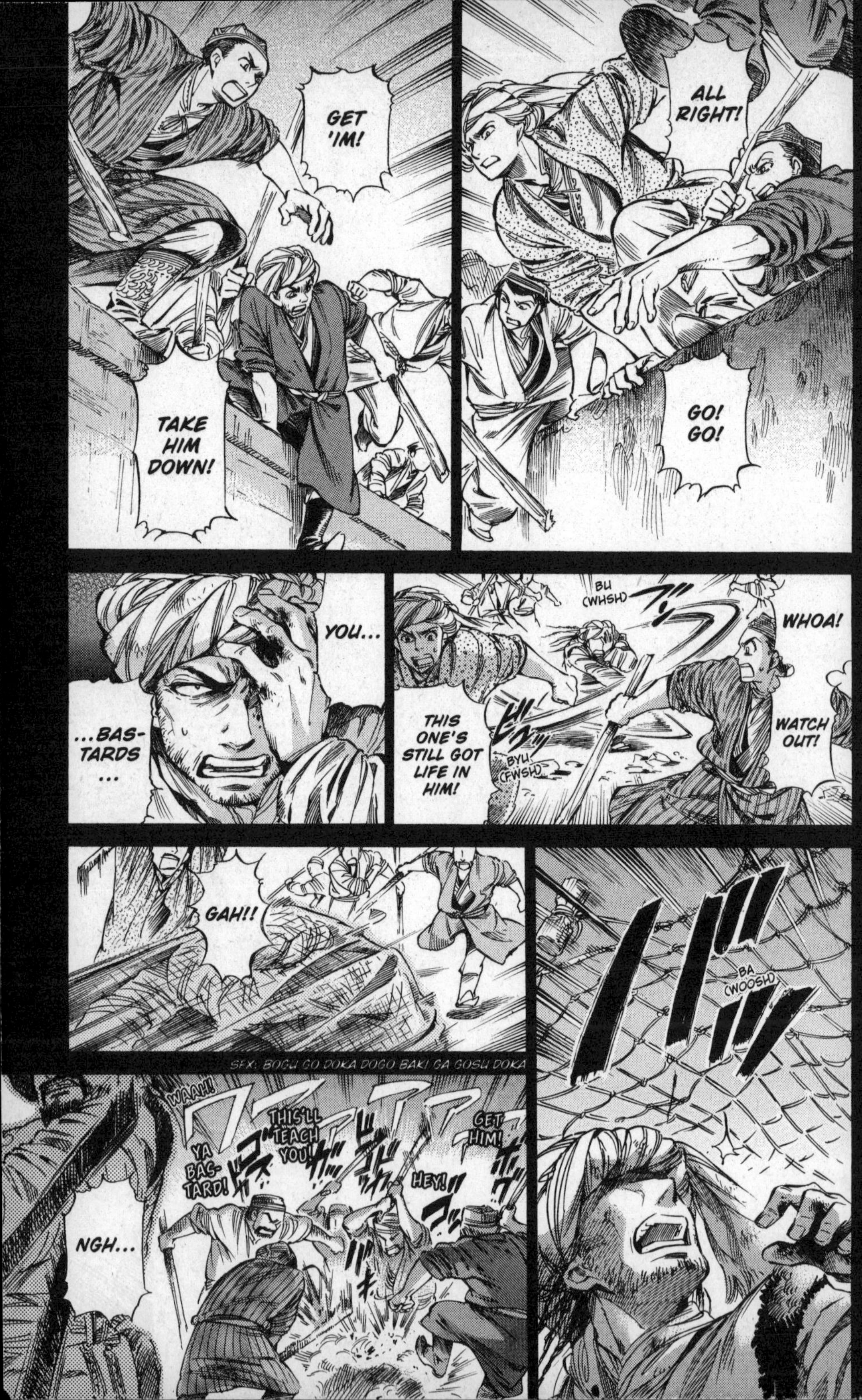
ALL RIGHT!
GO! GO!
GET 'IM!
TAKE HIM DOWN!
WHOA!
WATCH OUT!
BU (WHSH)
THIS ONE'S STILL GOT LIFE IN HIM!
BYU (FWSH)
YOU...
...BAS-TARDS...
BA (WOOSH)
GAH!!
SFX: BOGU GO DOKA DOGO BAKI GA GOSU DOKA
GET HIM!
HEY!
THIS'LL TEACH YOU!
WAAH!
YA BAS-TARD!
NGH...

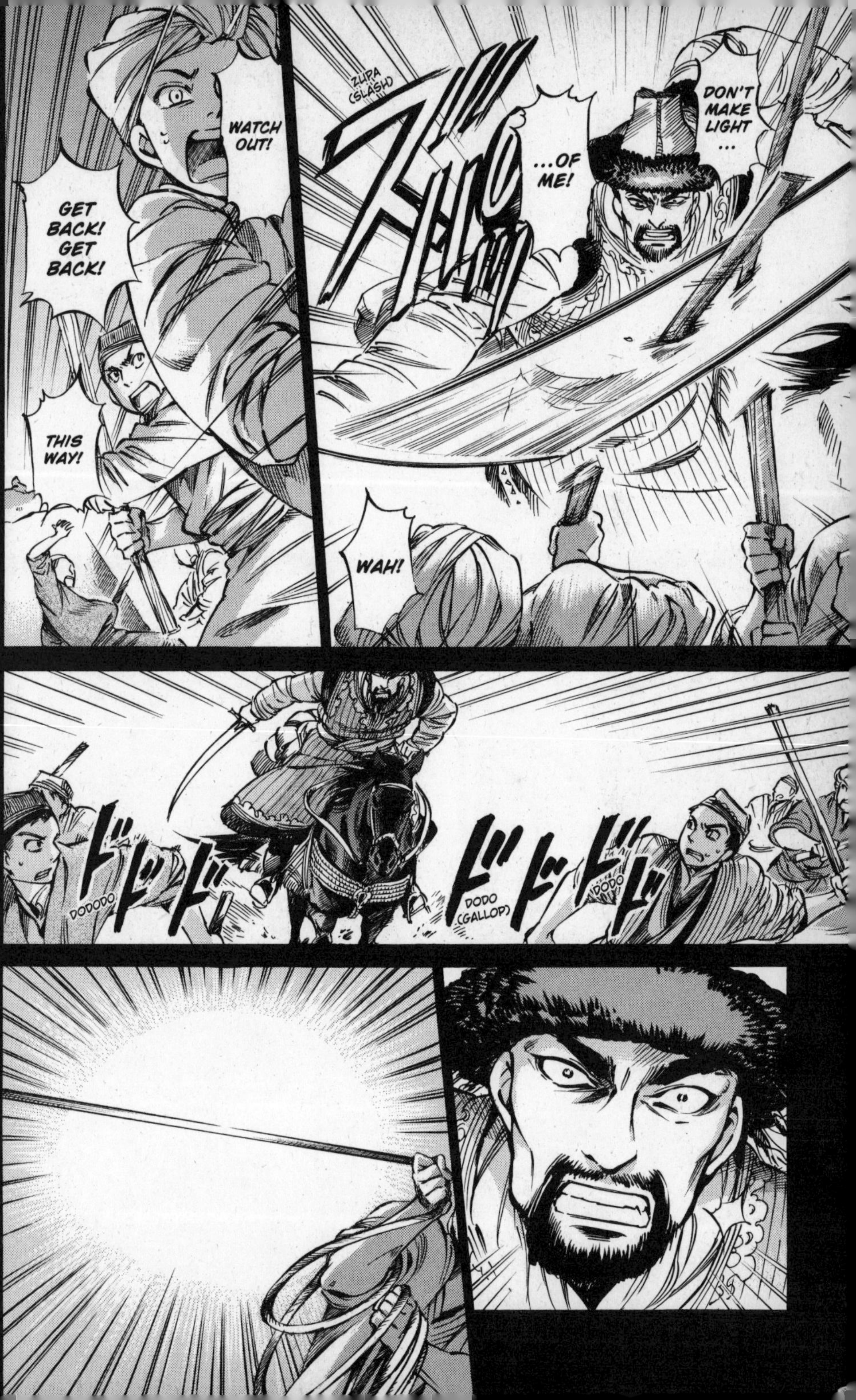
DON'T MAKE LIGHT ...
...OF ME!
ZUPA (SLASH)
WAH!
WATCH OUT!
GET BACK! GET BACK!
THIS WAY!
DODO
DODO (GALLOP)
DODODO

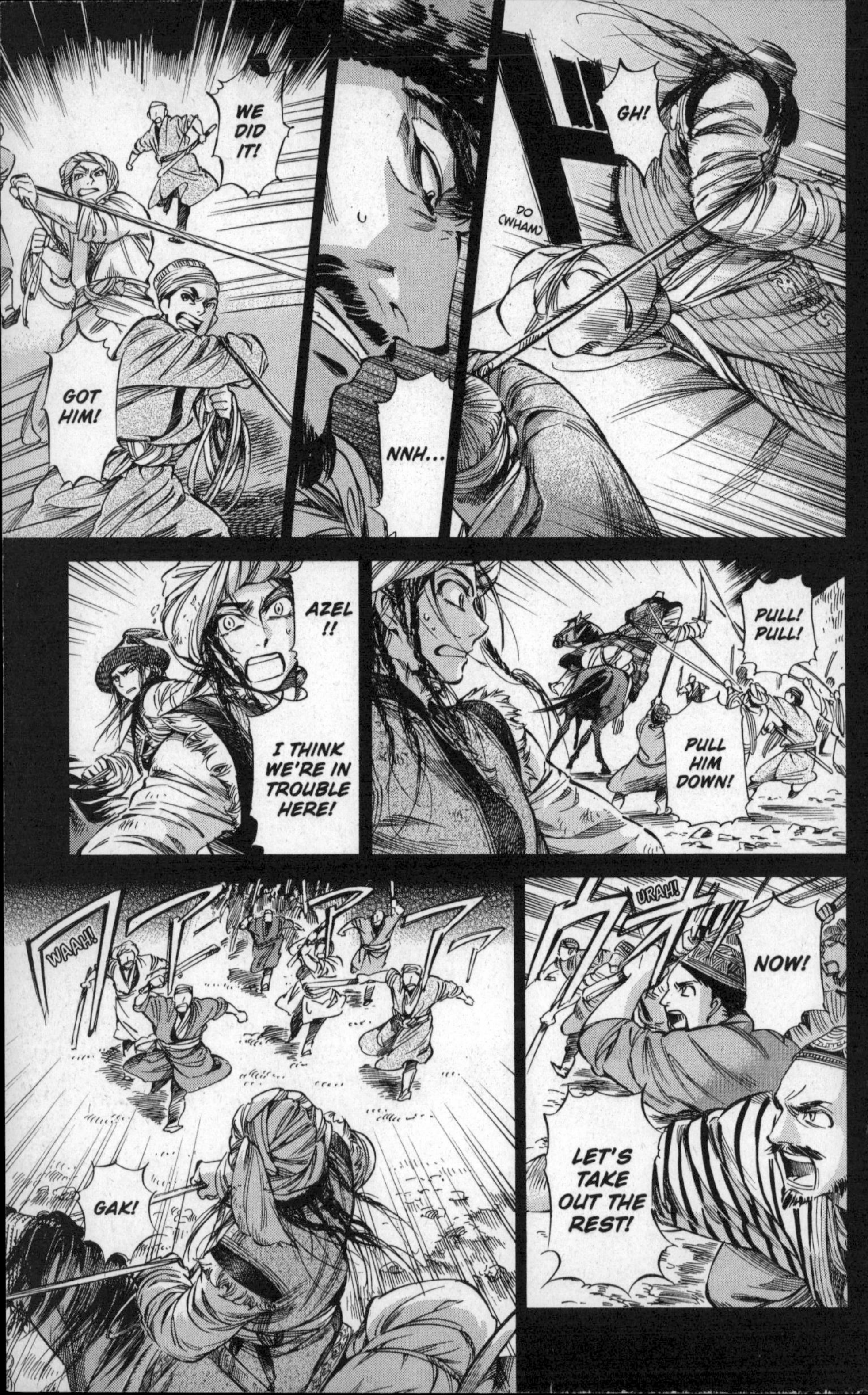
GH!
DO (WHAM)
NNH...
WE DID IT!
GOT HIM!
PULL! PULL!
PULL HIM DOWN!
AZEL !!
I THINK WE'RE IN TROUBLE HERE!
URAH!
NOW!
LET'S TAKE OUT THE REST!
WAAH!
GAK!

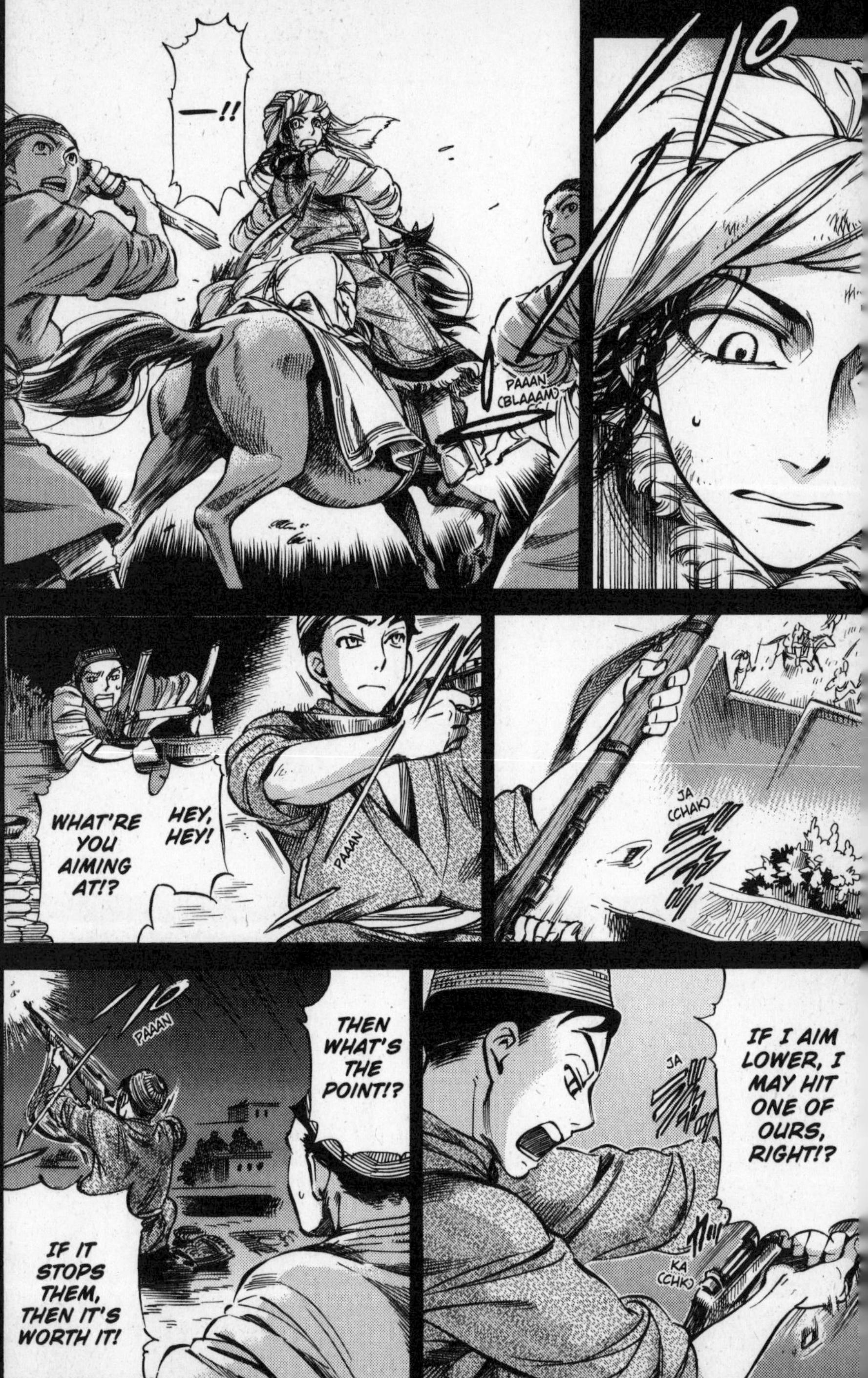
—!!
PAAAN (BLAAAM)
JA (CHAK)
HEY, HEY!
WHAT'RE YOU AIMING AT!?
PAAAN
IF I AIM LOWER, I MAY HIT ONE OF OURS, RIGHT!?
JA
KA (CHK)
PAAAN
THEN WHAT'S THE POINT!?
IF IT STOPS THEM, THEN IT'S WORTH IT!

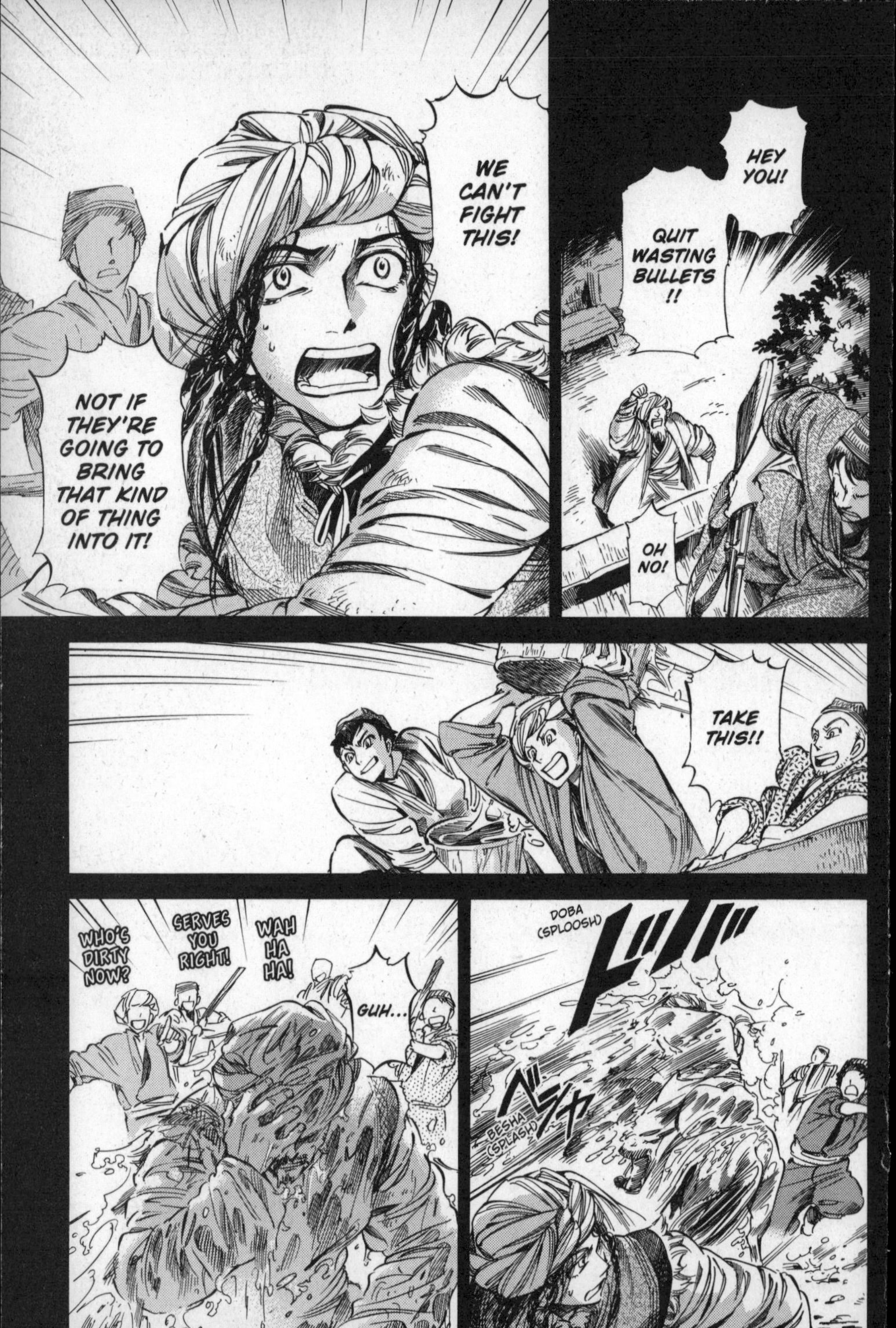
HEY YOU!
QUIT WASTING BULLETS!!
OH NO!
WE CAN'T FIGHT THIS!
NOT IF THEY'RE GOING TO BRING THAT KIND OF THING INTO IT!
TAKE THIS!!
DOBA (SPLOOSH)
ベシャ
BESHA (SPLASH)
WAH HA HA!
SERVES YOU RIGHT!
WHO'S DIRTY NOW?
GUH...

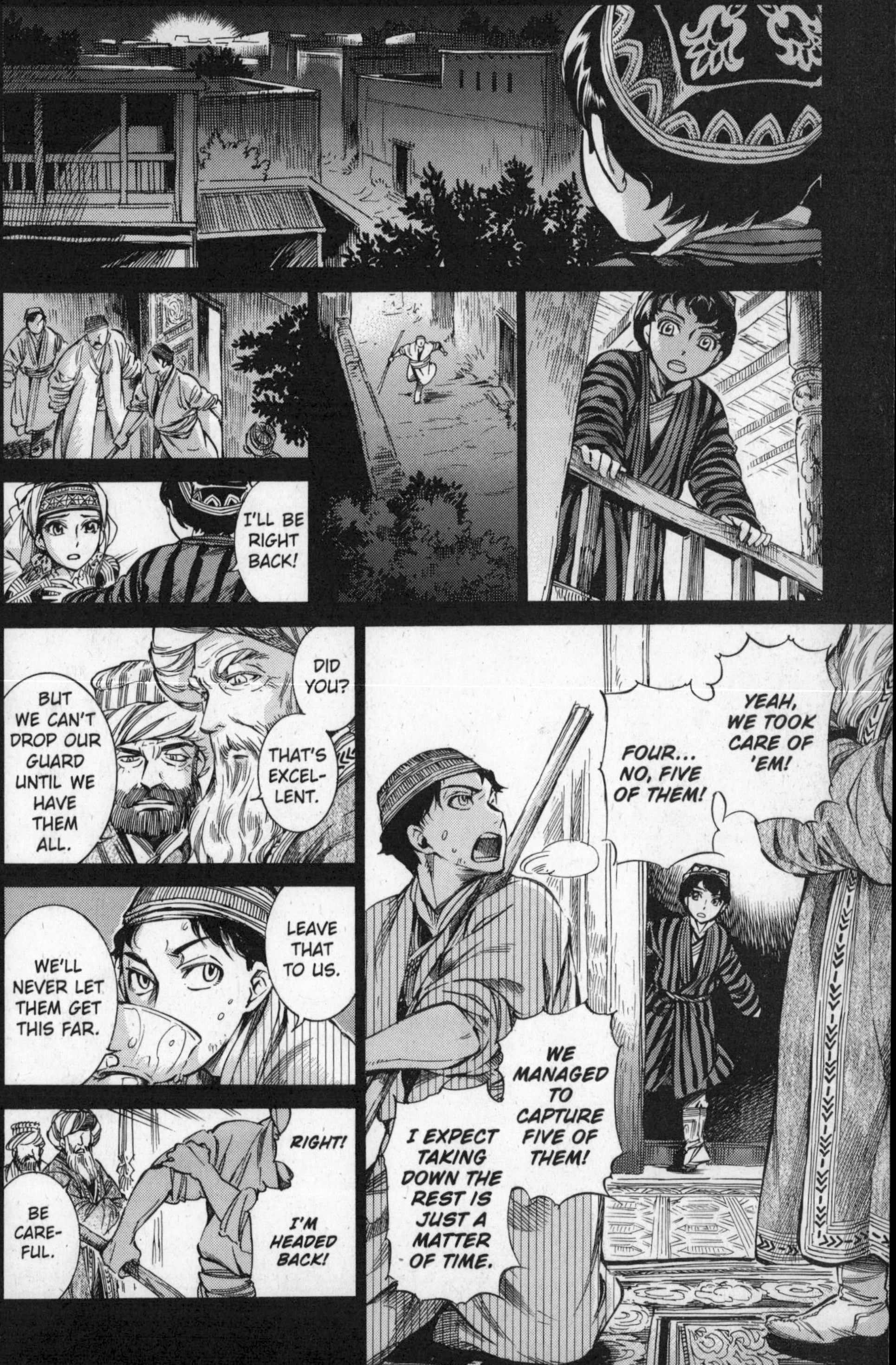
I'LL BE RIGHT BACK!
YEAH, WE TOOK CARE OF 'EM!
FOUR... NO, FIVE OF THEM!
WE MANAGED TO CAPTURE FIVE OF THEM!
I EXPECT TAKING DOWN THE REST IS JUST A MATTER OF TIME.
DID YOU?
THAT'S EXCEL-LENT.
BUT WE CAN'T DROP OUR GUARD UNTIL WE HAVE THEM ALL.
LEAVE THAT TO US.
WE'LL NEVER LET THEM GET THIS FAR.
RIGHT!
I'M HEADED BACK!
BE CARE-FUL.

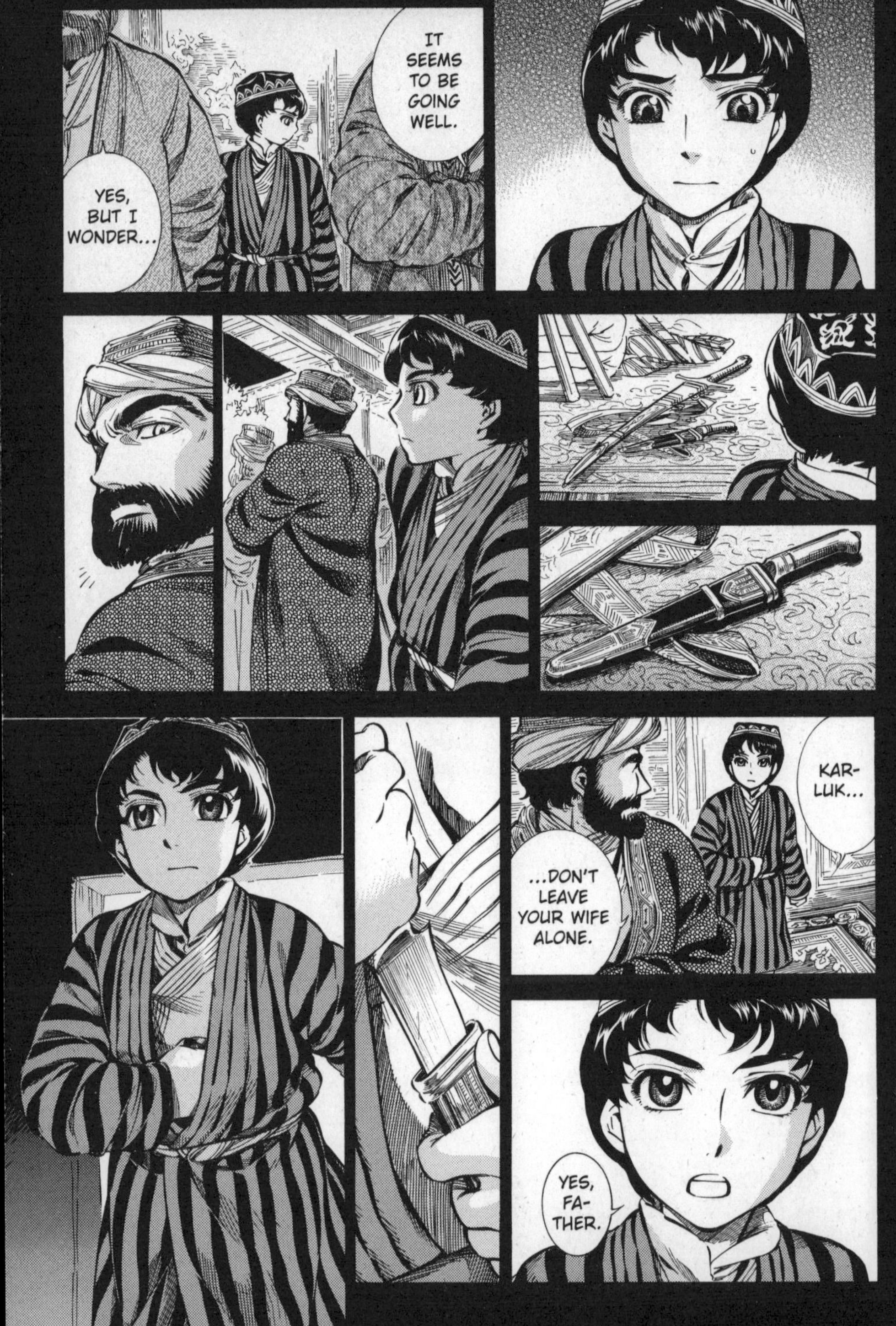
IT SEEMS TO BE GOING WELL.
YES, BUT I WONDER...
KAR-LUK...
...DON'T LEAVE YOUR WIFE ALONE.
YES, FA-THER.

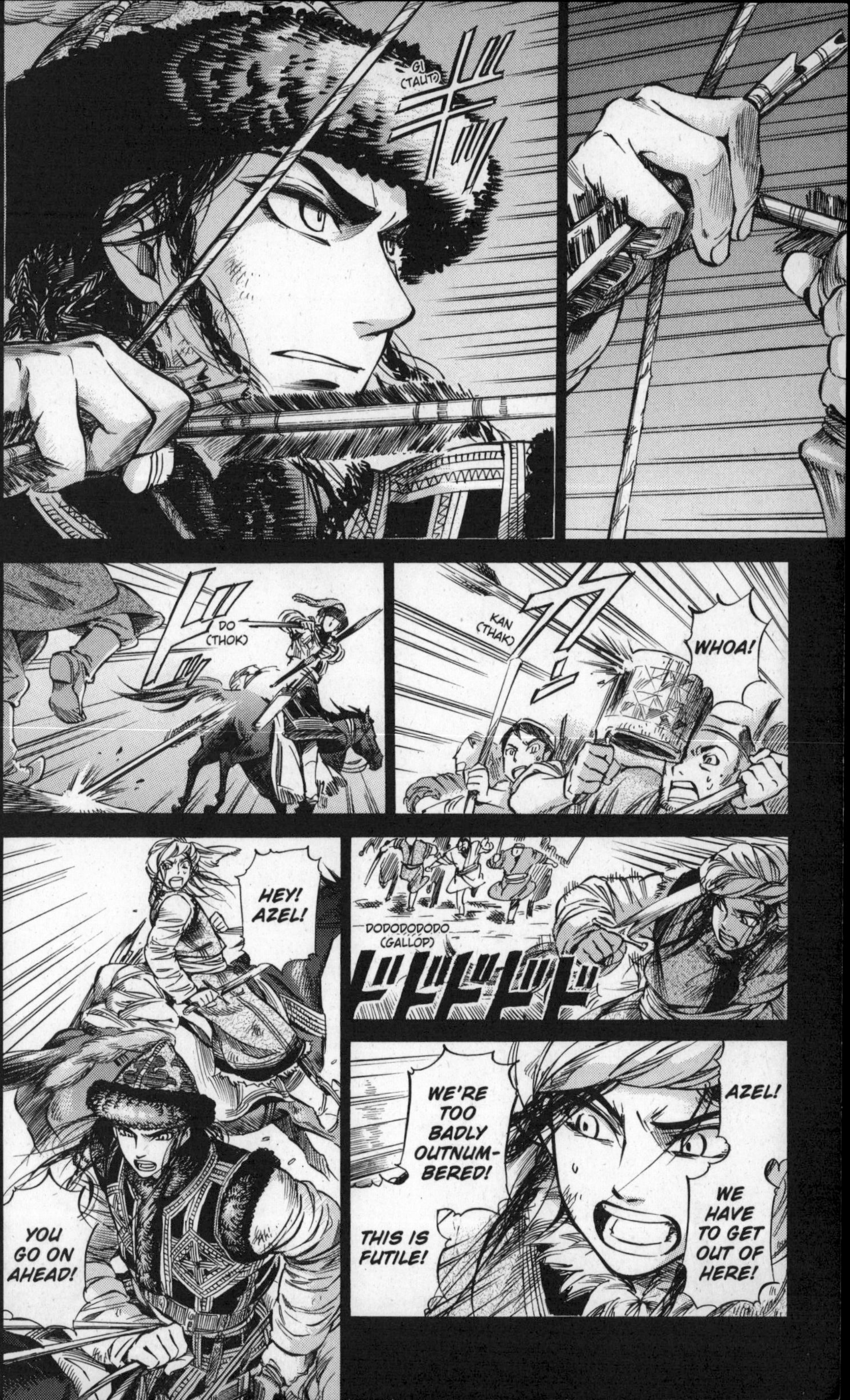
GI (TAUT)
KAN (THAK)
WHOA!
DO (THOK)
DODODODODO (GALLOP)
AZEL!
WE HAVE TO GET OUT OF HERE!
WE'RE TOO BADLY OUTNUMBERED!
THIS IS FUTILE!
HEY! AZEL!
YOU GO ON AHEAD!

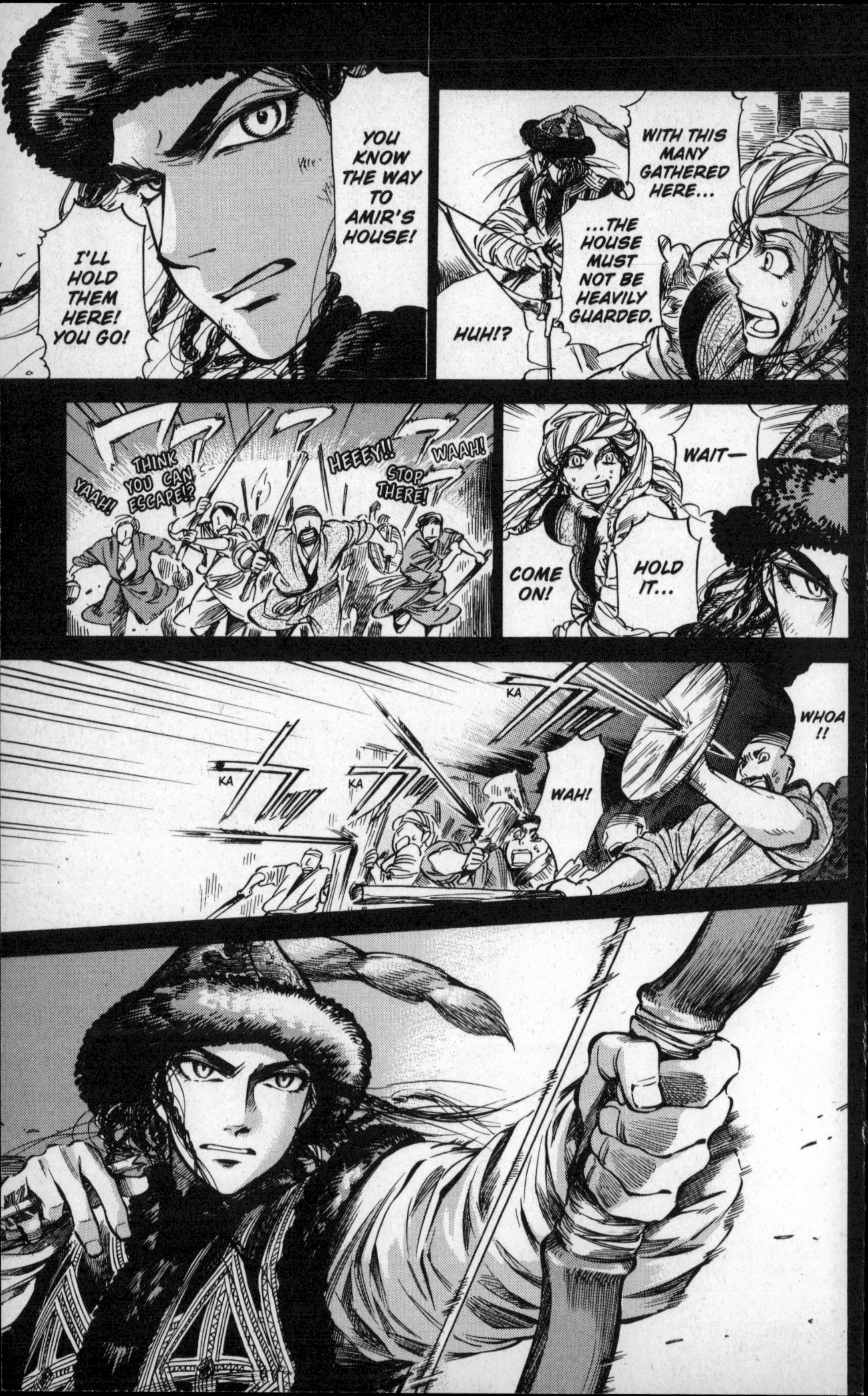
WITH THIS MANY GATHERED HERE...
...THE HOUSE MUST NOT BE HEAVILY GUARDED.
HUH!?
YOU KNOW THE WAY TO AMIR'S HOUSE!
I'LL HOLD THEM HERE! YOU GO!
WAIT—
HOLD IT...
COME ON!
WAAH!
STOP THERE!
HEEEY!!
THINK YOU CAN ESCAPE!?
YAAH!
WHOA !!
KA
WAH!
KA
KA

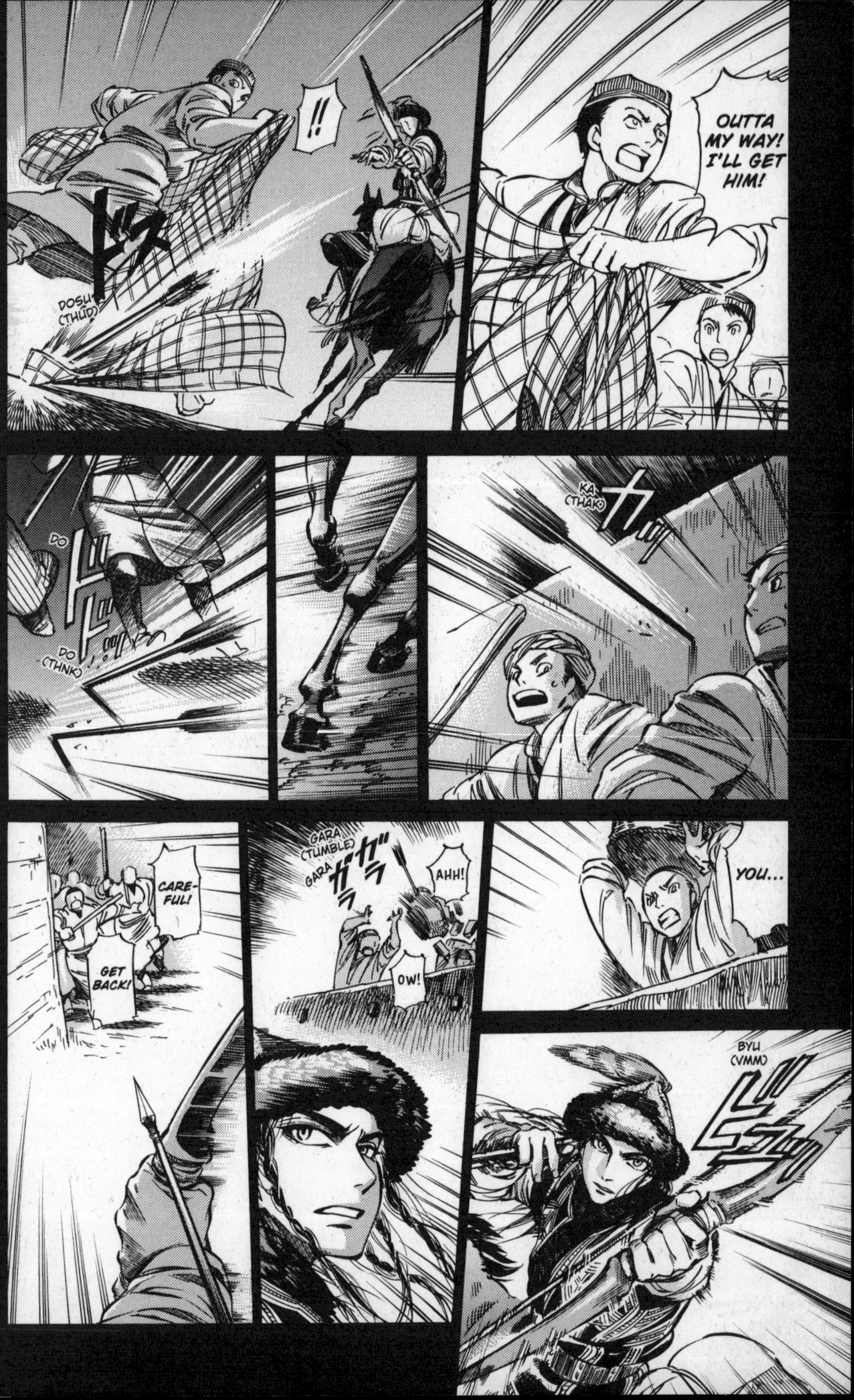
OUTTA MY WAY! I'LL GET HIM!
!!
DOSU (THUD)
KA (THAK)
DO (THNK) DO
YOU...
GARA (TUMBLE) GARA
AHH!
OW!
CARE-FUL!
GET BACK!
BYU (VMM)

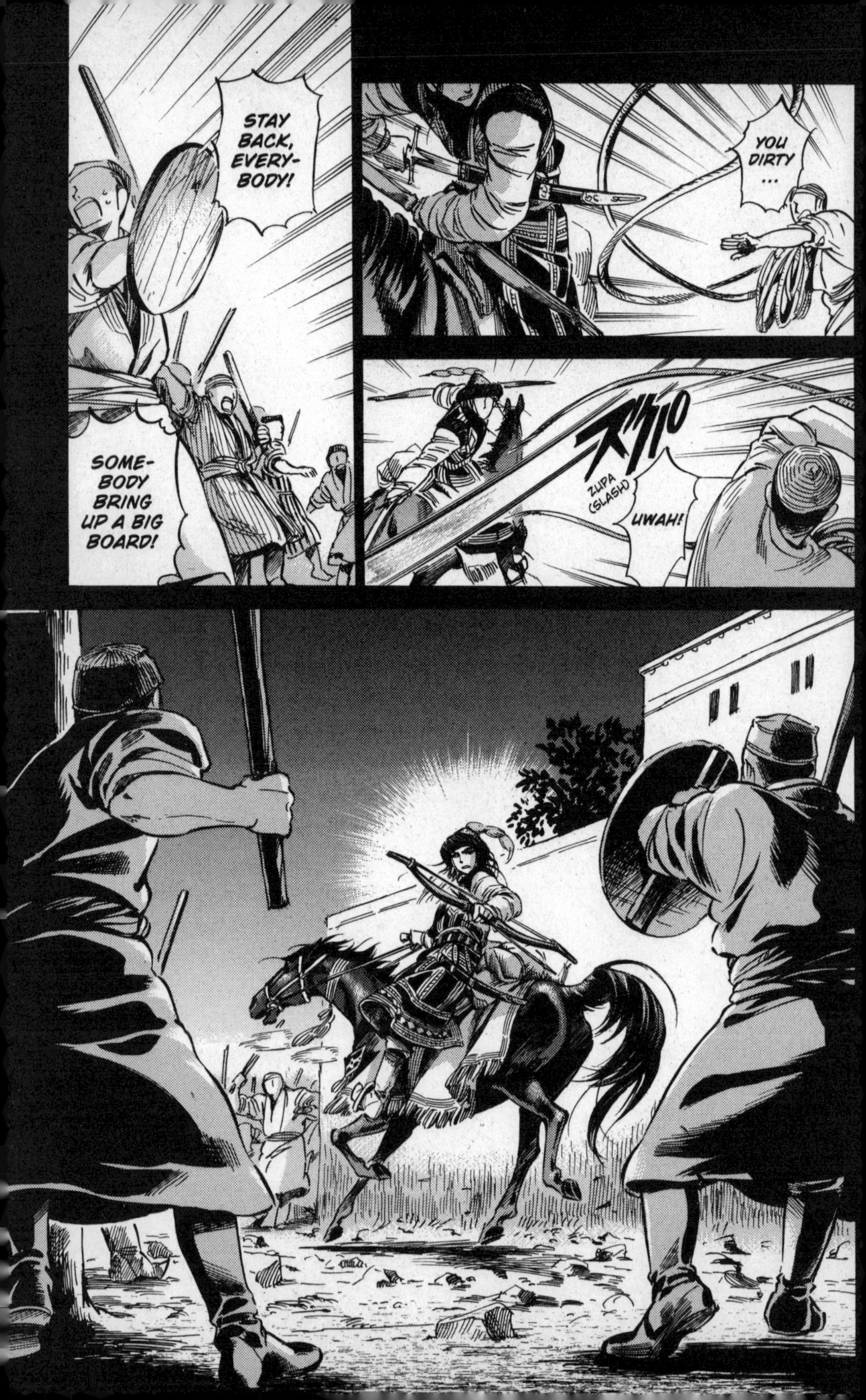
YOU DIRTY ...
ZUPA (SLASH)
UWAH!
STAY BACK, EVERY-BODY!
SOME-BODY BRING UP A BIG BOARD!

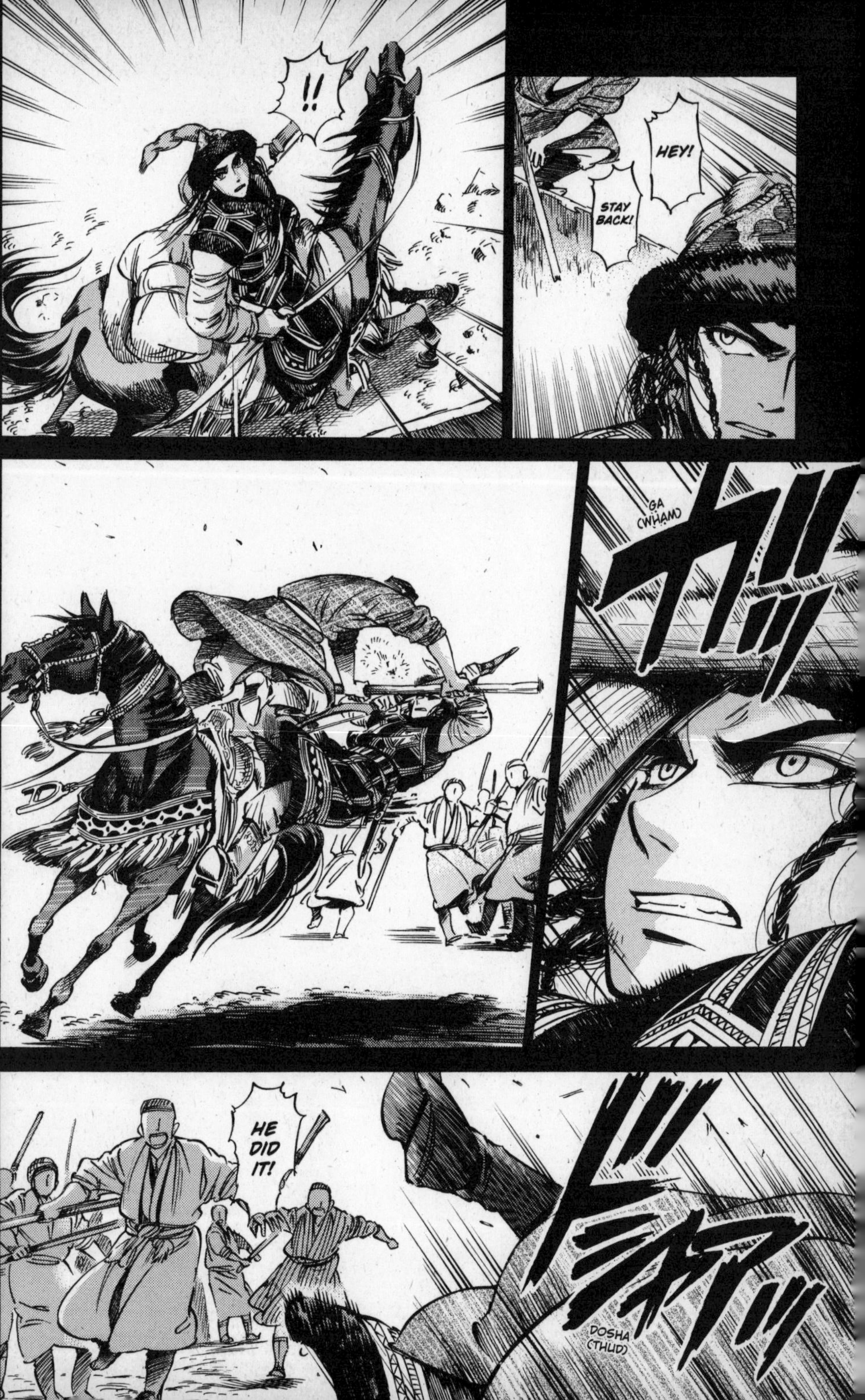
HEY!
STAY BACK!
!!
ガッ
GA (WHAM)
ドシャッ
DOSHA (THUD)
HE DID IT!

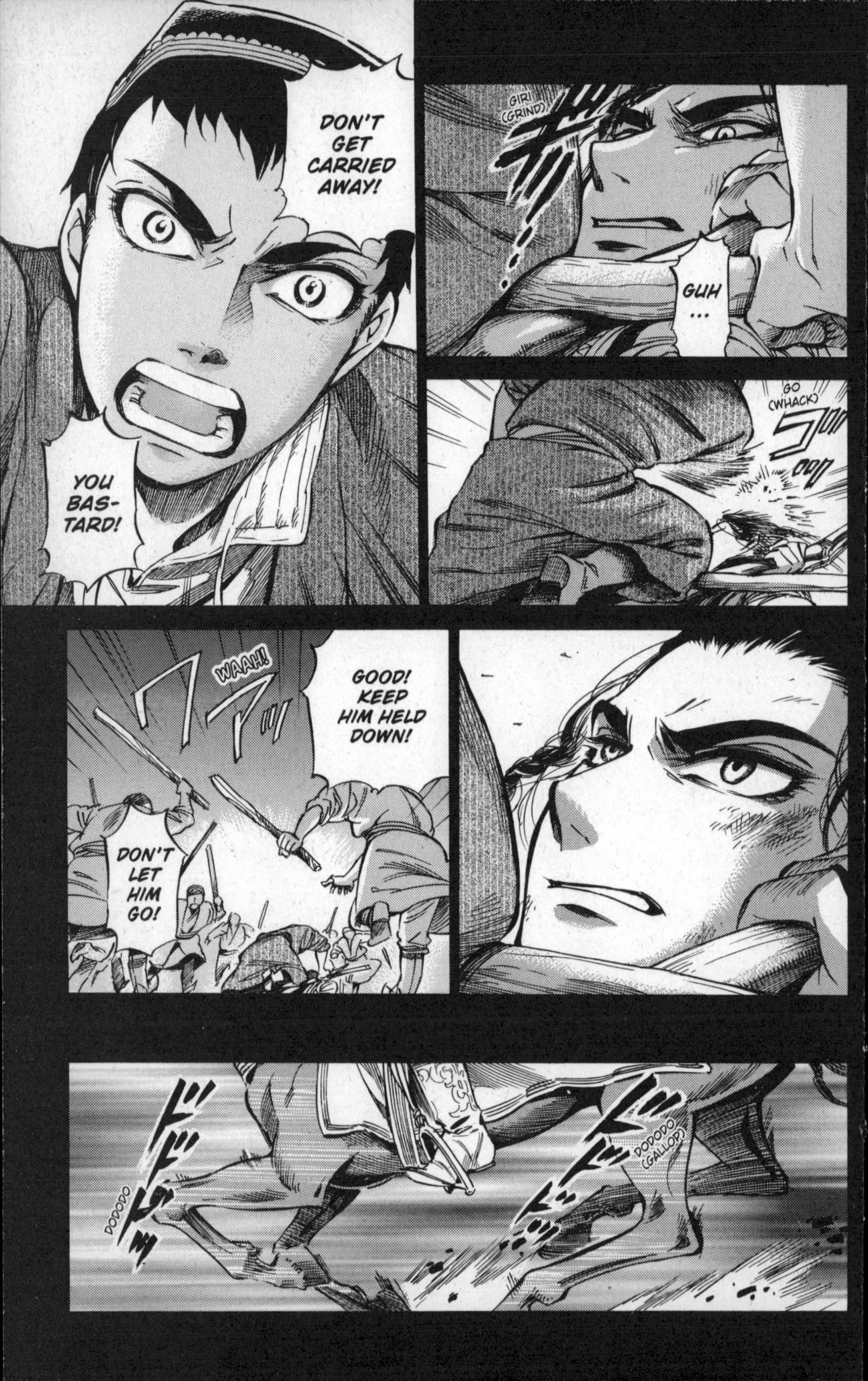
GIRI (GRIND)
GUH ...
GO (WHACK)
DON'T GET CARRIED AWAY!
YOU BAS-TARD!
WAAH!
GOOD! KEEP HIM HELD DOWN!
DON'T LET HIM GO!
DODODO (GALLOP)
DODODO

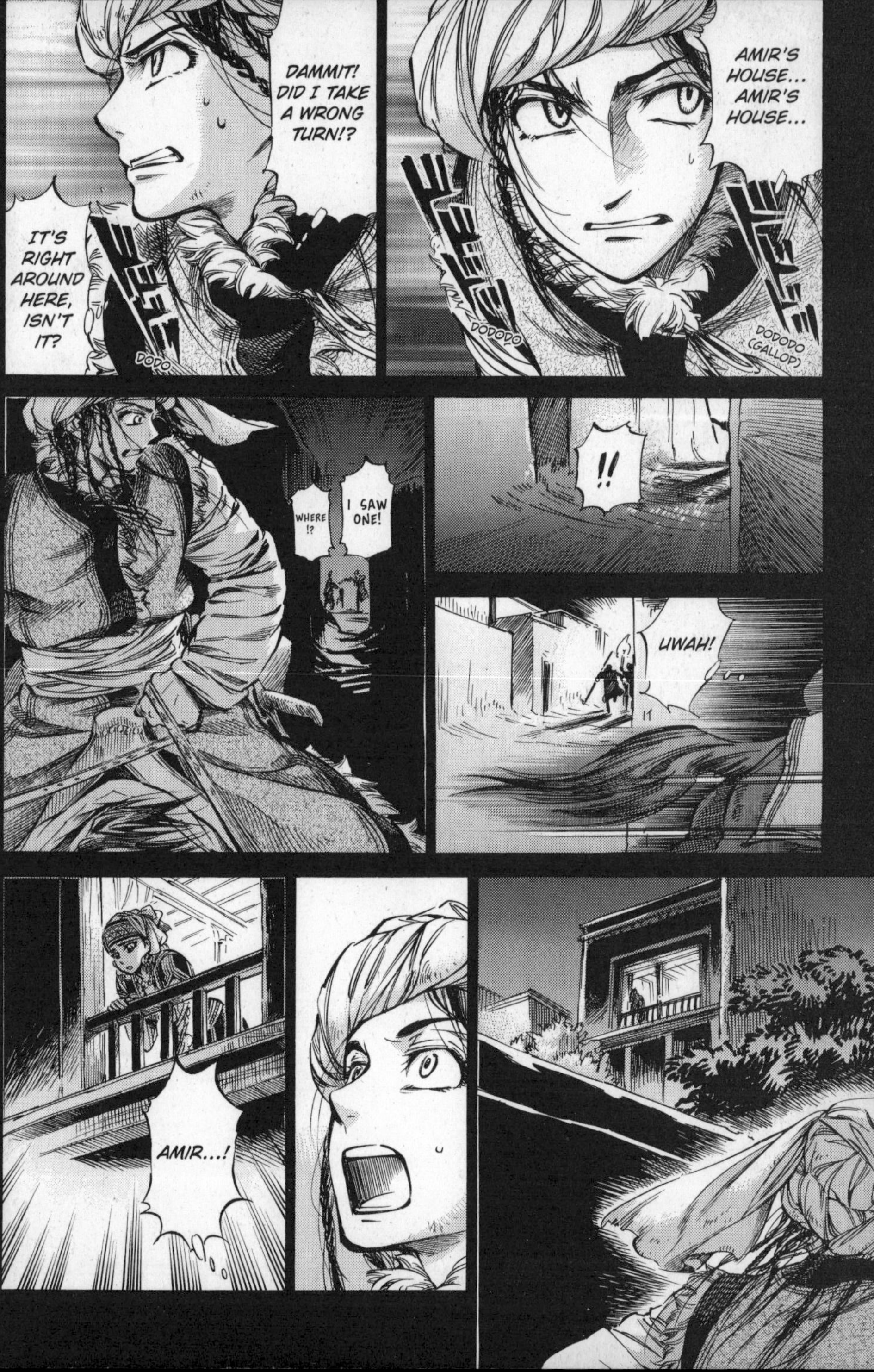
AMIR'S HOUSE... AMIR'S HOUSE...
DODODO (GALLOP)
DODODO
DAMMIT! DID I TAKE A WRONG TURN!?
IT'S RIGHT AROUND HERE, ISN'T IT?
DODO
!!
UWAH!
I SAW ONE!
WHERE !?
AMIR...!

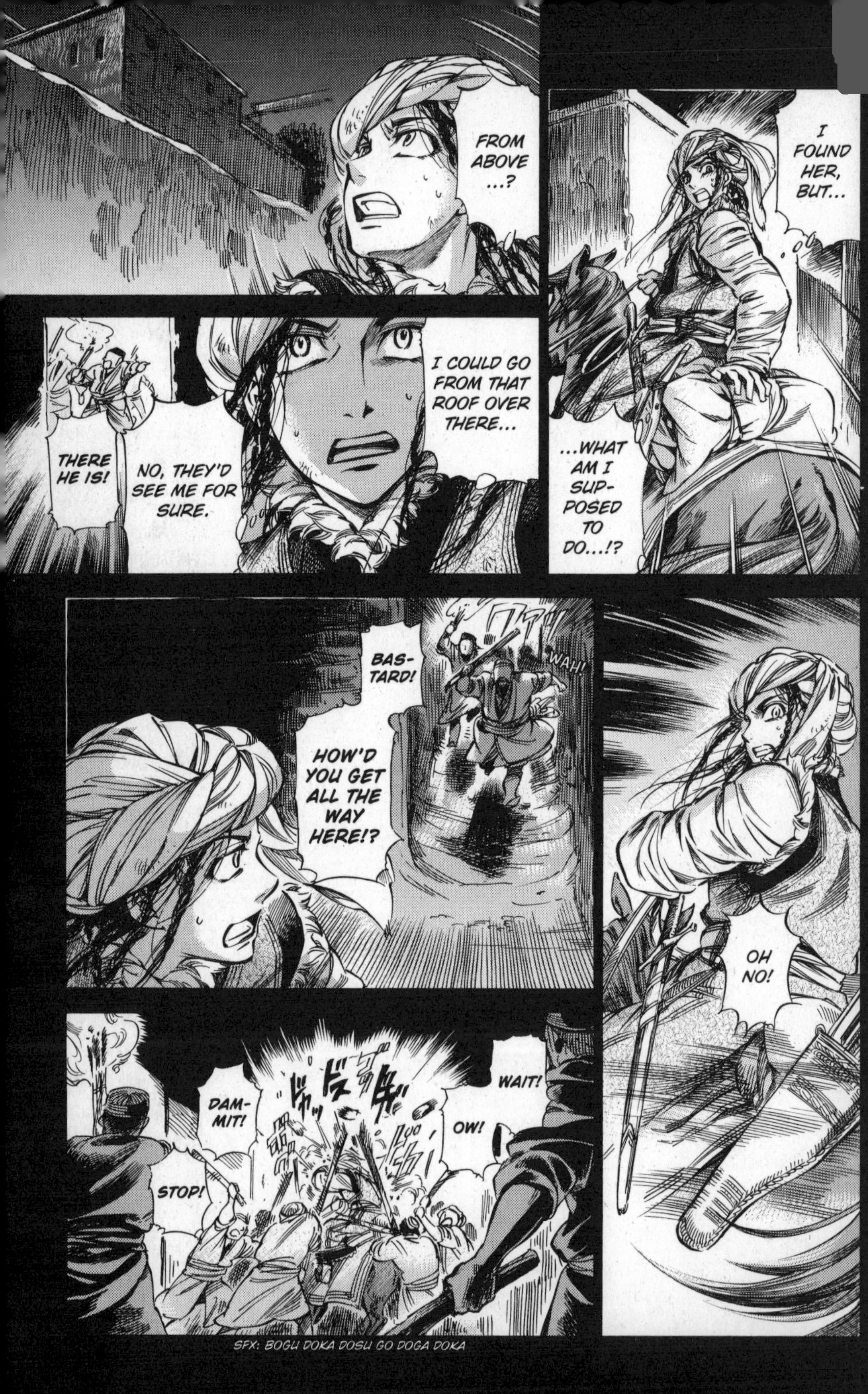
I FOUND HER, BUT...
...WHAT AM I SUP-POSED TO DO...!?
FROM ABOVE ...?
I COULD GO FROM THAT ROOF OVER THERE...
NO, THEY'D SEE ME FOR SURE.
THERE HE IS!
OH NO!
WAH!
BAS-TARD!
HOW'D YOU GET ALL THE WAY HERE!?
WAIT!
OW!
DAM-MIT!
STOP!

SFX: BOGU DOKA DOSU GO DOGA DOKA

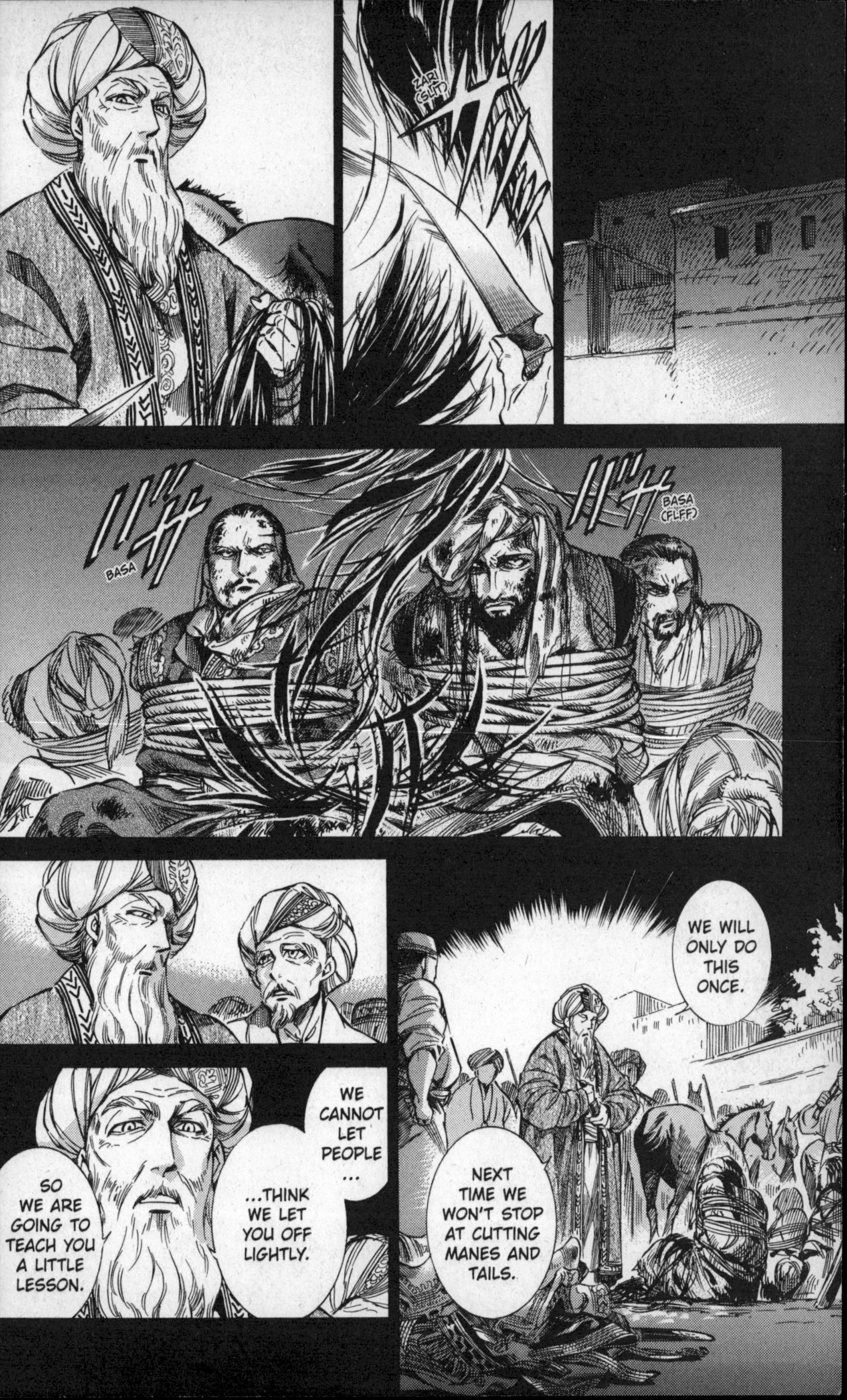
ZARI (SLIT)
BASA (FLFF)
BASA
WE WILL ONLY DO THIS ONCE.
NEXT TIME WE WON'T STOP AT CUTTING MANES AND TAILS.
WE CANNOT LET PEOPLE ...
...THINK WE LET YOU OFF LIGHTLY.
SO WE ARE GOING TO TEACH YOU A LITTLE LESSON.

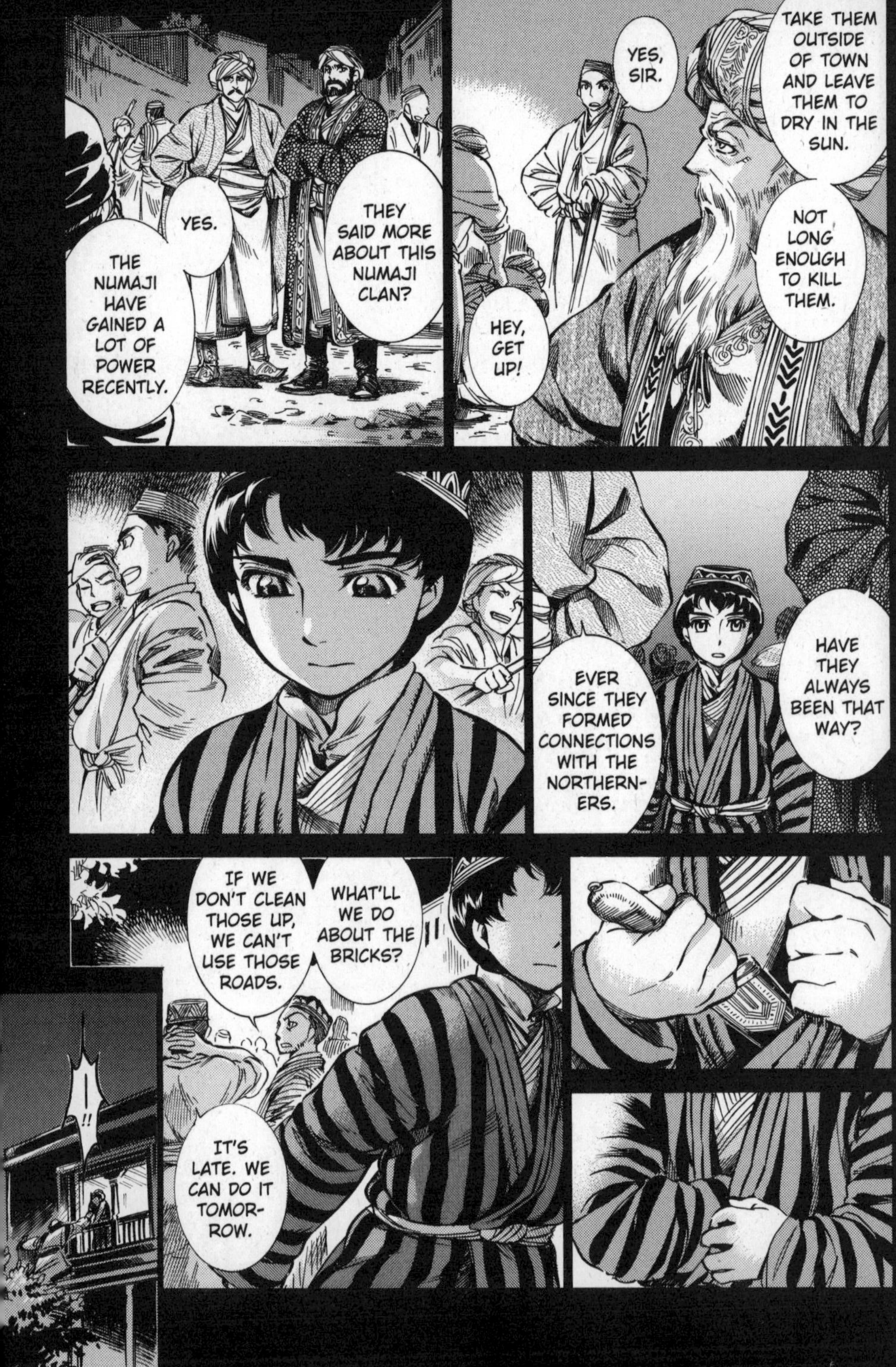
TAKE THEM OUTSIDE OF TOWN AND LEAVE THEM TO DRY IN THE SUN.
YES, SIR.
NOT LONG ENOUGH TO KILL THEM.
HEY, GET UP!
THEY SAID MORE ABOUT THIS NUMAJI CLAN?
YES.
THE NUMAJI HAVE GAINED A LOT OF POWER RECENTLY.
HAVE THEY ALWAYS BEEN THAT WAY?
EVER SINCE THEY FORMED CONNECTIONS WITH THE NORTHERN-ERS.
WHAT'LL WE DO ABOUT THE BRICKS?
IF WE DON'T CLEAN THOSE UP, WE CAN'T USE THOSE ROADS.
IT'S LATE. WE CAN DO IT TOMOR-ROW.
!
!!

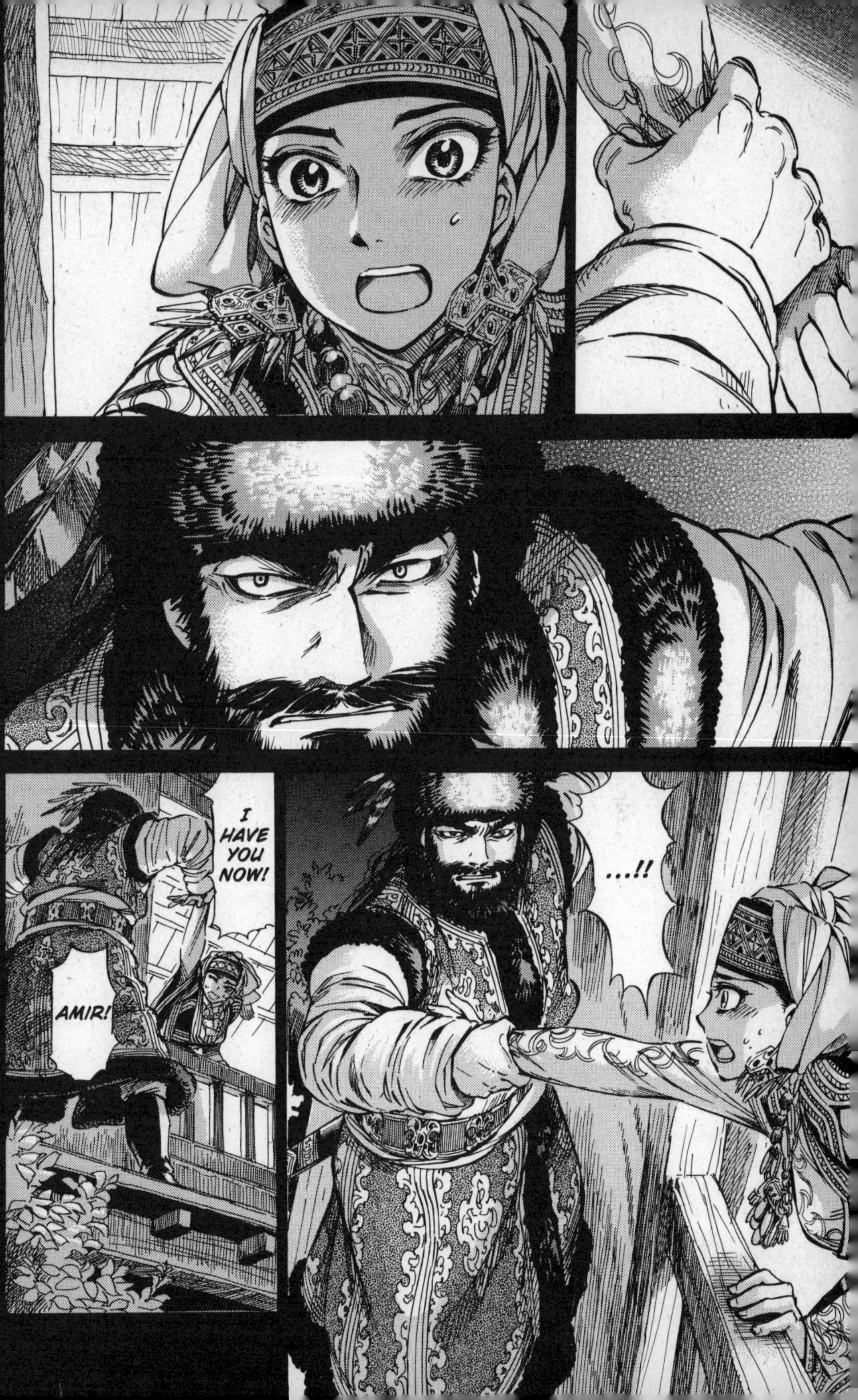
...!!
I HAVE YOU NOW!
AMIR!

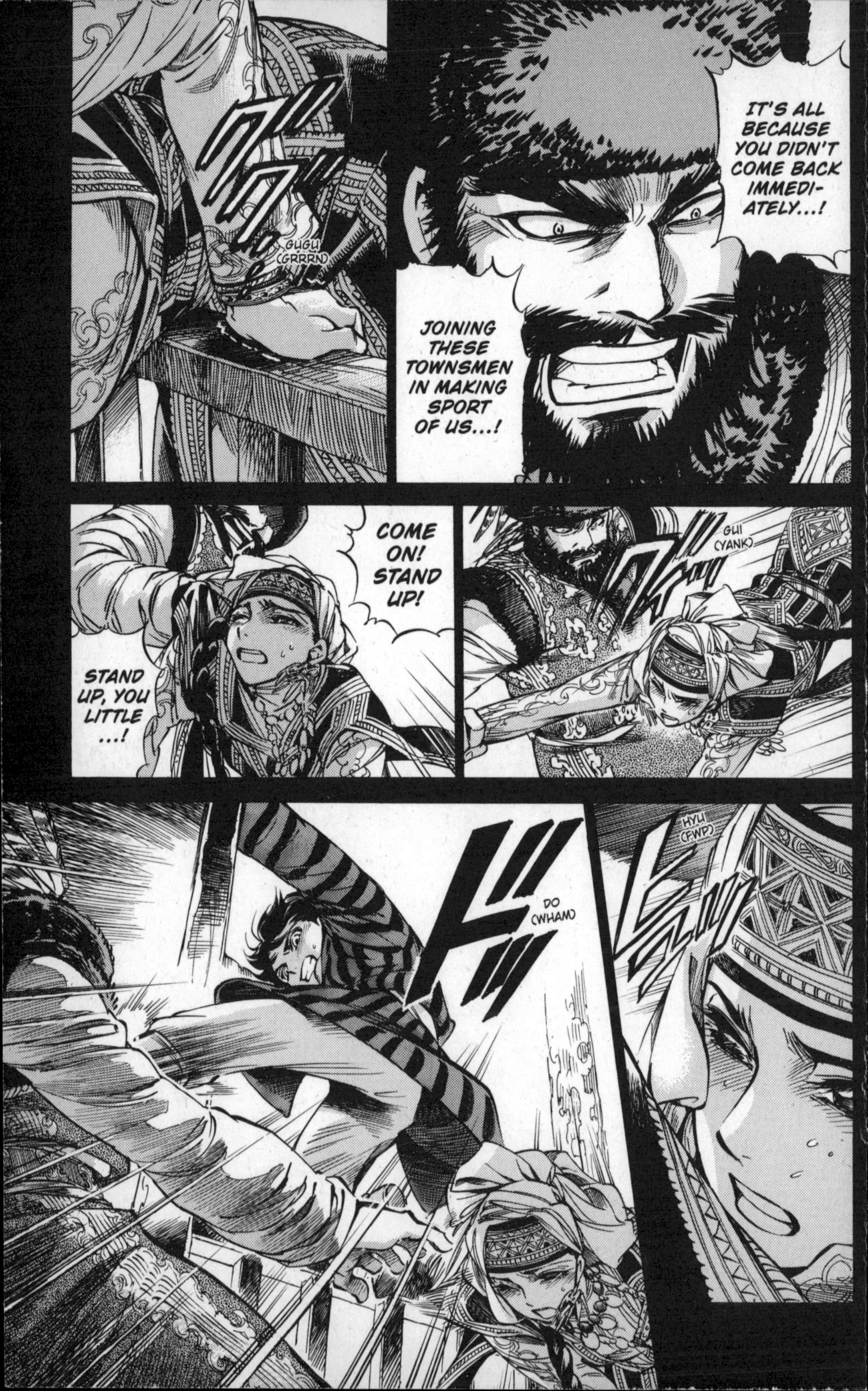
IT'S ALL BECAUSE YOU DIDN'T COME BACK IMMEDIATELY...!
JOINING THESE TOWNSMEN IN MAKING SPORT OF US...!
GUGU (GRRRN)
GUI (YANK)
COME ON! STAND UP!
STAND UP, YOU LITTLE ...!
HYU (FWP)
DO (WHAM)

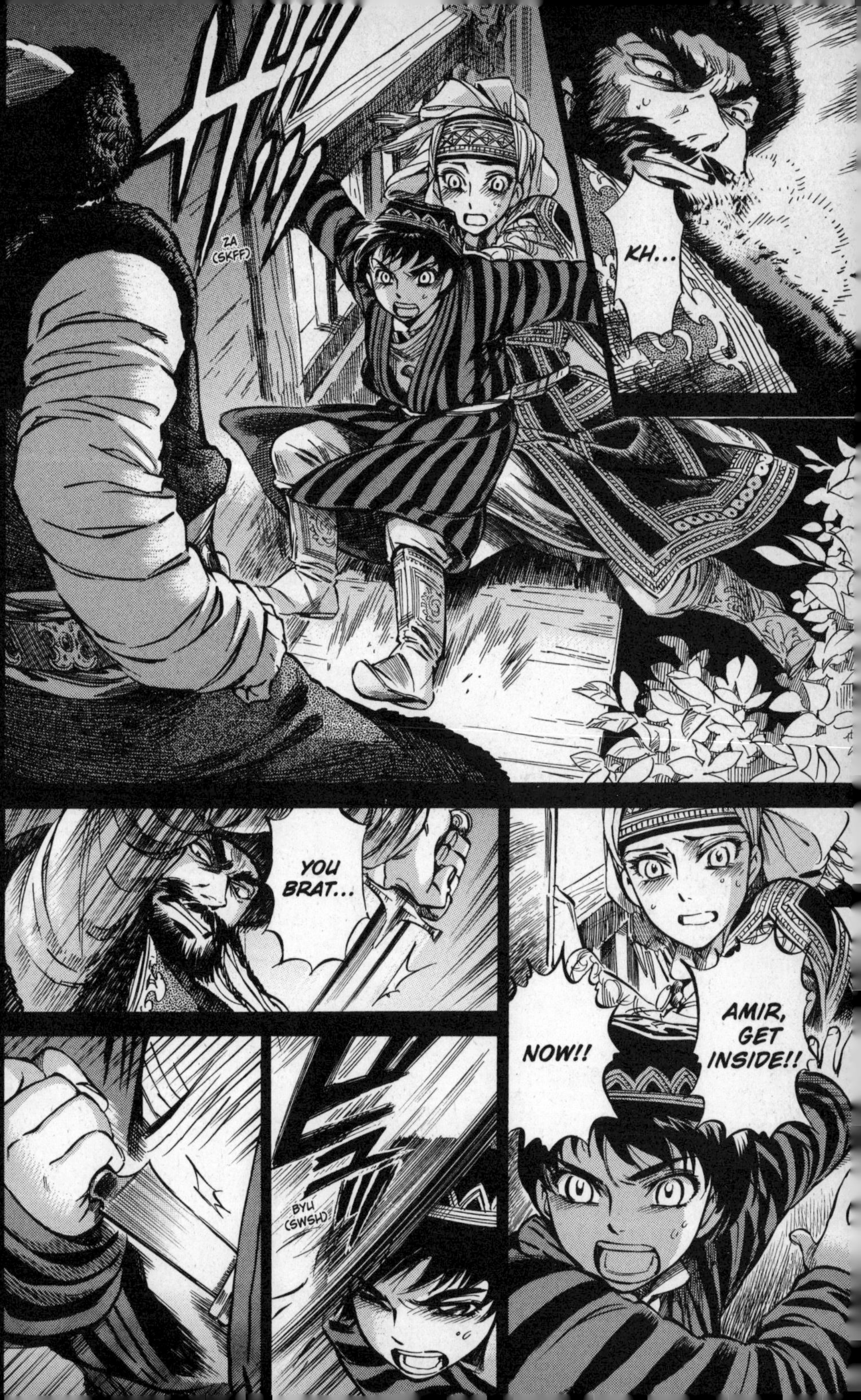
KH...
ZA (SKFF)
YOU BRAT...
AMIR, GET INSIDE!!
NOW!!
BYU (SWSH)

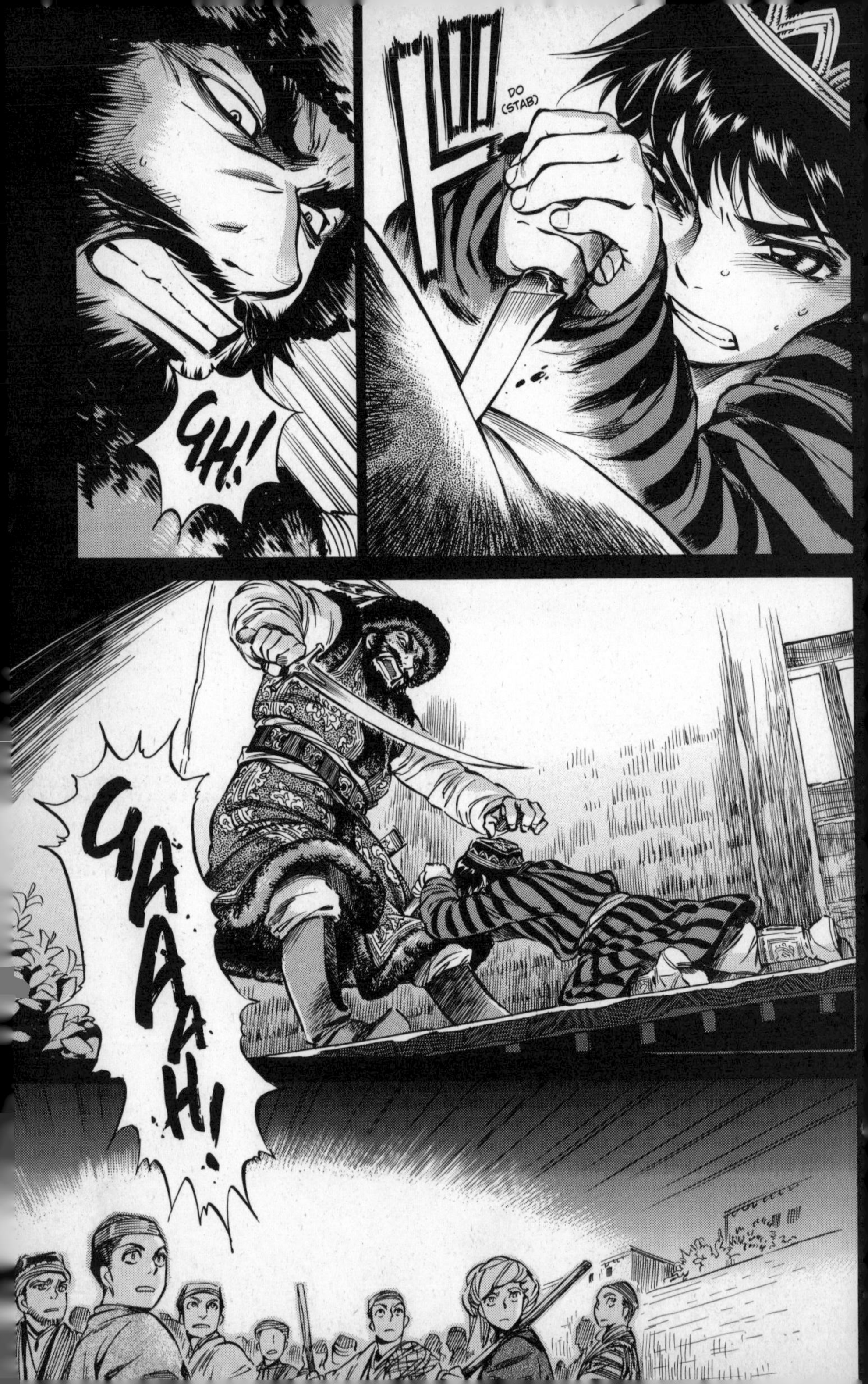
DO
(STAB)
GH!
UAAAAH!

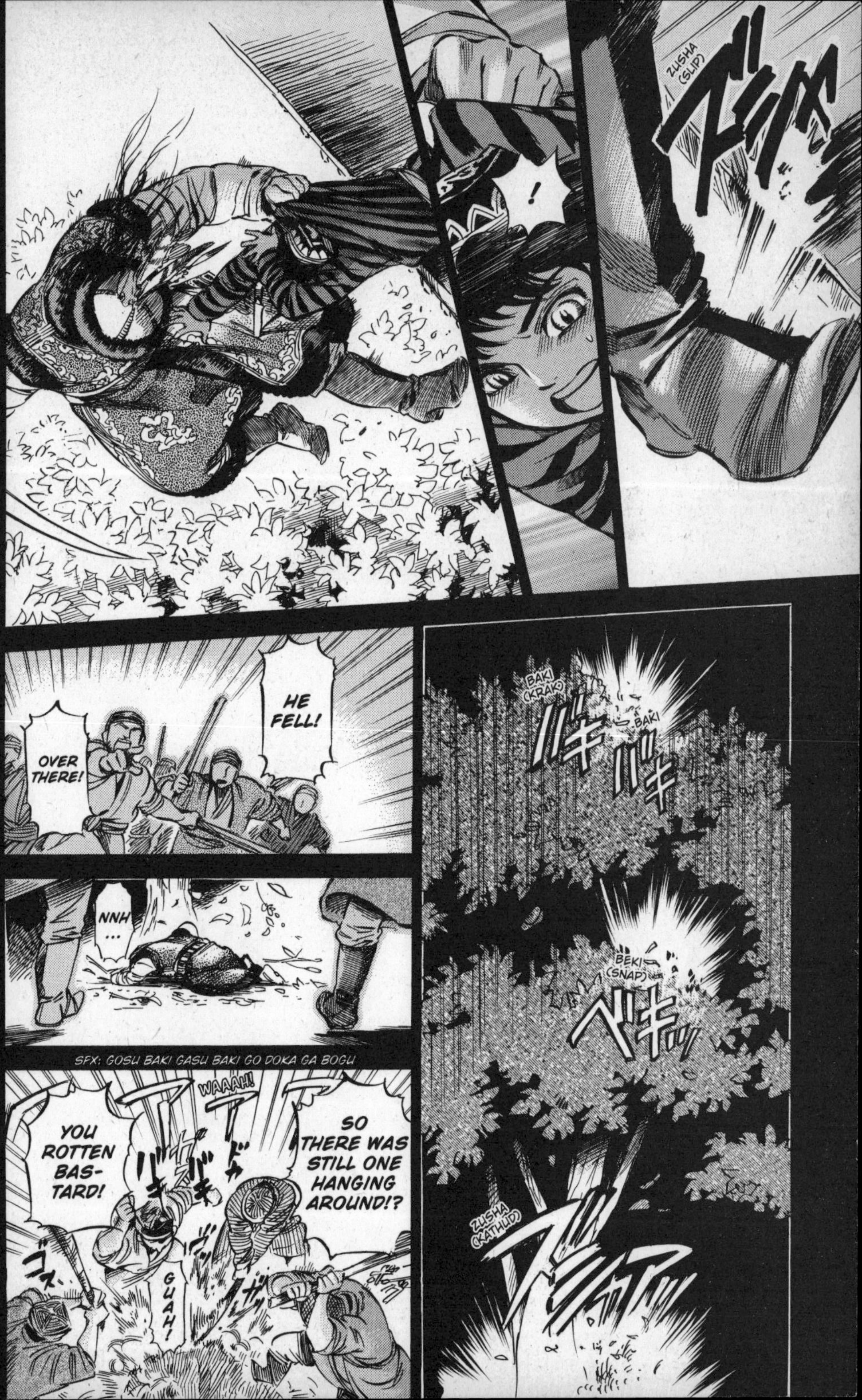
ZUSHA (SLIP)
!
BAKI (KRAK)
BAKI
BEKI (SNAP)
ZUSHA (KATHUD)
HE FELL!
OVER THERE!
NNH ...
SFX: GOSU BAKI GASU BAKI GO DOKA GA BOGU
SO THERE WAS STILL ONE HANGING AROUND!?
WAAAH!
YOU ROTTEN BAS-TARD!
GUAH!

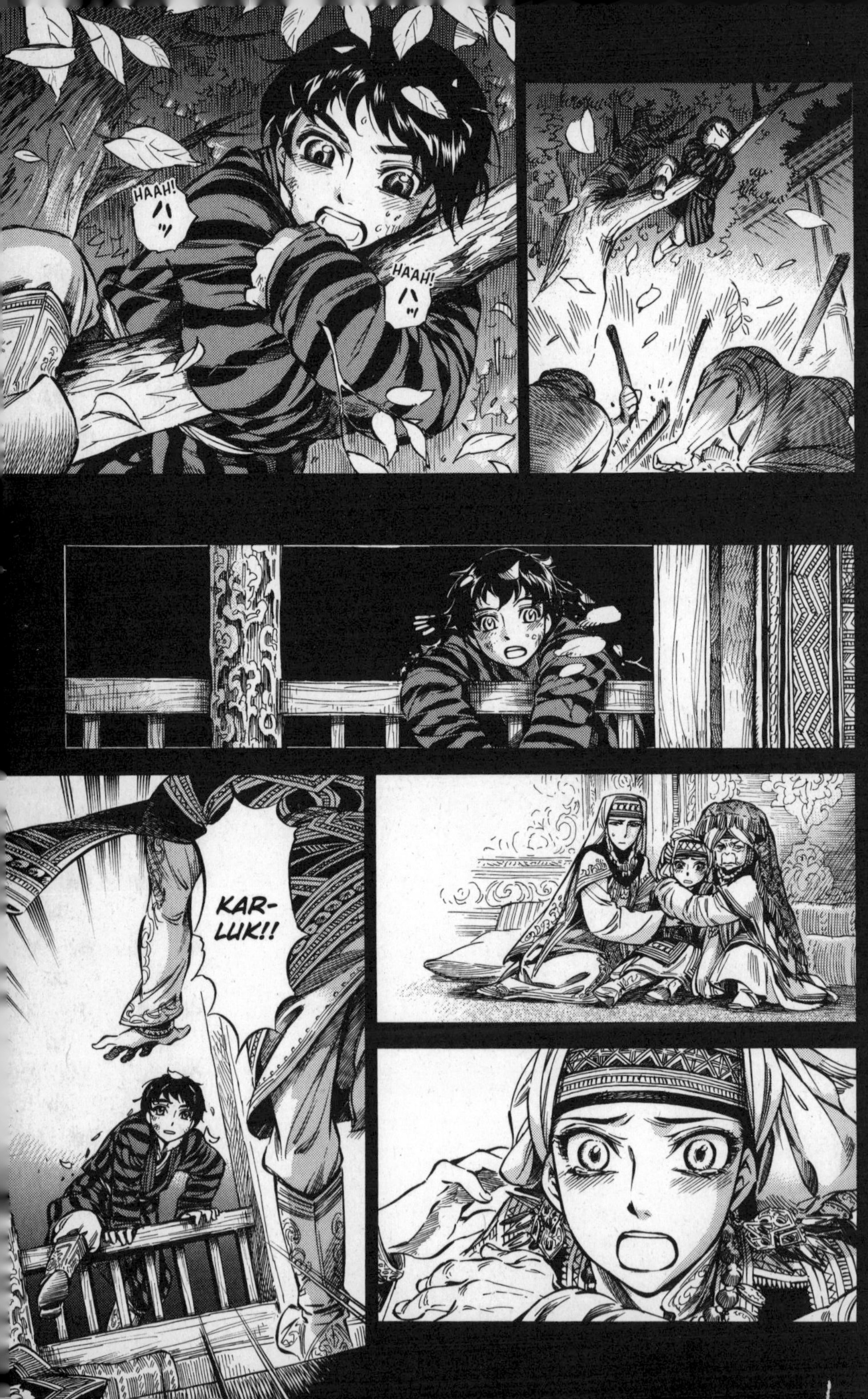
HAAH! ハッ
HA'AH! ハッ
KAR-
LUK!!

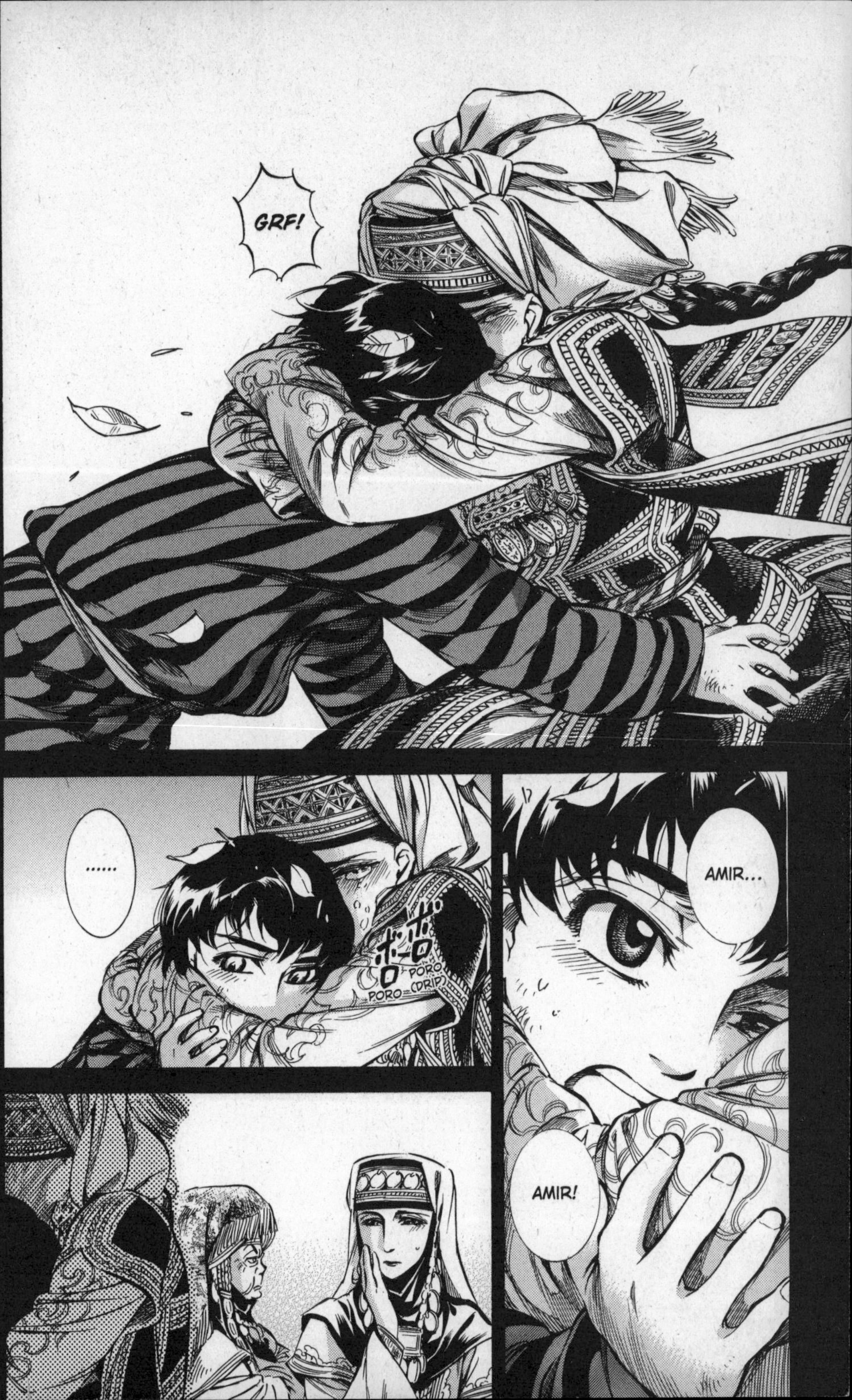
GRF!
AMIR...
AMIR!
......
PORO PORO (DRIP)

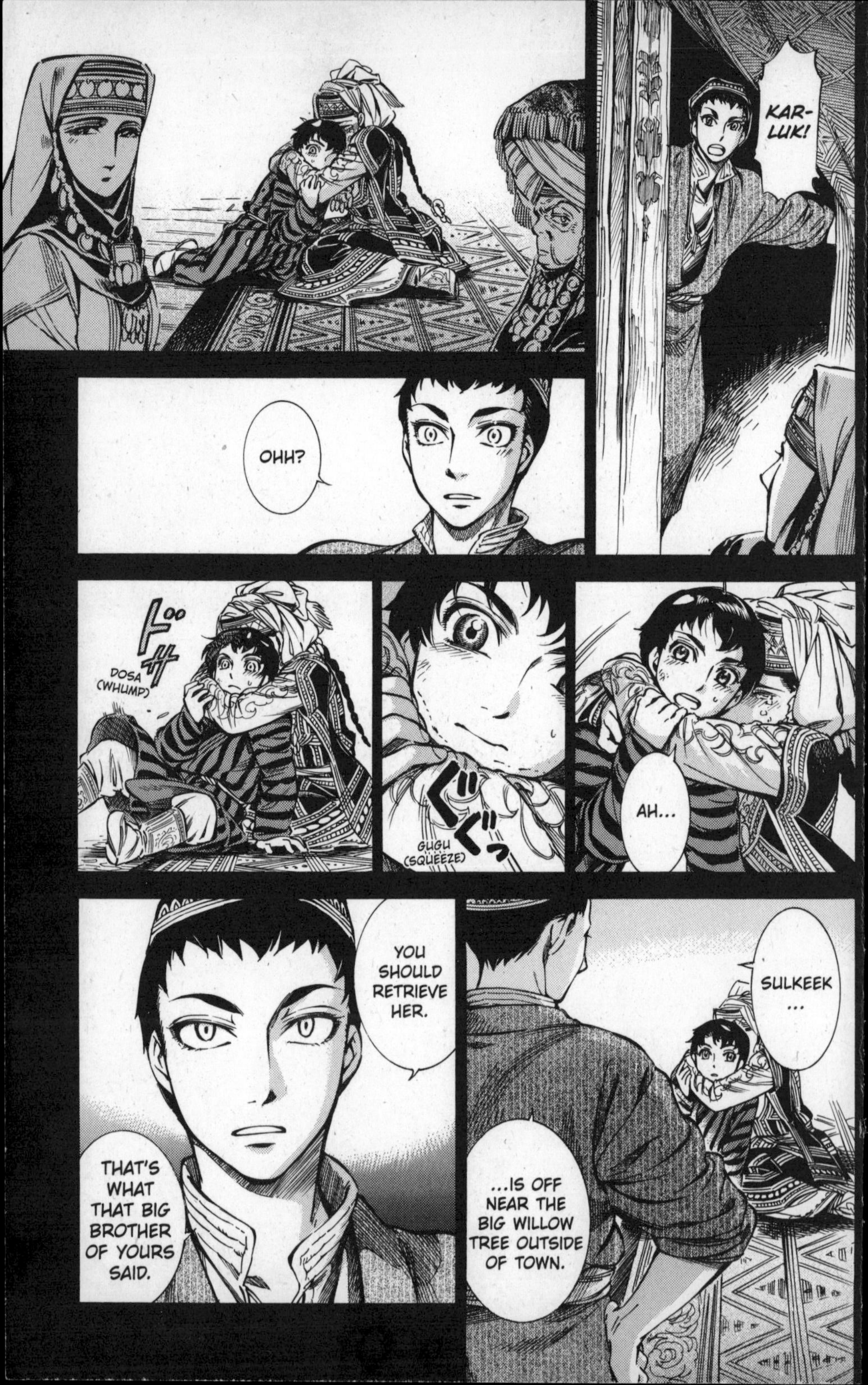
KAR-LUK!
OHH?
AH...
ぐぐっ
GUGU (SQUEEZE)
ドサ
DOSA (WHUMP)
SULKEEK ...
...IS OFF NEAR THE BIG WILLOW TREE OUTSIDE OF TOWN.
YOU SHOULD RETRIEVE HER.
THAT'S WHAT THAT BIG BROTHER OF YOURS SAID.

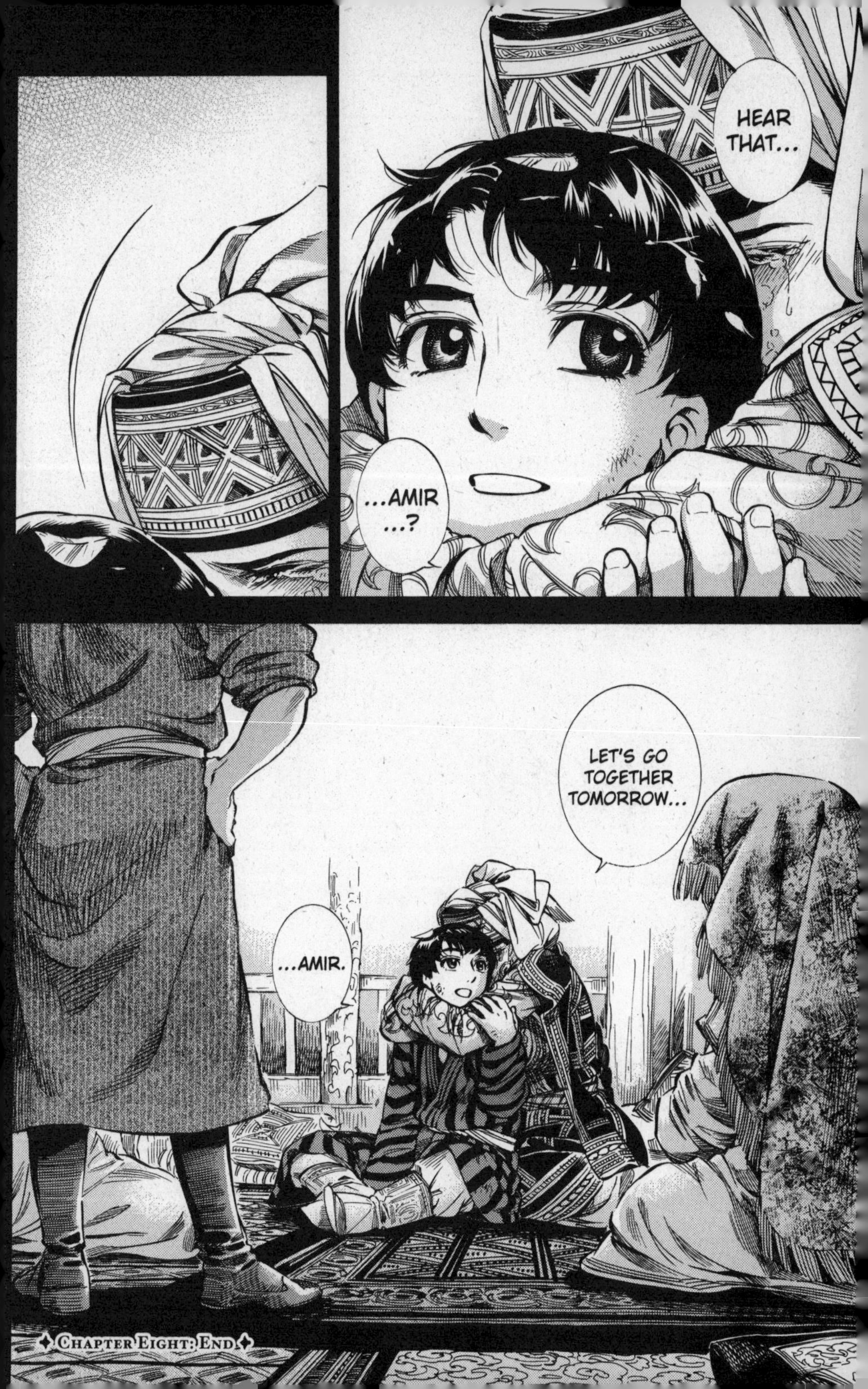
HEAR THAT...
...AMIR ...?
LET'S GO TOGETHER TOMORROW...
...AMIR.
✦ CHAPTER EIGHT: END ✦

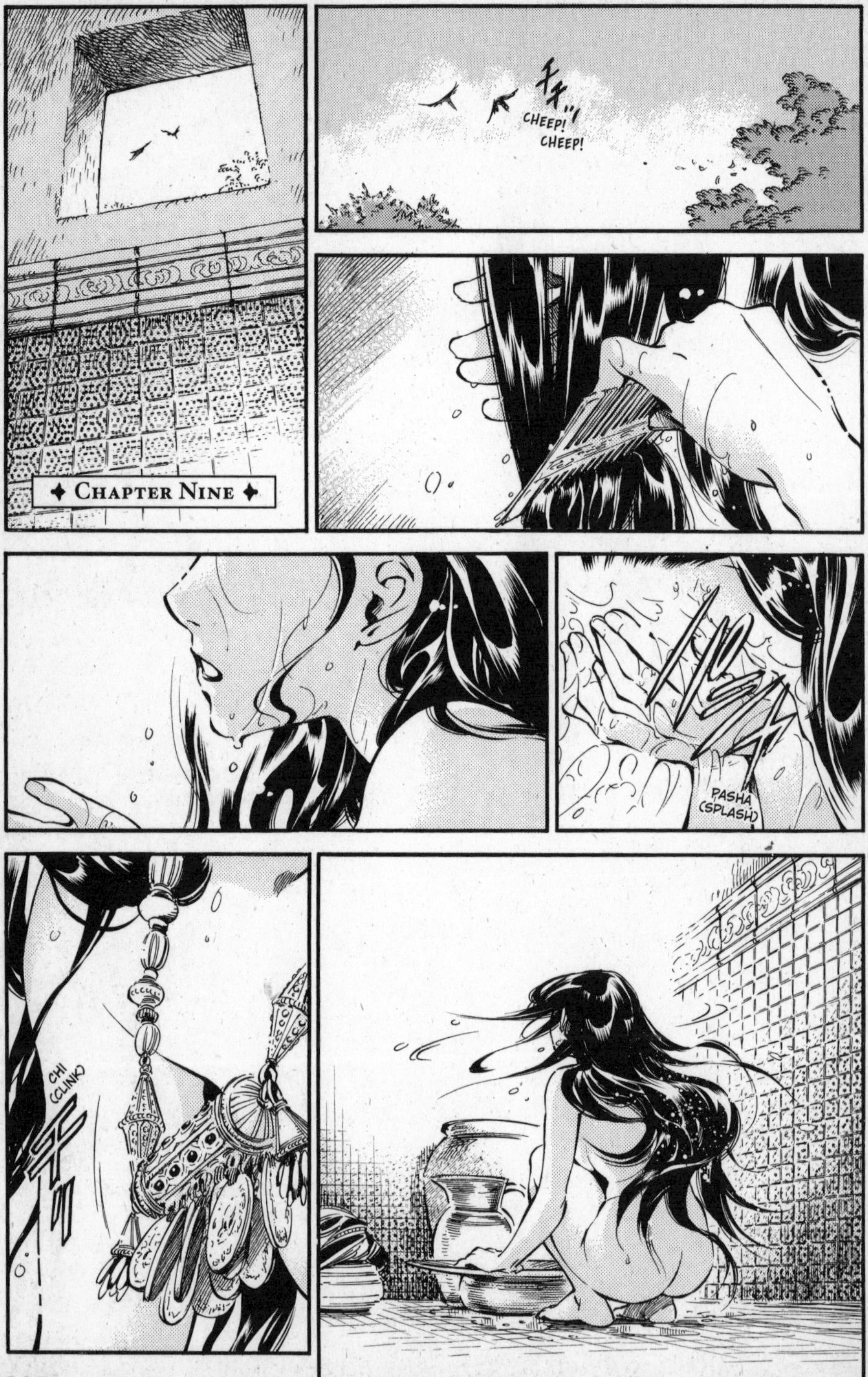
CHEEP! CHEEP!
Chapter Nine
PASHA (SPLASH)
CHI (CLINK)

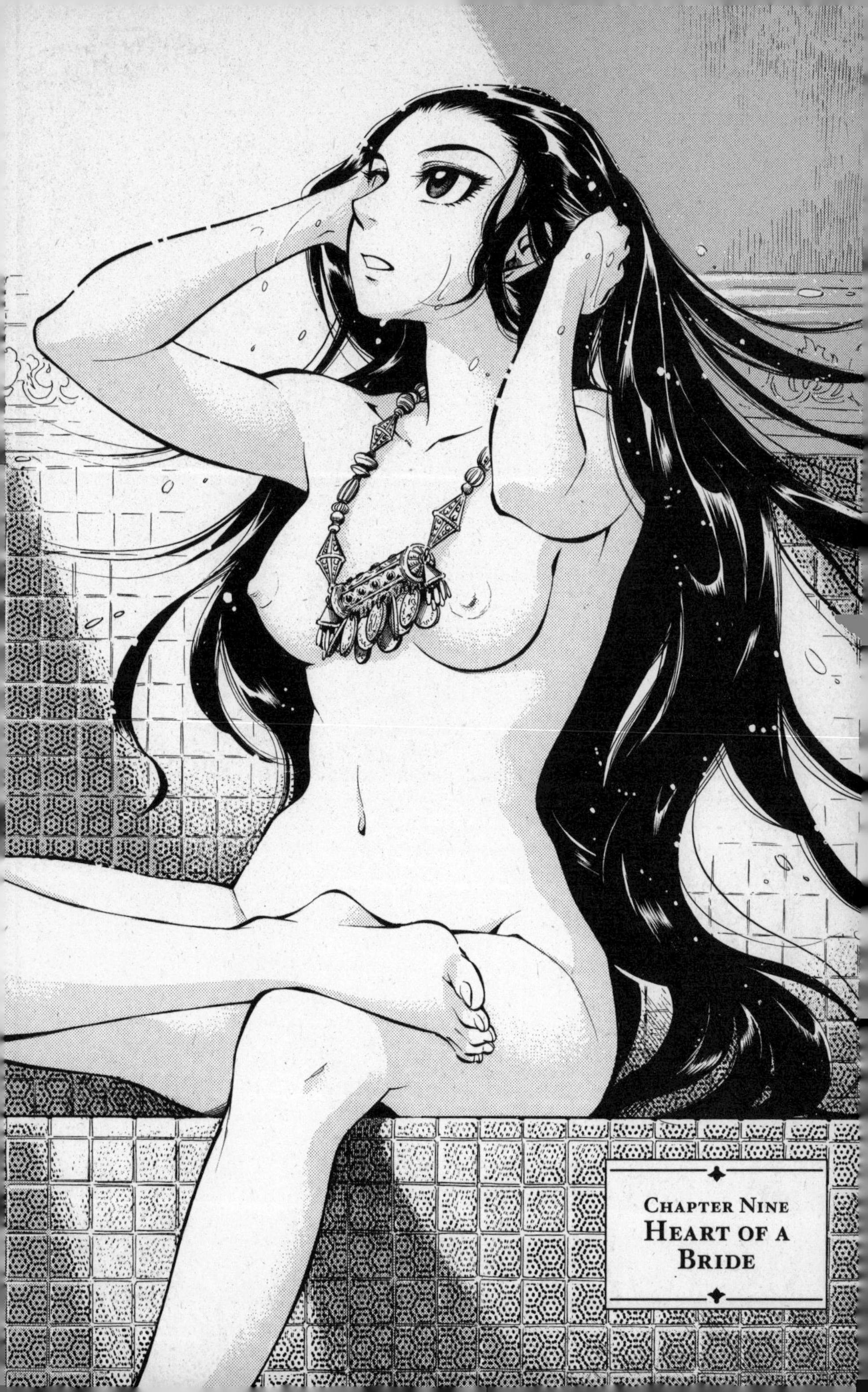
Chapter Nine
Heart of a
Bride

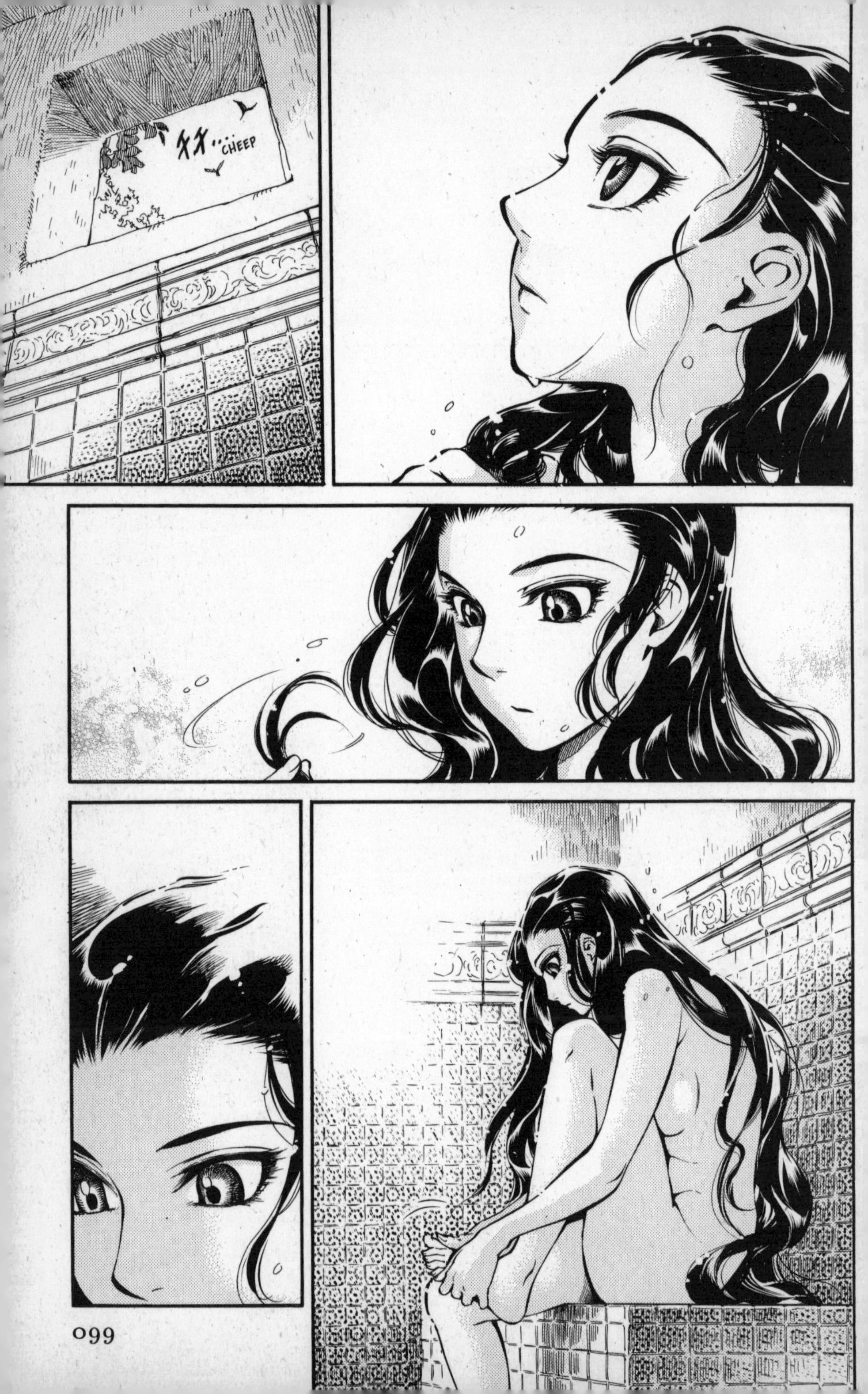
チチ…
CHEEP

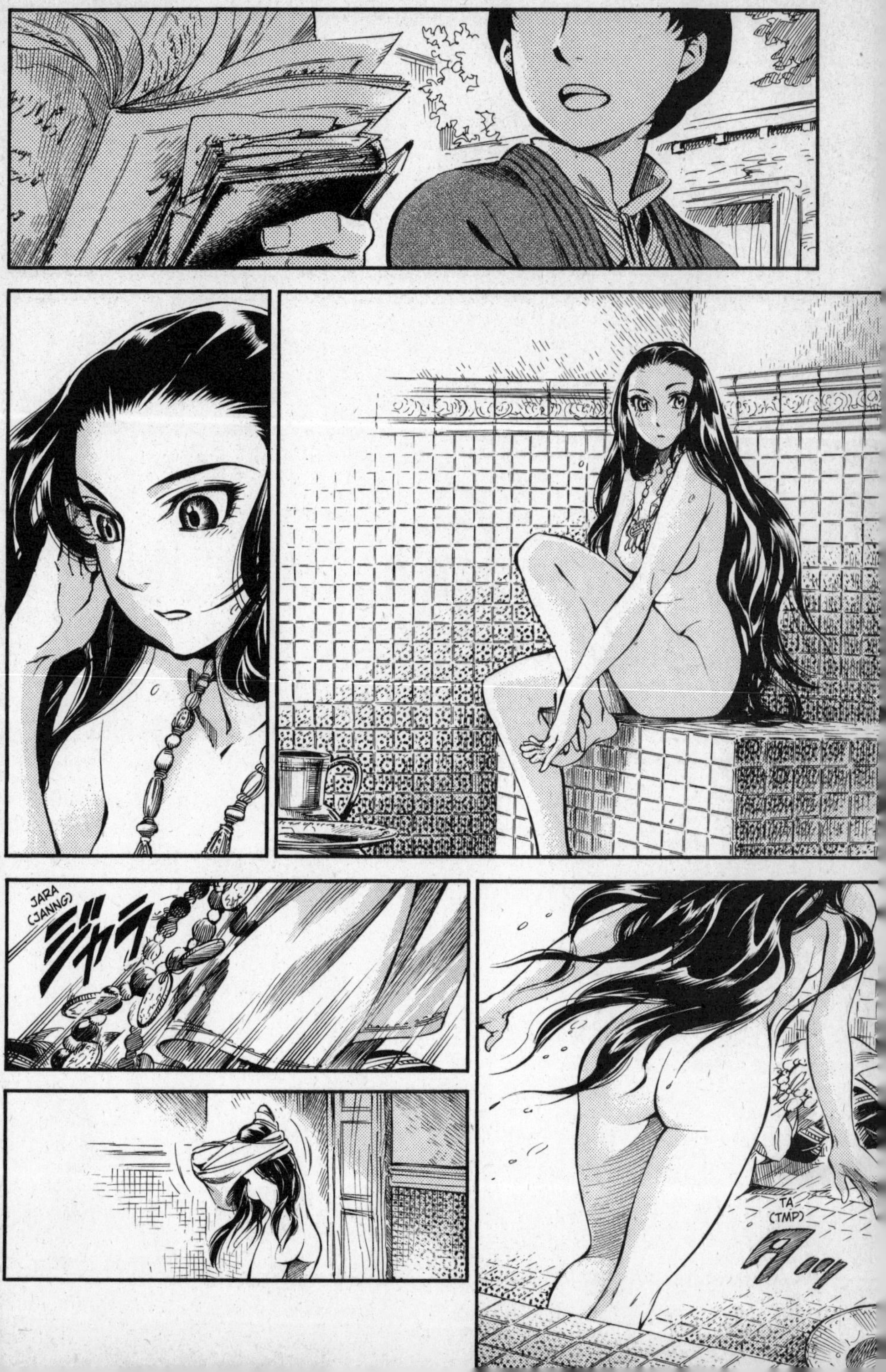
TA
(TMP)
タッ
JARA
(JANNG)
ジャラ

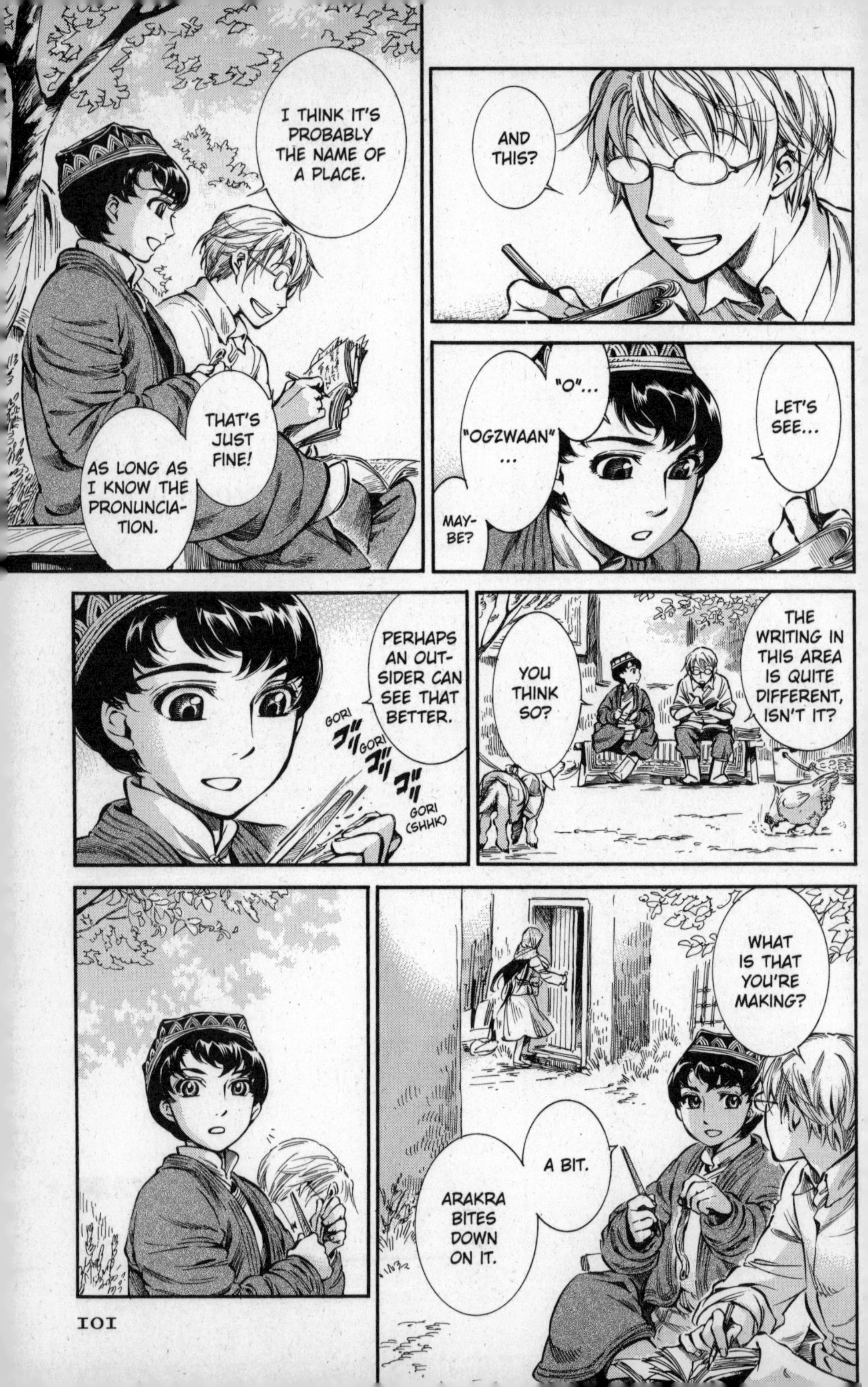
AND THIS?
LET'S SEE...
"O"...
"OGZWAAN" ...
MAY-BE?
I THINK IT'S PROBABLY THE NAME OF A PLACE.
THAT'S JUST FINE!
AS LONG AS I KNOW THE PRONUNCIA-TION.
THE WRITING IN THIS AREA IS QUITE DIFFERENT, ISN'T IT?
YOU THINK SO?
PERHAPS AN OUT-SIDER CAN SEE THAT BETTER.
GORI
GORI
GORI (SHHK)
WHAT IS THAT YOU'RE MAKING?
A BIT.
ARAKRA BITES DOWN ON IT.

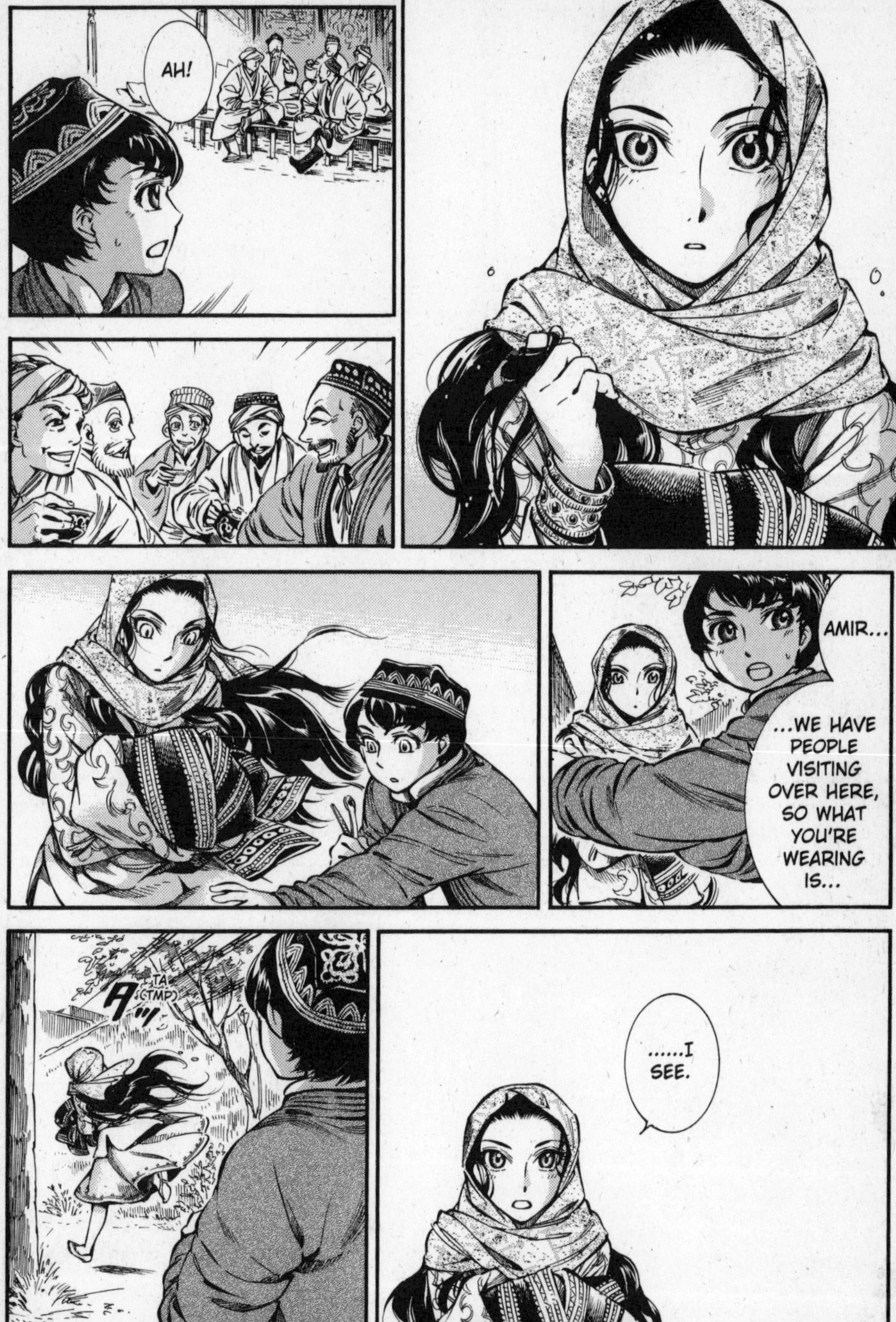
AH!
AMIR...
...WE HAVE PEOPLE VISITING OVER HERE, SO WHAT YOU'RE WEARING IS...
......I SEE.
TA (TMP)

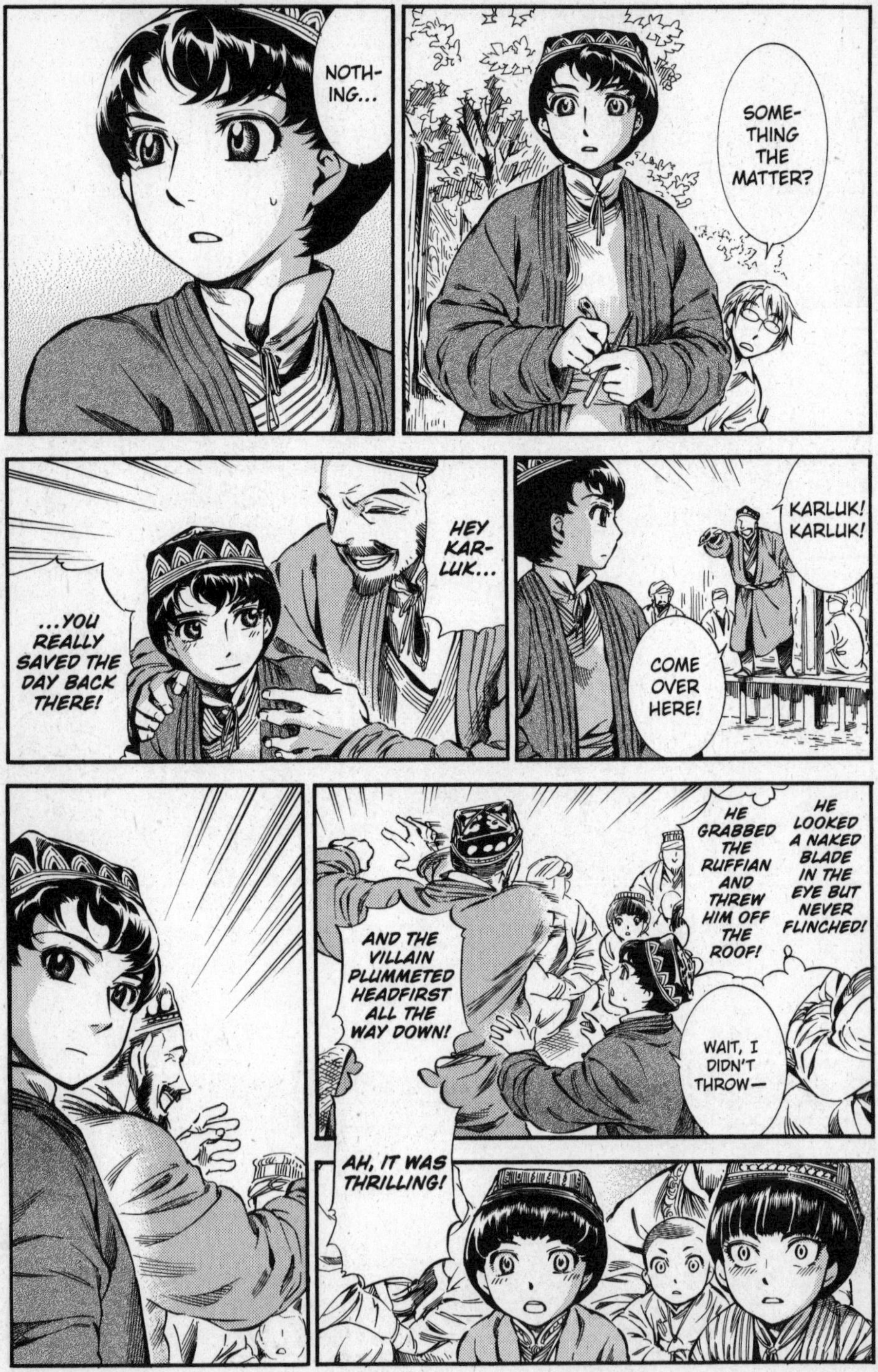
SOME-THING THE MATTER?
NOTH-ING...
KARLUK! KARLUK!
COME OVER HERE!
HEY KAR-LUK...
...YOU REALLY SAVED THE DAY BACK THERE!
HE LOOKED A NAKED BLADE IN THE EYE BUT NEVER FLINCHED!
HE GRABBED THE RUFFIAN AND THREW HIM OFF THE ROOF!
AND THE VILLAIN PLUMMETED HEADFIRST ALL THE WAY DOWN!
WAIT, I DIDN'T THROW—
AH, IT WAS THRILLING!

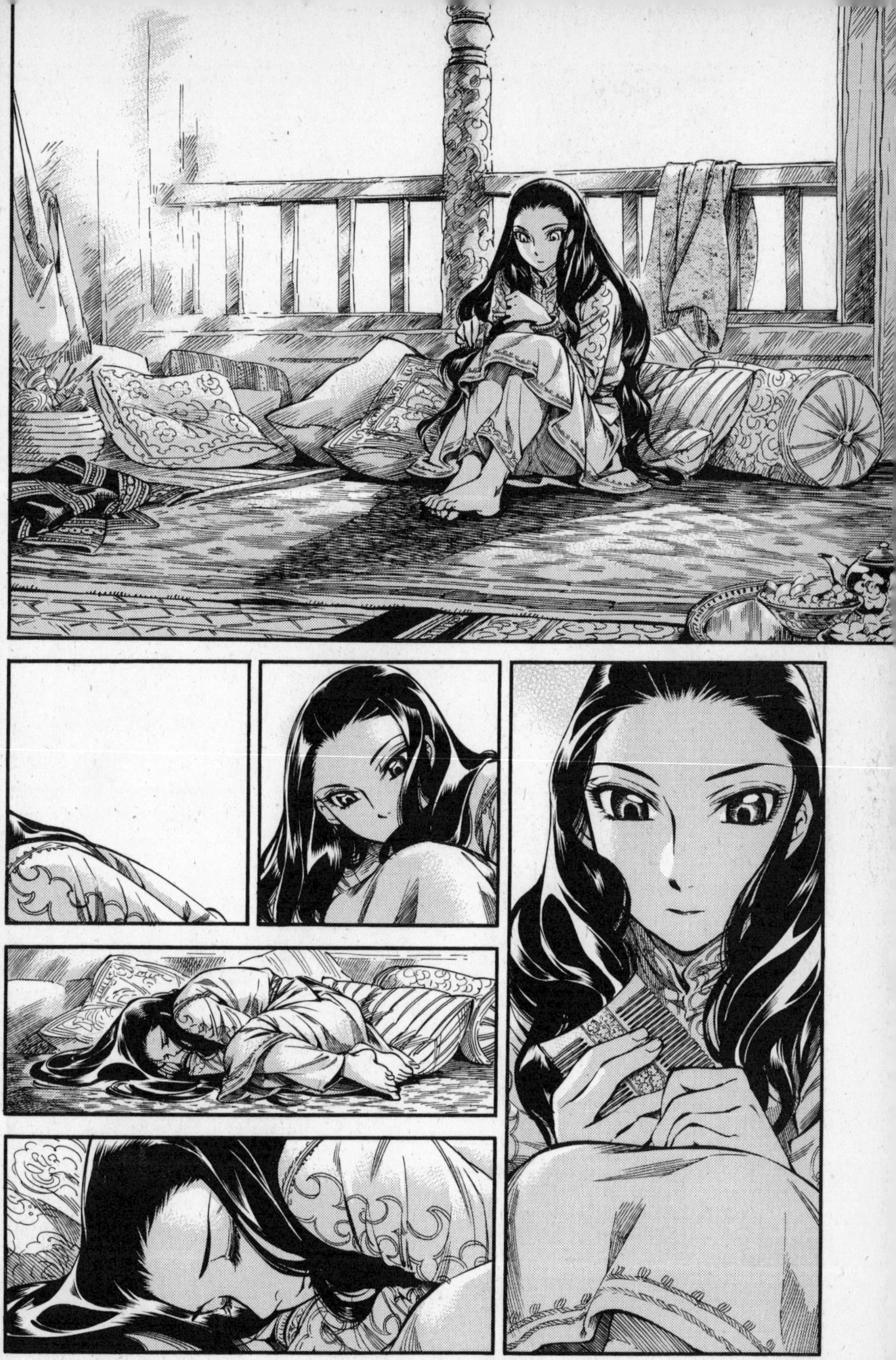

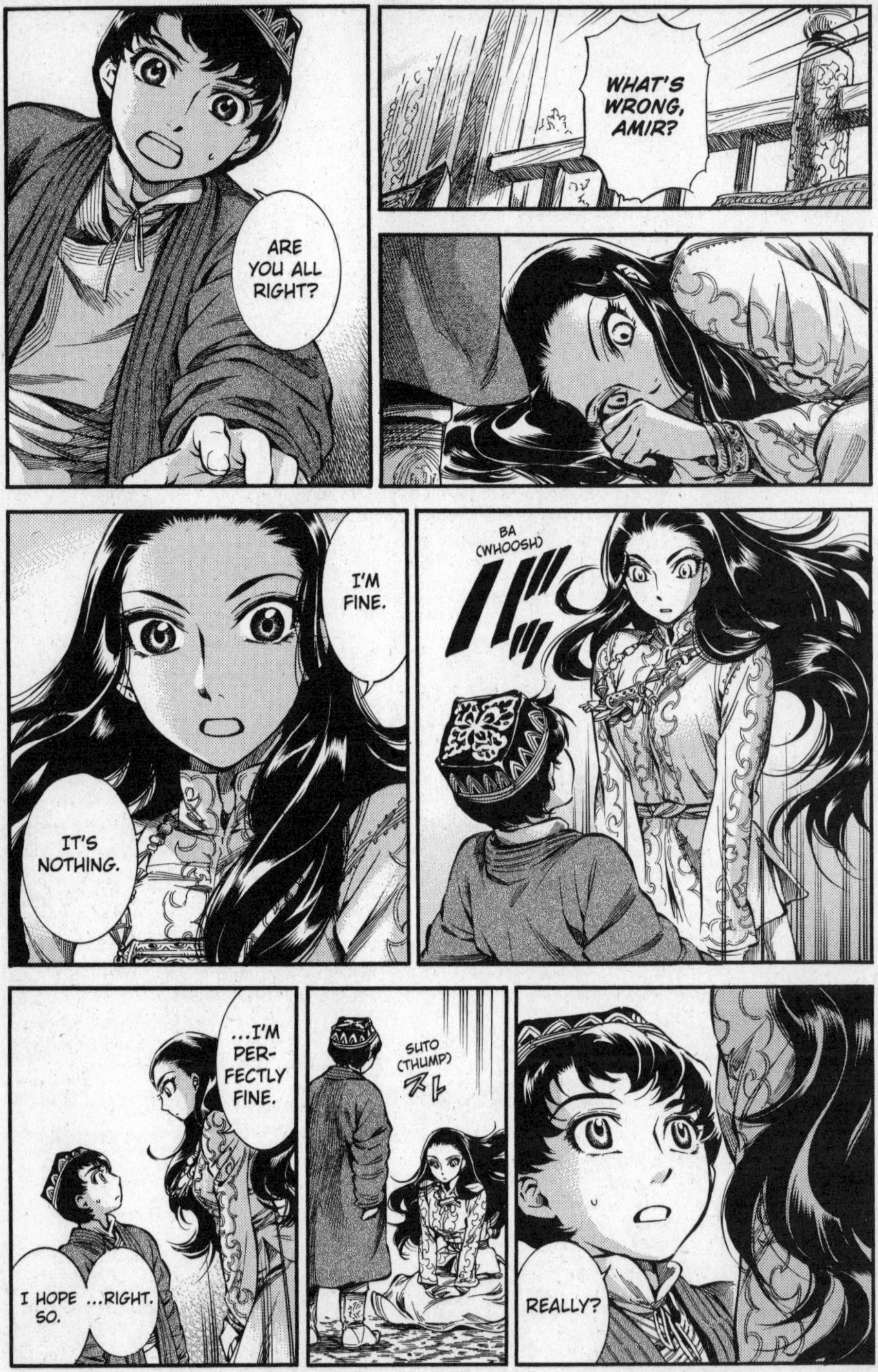
WHAT'S WRONG, AMIR?
ARE YOU ALL RIGHT?
BA (WHOOSH)
I'M FINE.
IT'S NOTHING.
REALLY?
SUTO (THUMP)
...I'M PER-FECTLY FINE.
...RIGHT.
I HOPE SO.

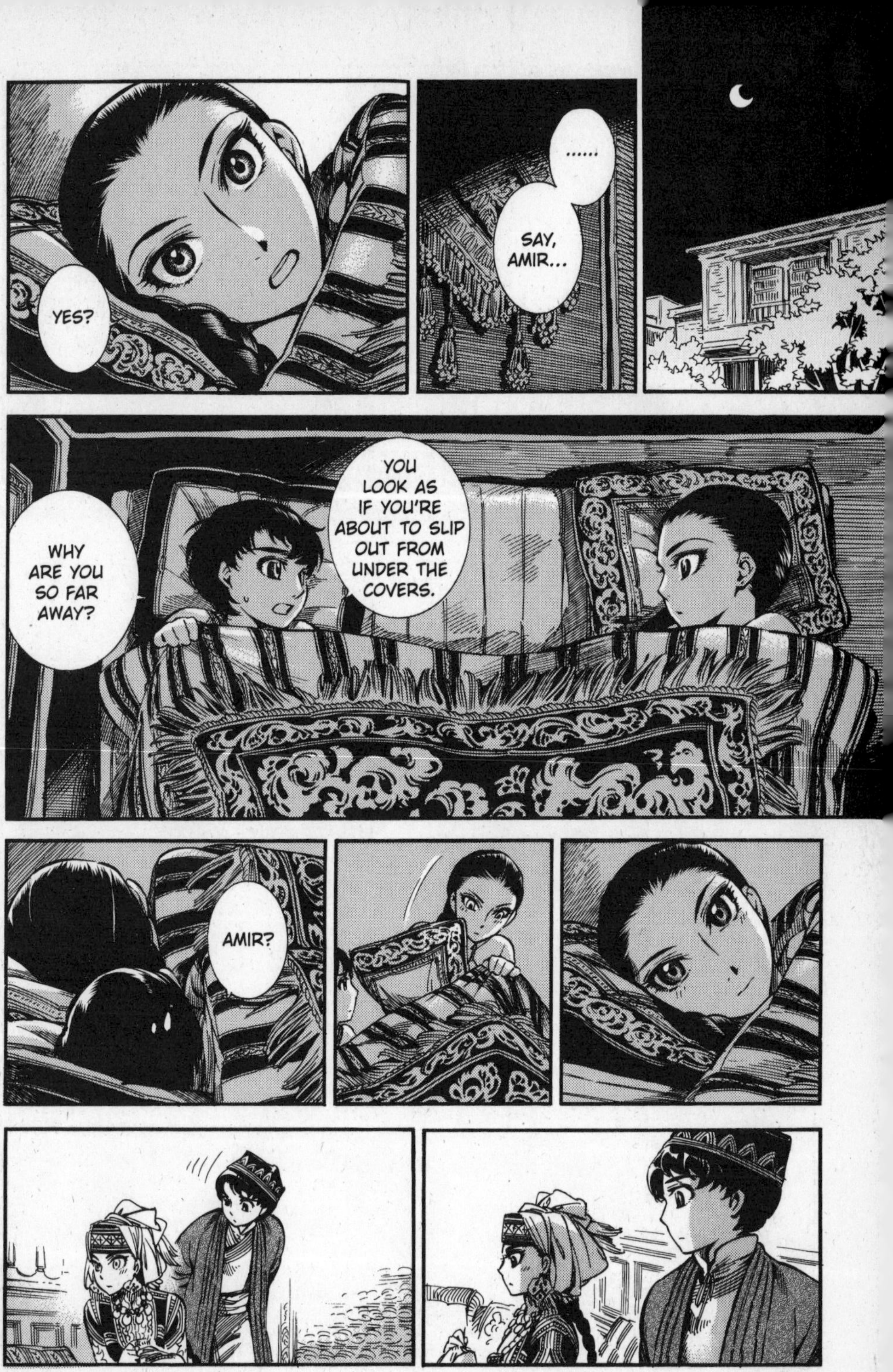
......
SAY, AMIR...
YES?
YOU LOOK AS IF YOU'RE ABOUT TO SLIP OUT FROM UNDER THE COVERS.
WHY ARE YOU SO FAR AWAY?
AMIR?

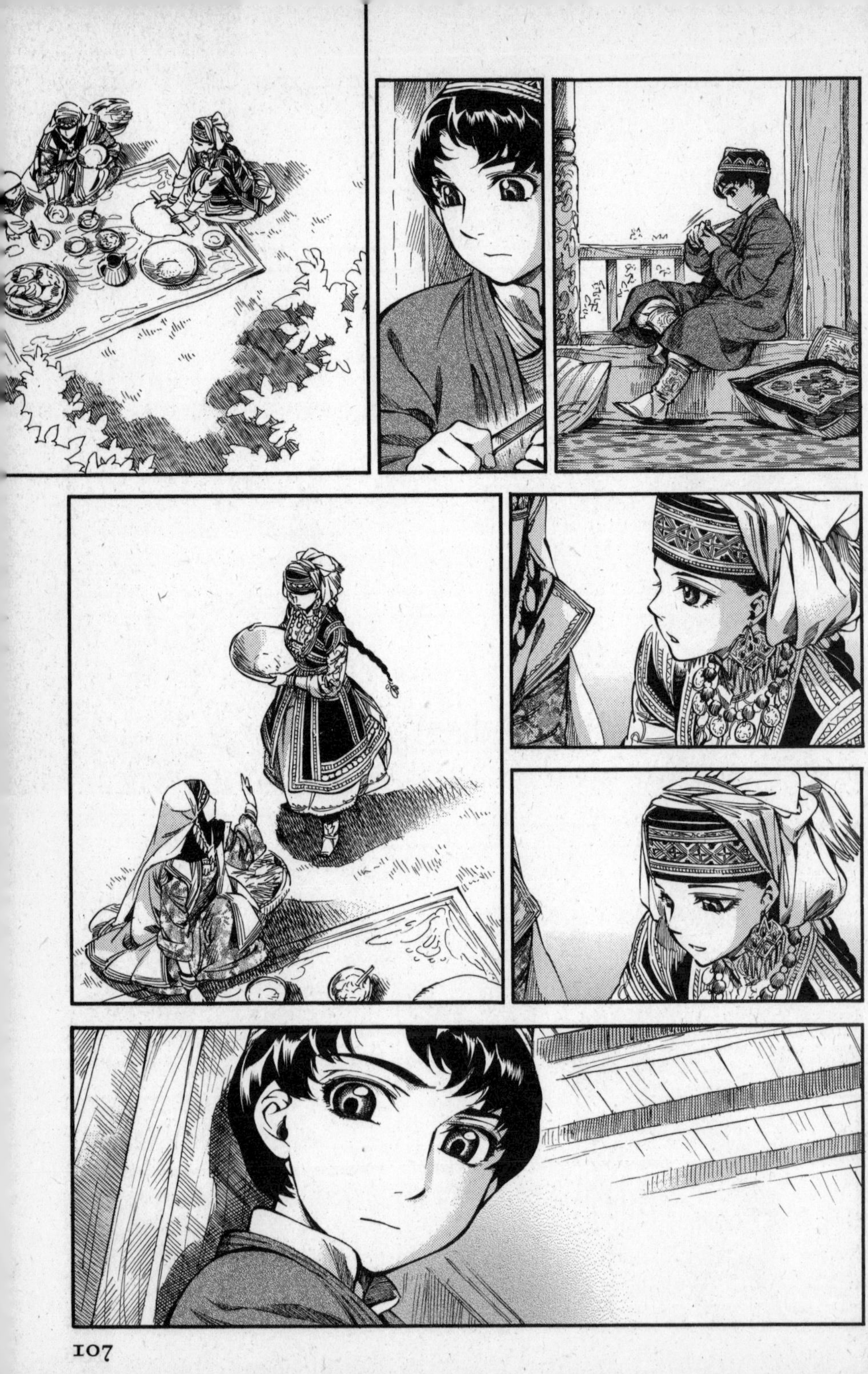

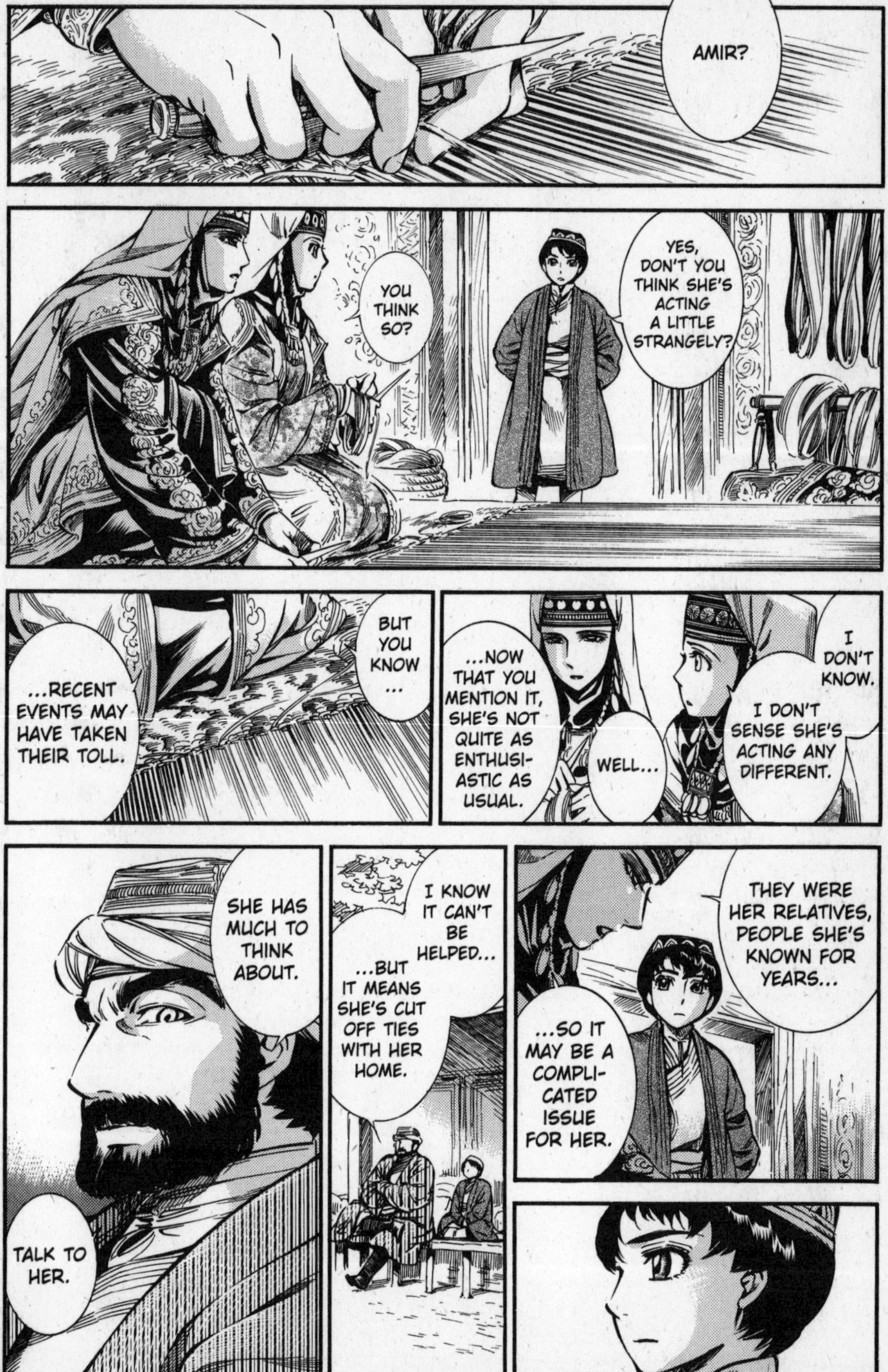
AMIR?
YES, DON'T YOU THINK SHE'S ACTING A LITTLE STRANGELY?
YOU THINK SO?
I DON'T KNOW.
I DON'T SENSE SHE'S ACTING ANY DIFFERENT.
WELL...
...NOW THAT YOU MENTION IT, SHE'S NOT QUITE AS ENTHUSIASTIC AS USUAL.
BUT YOU KNOW...
...RECENT EVENTS MAY HAVE TAKEN THEIR TOLL.
THEY WERE HER RELATIVES, PEOPLE SHE'S KNOWN FOR YEARS...
...SO IT MAY BE A COMPLICATED ISSUE FOR HER.
I KNOW IT CAN'T BE HELPED...
...BUT IT MEANS SHE'S CUT OFF TIES WITH HER HOME.
SHE HAS MUCH TO THINK ABOUT.
TALK TO HER.

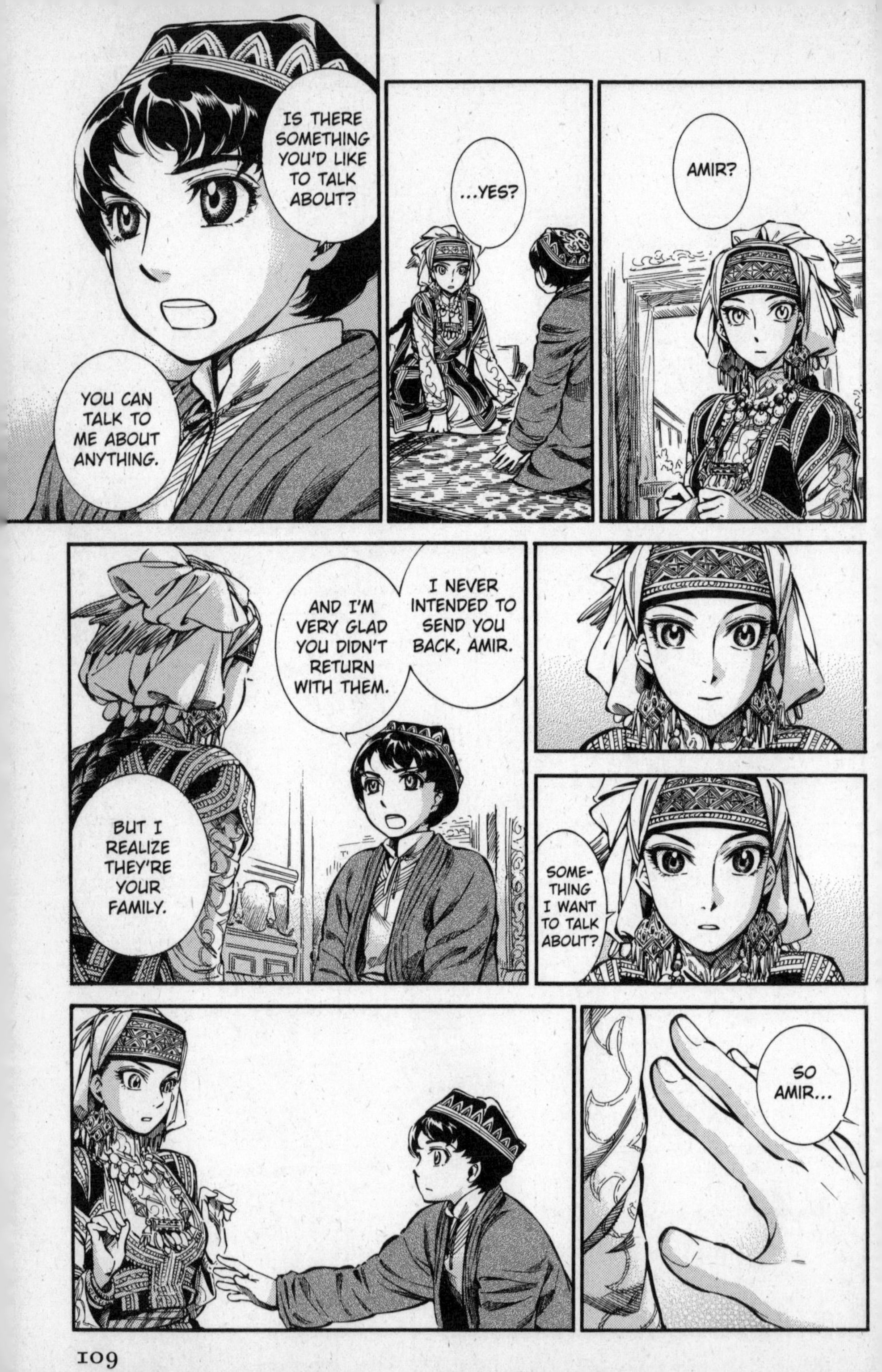
AMIR?
...YES?
IS THERE SOMETHING YOU'D LIKE TO TALK ABOUT?
YOU CAN TALK TO ME ABOUT ANYTHING.
SOME-THING I WANT TO TALK ABOUT?
I NEVER INTENDED TO SEND YOU BACK, AMIR.
AND I'M VERY GLAD YOU DIDN'T RETURN WITH THEM.
BUT I REALIZE THEY'RE YOUR FAMILY.
SO AMIR...

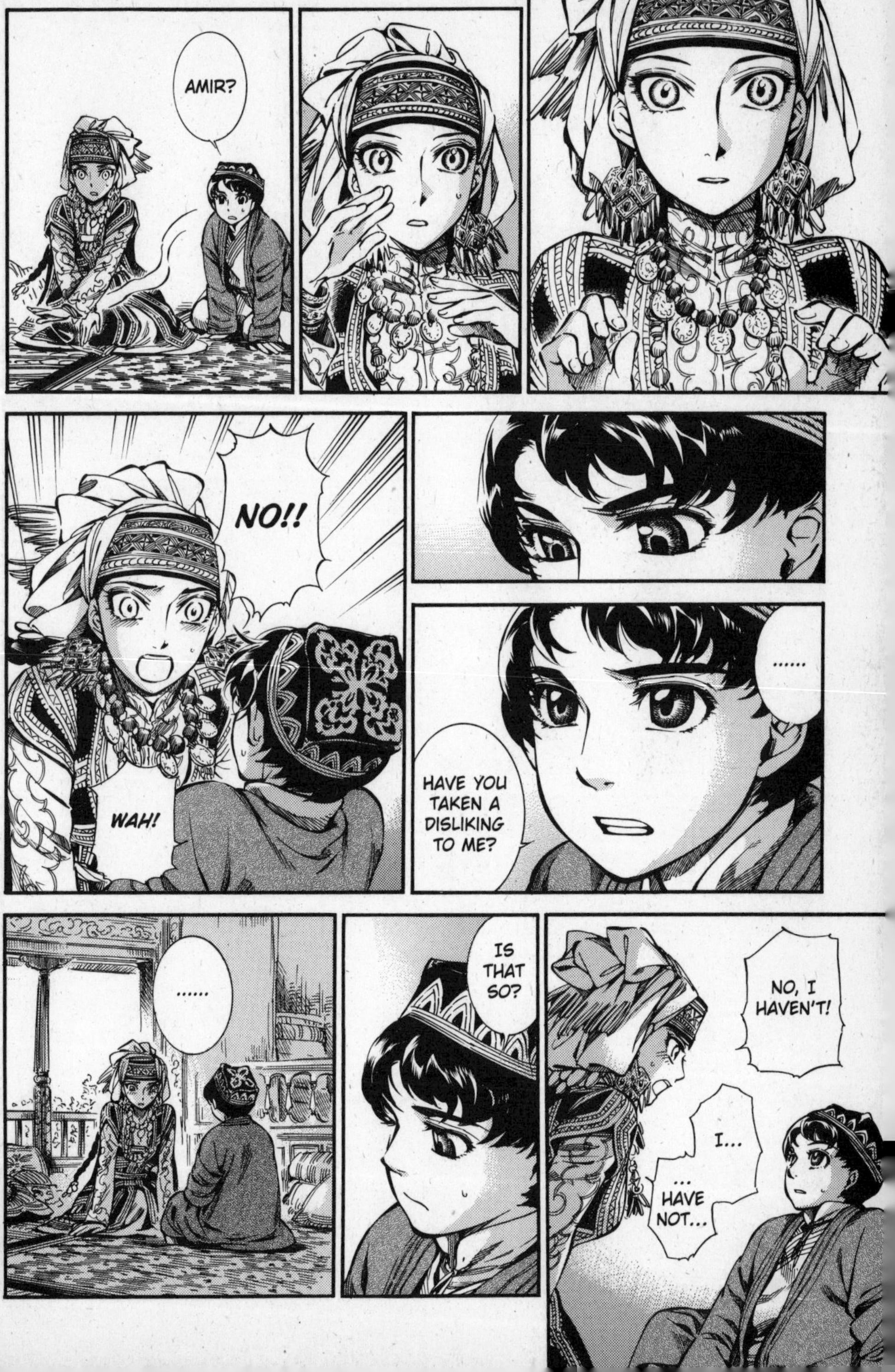
AMIR?
......
HAVE YOU TAKEN A DISLIKING TO ME?
NO!!
WAH!
NO, I HAVEN'T!
I...
... HAVE NOT...
IS THAT SO?
......

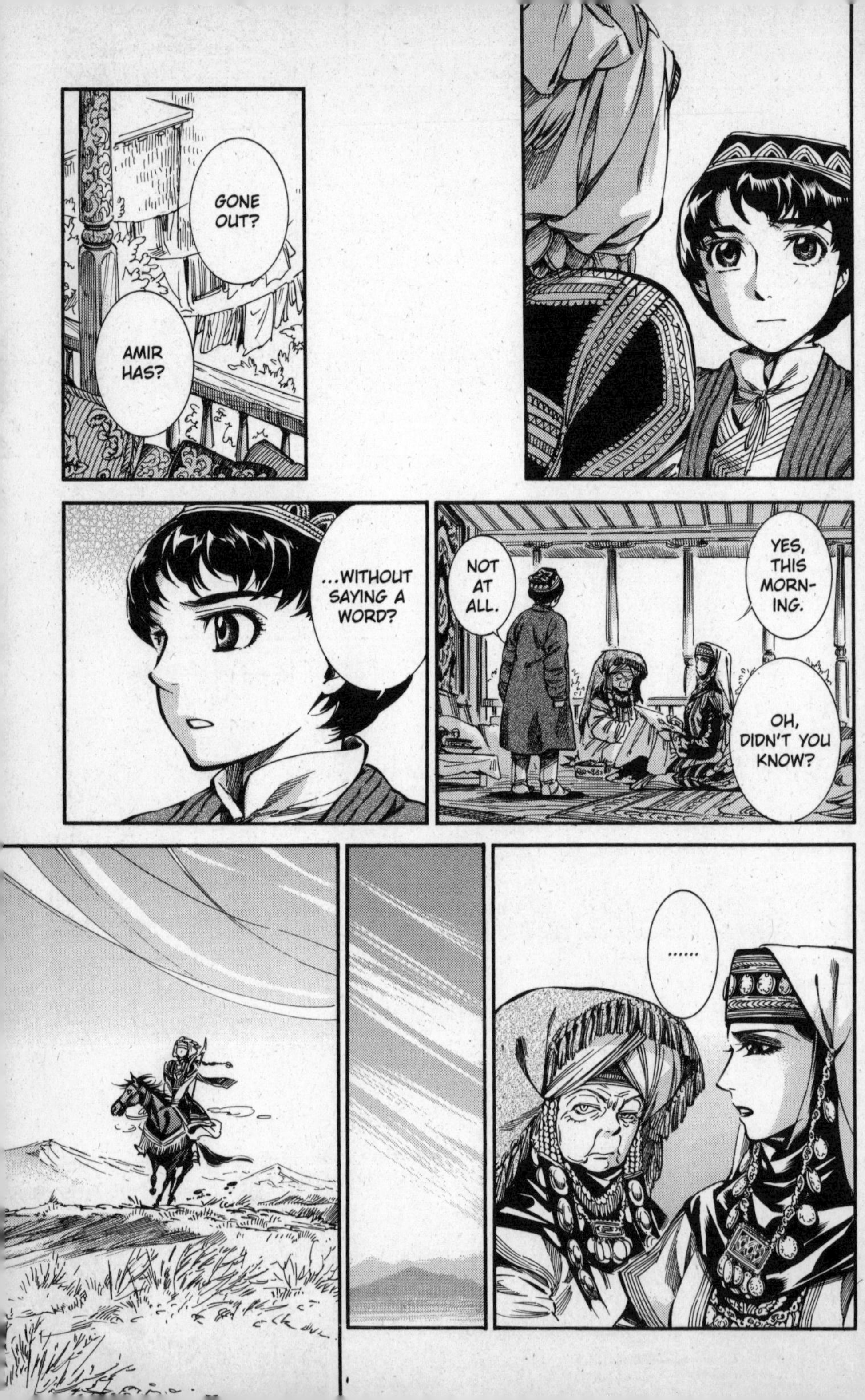
GONE OUT?
AMIR HAS?
YES, THIS MORN-ING.
OH, DIDN'T YOU KNOW?
NOT AT ALL.
...WITHOUT SAYING A WORD?
......

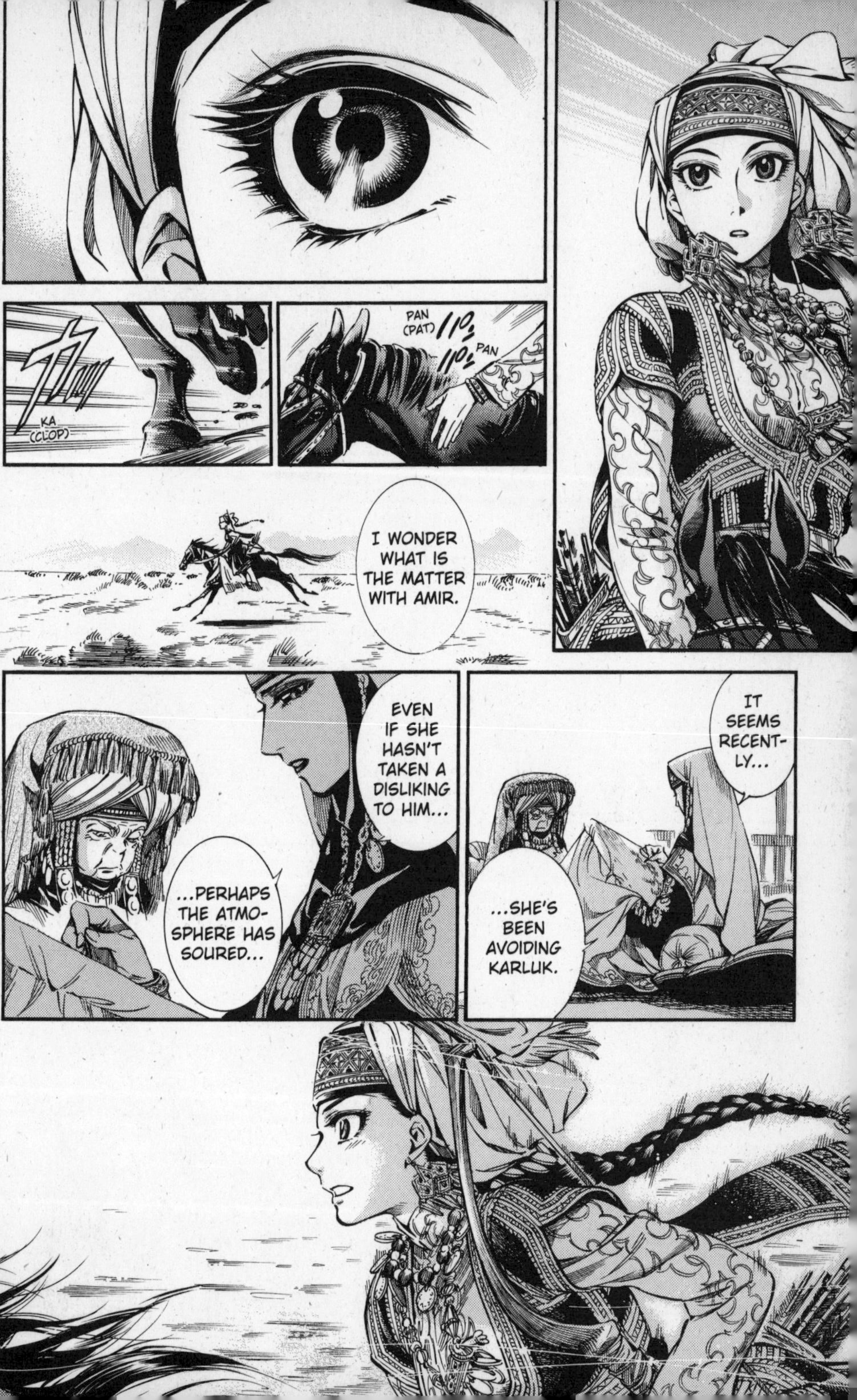
PAN (PAT)
PAN
KA (CLOP)
I WONDER WHAT IS THE MATTER WITH AMIR.
IT SEEMS RECENTLY...
...SHE'S BEEN AVOIDING KARLUK.
EVEN IF SHE HASN'T TAKEN A DISLIKING TO HIM...
...PERHAPS THE ATMOSPHERE HAS SOURED...

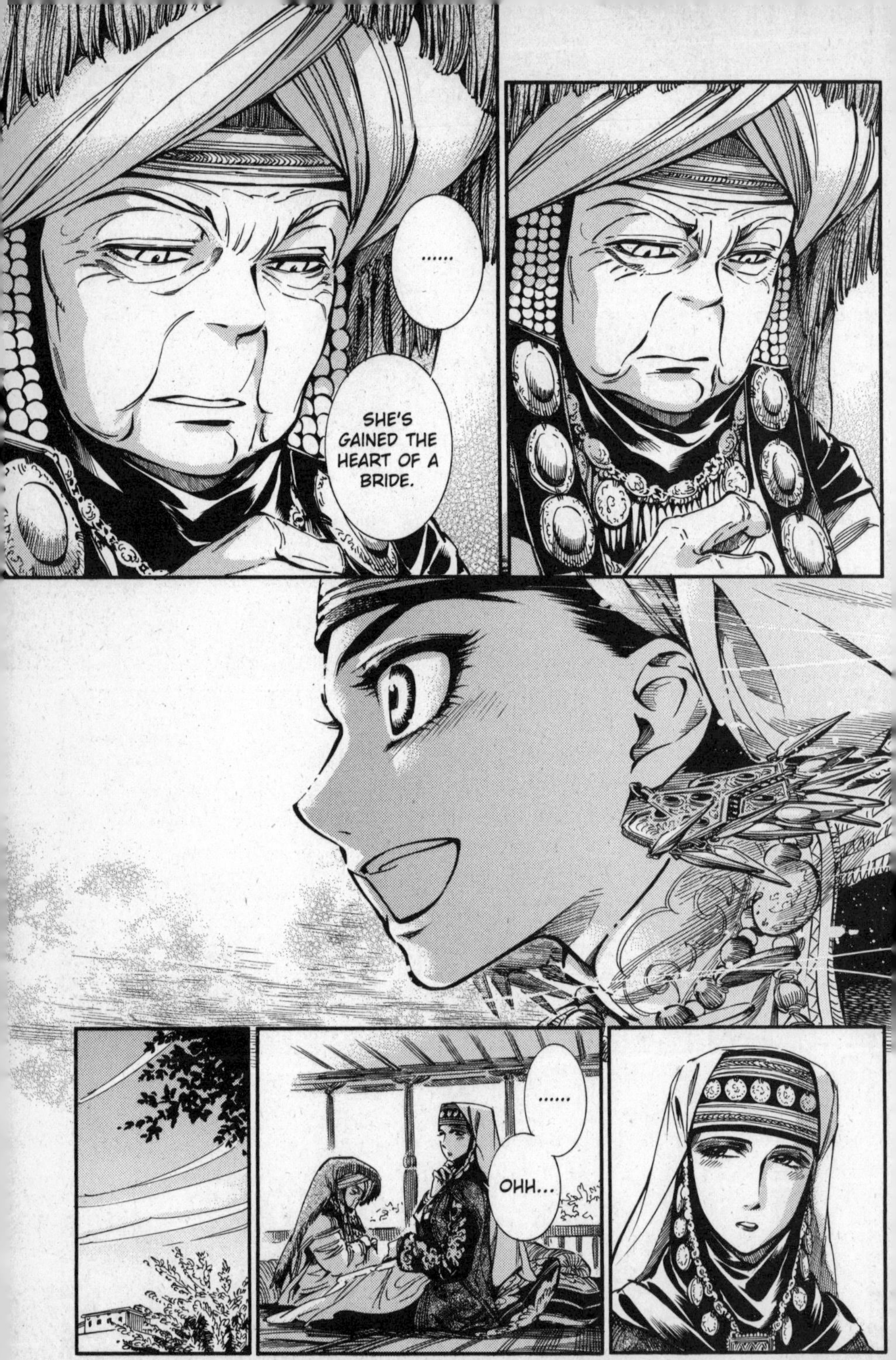
......
SHE'S GAINED THE HEART OF A BRIDE.
......
OHH...

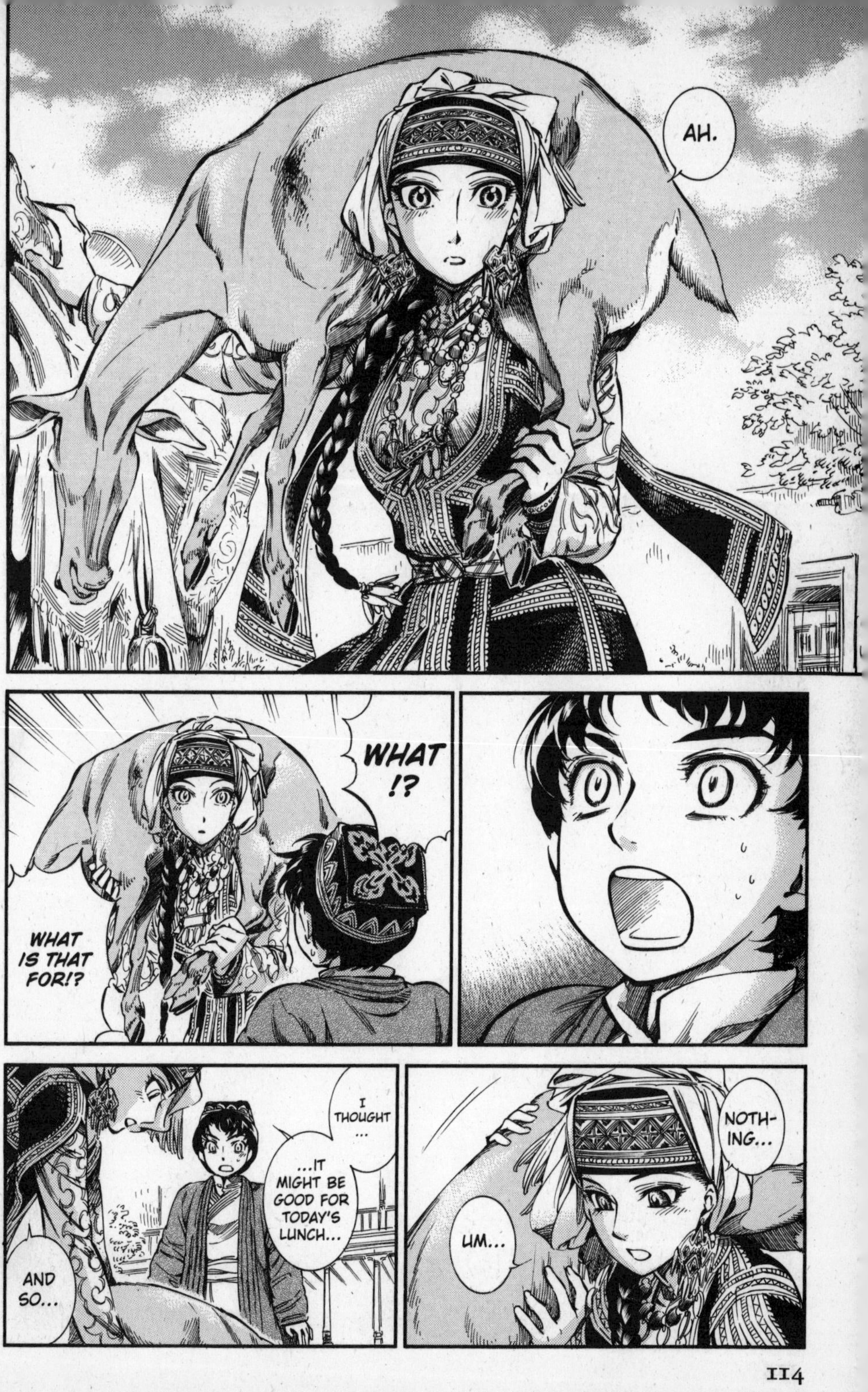
AH.
WHAT !?
WHAT IS THAT FOR!?
NOTH-ING...
UM...
I THOUGHT...
...IT MIGHT BE GOOD FOR TODAY'S LUNCH...
AND SO...

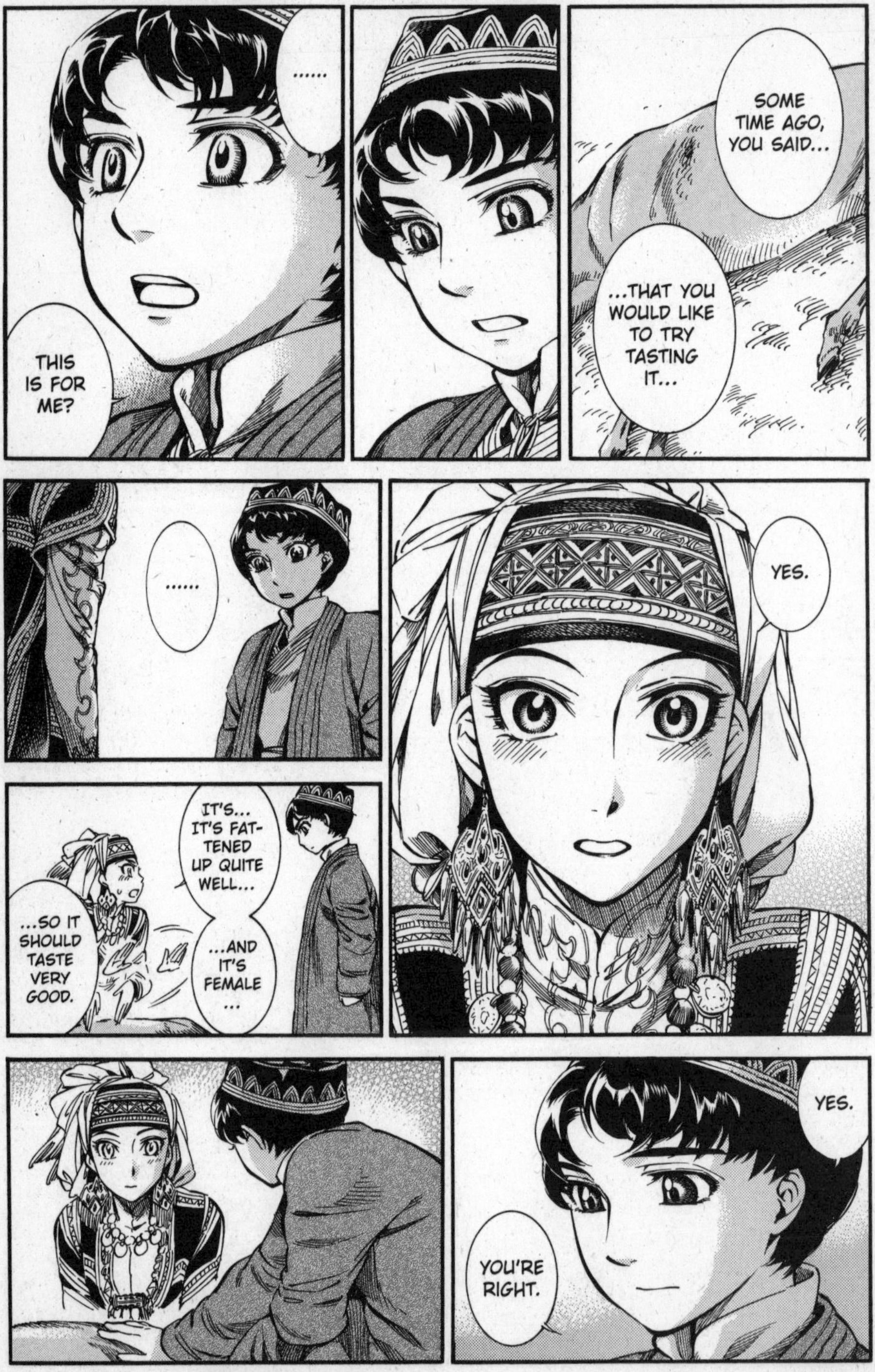
SOME TIME AGO, YOU SAID...
...THAT YOU WOULD LIKE TO TRY TASTING IT...
......
THIS IS FOR ME?
YES.
......
IT'S... IT'S FAT-TENED UP QUITE WELL...
...AND IT'S FEMALE ...
...SO IT SHOULD TASTE VERY GOOD.
YES.
YOU'RE RIGHT.

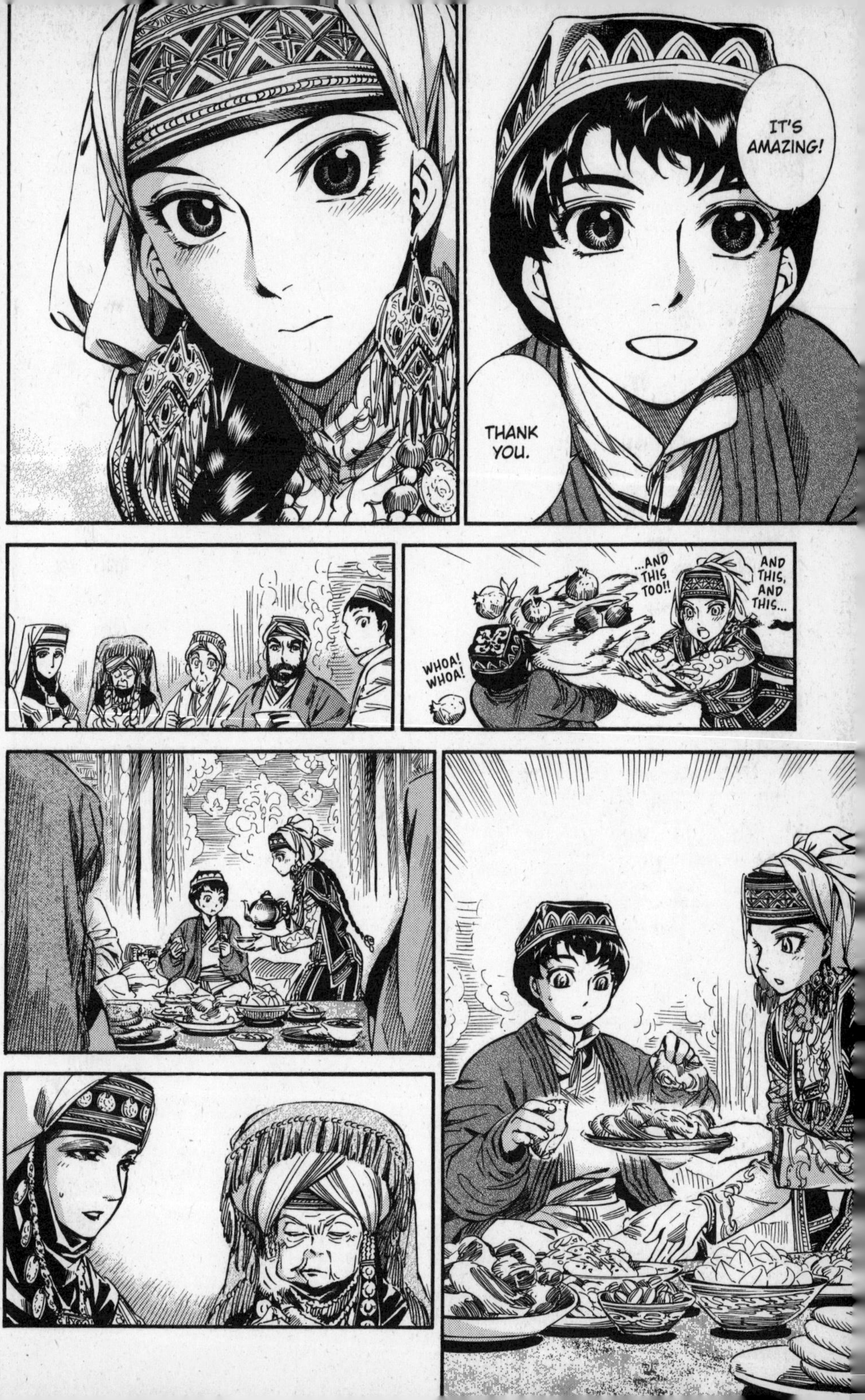
IT'S AMAZING!
THANK YOU.
AND THIS, AND THIS...
...AND THIS TOO!!
WHOA! WHOA!

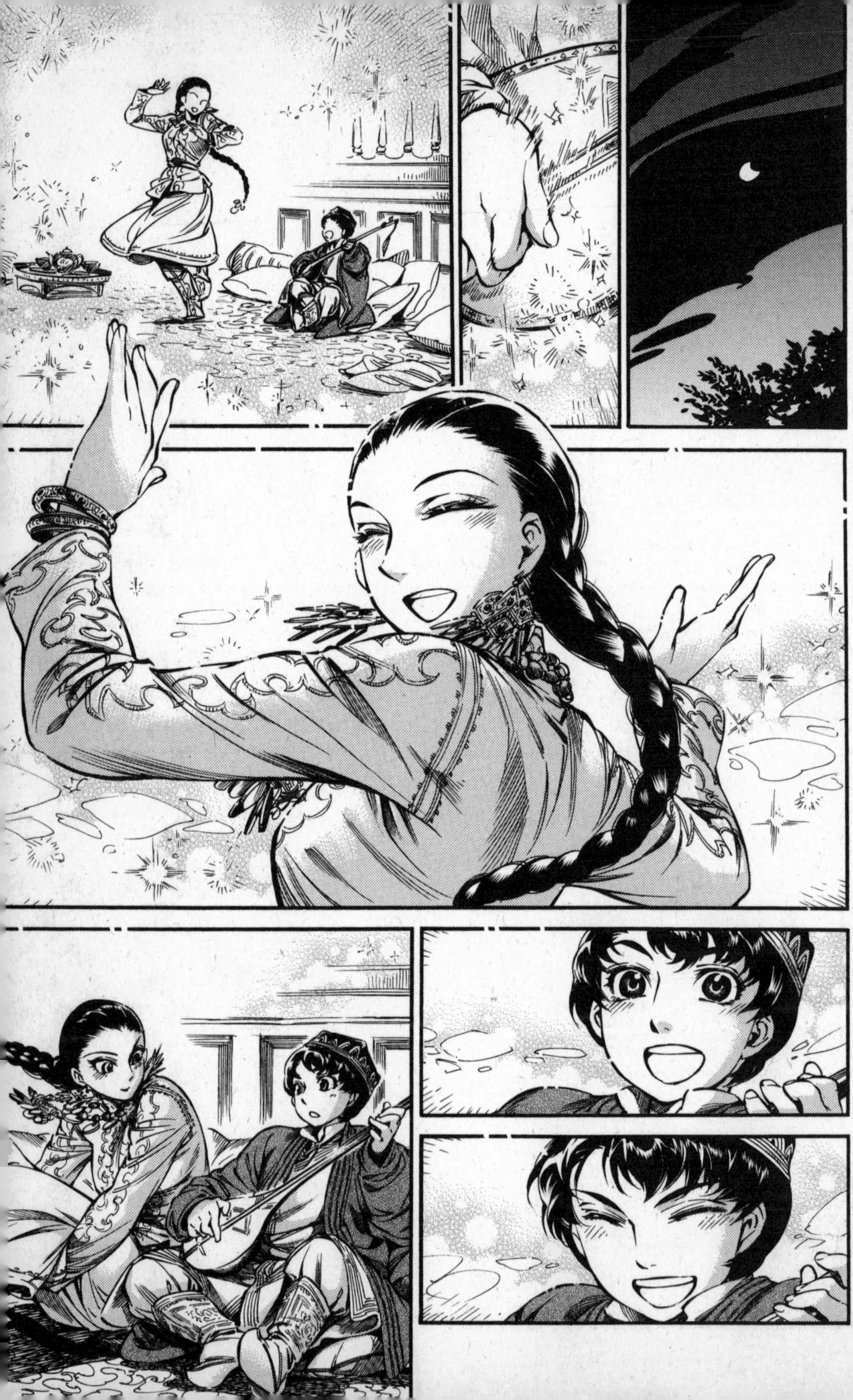

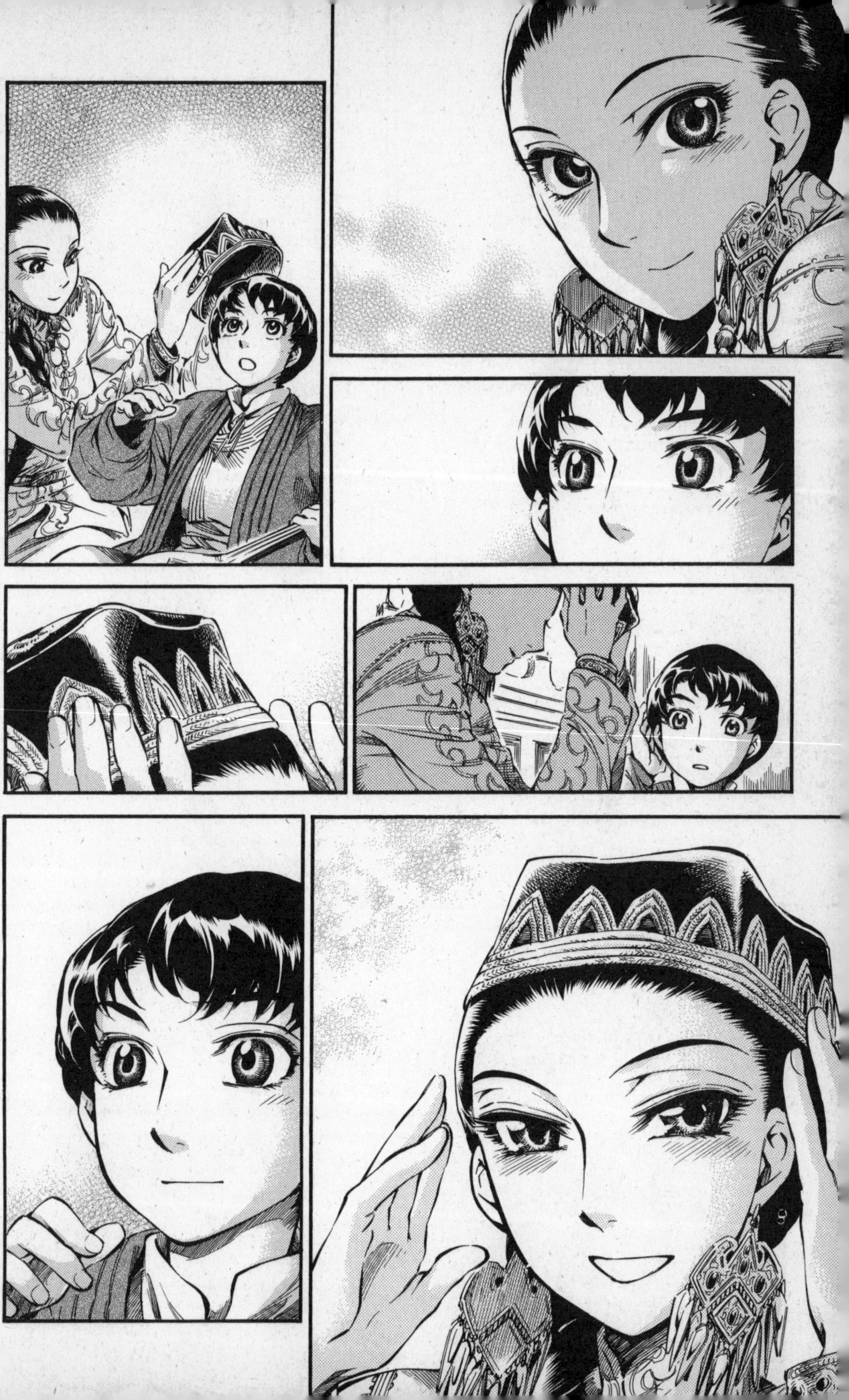

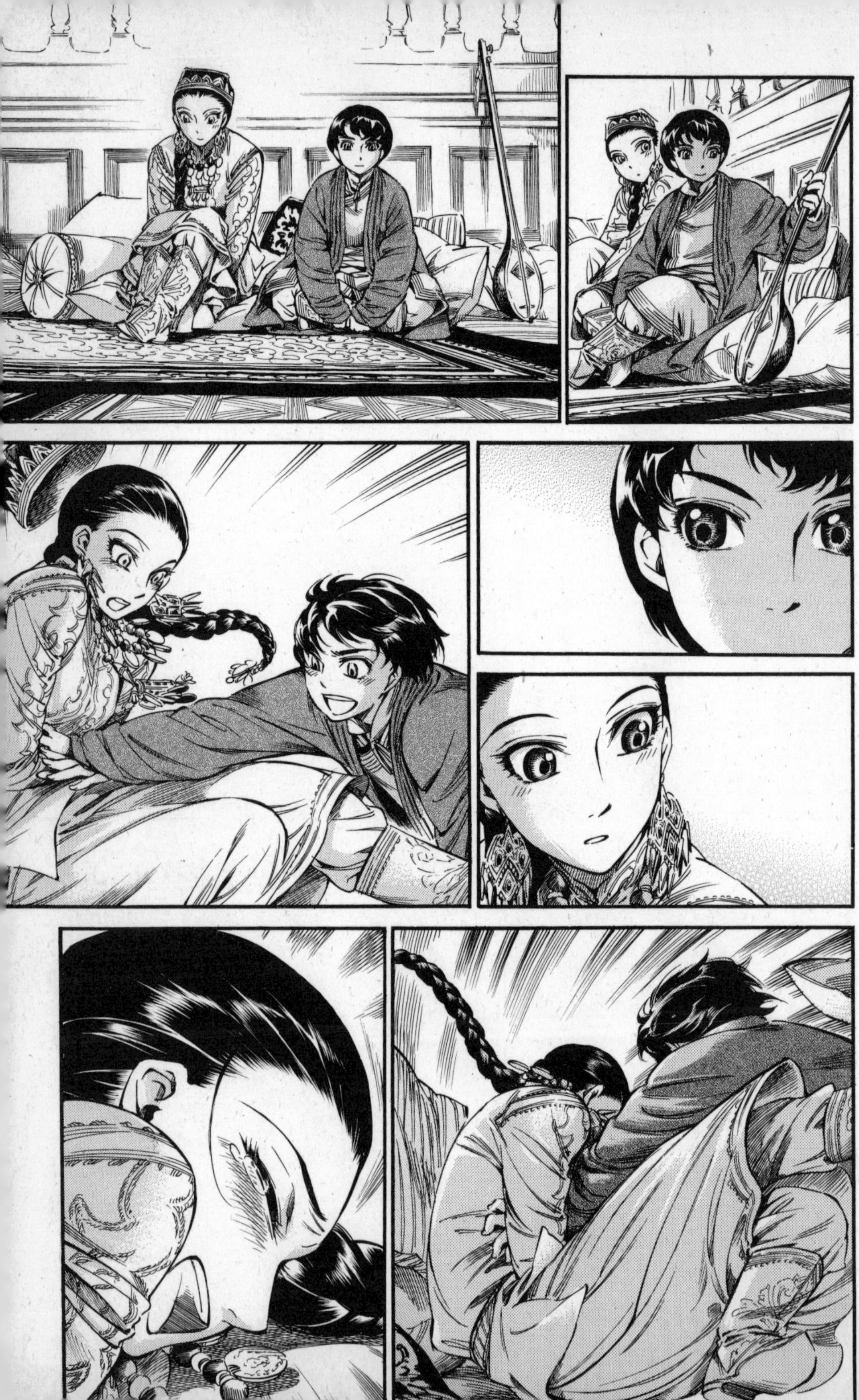

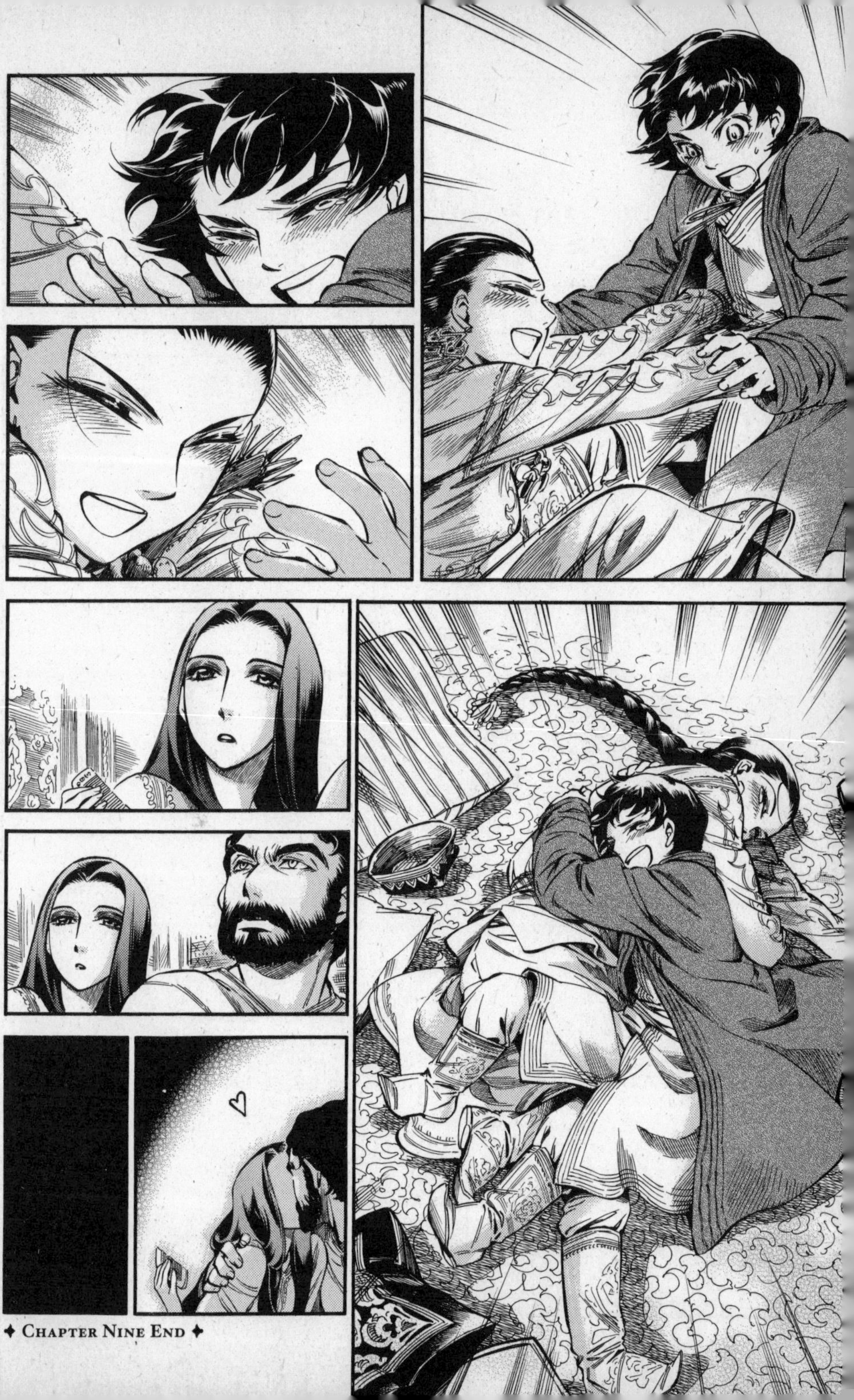

✦ Chapter Nine End ✦

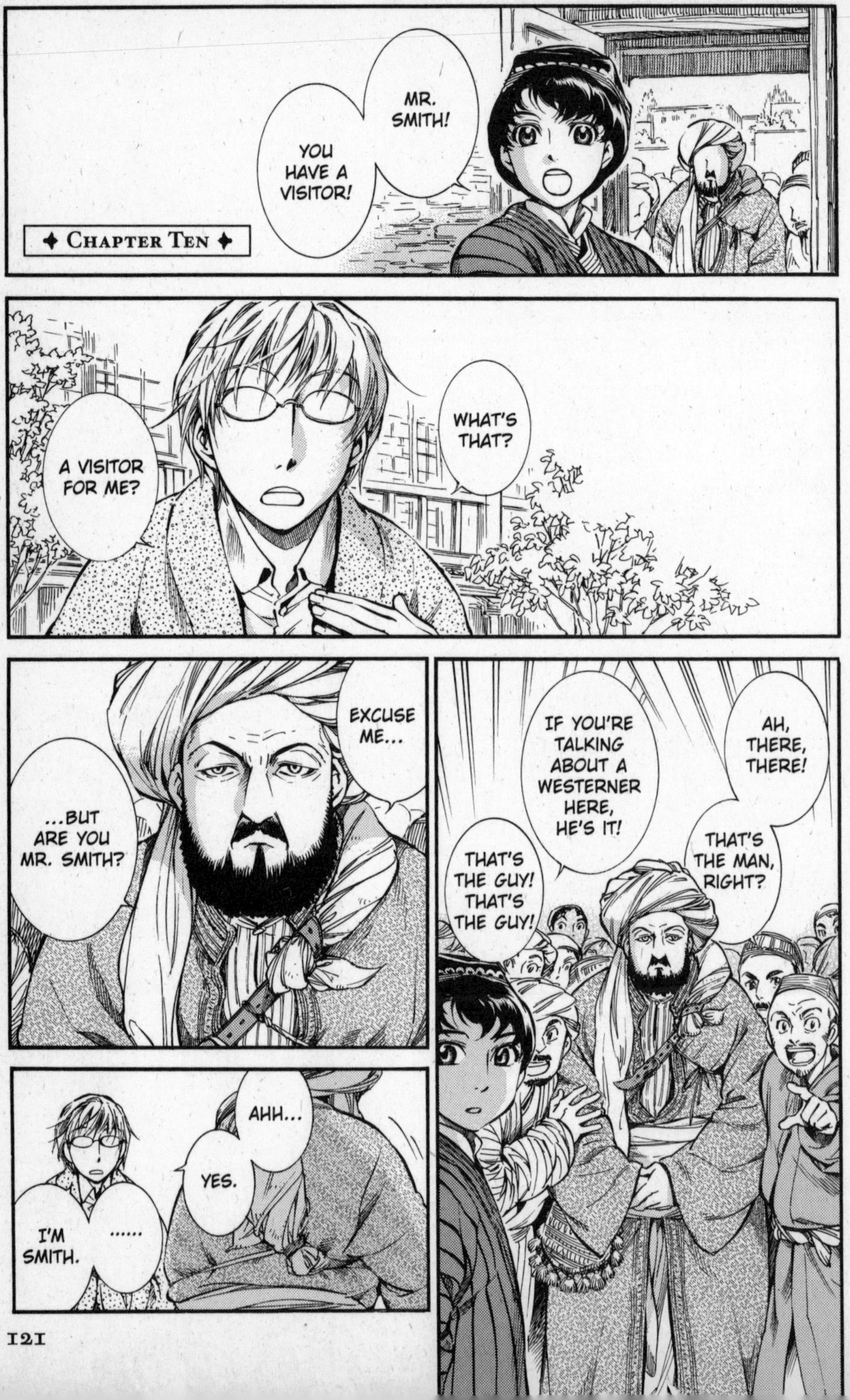
MR. SMITH!
YOU HAVE A VISITOR!
✦ CHAPTER TEN ✦
WHAT'S THAT?
A VISITOR FOR ME?
AH, THERE, THERE!
THAT'S THE MAN, RIGHT?
IF YOU'RE TALKING ABOUT A WESTERNER HERE, HE'S IT!
THAT'S THE GUY! THAT'S THE GUY!
EXCUSE ME...
...BUT ARE YOU MR. SMITH?
AHH...
YES.
......
I'M SMITH.

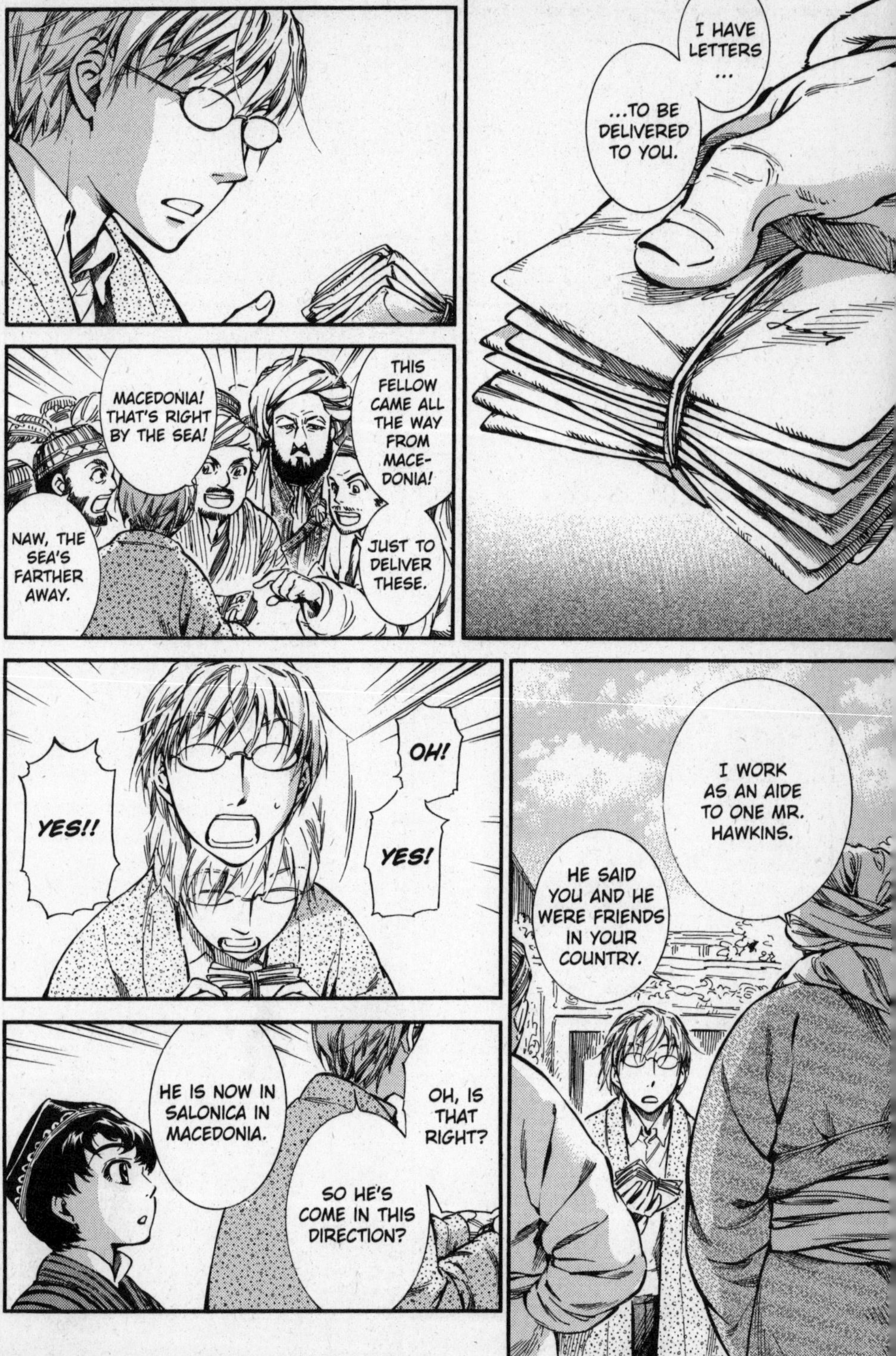
I HAVE LETTERS ...
...TO BE DELIVERED TO YOU.
THIS FELLOW CAME ALL THE WAY FROM MACE-DONIA!
MACEDONIA! THAT'S RIGHT BY THE SEA!
JUST TO DELIVER THESE.
NAW, THE SEA'S FARTHER AWAY.
I WORK AS AN AIDE TO ONE MR. HAWKINS.
HE SAID YOU AND HE WERE FRIENDS IN YOUR COUNTRY.
OH! YES!
YES!!
OH, IS THAT RIGHT?
HE IS NOW IN SALONICA IN MACEDONIA.
SO HE'S COME IN THIS DIRECTION?

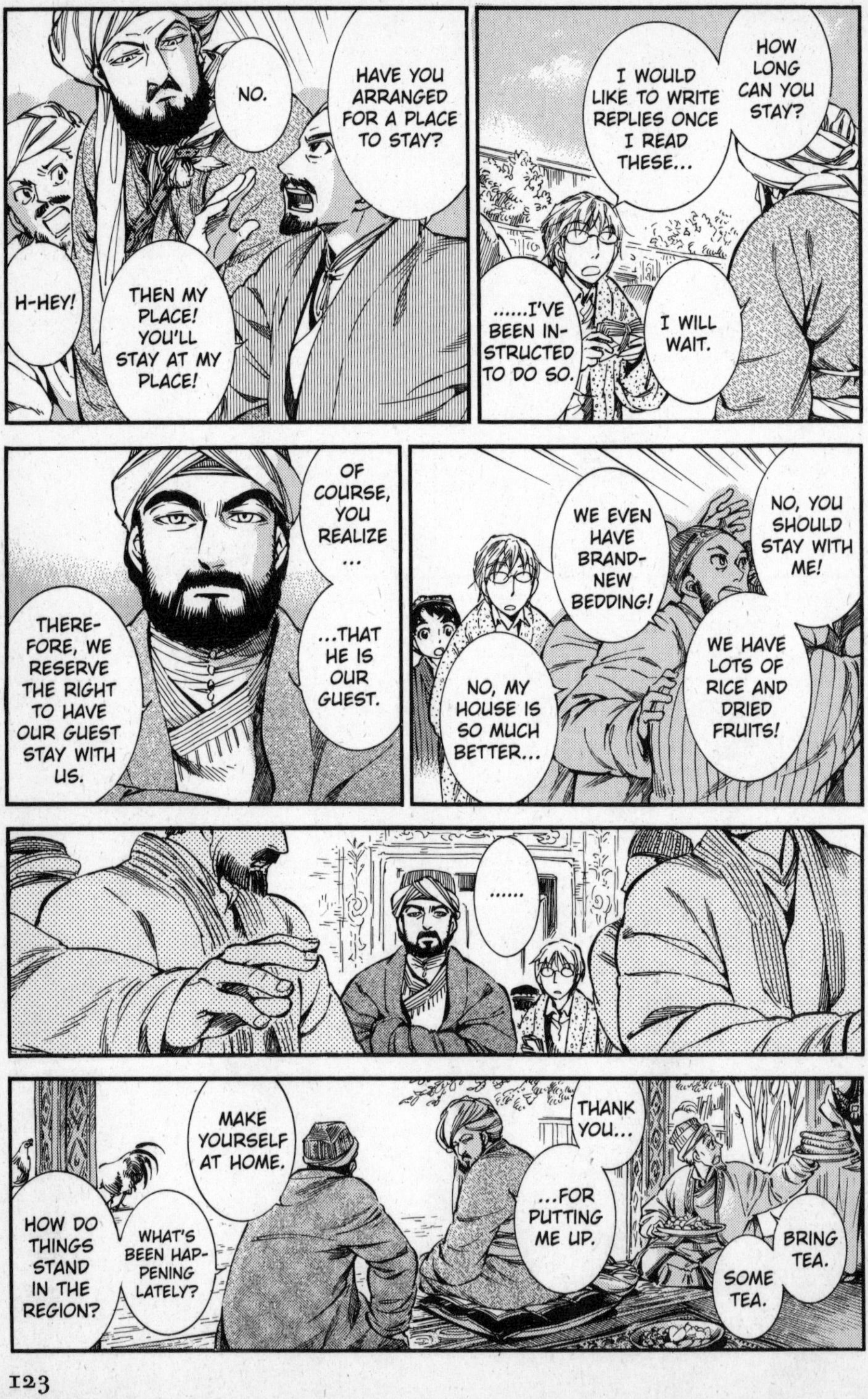
HOW LONG CAN YOU STAY?
I WOULD LIKE TO WRITE REPLIES ONCE I READ THESE...
I WILL WAIT.
......I'VE BEEN IN-STRUCTED TO DO SO.
HAVE YOU ARRANGED FOR A PLACE TO STAY?
NO.
THEN MY PLACE! YOU'LL STAY AT MY PLACE!
H-HEY!
NO, YOU SHOULD STAY WITH ME!
WE EVEN HAVE BRAND-NEW BEDDING!
WE HAVE LOTS OF RICE AND DRIED FRUITS!
NO, MY HOUSE IS SO MUCH BETTER...
OF COURSE, YOU REALIZE ...
...THAT HE IS OUR GUEST.
THERE-FORE, WE RESERVE THE RIGHT TO HAVE OUR GUEST STAY WITH US.
......
BRING TEA.
SOME TEA.
THANK YOU...
...FOR PUTTING ME UP.
MAKE YOURSELF AT HOME.
WHAT'S BEEN HAP-PENING LATELY?
HOW DO THINGS STAND IN THE REGION?

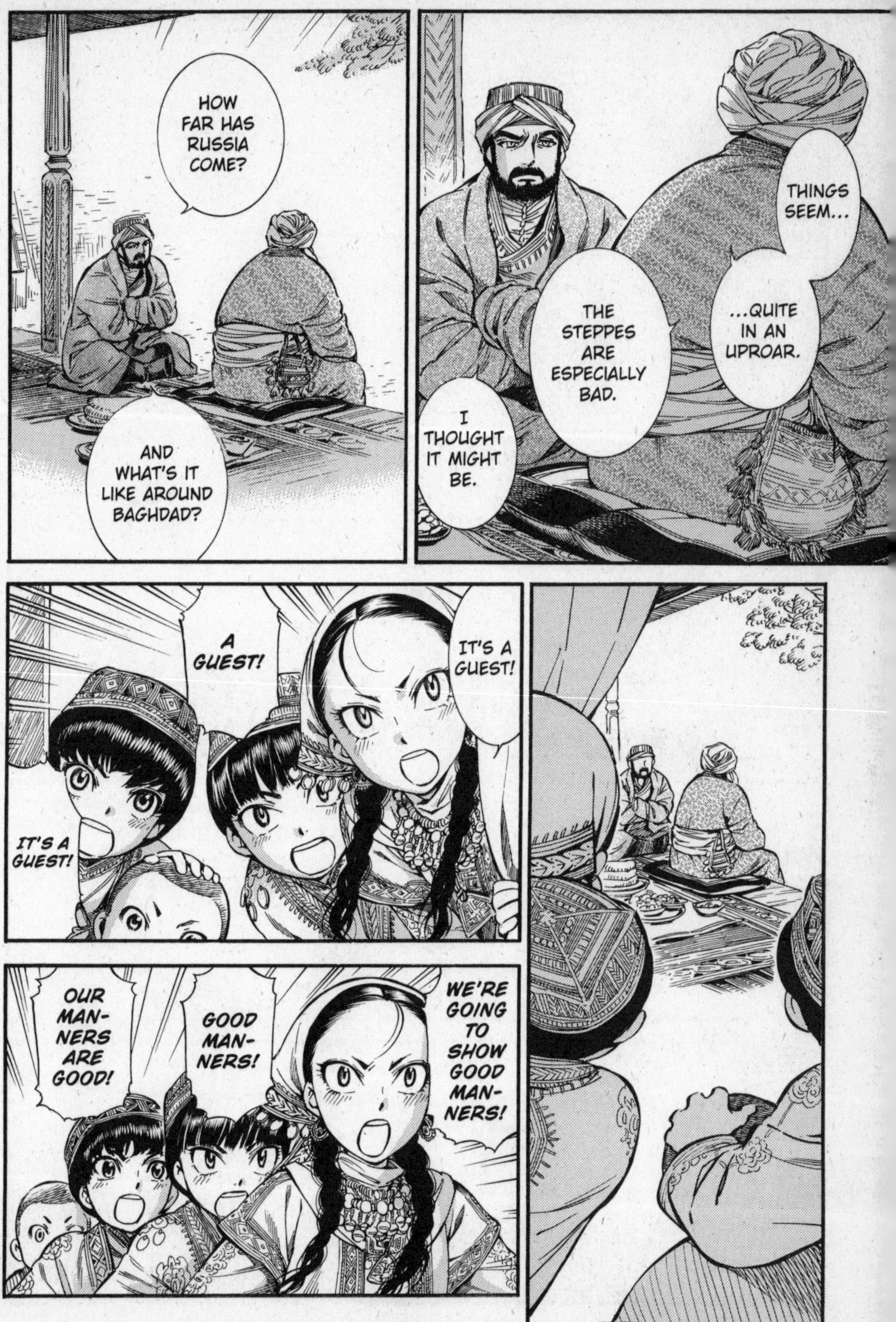
THINGS SEEM...
...QUITE IN AN UPROAR.
THE STEPPES ARE ESPECIALLY BAD.
I THOUGHT IT MIGHT BE.
HOW FAR HAS RUSSIA COME?
AND WHAT'S IT LIKE AROUND BAGHDAD?
IT'S A GUEST!
A GUEST!
IT'S A GUEST!
WE'RE GOING TO SHOW GOOD MAN-NERS!
GOOD MAN-NERS!
OUR MAN-NERS ARE GOOD!

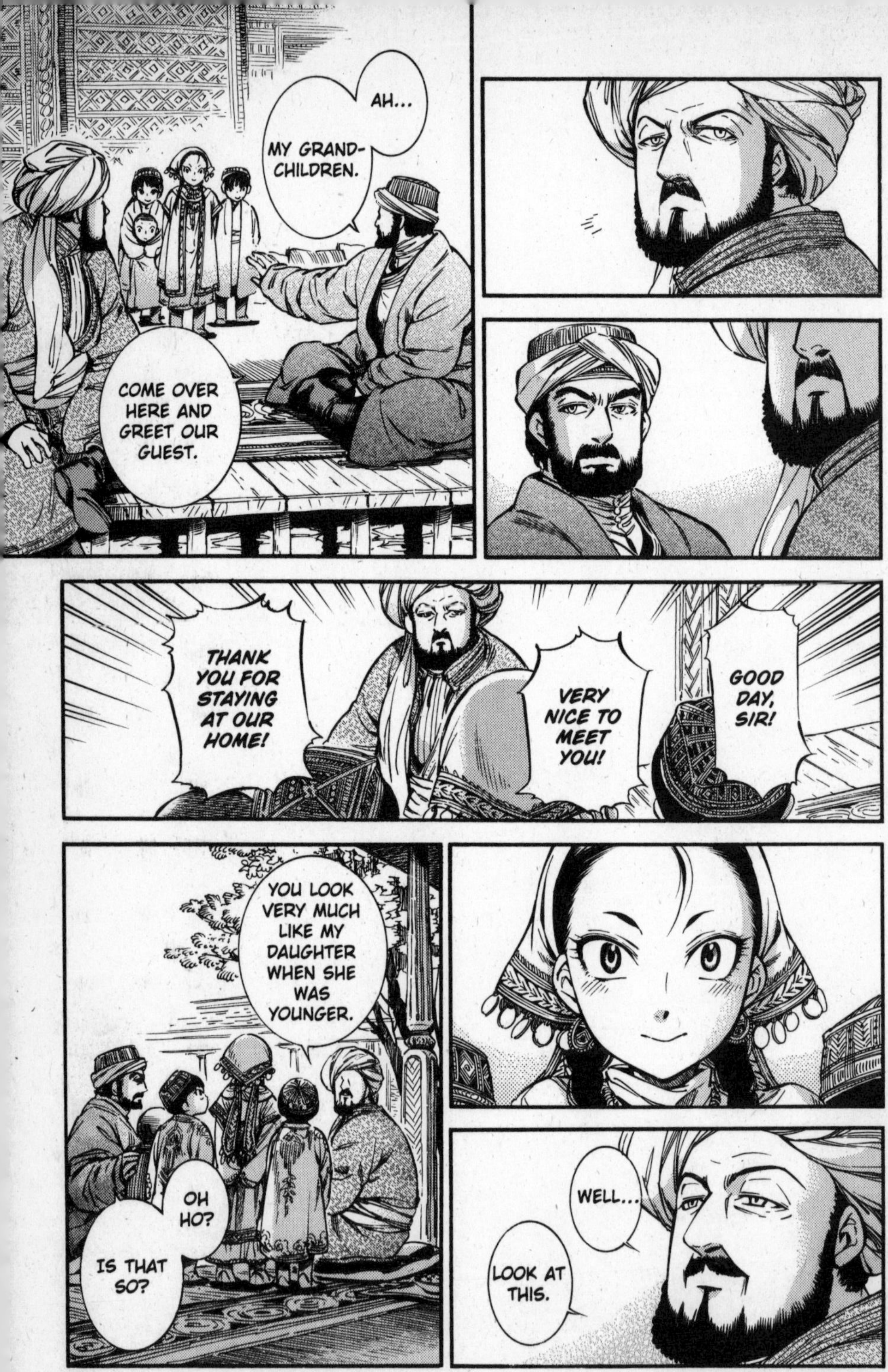
AH...
MY GRAND-CHILDREN.
COME OVER HERE AND GREET OUR GUEST.
GOOD DAY, SIR!
VERY NICE TO MEET YOU!
THANK YOU FOR STAYING AT OUR HOME!
WELL...
LOOK AT THIS.
YOU LOOK VERY MUCH LIKE MY DAUGHTER WHEN SHE WAS YOUNGER.
OH HO?
IS THAT SO?

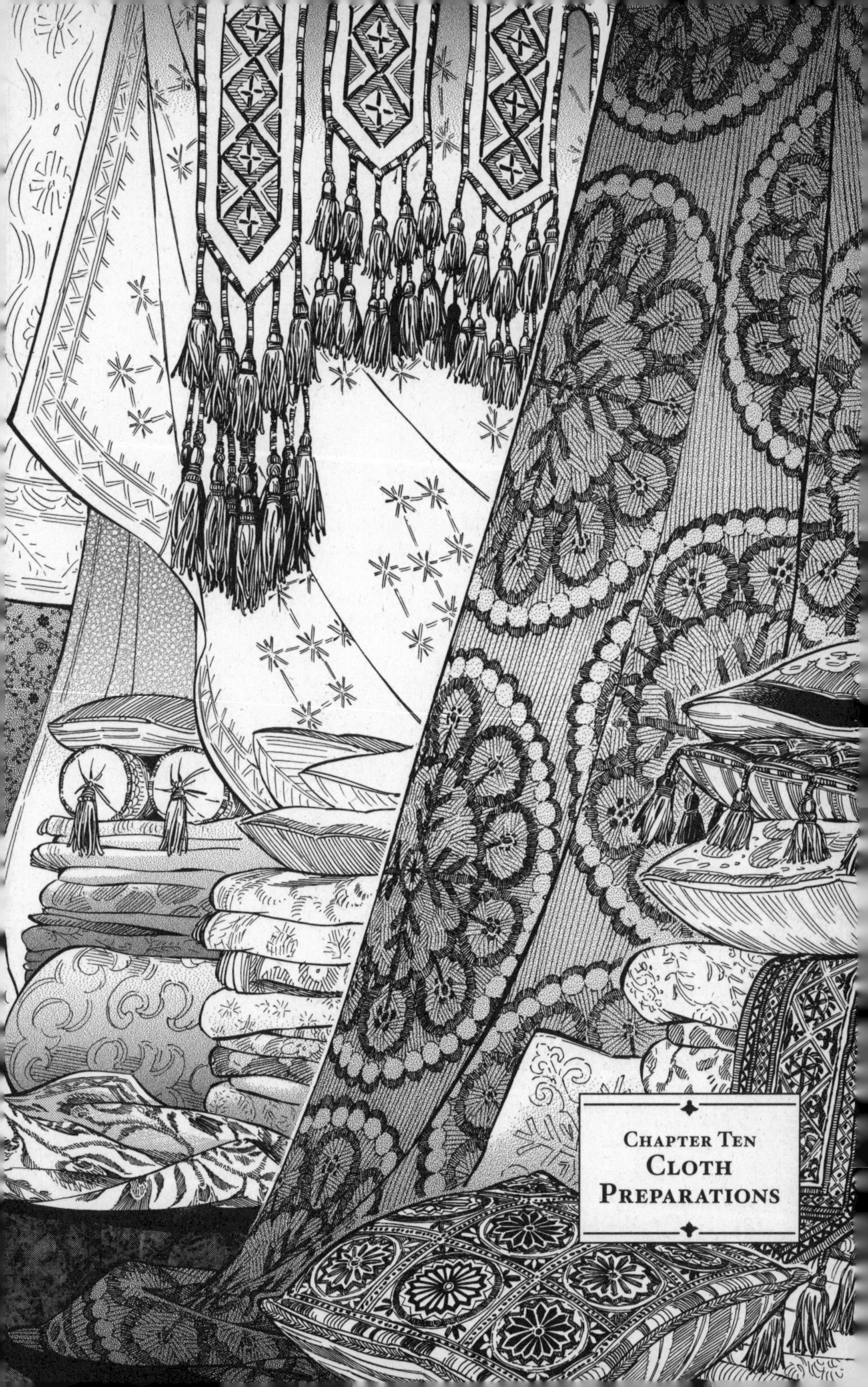

Chapter Ten
Cloth Preparations

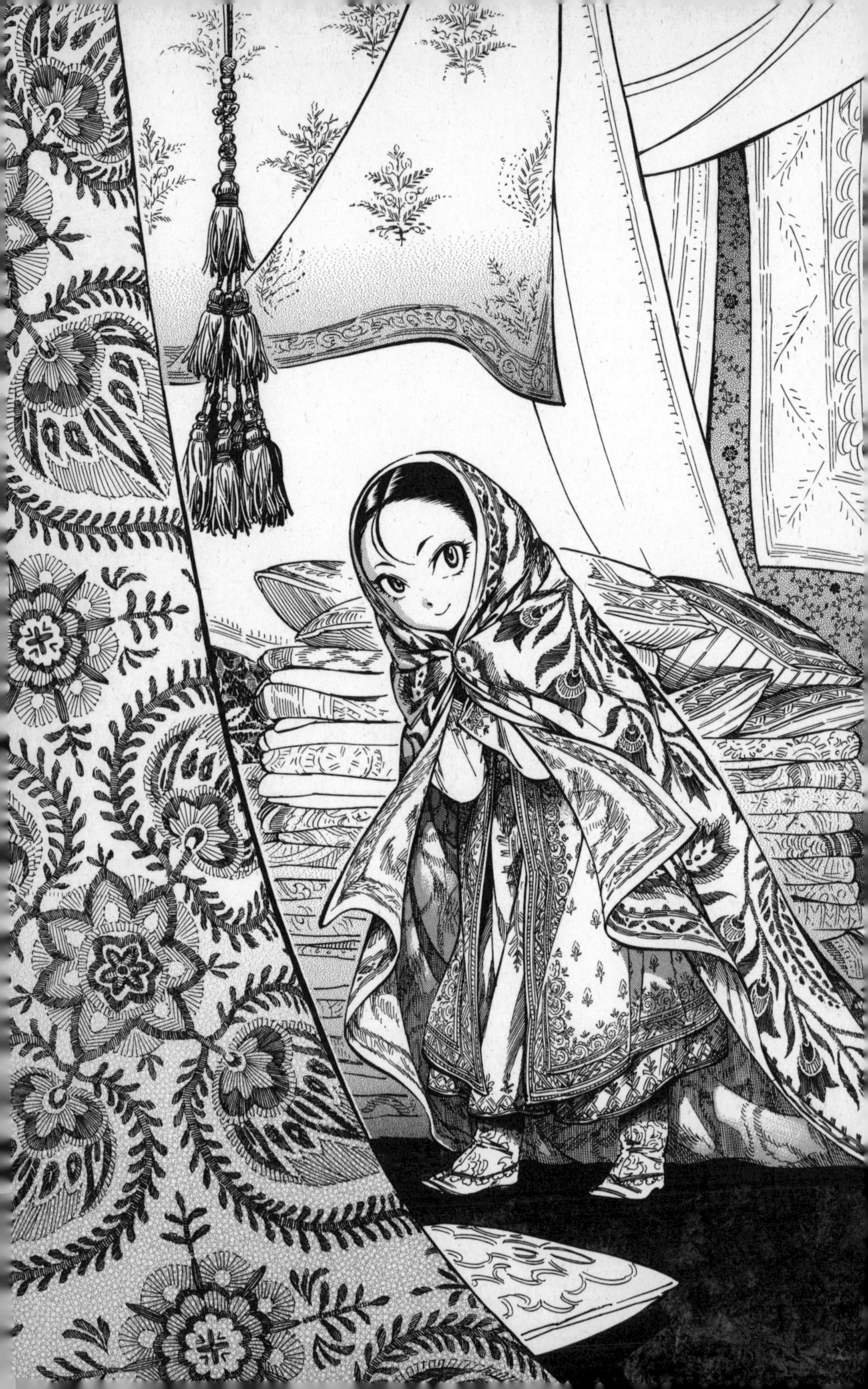

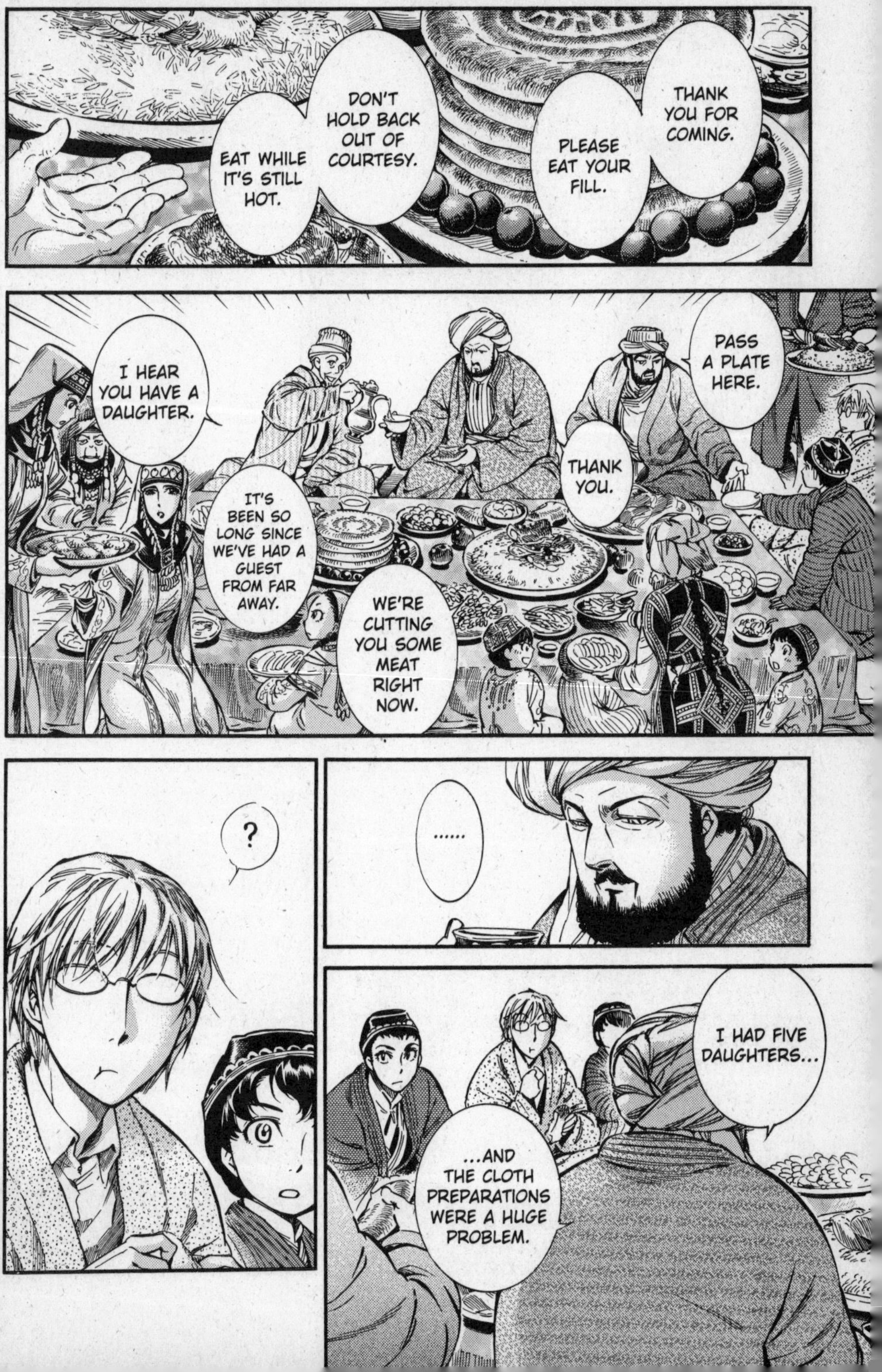
THANK YOU FOR COMING.
PLEASE EAT YOUR FILL.
DON'T HOLD BACK OUT OF COURTESY.
EAT WHILE IT'S STILL HOT.
PASS A PLATE HERE.
THANK YOU.
I HEAR YOU HAVE A DAUGHTER.
IT'S BEEN SO LONG SINCE WE'VE HAD A GUEST FROM FAR AWAY.
WE'RE CUTTING YOU SOME MEAT RIGHT NOW.
......
?
I HAD FIVE DAUGHTERS...
...AND THE CLOTH PREPARATIONS WERE A HUGE PROBLEM.

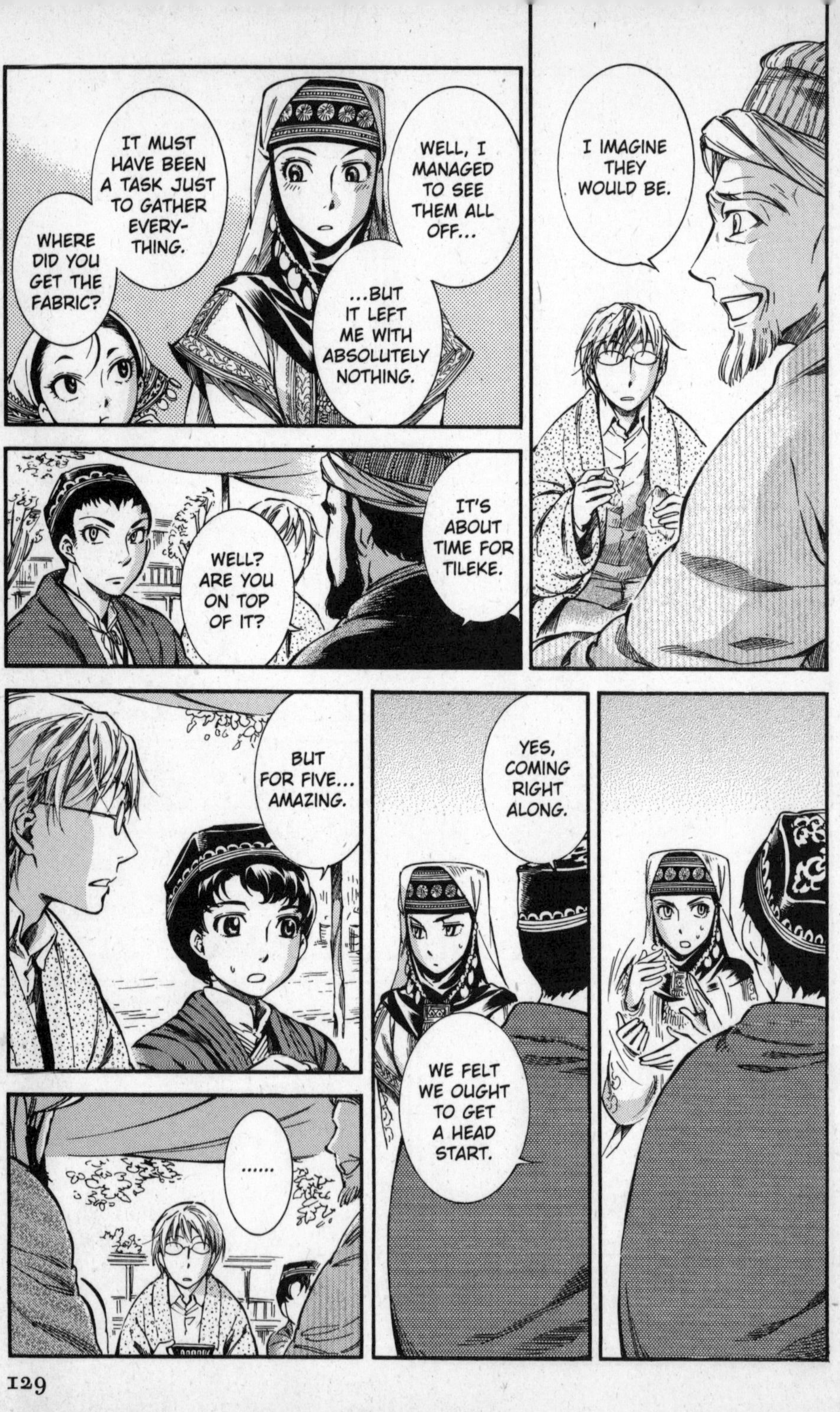
I IMAGINE THEY WOULD BE.
WELL, I MANAGED TO SEE THEM ALL OFF...
...BUT IT LEFT ME WITH ABSOLUTELY NOTHING.
IT MUST HAVE BEEN A TASK JUST TO GATHER EVERY-THING.
WHERE DID YOU GET THE FABRIC?
IT'S ABOUT TIME FOR TILEKE.
WELL? ARE YOU ON TOP OF IT?
YES, COMING RIGHT ALONG.
WE FELT WE OUGHT TO GET A HEAD START.
BUT FOR FIVE... AMAZING.
......

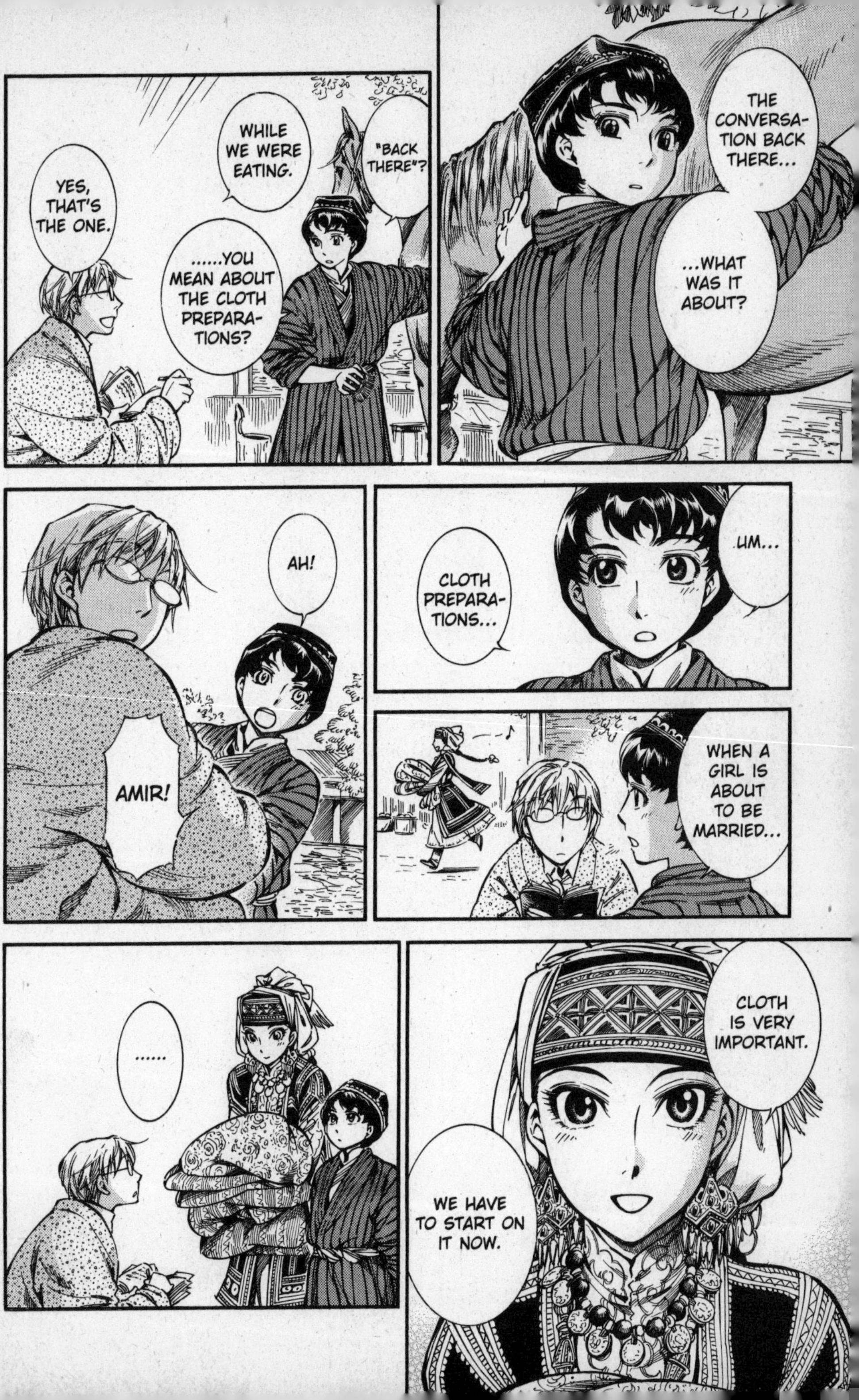
THE CONVERSATION BACK THERE...
...WHAT WAS IT ABOUT?
"BACK THERE"?
WHILE WE WERE EATING.
......YOU MEAN ABOUT THE CLOTH PREPARATIONS?
YES, THAT'S THE ONE.
UM...
CLOTH PREPARATIONS...
WHEN A GIRL IS ABOUT TO BE MARRIED...
AH!
AMIR!
CLOTH IS VERY IMPORTANT.
WE HAVE TO START ON IT NOW.
......

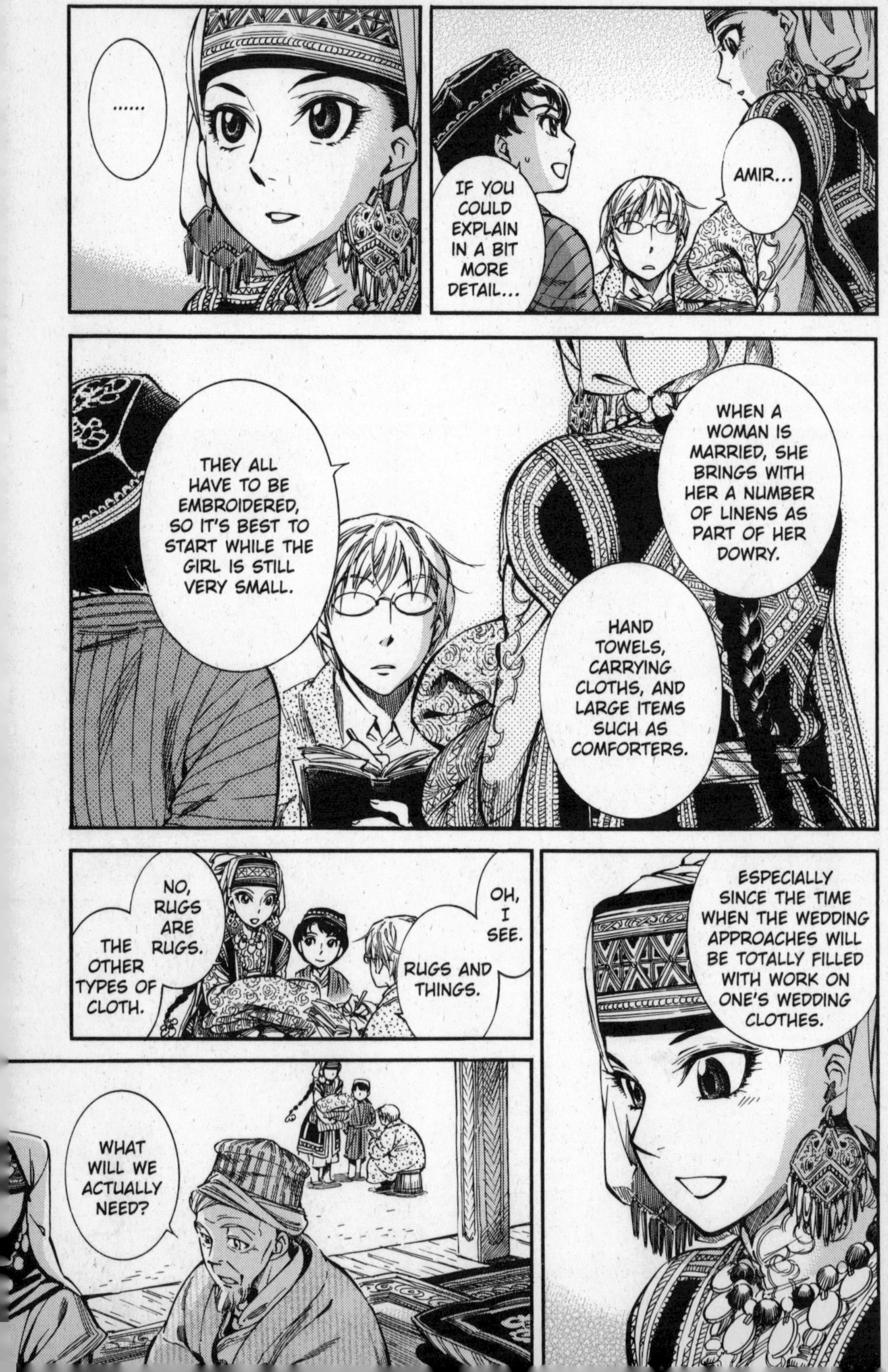
AMIR...
IF YOU COULD EXPLAIN IN A BIT MORE DETAIL...
......
WHEN A WOMAN IS MARRIED, SHE BRINGS WITH HER A NUMBER OF LINENS AS PART OF HER DOWRY.
HAND TOWELS, CARRYING CLOTHS, AND LARGE ITEMS SUCH AS COMFORTERS.
THEY ALL HAVE TO BE EMBROIDERED, SO IT'S BEST TO START WHILE THE GIRL IS STILL VERY SMALL.
ESPECIALLY SINCE THE TIME WHEN THE WEDDING APPROACHES WILL BE TOTALLY FILLED WITH WORK ON ONE'S WEDDING CLOTHES.
OH, I SEE.
RUGS AND THINGS.
NO, RUGS ARE RUGS.
THE OTHER TYPES OF CLOTH.
WHAT WILL WE ACTUALLY NEED?

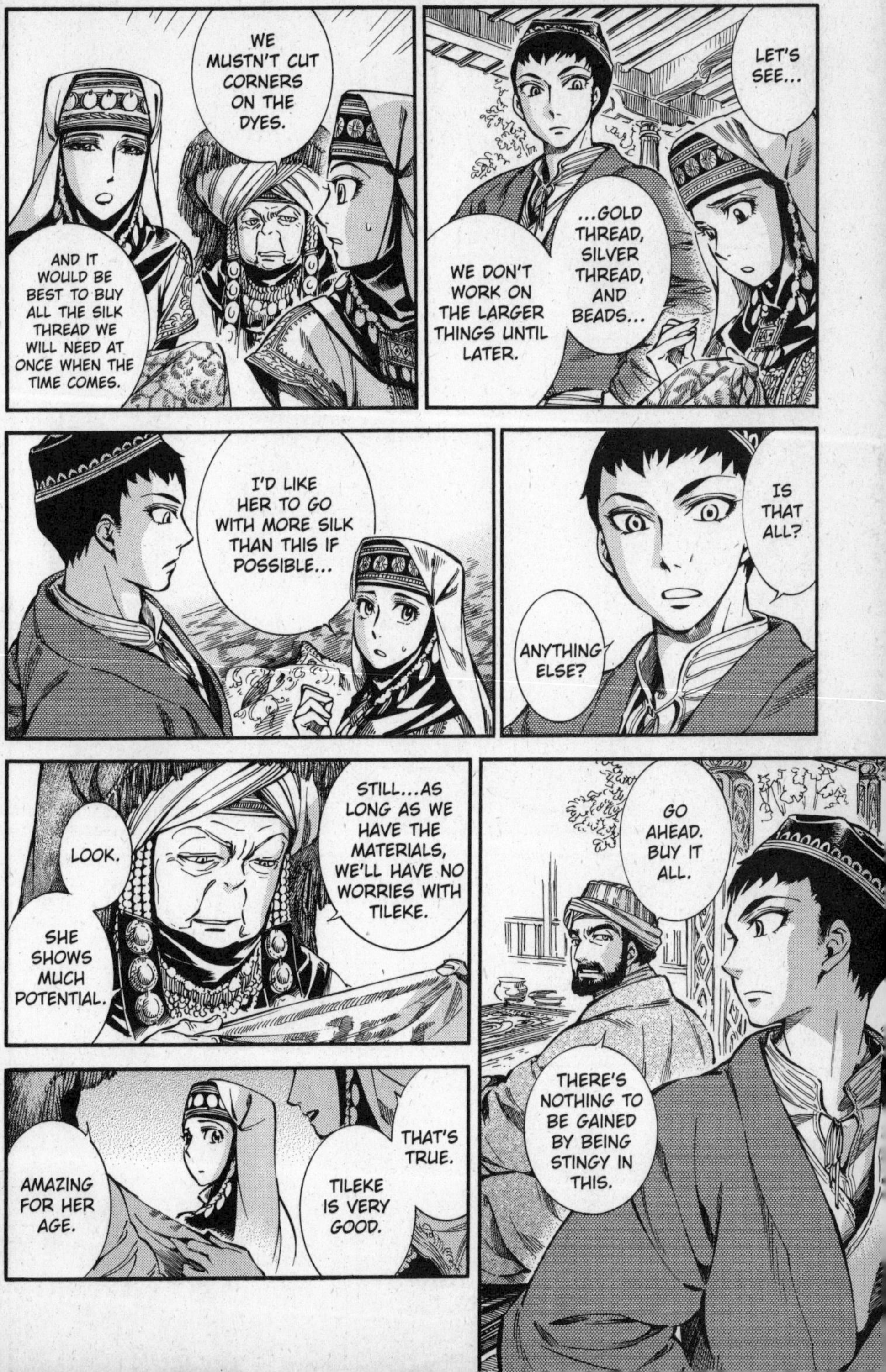
LET'S SEE...
...GOLD THREAD, SILVER THREAD, AND BEADS...
WE DON'T WORK ON THE LARGER THINGS UNTIL LATER.
WE MUSTN'T CUT CORNERS ON THE DYES.
AND IT WOULD BE BEST TO BUY ALL THE SILK THREAD WE WILL NEED AT ONCE WHEN THE TIME COMES.
IS THAT ALL?
ANYTHING ELSE?
I'D LIKE HER TO GO WITH MORE SILK THAN THIS IF POSSIBLE...
GO AHEAD. BUY IT ALL.
THERE'S NOTHING TO BE GAINED BY BEING STINGY IN THIS.
STILL...AS LONG AS WE HAVE THE MATERIALS, WE'LL HAVE NO WORRIES WITH TILEKE.
LOOK.
SHE SHOWS MUCH POTENTIAL.
THAT'S TRUE.
TILEKE IS VERY GOOD.
AMAZING FOR HER AGE.

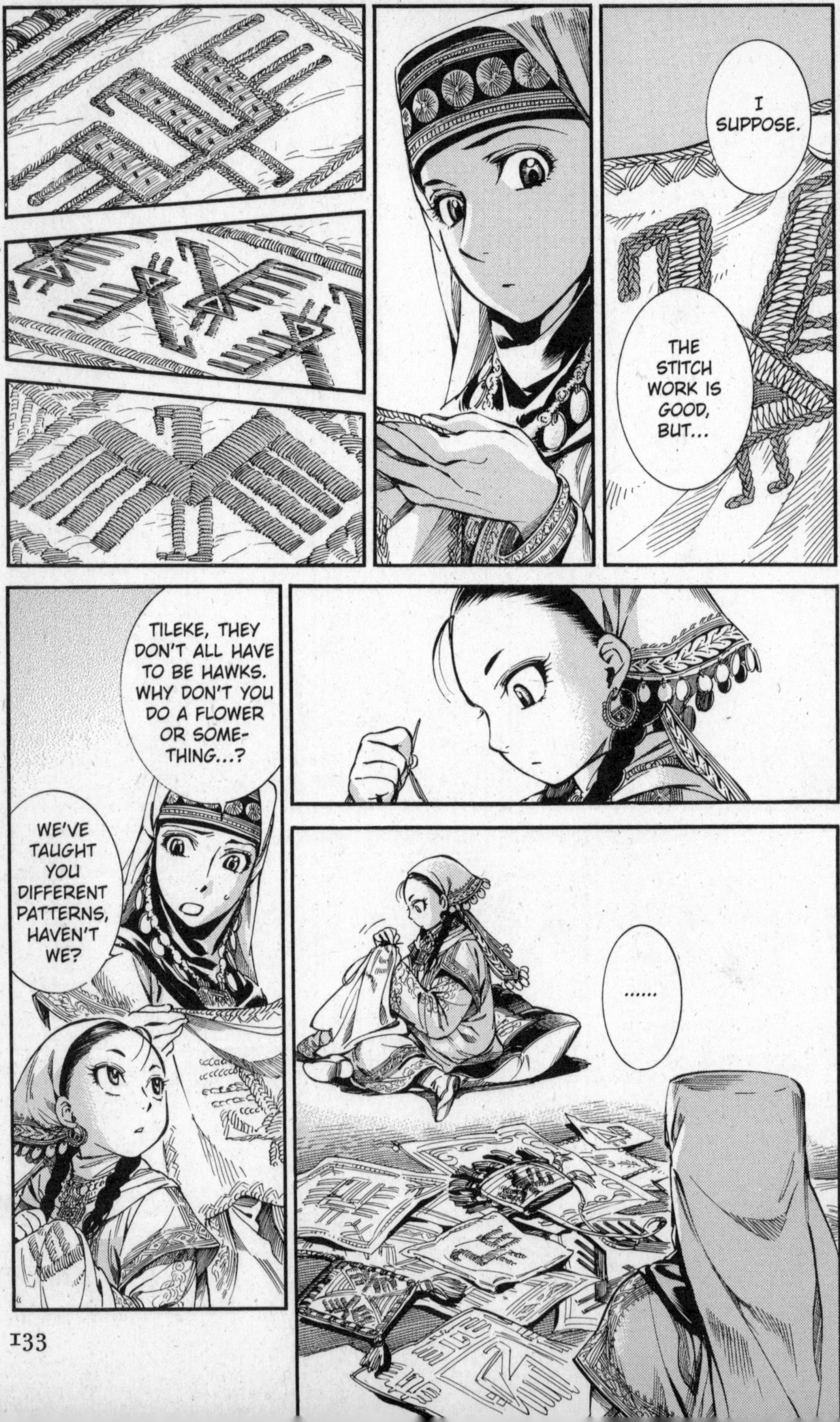
I SUPPOSE.
THE STITCH WORK IS GOOD, BUT...
TILEKE, THEY DON'T ALL HAVE TO BE HAWKS. WHY DON'T YOU DO A FLOWER OR SOME-THING...?
WE'VE TAUGHT YOU DIFFERENT PATTERNS, HAVEN'T WE?
......

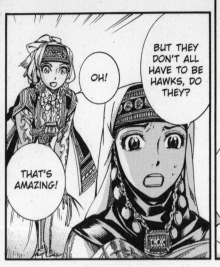

......
I LIKE DOING HAWKS.
BUT THEY DON'T ALL HAVE TO BE HAWKS, DO THEY?
OH!
THAT'S AMAZING!
AMIR!
EXCELLENT TIMING!
COULD YOU SHOW MY DAUGHTER YOUR EM-BROIDERY?
SEE, TILEKE?
JUST LOOK AT WHAT AMIR HAS!
BIRDS
DEER
RAMS
A HORSE-MAN

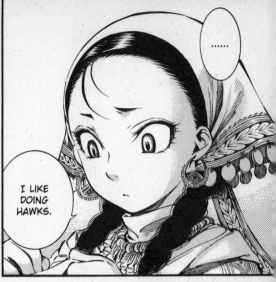

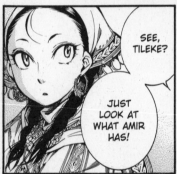

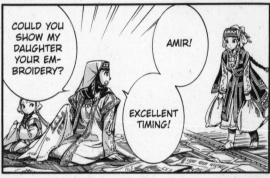

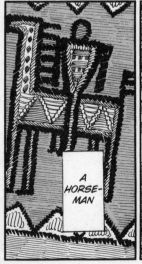

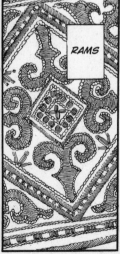

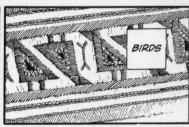

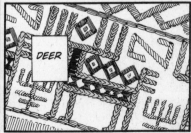

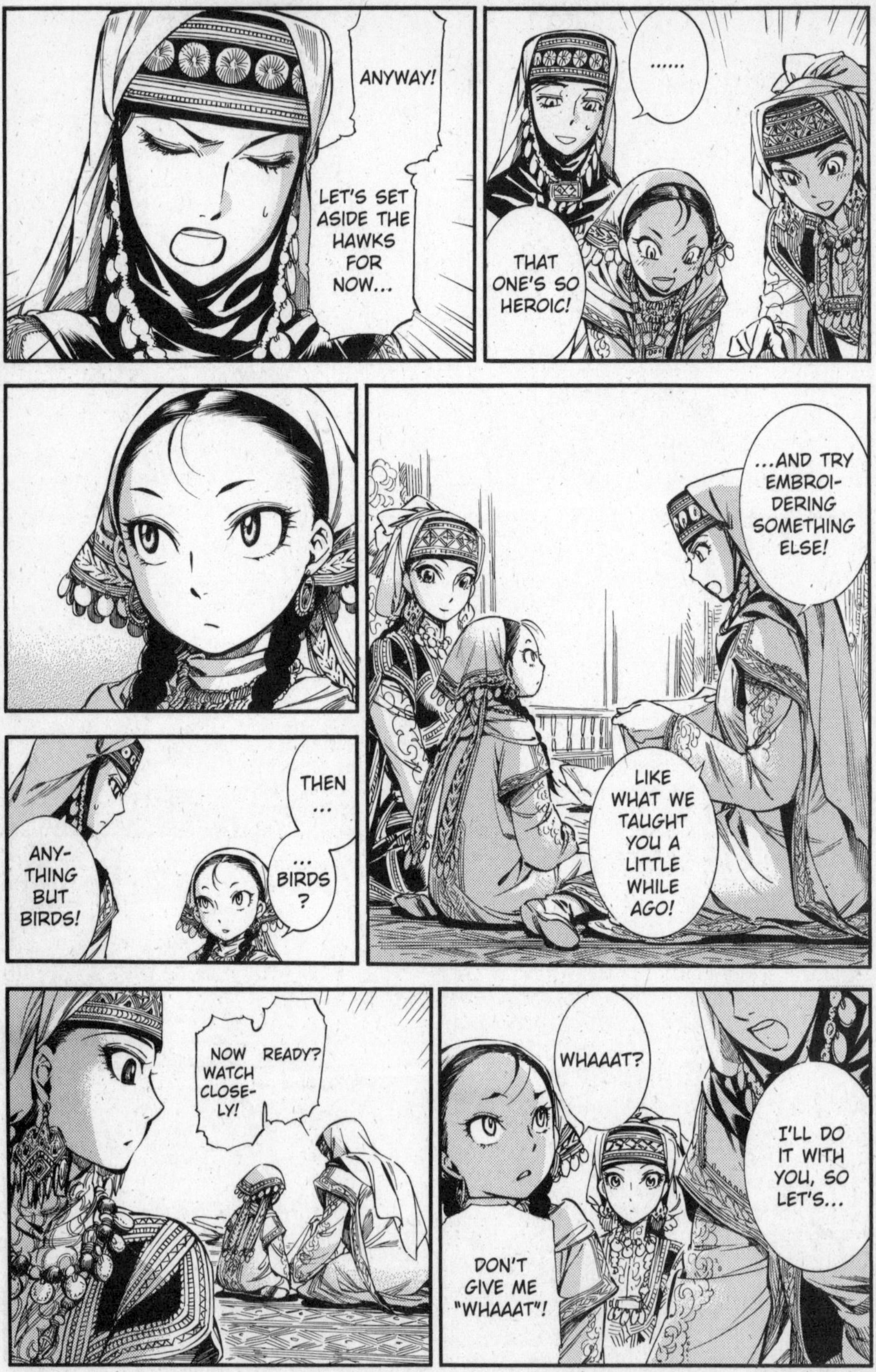
......
THAT ONE'S SO HEROIC!
ANYWAY!
LET'S SET ASIDE THE HAWKS FOR NOW...
...AND TRY EMBROIDERING SOMETHING ELSE!
LIKE WHAT WE TAUGHT YOU A LITTLE WHILE AGO!
THEN ...
... BIRDS ?
ANYTHING BUT BIRDS!
WHAAAT?
I'LL DO IT WITH YOU, SO LET'S...
DON'T GIVE ME "WHAAAT"!
READY?
NOW WATCH CLOSELY!

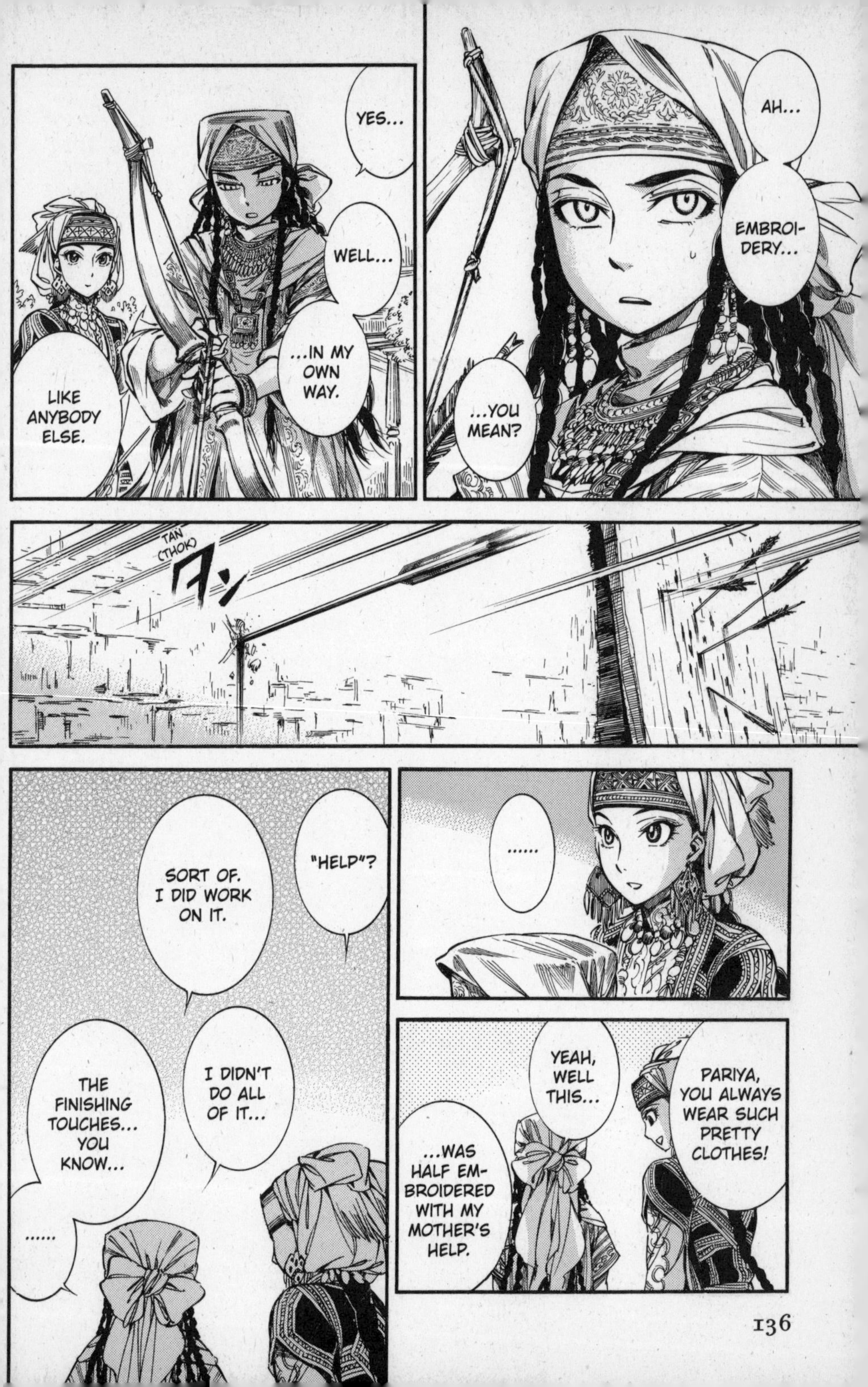
AH...
EMBROI-DERY...
...YOU MEAN?
YES...
WELL...
...IN MY OWN WAY.
LIKE ANYBODY ELSE.
TAN (THOK)
......
PARIYA, YOU ALWAYS WEAR SUCH PRETTY CLOTHES!
YEAH, WELL THIS...
...WAS HALF EMBROIDERED WITH MY MOTHER'S HELP.
"HELP"?
SORT OF. I DID WORK ON IT.
I DIDN'T DO ALL OF IT...
THE FINISHING TOUCHES... YOU KNOW...
......

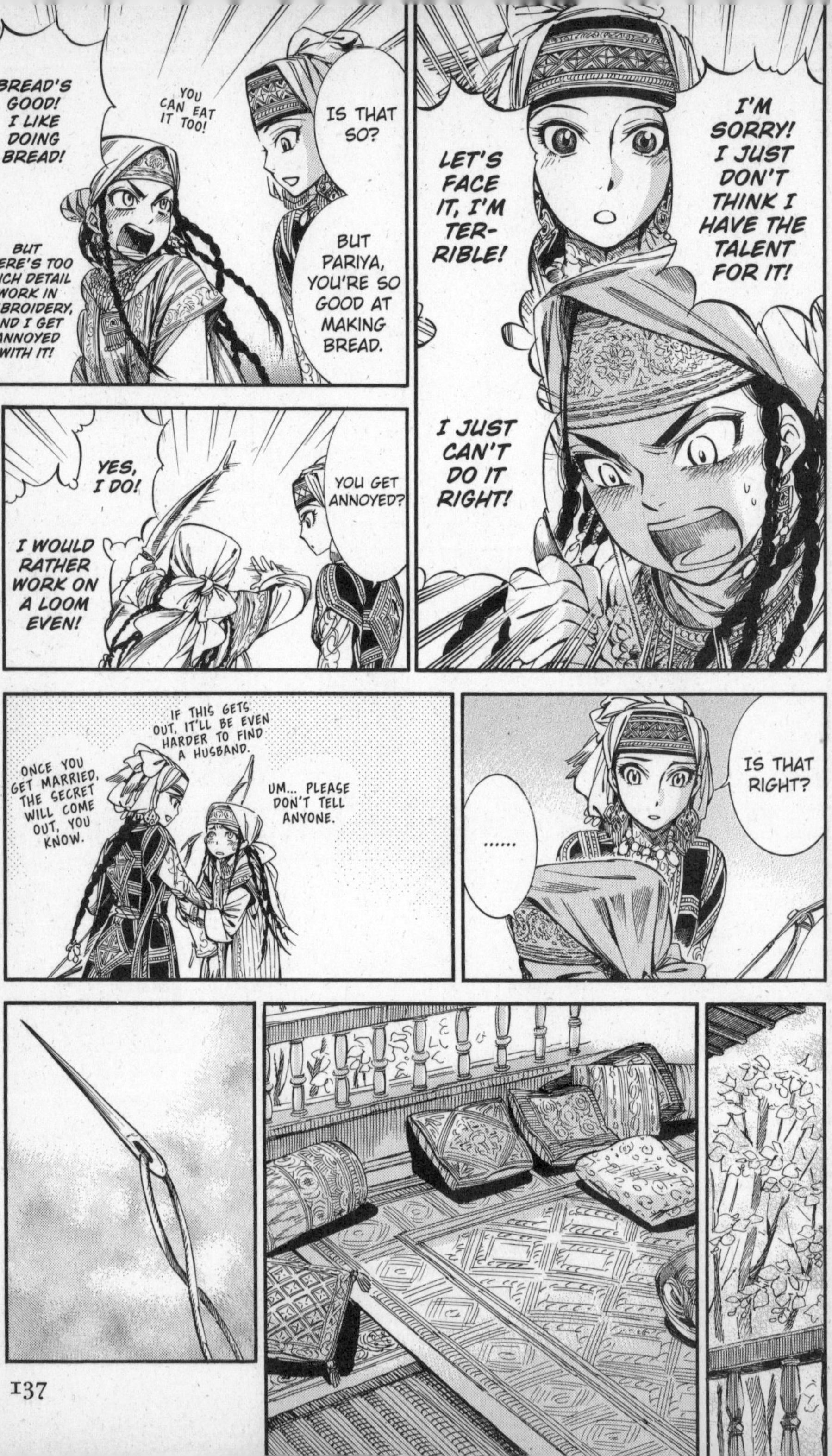
I'M SORRY! I JUST DON'T THINK I HAVE THE TALENT FOR IT!
LET'S FACE IT, I'M TERRIBLE!
I JUST CAN'T DO IT RIGHT!
IS THAT SO?
BUT PARIYA, YOU'RE SO GOOD AT MAKING BREAD.
BREAD'S GOOD! I LIKE DOING BREAD!
YOU CAN EAT IT TOO!
BUT THERE'S TOO MUCH DETAIL WORK IN EMBROIDERY, AND I GET ANNOYED WITH IT!
YOU GET ANNOYED?
YES, I DO!
I WOULD RATHER WORK ON A LOOM EVEN!
IS THAT RIGHT?
......
UM... PLEASE DON'T TELL ANYONE.
IF THIS GETS OUT, IT'LL BE EVEN HARDER TO FIND A HUSBAND.
ONCE YOU GET MARRIED, THE SECRET WILL COME OUT, YOU KNOW.

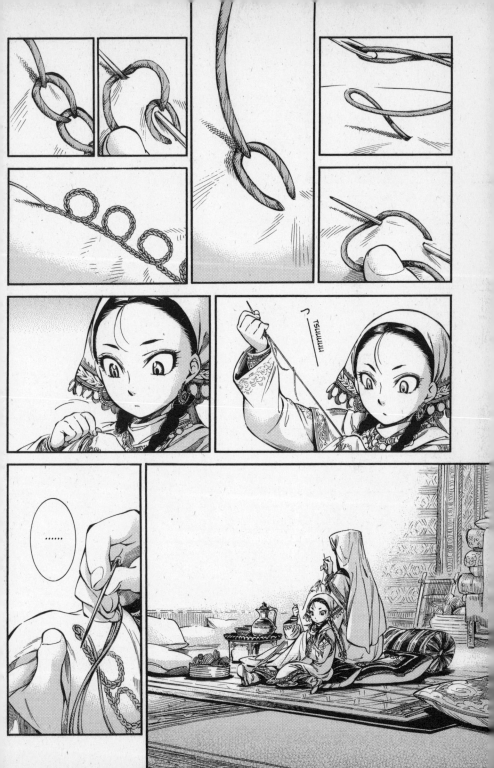

TSHHHH

……

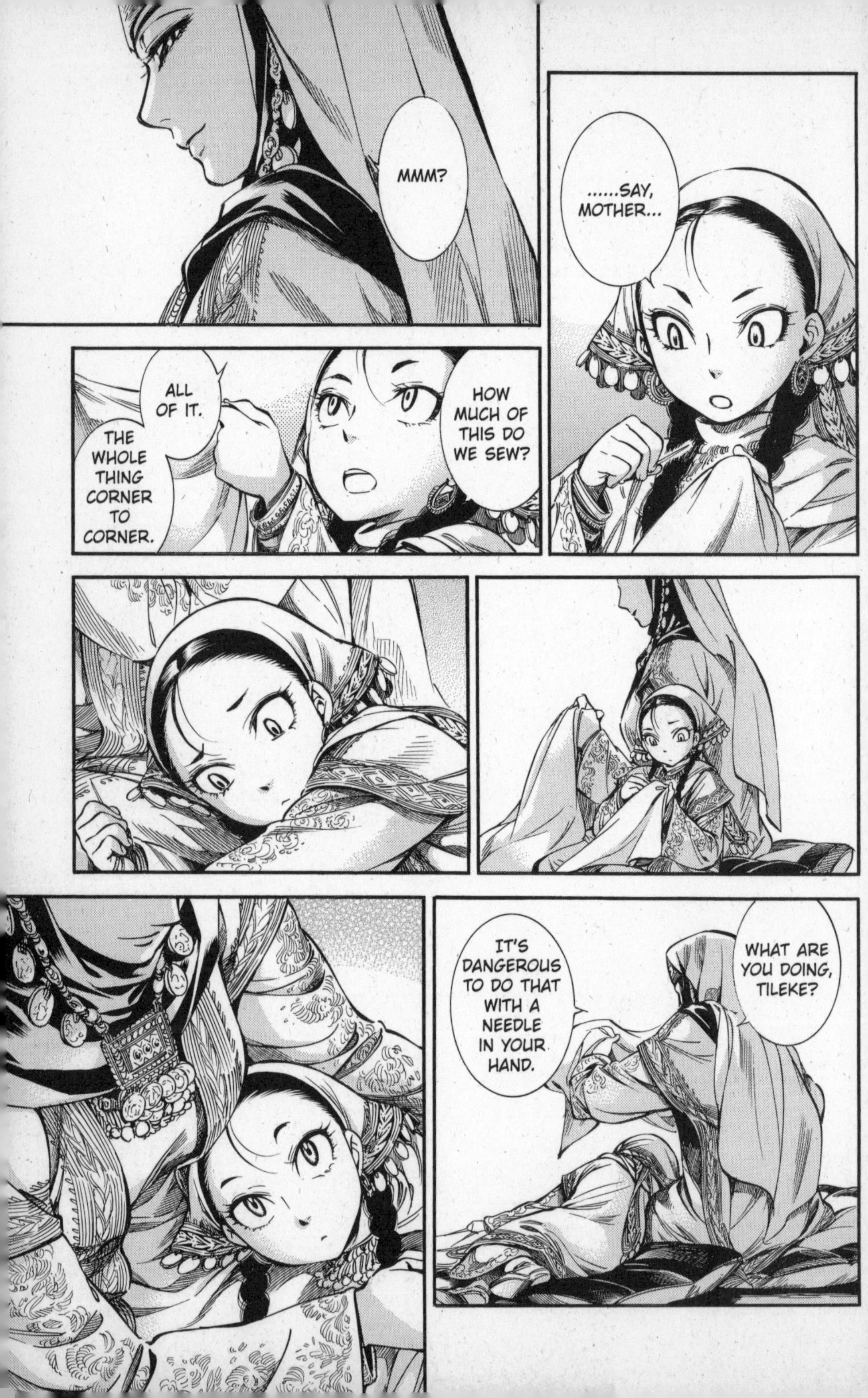
......SAY, MOTHER...
MMM?
HOW MUCH OF THIS DO WE SEW?
ALL OF IT.
THE WHOLE THING CORNER TO CORNER.
WHAT ARE YOU DOING, TILEKE?
IT'S DANGEROUS TO DO THAT WITH A NEEDLE IN YOUR HAND.

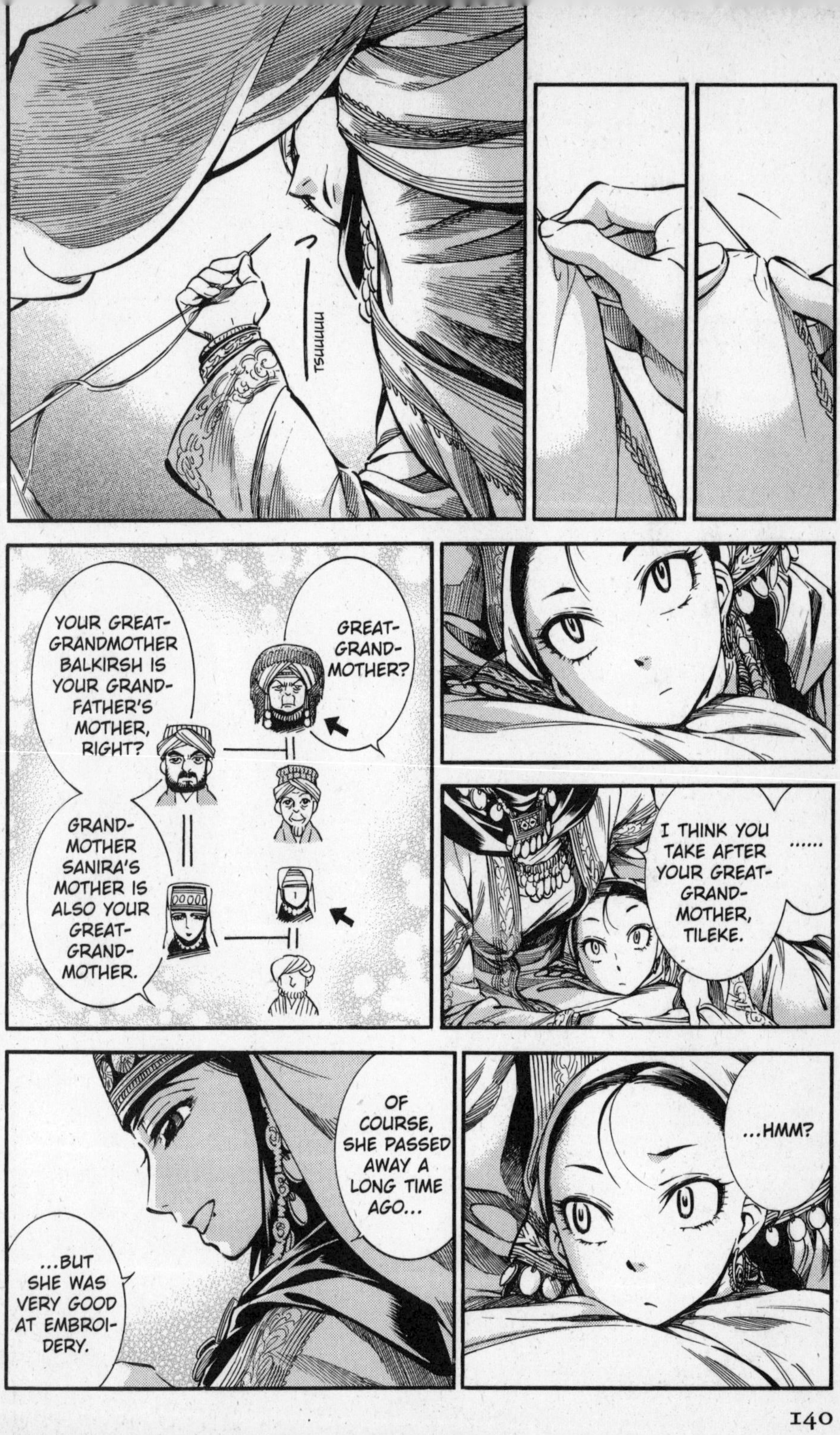
TSUUUUU
......
I THINK YOU TAKE AFTER YOUR GREAT-GRANDMOTHER, TILEKE.
GREAT-GRANDMOTHER?
YOUR GREAT-GRANDMOTHER BALKIRSH IS YOUR GRANDFATHER'S MOTHER, RIGHT?
GRANDMOTHER SANIRA'S MOTHER IS ALSO YOUR GREAT-GRANDMOTHER.
...HMM?
OF COURSE, SHE PASSED AWAY A LONG TIME AGO...
...BUT SHE WAS VERY GOOD AT EMBROIDERY.

REALLY!?

I HEAR SHE WAS ESPECIALLY GOOD AT ANIMALS.

THEY SAY HER BIRDS FLEW RIGHT OFF THE CLOTH.

SHE WAS JUST THAT GOOD.

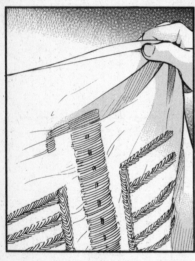

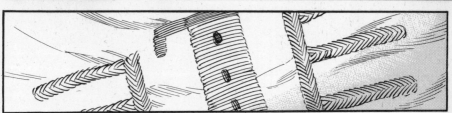

NOW SIT UP STRAIGHT.

AND DO YOUR SEWING.

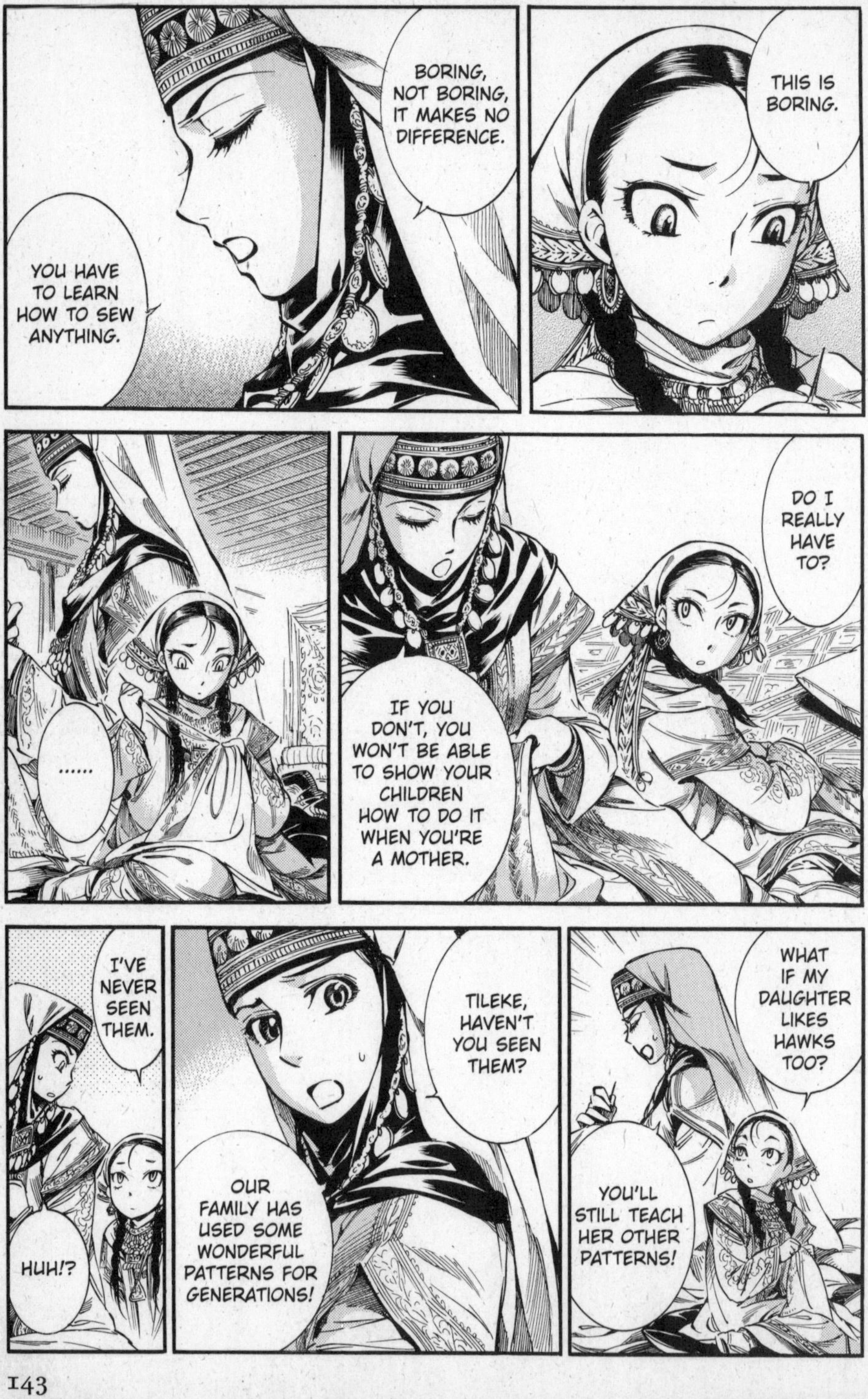
THIS IS BORING.
BORING, NOT BORING, IT MAKES NO DIFFERENCE.
YOU HAVE TO LEARN HOW TO SEW ANYTHING.
DO I REALLY HAVE TO?
IF YOU DON'T, YOU WON'T BE ABLE TO SHOW YOUR CHILDREN HOW TO DO IT WHEN YOU'RE A MOTHER.
......
WHAT IF MY DAUGHTER LIKES HAWKS TOO?
YOU'LL STILL TEACH HER OTHER PATTERNS!
TILEKE, HAVEN'T YOU SEEN THEM?
OUR FAMILY HAS USED SOME WONDERFUL PATTERNS FOR GENERATIONS!
I'VE NEVER SEEN THEM.
HUH!?

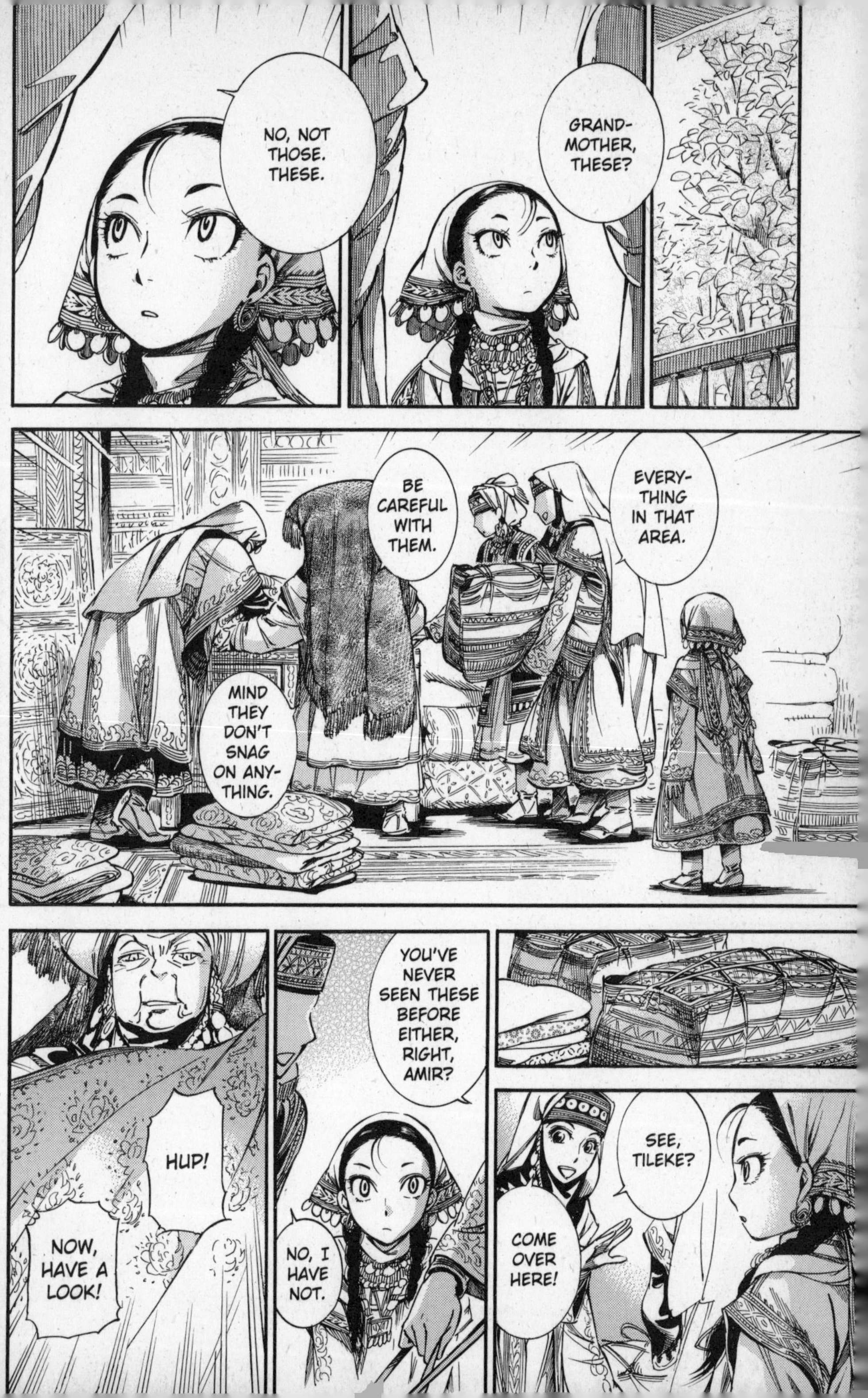
GRAND-MOTHER, THESE?
NO, NOT THOSE. THESE.
EVERY-THING IN THAT AREA.
BE CAREFUL WITH THEM.
MIND THEY DON'T SNAG ON ANY-THING.
SEE, TILEKE?
COME OVER HERE!
YOU'VE NEVER SEEN THESE BEFORE EITHER, RIGHT, AMIR?
NO, I HAVE NOT.
HUP!
NOW, HAVE A LOOK!

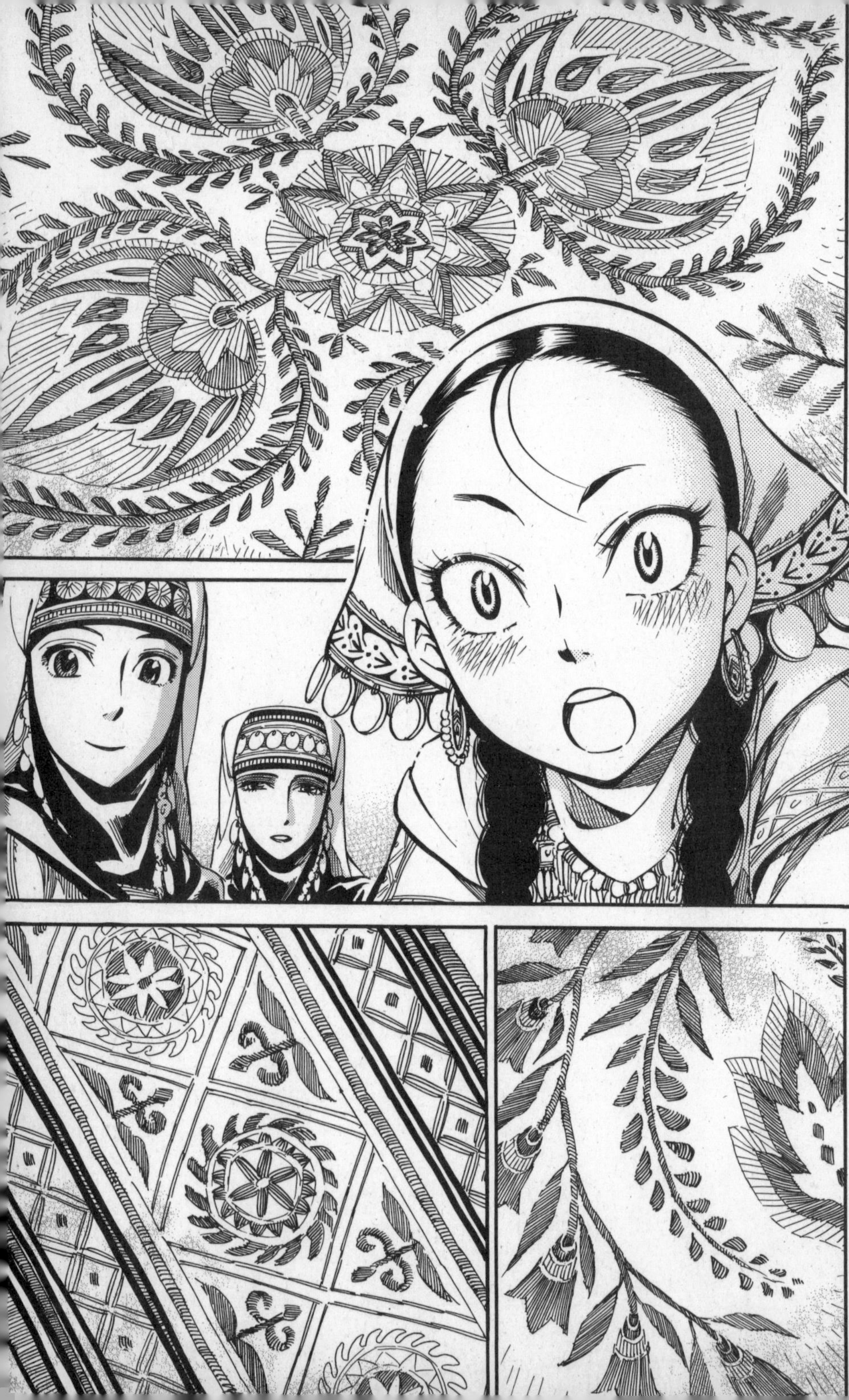

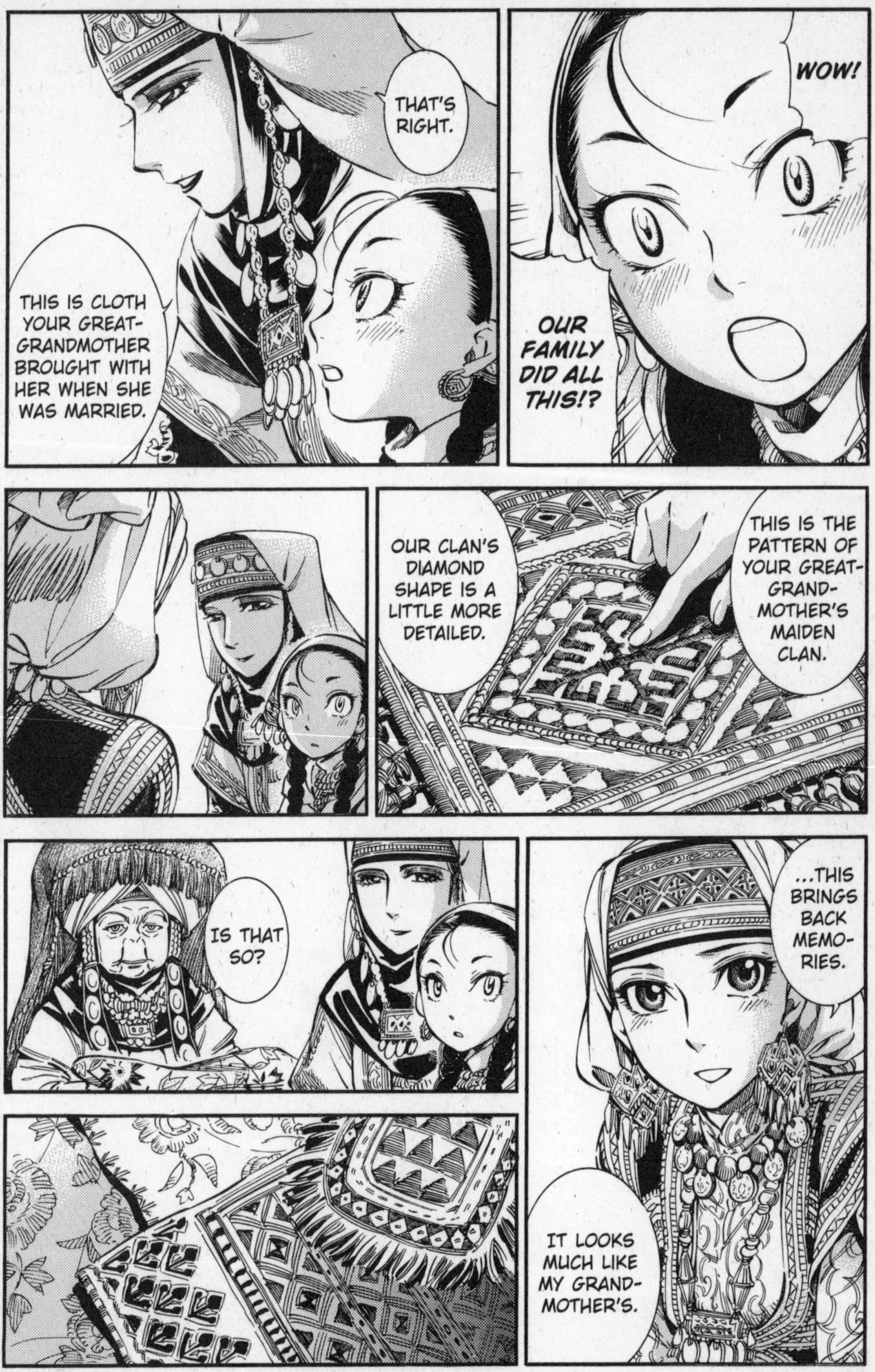
WOW!
OUR FAMILY DID ALL THIS!?
THAT'S RIGHT.
THIS IS CLOTH YOUR GREAT-GRANDMOTHER BROUGHT WITH HER WHEN SHE WAS MARRIED.
THIS IS THE PATTERN OF YOUR GREAT-GRAND-MOTHER'S MAIDEN CLAN.
OUR CLAN'S DIAMOND SHAPE IS A LITTLE MORE DETAILED.
...THIS BRINGS BACK MEMO-RIES.
IT LOOKS MUCH LIKE MY GRAND-MOTHER'S.
IS THAT SO?

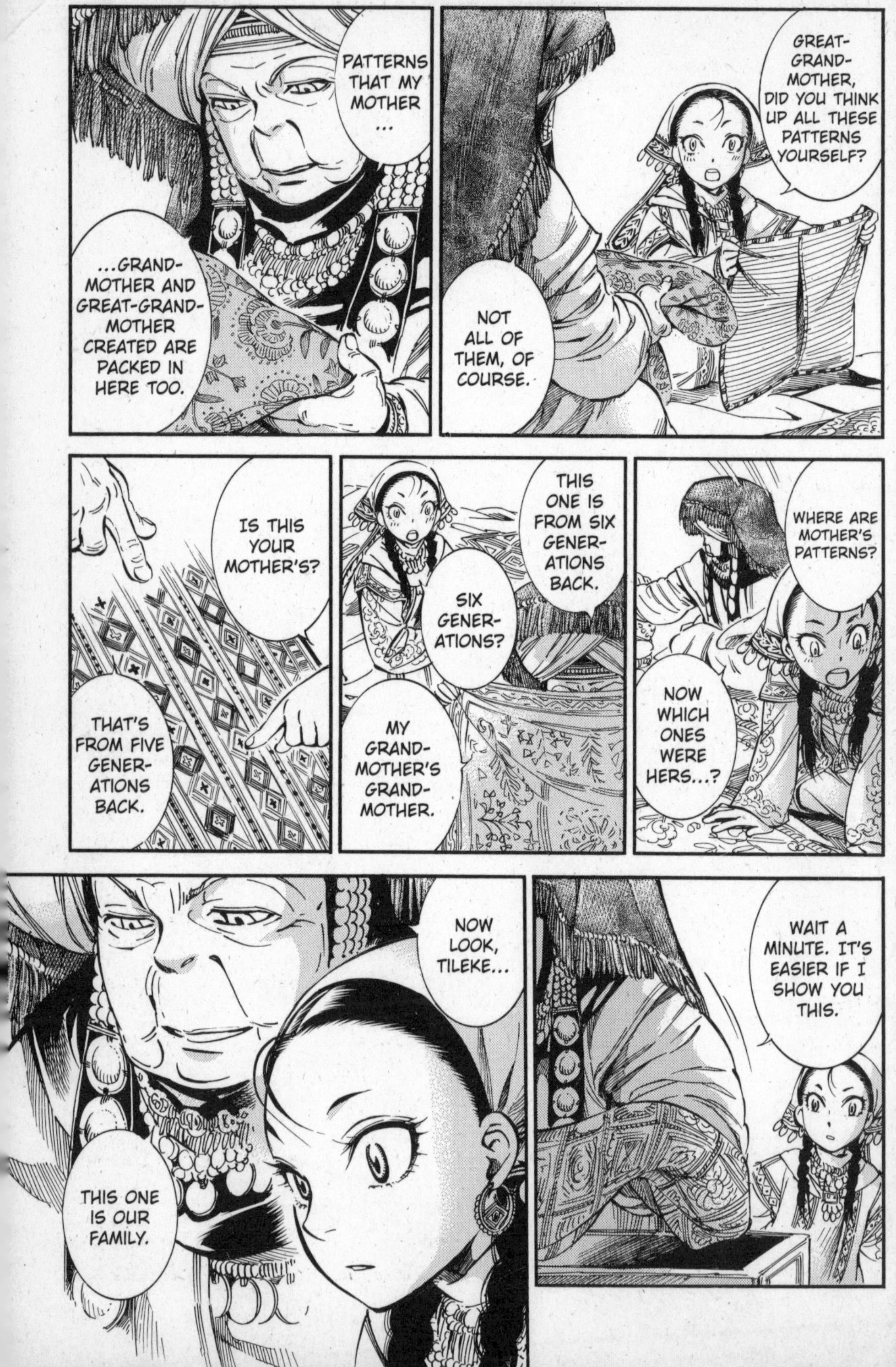
GREAT-GRANDMOTHER, DID YOU THINK UP ALL THESE PATTERNS YOURSELF?
NOT ALL OF THEM, OF COURSE.
PATTERNS THAT MY MOTHER ...
...GRANDMOTHER AND GREAT-GRANDMOTHER CREATED ARE PACKED IN HERE TOO.
WHERE ARE MOTHER'S PATTERNS?
NOW WHICH ONES WERE HERS...?
THIS ONE IS FROM SIX GENERATIONS BACK.
SIX GENERATIONS?
MY GRANDMOTHER'S GRANDMOTHER.
IS THIS YOUR MOTHER'S?
THAT'S FROM FIVE GENERATIONS BACK.
WAIT A MINUTE. IT'S EASIER IF I SHOW YOU THIS.
NOW LOOK, TILEKE...
THIS ONE IS OUR FAMILY.

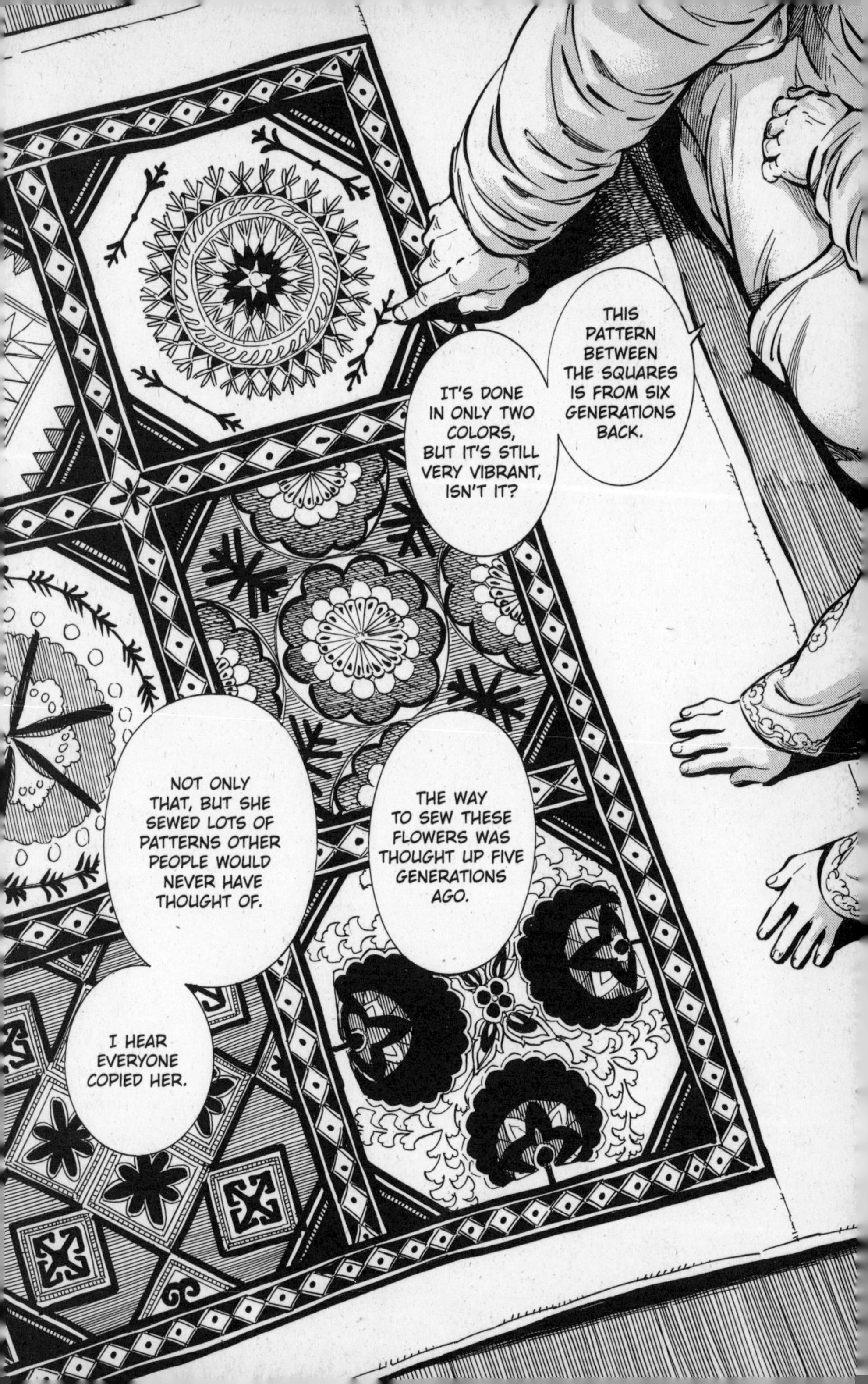
THIS PATTERN BETWEEN THE SQUARES IS FROM SIX GENERATIONS BACK.
IT'S DONE IN ONLY TWO COLORS, BUT IT'S STILL VERY VIBRANT, ISN'T IT?
THE WAY TO SEW THESE FLOWERS WAS THOUGHT UP FIVE GENERATIONS AGO.
NOT ONLY THAT, BUT SHE SEWED LOTS OF PATTERNS OTHER PEOPLE WOULD NEVER HAVE THOUGHT OF.
I HEAR EVERYONE COPIED HER.

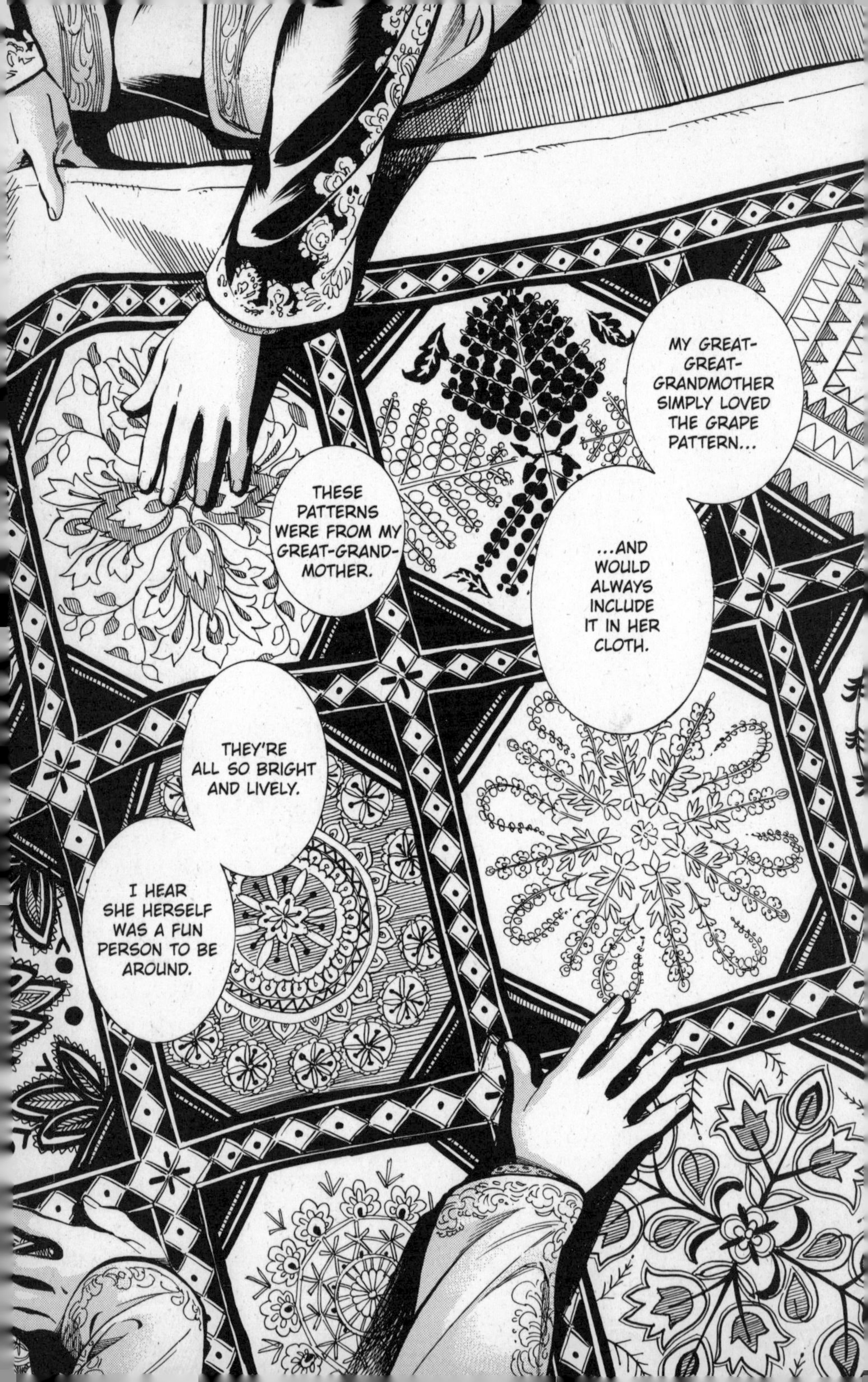
MY GREAT-GREAT-GRANDMOTHER SIMPLY LOVED THE GRAPE PATTERN...
THESE PATTERNS WERE FROM MY GREAT-GRAND-MOTHER.
...AND WOULD ALWAYS INCLUDE IT IN HER CLOTH.
THEY'RE ALL SO BRIGHT AND LIVELY.
I HEAR SHE HERSELF WAS A FUN PERSON TO BE AROUND.

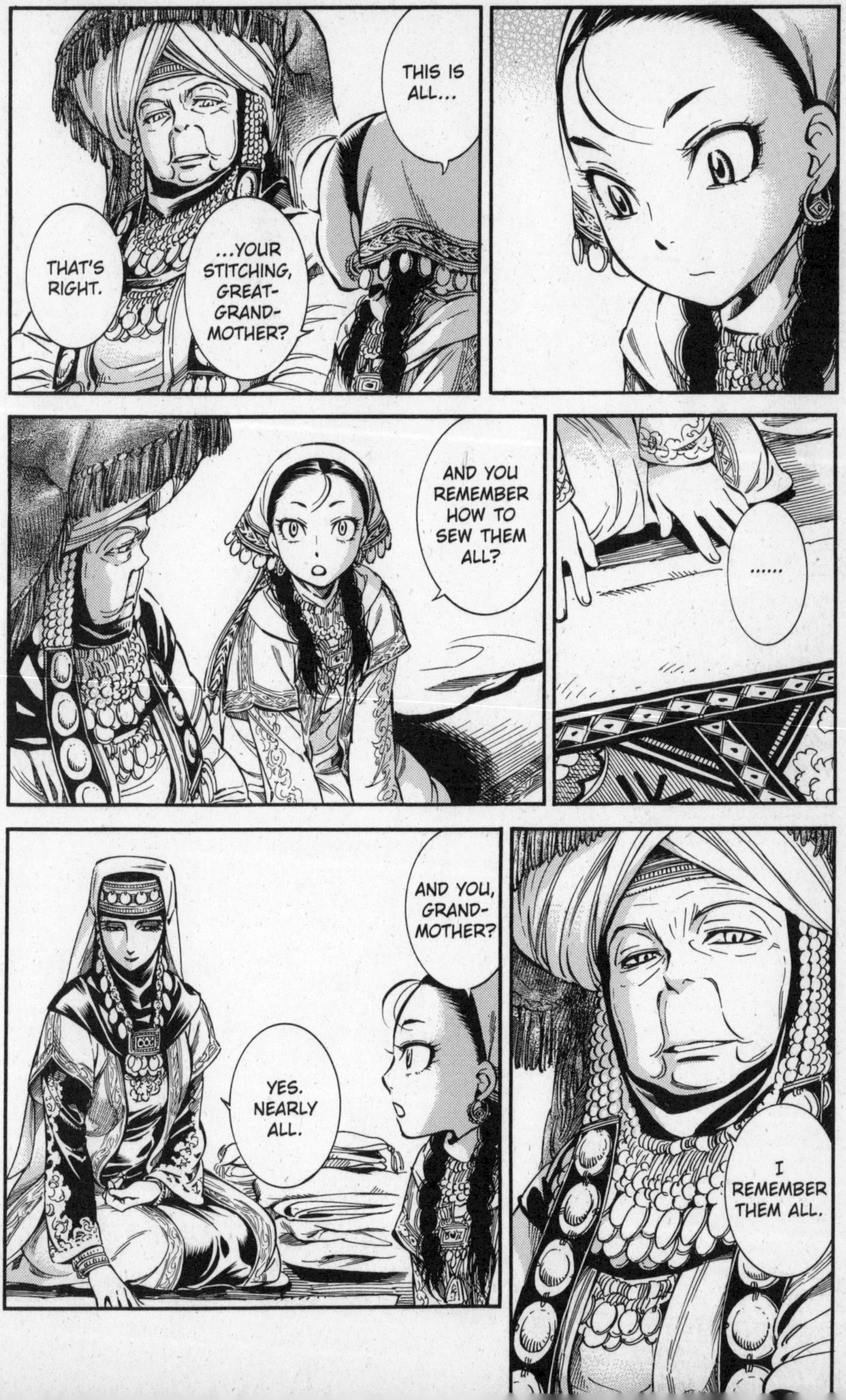
THIS IS ALL...
...YOUR STITCHING, GREAT-GRANDMOTHER?
THAT'S RIGHT.
......
AND YOU REMEMBER HOW TO SEW THEM ALL?
I REMEMBER THEM ALL.
AND YOU, GRANDMOTHER?
YES. NEARLY ALL.

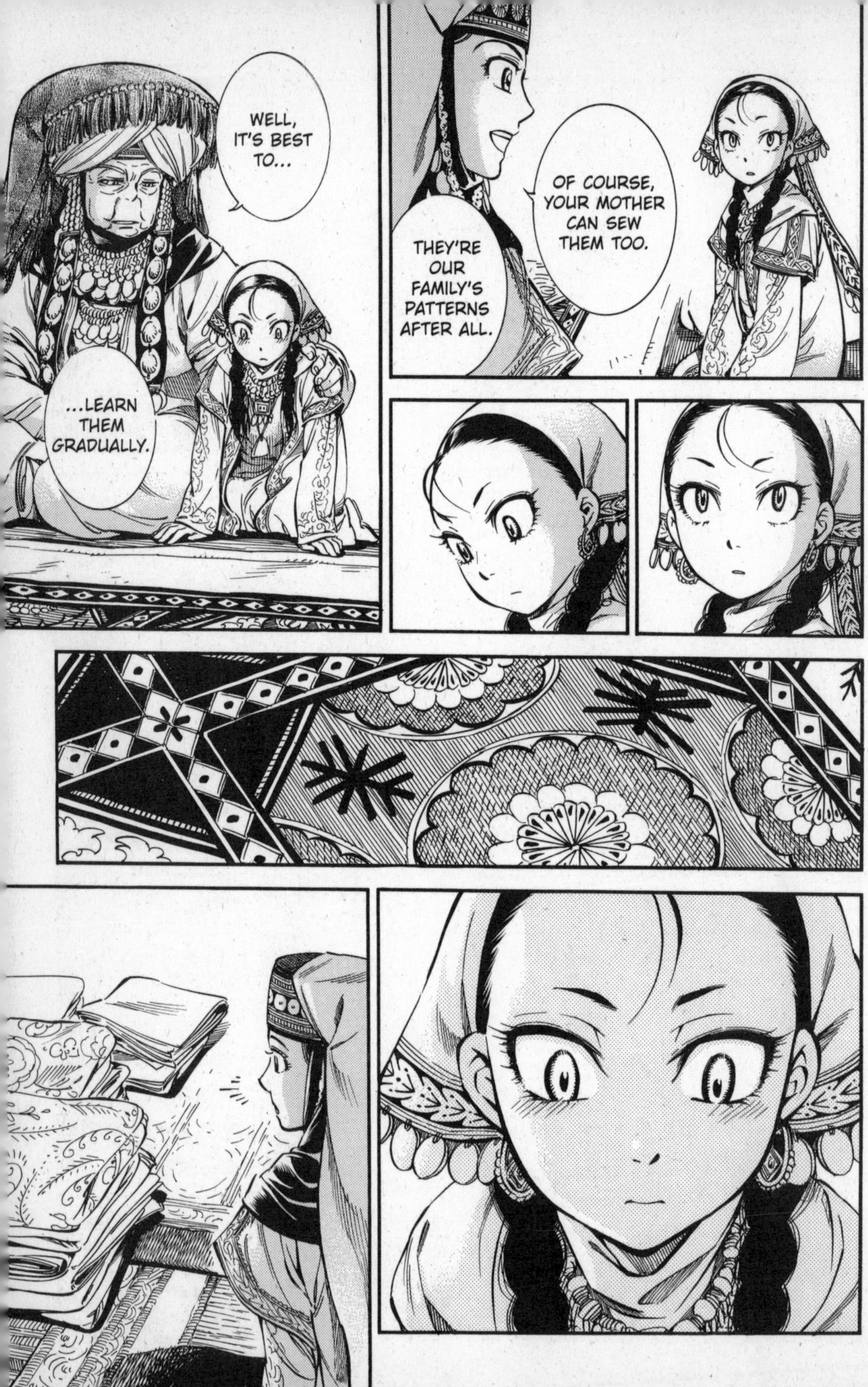
OF COURSE, YOUR MOTHER CAN SEW THEM TOO.
THEY'RE OUR FAMILY'S PATTERNS AFTER ALL.
WELL, IT'S BEST TO...
...LEARN THEM GRADUALLY.

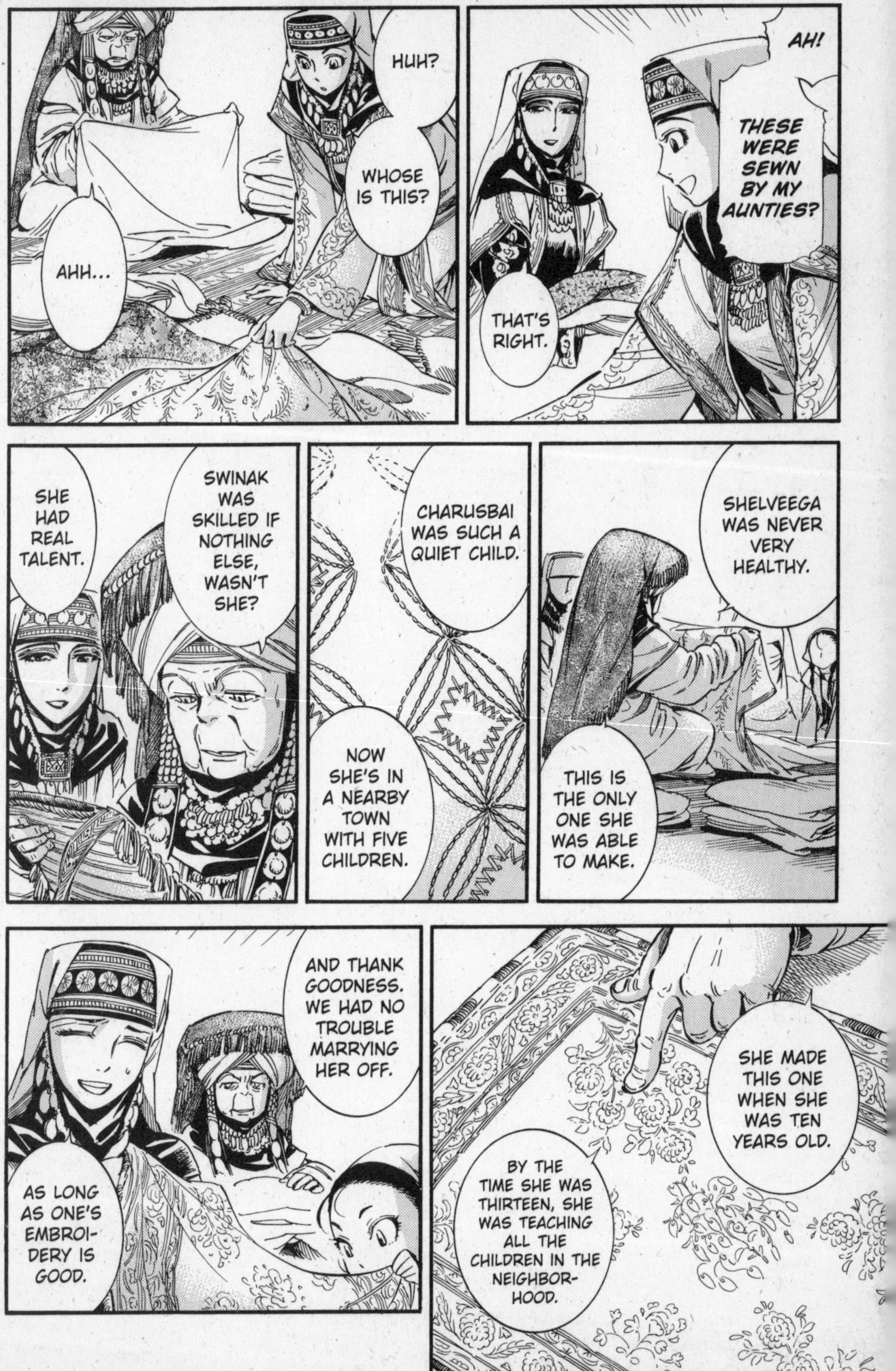
AH!
THESE WERE SEWN BY MY AUNTIES?
THAT'S RIGHT.
HUH?
WHOSE IS THIS?
AHH...
SHELVEEGA WAS NEVER VERY HEALTHY.
THIS IS THE ONLY ONE SHE WAS ABLE TO MAKE.
CHARUSBAI WAS SUCH A QUIET CHILD.
NOW SHE'S IN A NEARBY TOWN WITH FIVE CHILDREN.
SWINAK WAS SKILLED IF NOTHING ELSE, WASN'T SHE?
SHE HAD REAL TALENT.
SHE MADE THIS ONE WHEN SHE WAS TEN YEARS OLD.
BY THE TIME SHE WAS THIRTEEN, SHE WAS TEACHING ALL THE CHILDREN IN THE NEIGHBOR-HOOD.
AND THANK GOODNESS. WE HAD NO TROUBLE MARRYING HER OFF.
AS LONG AS ONE'S EMBROIDERY IS GOOD.

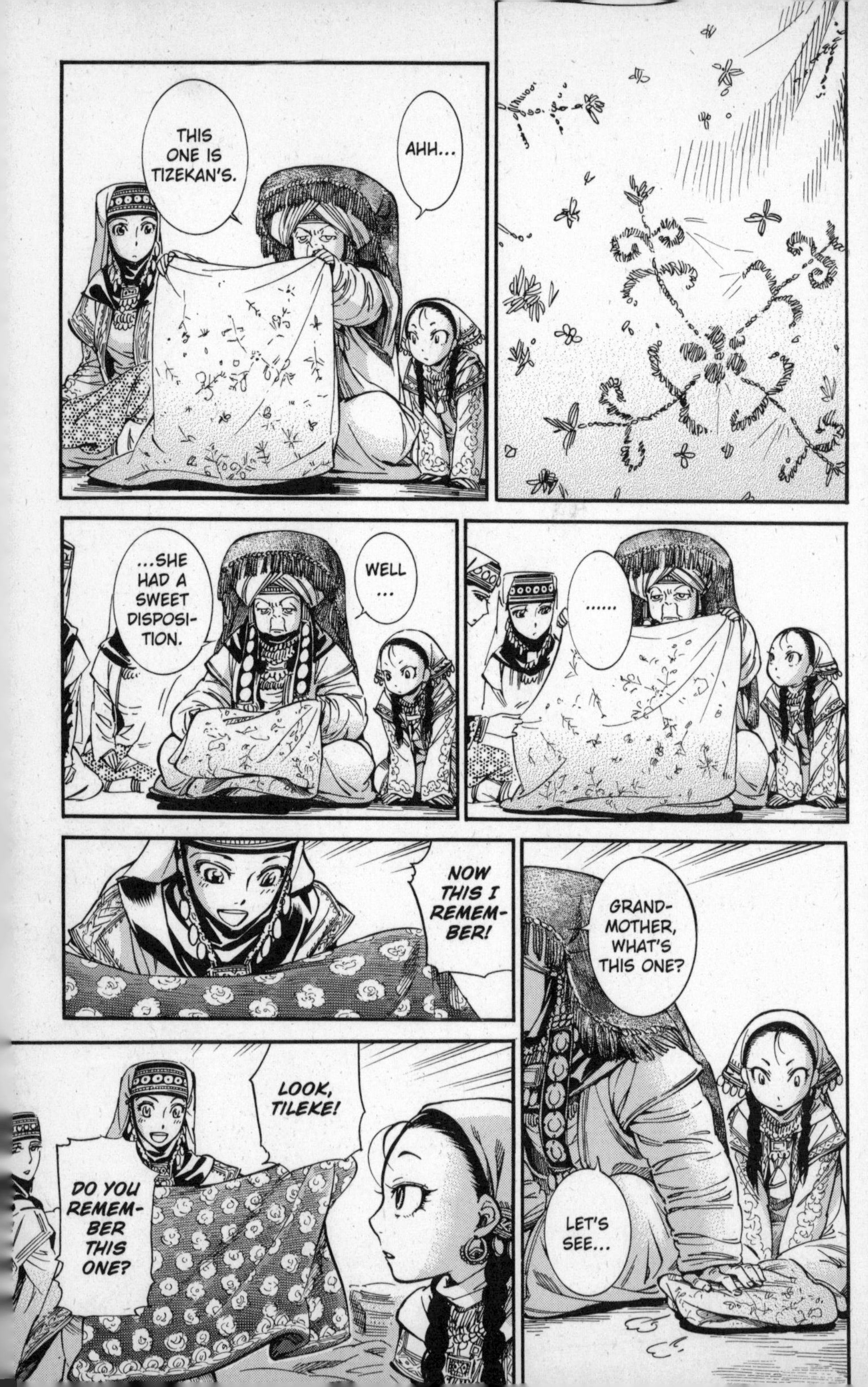
THIS ONE IS TIZEKAN'S.
AHH...
......
WELL ...
...SHE HAD A SWEET DISPOSITION.
GRANDMOTHER, WHAT'S THIS ONE?
LET'S SEE...
NOW THIS I REMEMBER!
LOOK, TILEKE!
DO YOU REMEMBER THIS ONE?

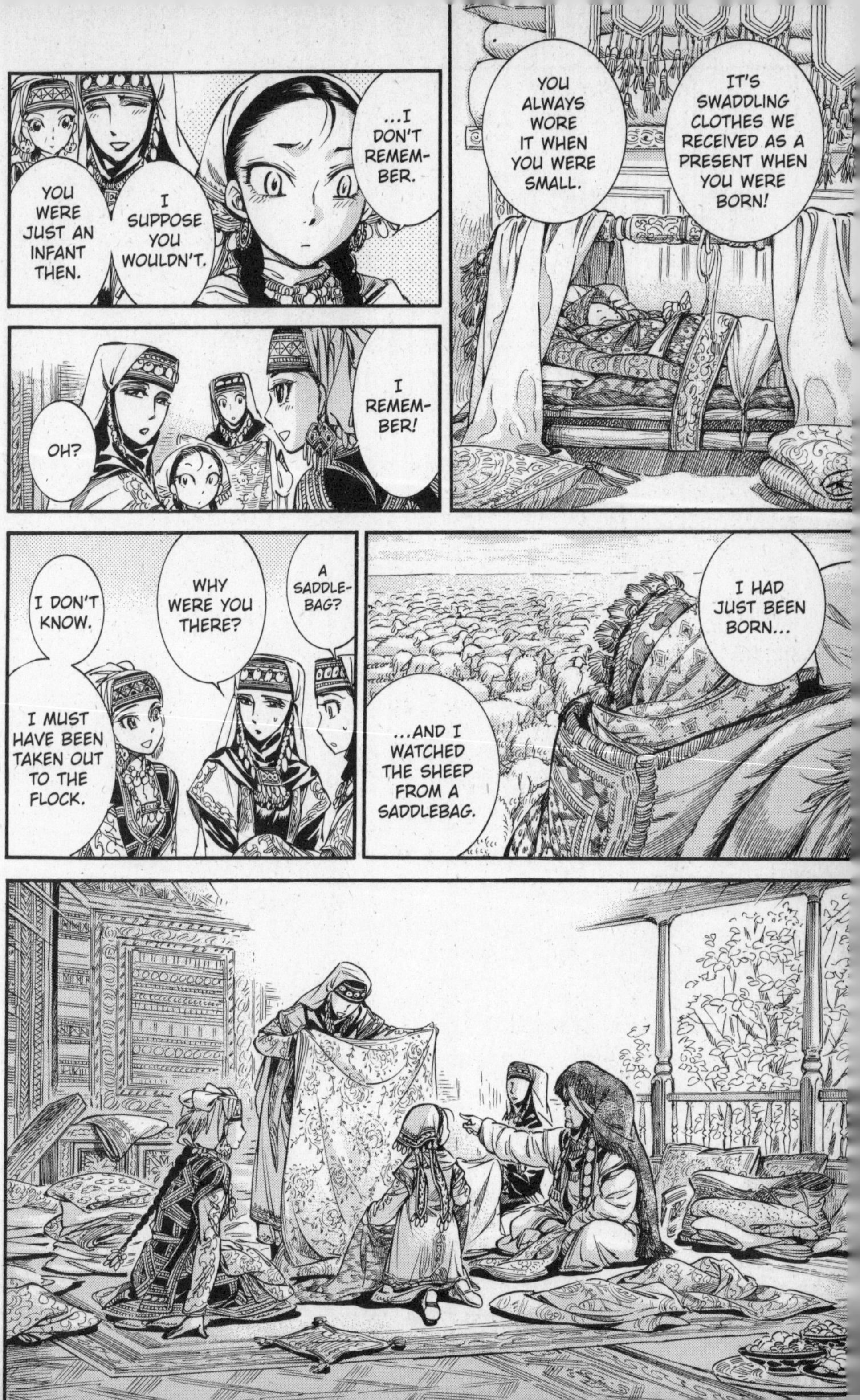
IT'S SWADDLING CLOTHES WE RECEIVED AS A PRESENT WHEN YOU WERE BORN!
YOU ALWAYS WORE IT WHEN YOU WERE SMALL.
...I DON'T REMEMBER.
I SUPPOSE YOU WOULDN'T.
YOU WERE JUST AN INFANT THEN.
I REMEMBER!
OH?
I HAD JUST BEEN BORN...
...AND I WATCHED THE SHEEP FROM A SADDLEBAG.
A SADDLEBAG?
WHY WERE YOU THERE?
I DON'T KNOW.
I MUST HAVE BEEN TAKEN OUT TO THE FLOCK.

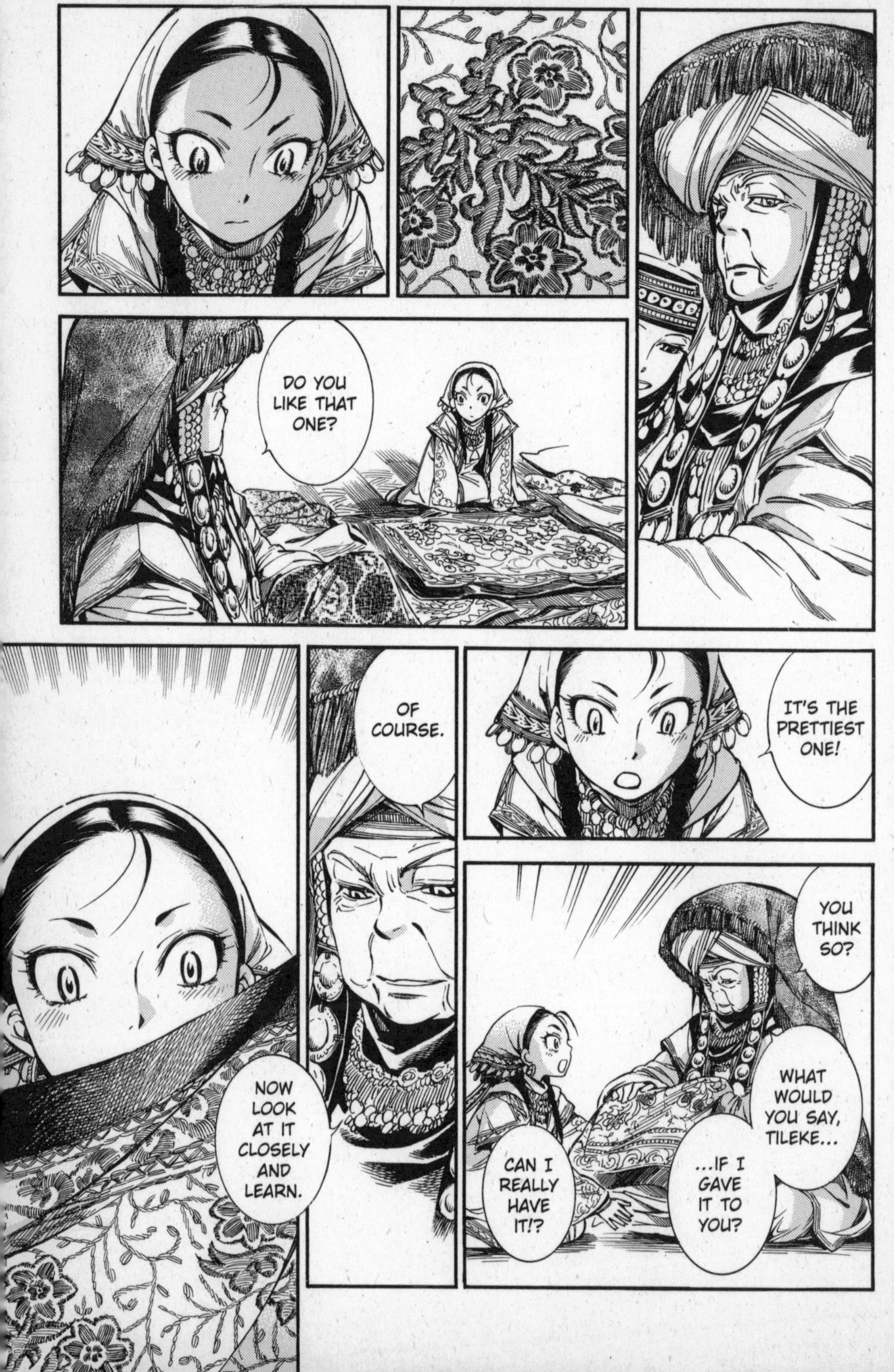
DO YOU LIKE THAT ONE?
IT'S THE PRETTIEST ONE!
YOU THINK SO?
WHAT WOULD YOU SAY, TILEKE...
...IF I GAVE IT TO YOU?
CAN I REALLY HAVE IT!?
OF COURSE.
NOW LOOK AT IT CLOSELY AND LEARN.

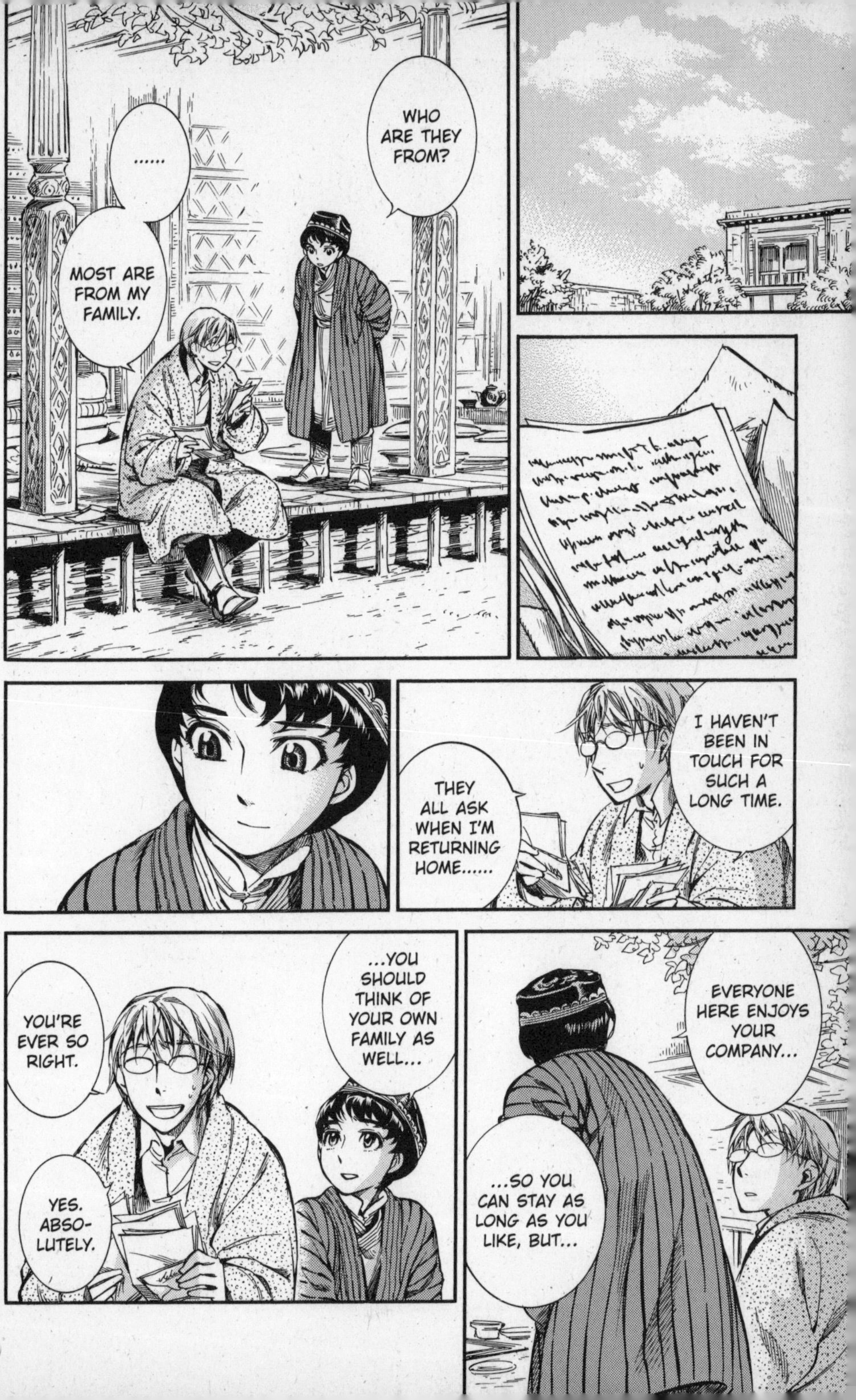
WHO ARE THEY FROM?
......
MOST ARE FROM MY FAMILY.
I HAVEN'T BEEN IN TOUCH FOR SUCH A LONG TIME.
THEY ALL ASK WHEN I'M RETURNING HOME......
EVERYONE HERE ENJOYS YOUR COMPANY...
...SO YOU CAN STAY AS LONG AS YOU LIKE, BUT...
...YOU SHOULD THINK OF YOUR OWN FAMILY AS WELL...
YOU'RE EVER SO RIGHT.
YES. ABSO-LUTELY.

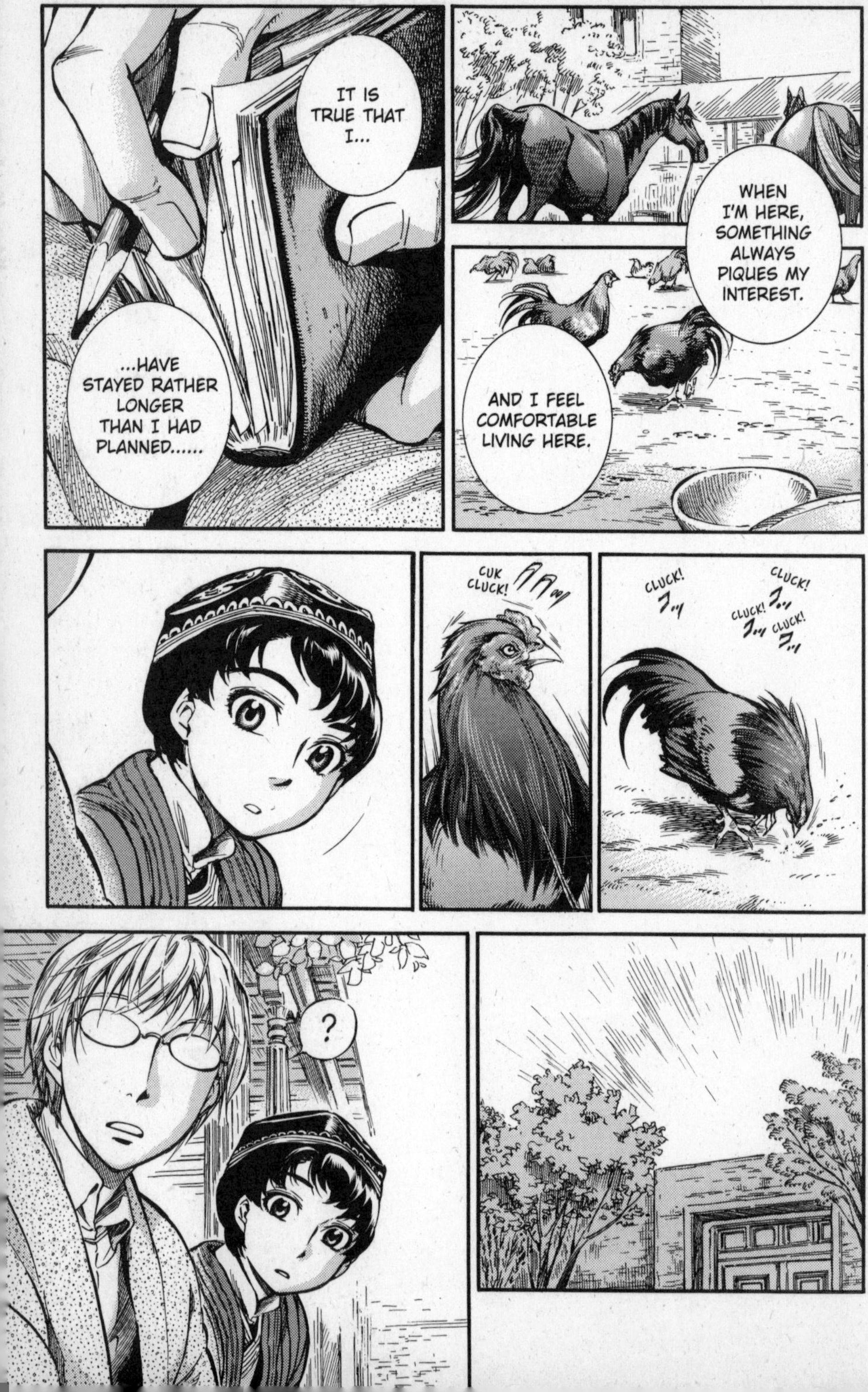
WHEN I'M HERE, SOMETHING ALWAYS PIQUES MY INTEREST.
AND I FEEL COMFORTABLE LIVING HERE.
IT IS TRUE THAT I...
...HAVE STAYED RATHER LONGER THAN I HAD PLANNED......
CLUCK!
CLUCK!
CLUCK!
CLUCK!
CUK CLUCK!
?

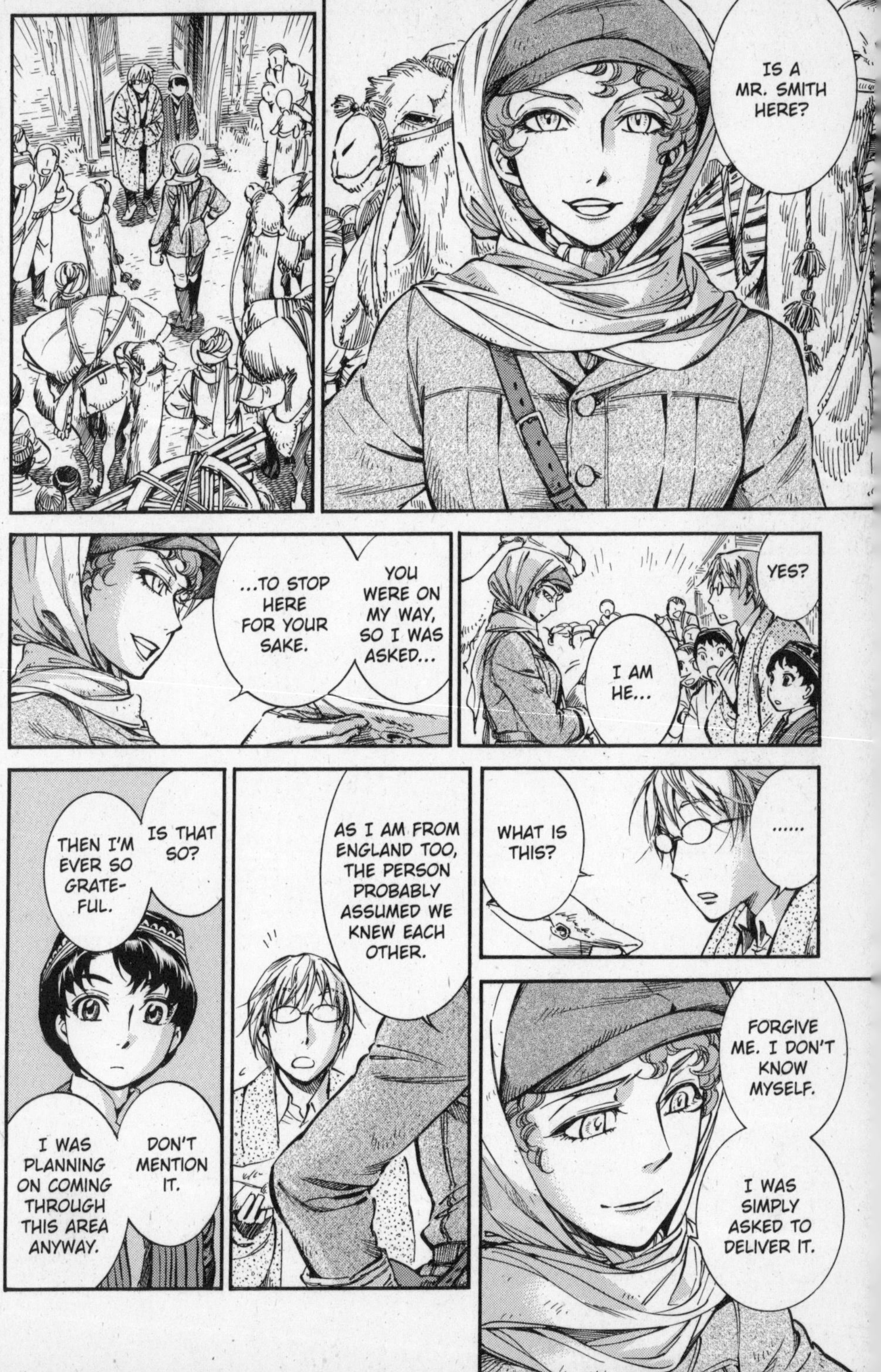
IS A MR. SMITH HERE?
YES?
I AM HE...
YOU WERE ON MY WAY, SO I WAS ASKED...
...TO STOP HERE FOR YOUR SAKE.
......
WHAT IS THIS?
FORGIVE ME. I DON'T KNOW MYSELF.
I WAS SIMPLY ASKED TO DELIVER IT.
AS I AM FROM ENGLAND TOO, THE PERSON PROBABLY ASSUMED WE KNEW EACH OTHER.
IS THAT SO?
THEN I'M EVER SO GRATEFUL.
DON'T MENTION IT.
I WAS PLANNING ON COMING THROUGH THIS AREA ANYWAY.

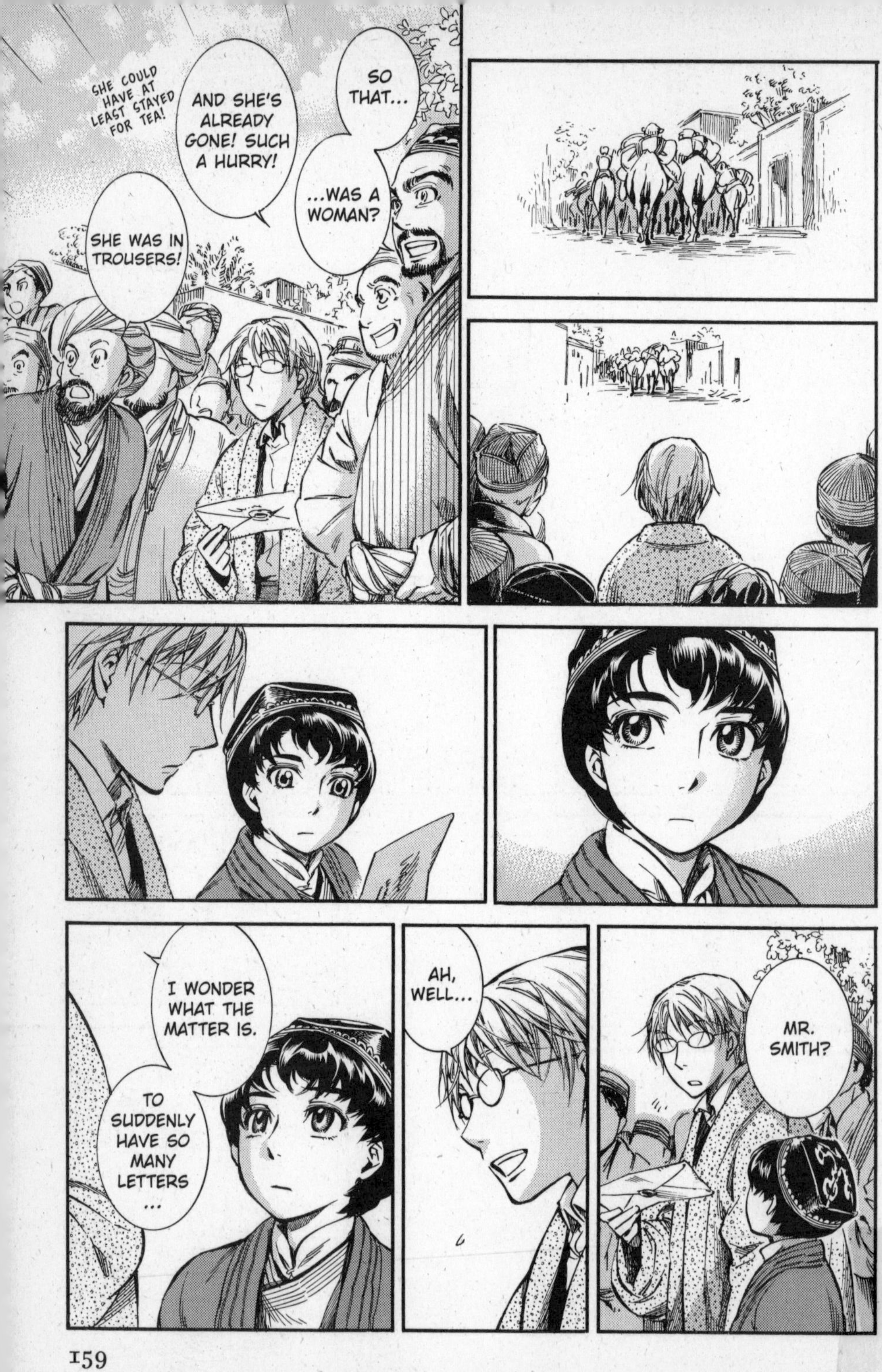

SO THAT...
...WAS A WOMAN?
AND SHE'S ALREADY GONE! SUCH A HURRY!
SHE COULD HAVE AT LEAST STAYED FOR TEA!
SHE WAS IN TROUSERS!
MR. SMITH?
AH, WELL...
I WONDER WHAT THE MATTER IS.
TO SUDDENLY HAVE SO MANY LETTERS ...

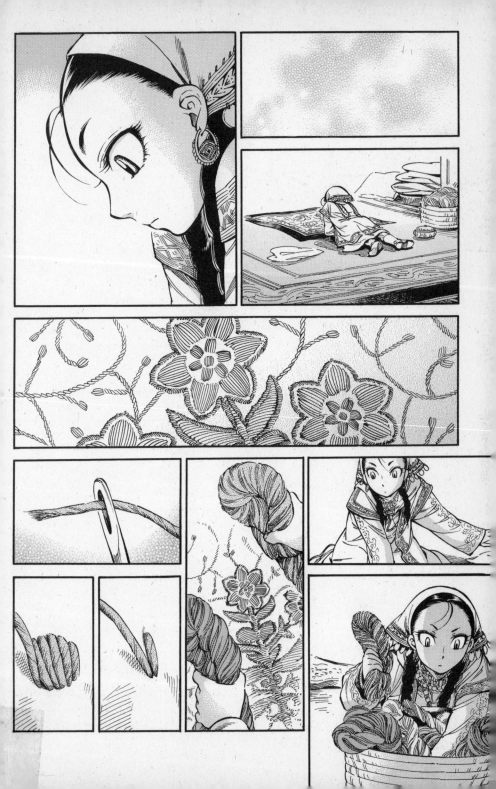

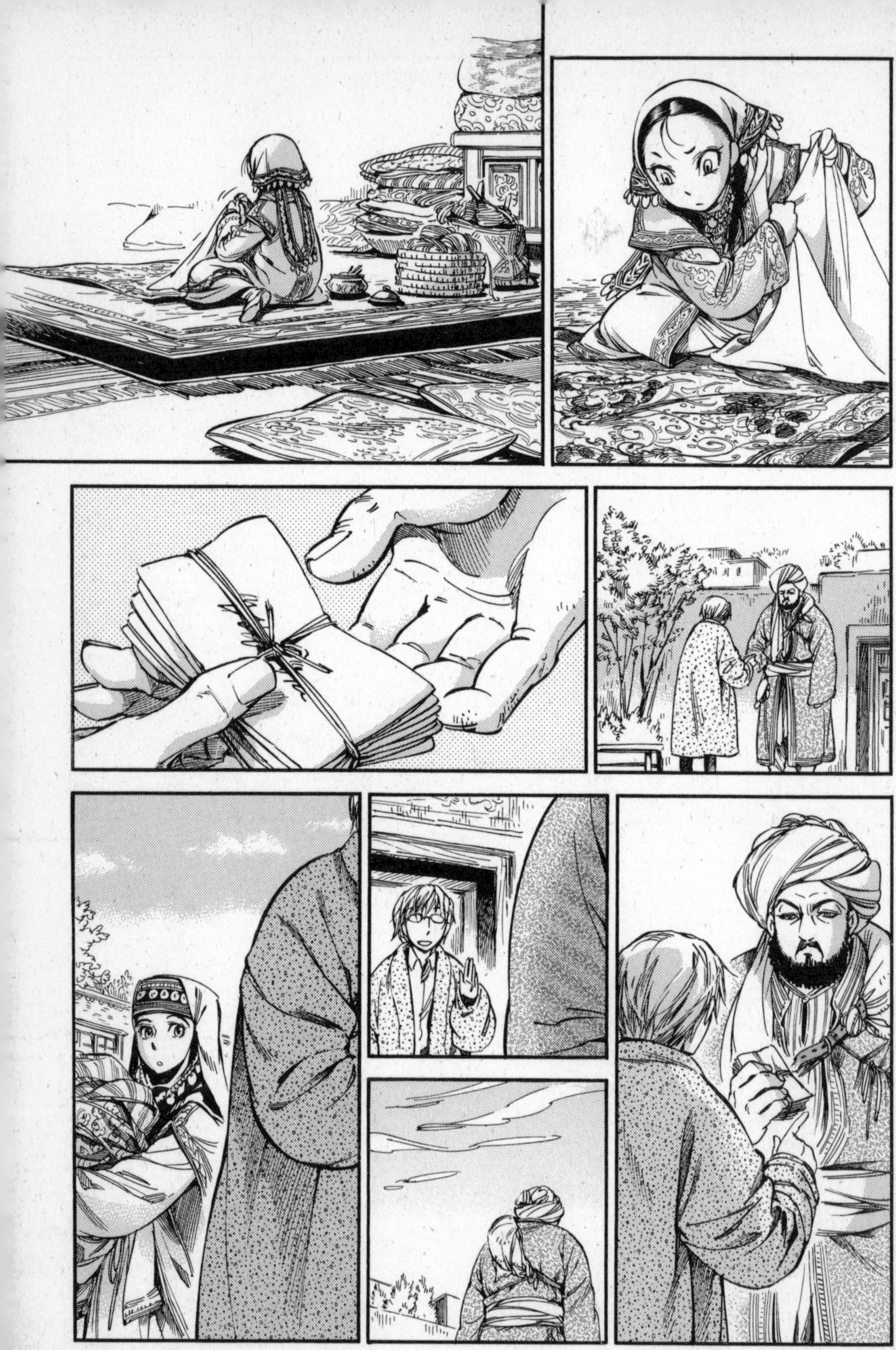

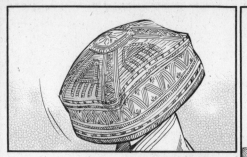

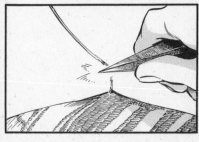

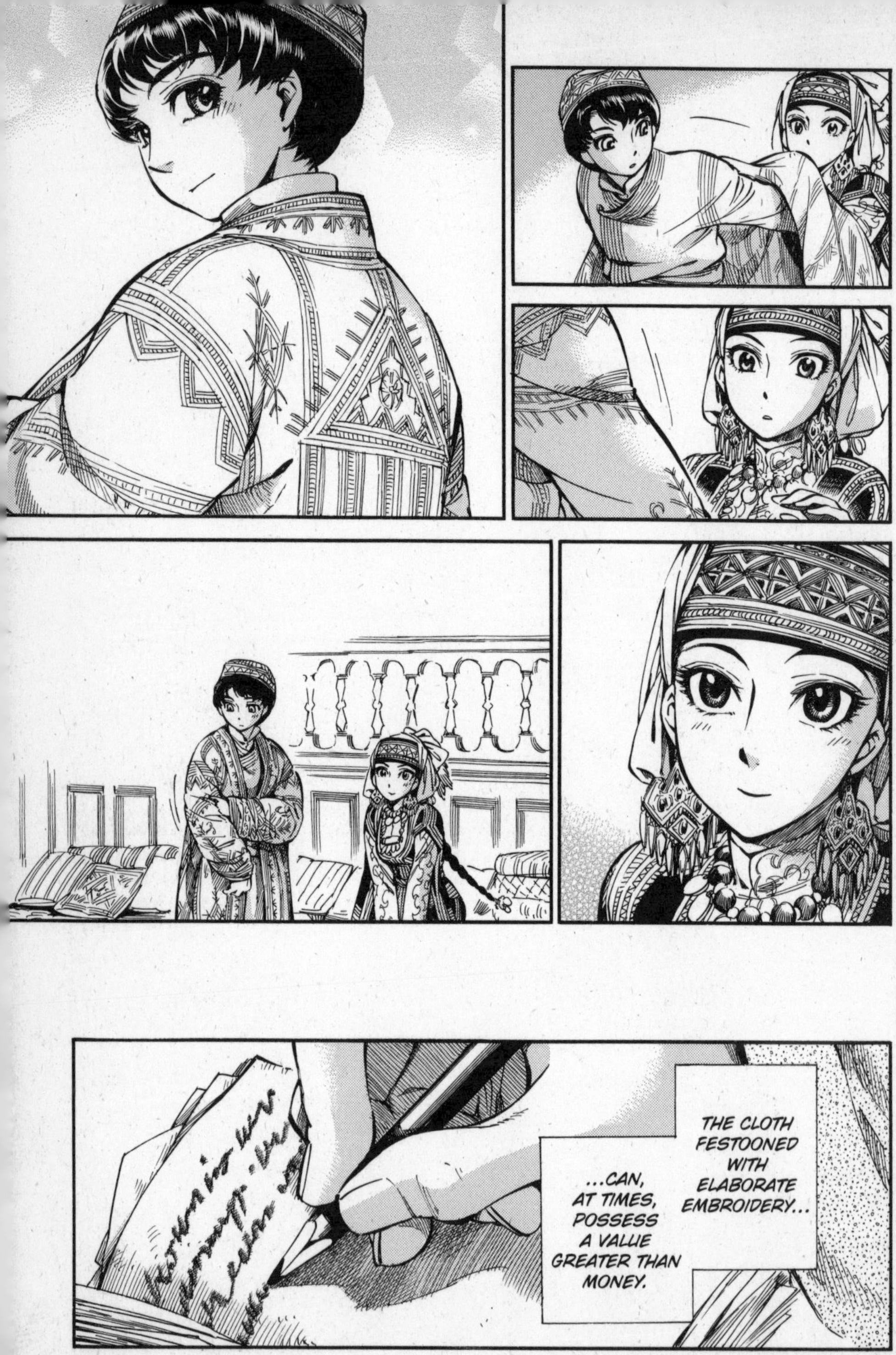
THE CLOTH FESTOONED WITH ELABORATE EMBROIDERY...
...CAN, AT TIMES, POSSESS A VALUE GREATER THAN MONEY.

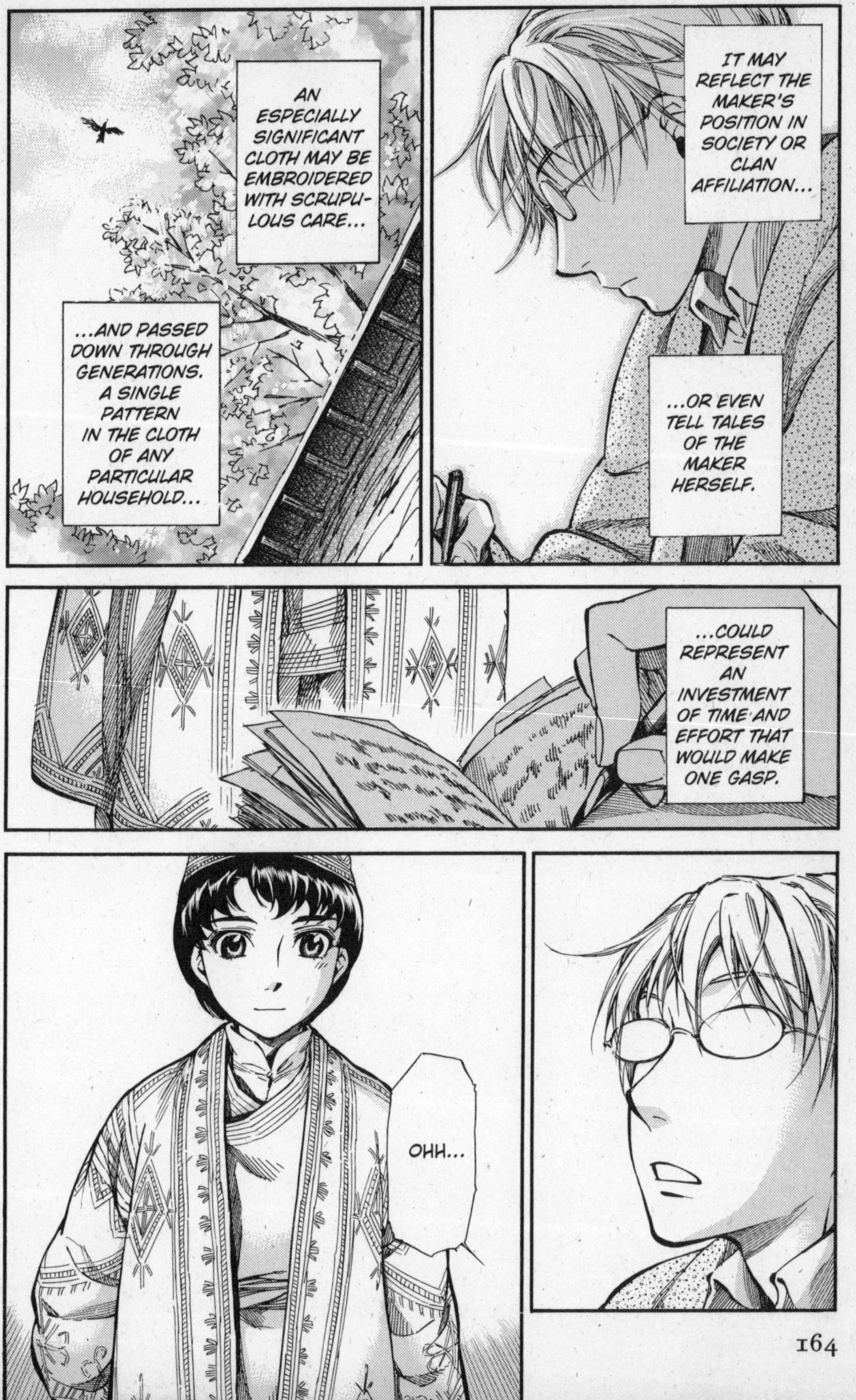
IT MAY REFLECT THE MAKER'S POSITION IN SOCIETY OR CLAN AFFILIATION...
...OR EVEN TELL TALES OF THE MAKER HERSELF.
AN ESPECIALLY SIGNIFICANT CLOTH MAY BE EMBROIDERED WITH SCRUPULOUS CARE...
...AND PASSED DOWN THROUGH GENERATIONS. A SINGLE PATTERN IN THE CLOTH OF ANY PARTICULAR HOUSEHOLD...
...COULD REPRESENT AN INVESTMENT OF TIME AND EFFORT THAT WOULD MAKE ONE GASP.
OHH...

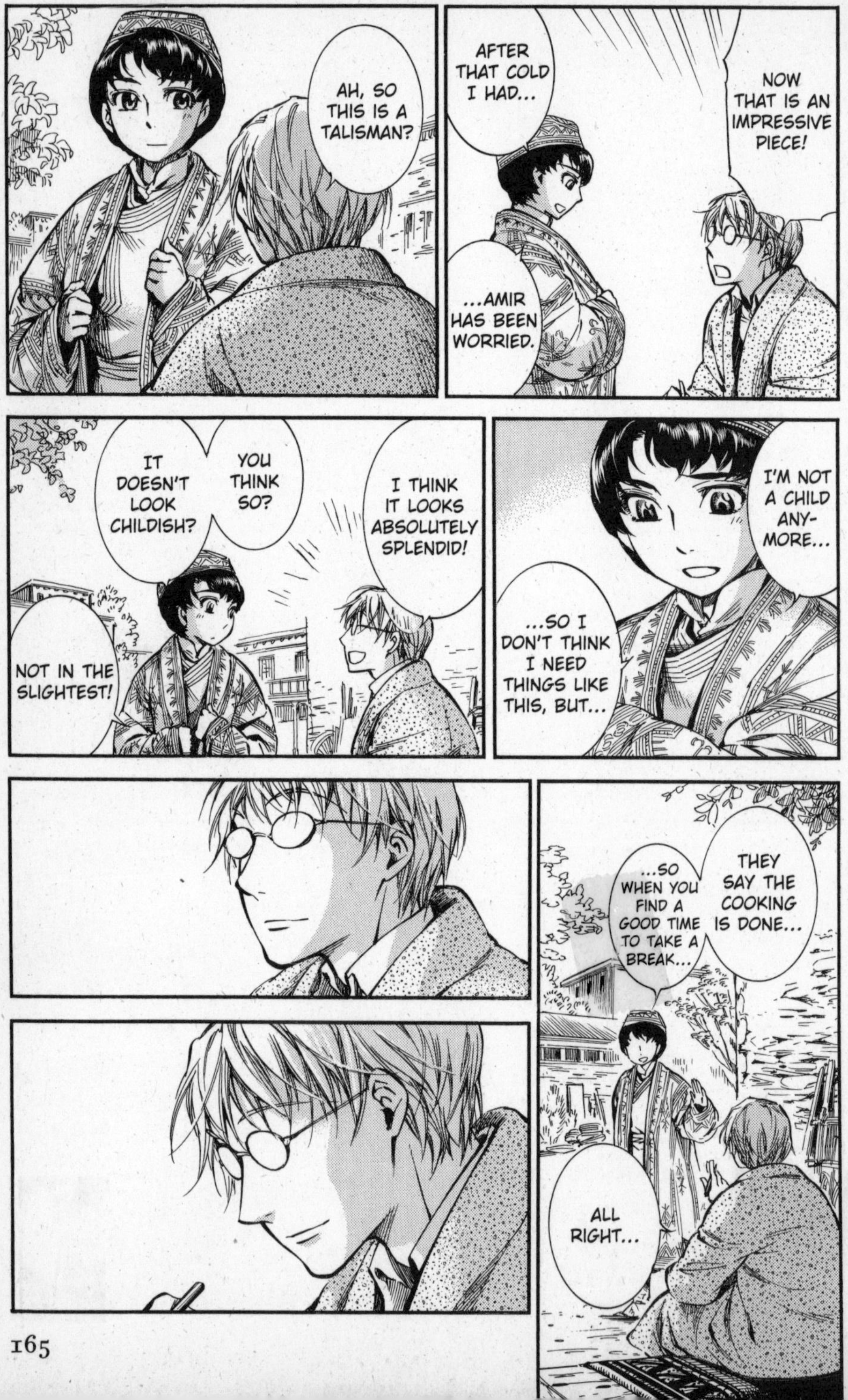
NOW THAT IS AN IMPRESSIVE PIECE!
AFTER THAT COLD I HAD...
...AMIR HAS BEEN WORRIED.
AH, SO THIS IS A TALISMAN?
I'M NOT A CHILD ANYMORE...
...SO I DON'T THINK I NEED THINGS LIKE THIS, BUT...
I THINK IT LOOKS ABSOLUTELY SPLENDID!
YOU THINK SO?
IT DOESN'T LOOK CHILDISH?
NOT IN THE SLIGHTEST!
THEY SAY THE COOKING IS DONE...
...SO WHEN YOU FIND A GOOD TIME TO TAKE A BREAK...
ALL RIGHT...

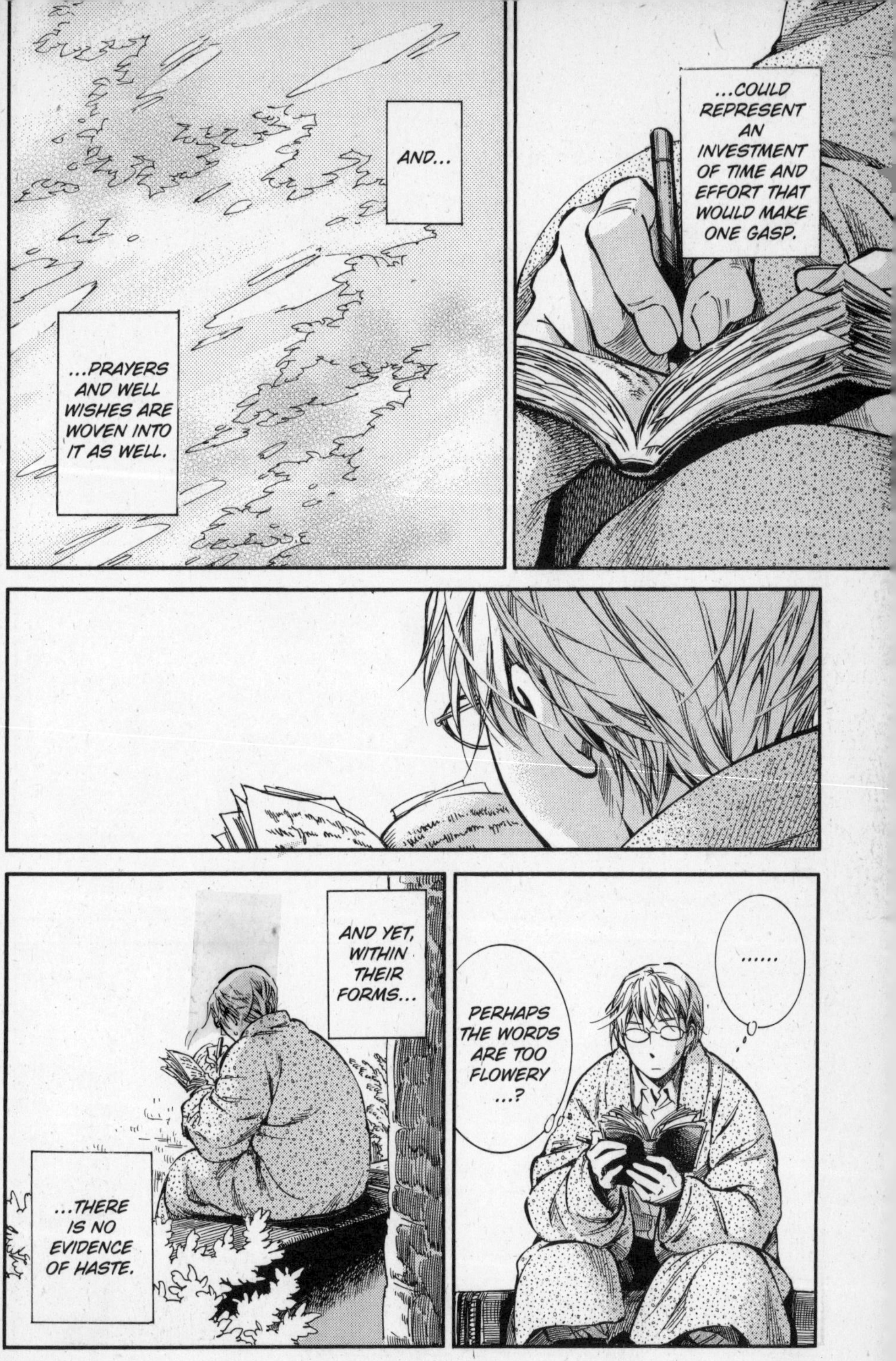
...COULD REPRESENT AN INVESTMENT OF TIME AND EFFORT THAT WOULD MAKE ONE GASP.
AND...
...PRAYERS AND WELL WISHES ARE WOVEN INTO IT AS WELL.
......
PERHAPS THE WORDS ARE TOO FLOWERY ...?
AND YET, WITHIN THEIR FORMS...
...THERE IS NO EVIDENCE OF HASTE.

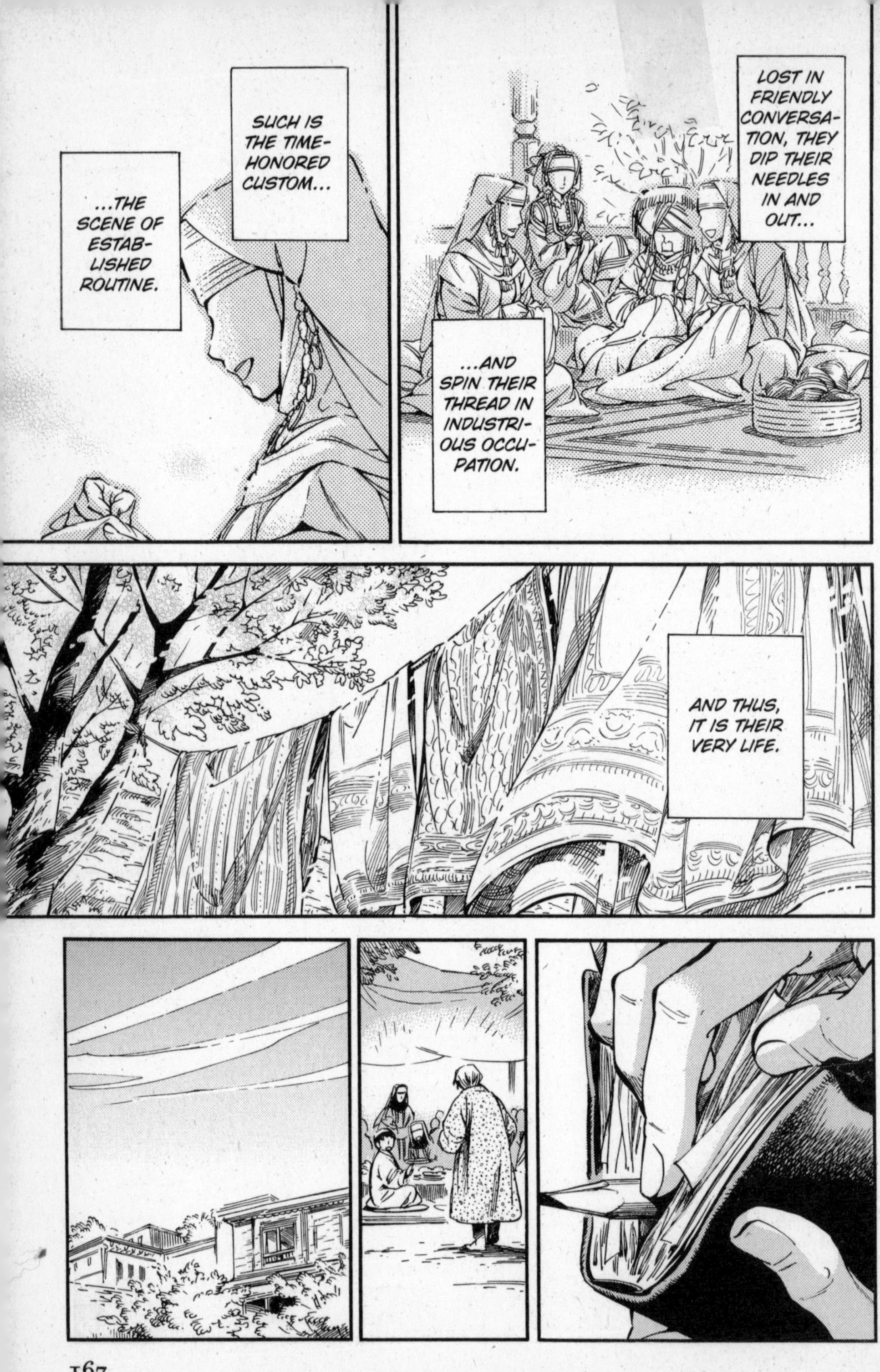
LOST IN FRIENDLY CONVERSA-TION, THEY DIP THEIR NEEDLES IN AND OUT...
...AND SPIN THEIR THREAD IN INDUSTRI-OUS OCCU-PATION.
SUCH IS THE TIME-HONORED CUSTOM...
...THE SCENE OF ESTAB-LISHED ROUTINE.
AND THUS, IT IS THEIR VERY LIFE.

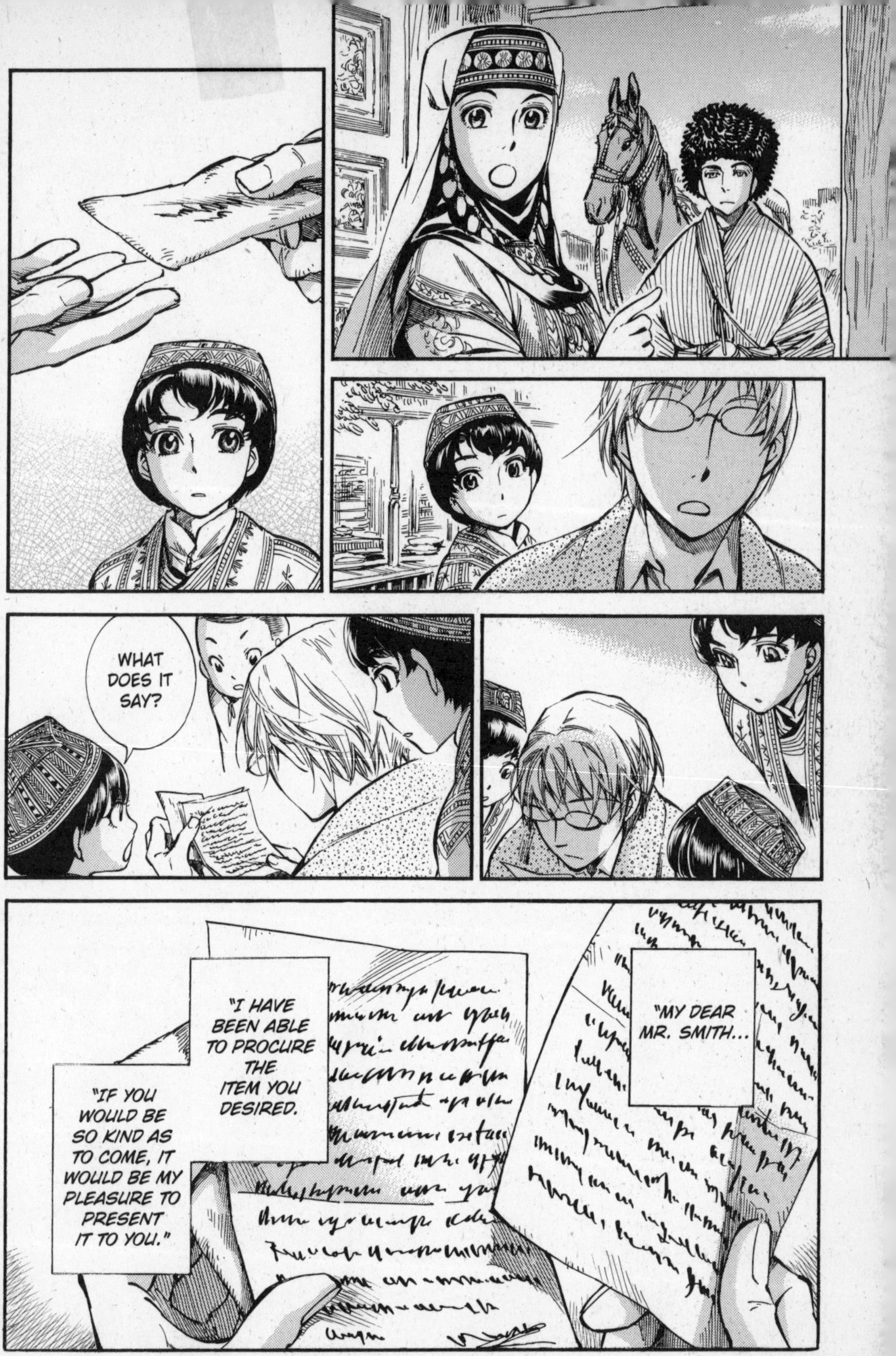
WHAT DOES IT SAY?
"MY DEAR MR. SMITH...
"I HAVE BEEN ABLE TO PROCURE THE ITEM YOU DESIRED.
"IF YOU WOULD BE SO KIND AS TO COME, IT WOULD BE MY PLEASURE TO PRESENT IT TO YOU."

✦ Chapter Ten End ✦

Chapter Eleven
Departure

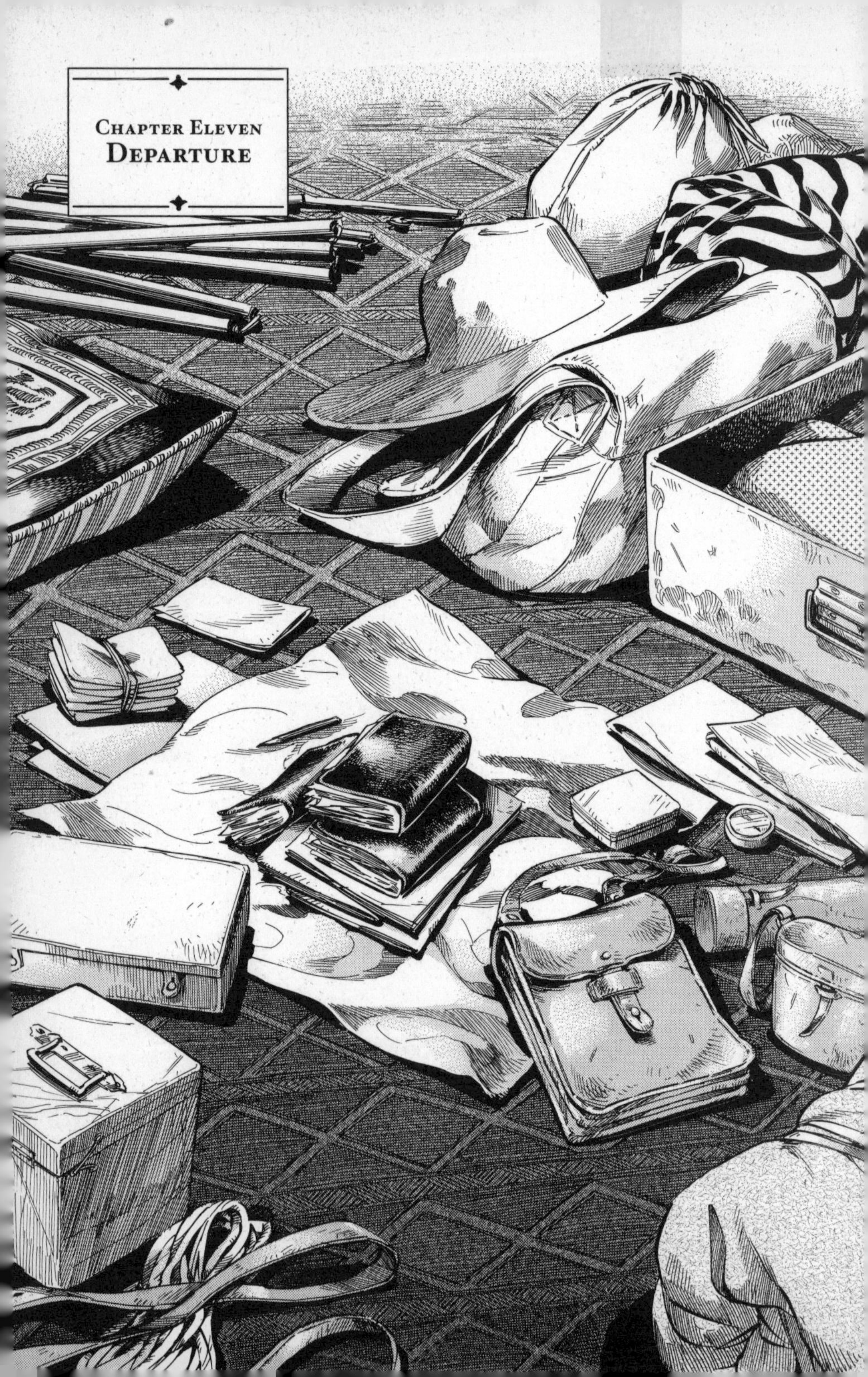

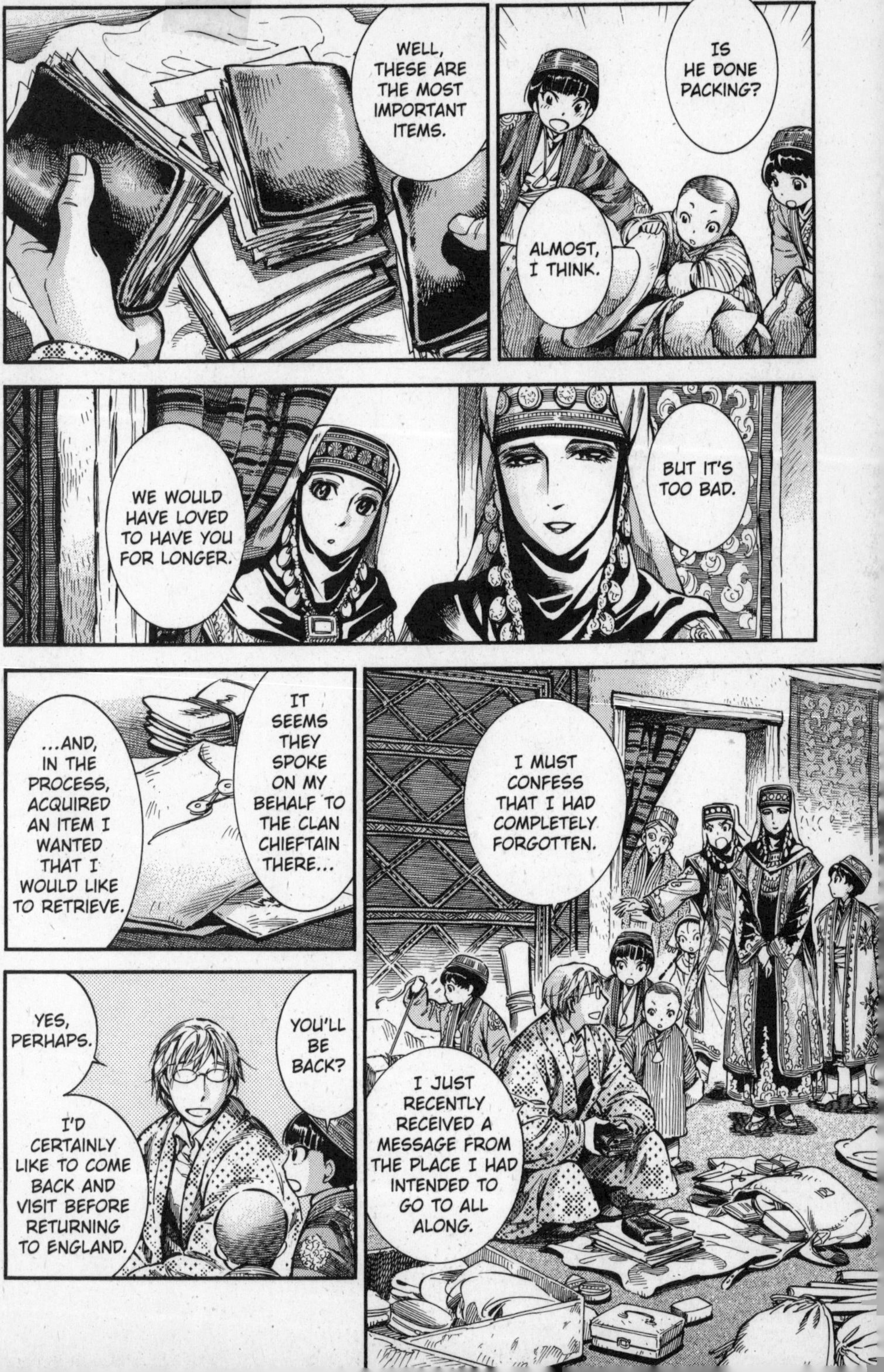
IS HE DONE PACKING?
ALMOST, I THINK.
WELL, THESE ARE THE MOST IMPORTANT ITEMS.
BUT IT'S TOO BAD.
WE WOULD HAVE LOVED TO HAVE YOU FOR LONGER.
I MUST CONFESS THAT I HAD COMPLETELY FORGOTTEN.
I JUST RECENTLY RECEIVED A MESSAGE FROM THE PLACE I HAD INTENDED TO GO TO ALL ALONG.
IT SEEMS THEY SPOKE ON MY BEHALF TO THE CLAN CHIEFTAIN THERE...
...AND, IN THE PROCESS, ACQUIRED AN ITEM I WANTED THAT I WOULD LIKE TO RETRIEVE.
YOU'LL BE BACK?
YES, PERHAPS.
I'D CERTAINLY LIKE TO COME BACK AND VISIT BEFORE RETURNING TO ENGLAND.

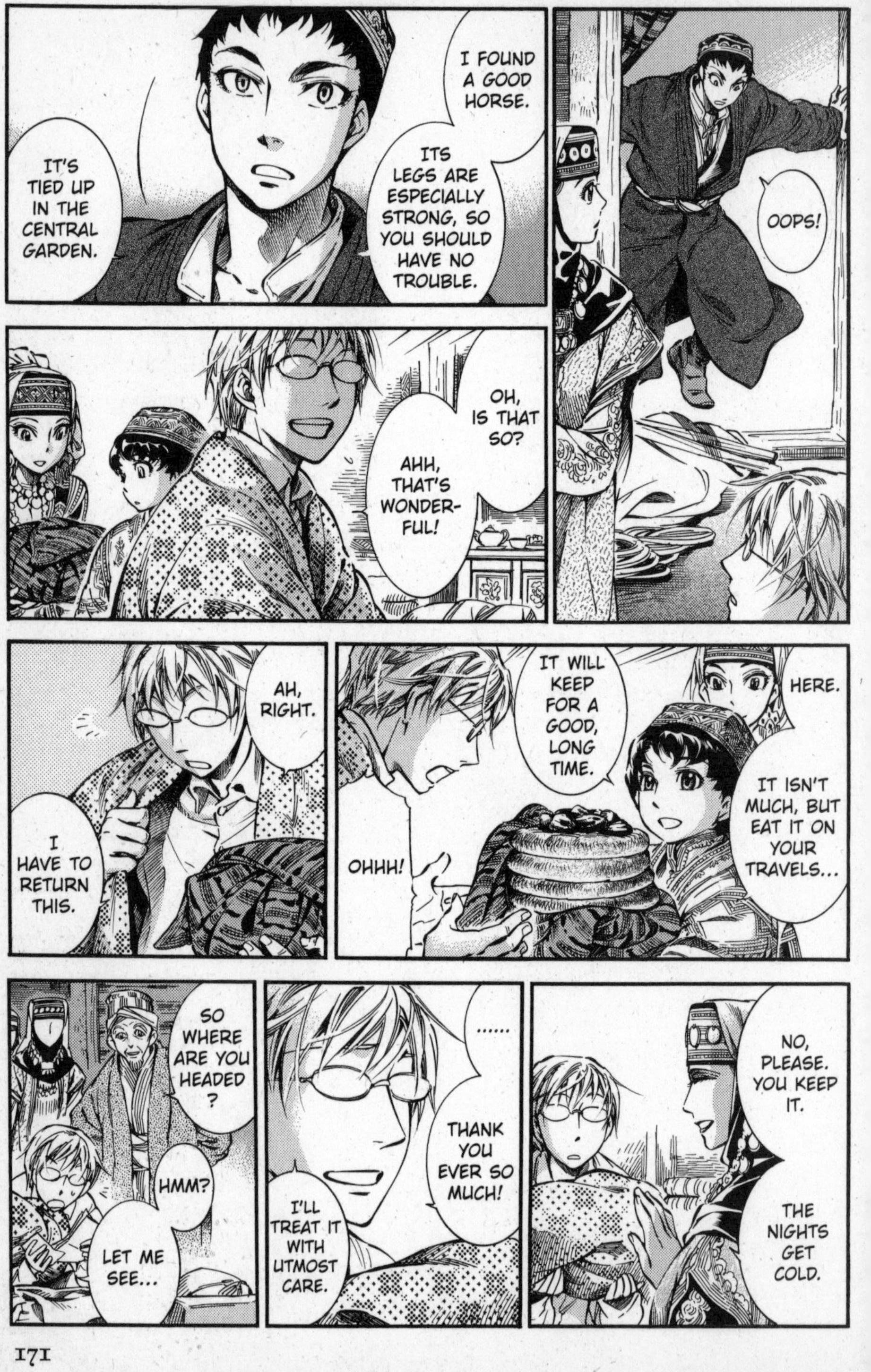
OOPS!
I FOUND A GOOD HORSE.
ITS LEGS ARE ESPECIALLY STRONG, SO YOU SHOULD HAVE NO TROUBLE.
IT'S TIED UP IN THE CENTRAL GARDEN.
OH, IS THAT SO?
AHH, THAT'S WONDERFUL!
HERE.
IT ISN'T MUCH, BUT EAT IT ON YOUR TRAVELS...
IT WILL KEEP FOR A GOOD, LONG TIME.
OHHH!
AH, RIGHT.
I HAVE TO RETURN THIS.
NO, PLEASE. YOU KEEP IT.
THE NIGHTS GET COLD.
......
THANK YOU EVER SO MUCH!
I'LL TREAT IT WITH UTMOST CARE.
SO WHERE ARE YOU HEADED?
HMM?
LET ME SEE...

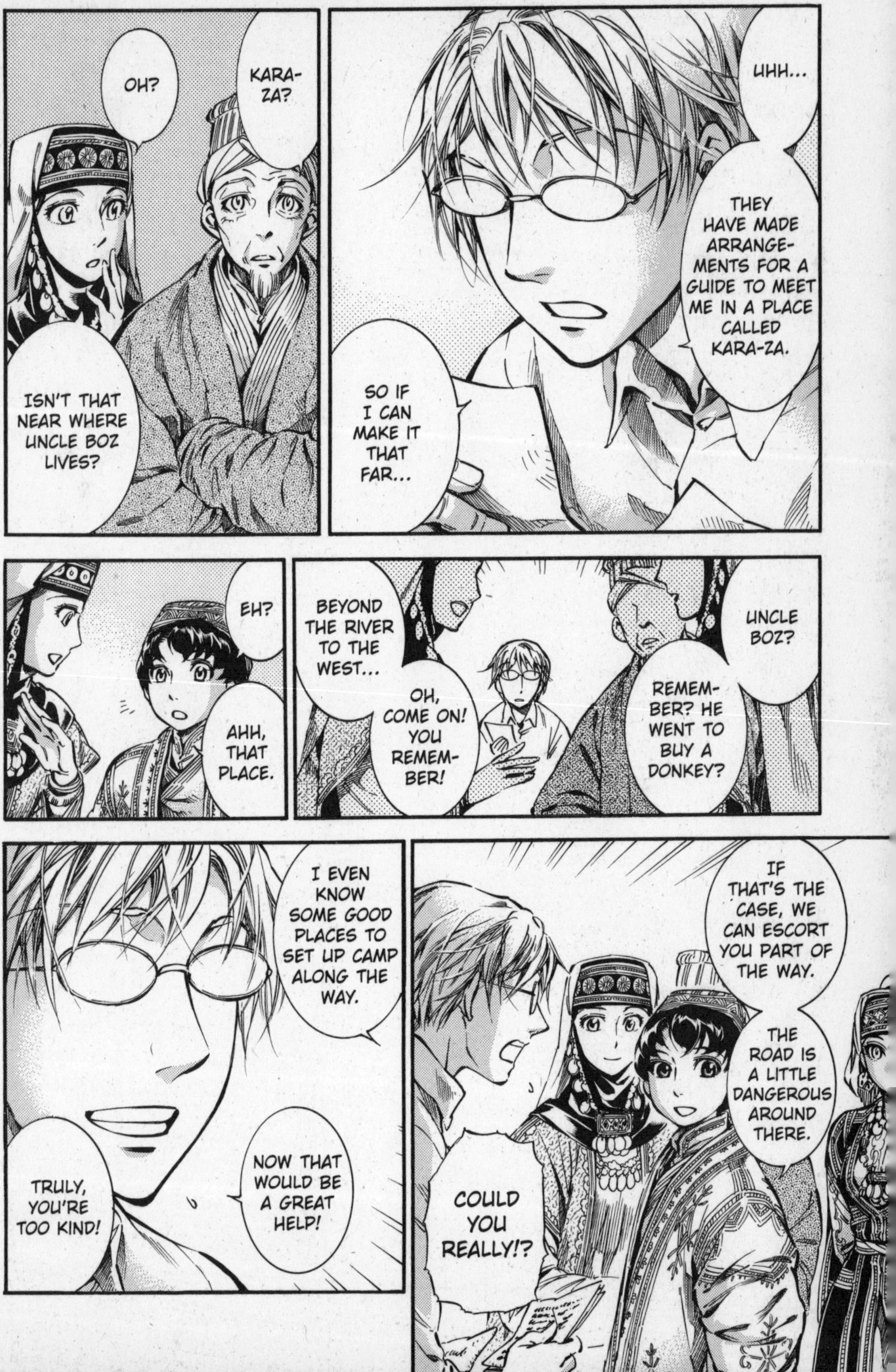
UHH...
THEY HAVE MADE ARRANGEMENTS FOR A GUIDE TO MEET ME IN A PLACE CALLED KARA-ZA.
SO IF I CAN MAKE IT THAT FAR...
KARA-ZA?
OH?
ISN'T THAT NEAR WHERE UNCLE BOZ LIVES?
UNCLE BOZ?
REMEMBER? HE WENT TO BUY A DONKEY?
BEYOND THE RIVER TO THE WEST...
OH, COME ON! YOU REMEMBER!
EH?
AHH, THAT PLACE.
IF THAT'S THE CASE, WE CAN ESCORT YOU PART OF THE WAY.
THE ROAD IS A LITTLE DANGEROUS AROUND THERE.
COULD YOU REALLY!?
I EVEN KNOW SOME GOOD PLACES TO SET UP CAMP ALONG THE WAY.
NOW THAT WOULD BE A GREAT HELP!
TRULY, YOU'RE TOO KIND!

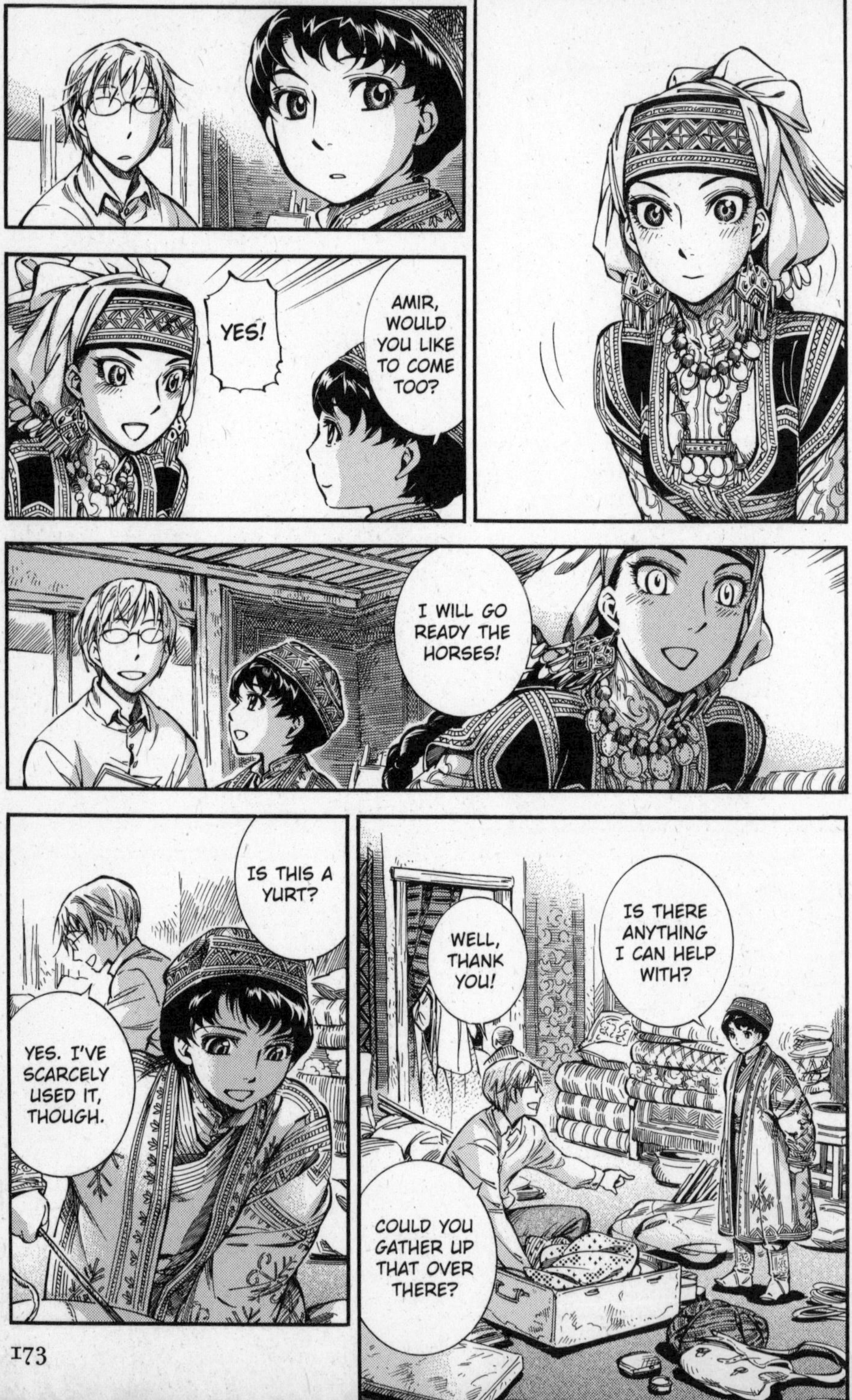
AMIR, WOULD YOU LIKE TO COME TOO?
YES!
I WILL GO READY THE HORSES!
IS THERE ANYTHING I CAN HELP WITH?
WELL, THANK YOU!
COULD YOU GATHER UP THAT OVER THERE?
IS THIS A YURT?
YES. I'VE SCARCELY USED IT, THOUGH.

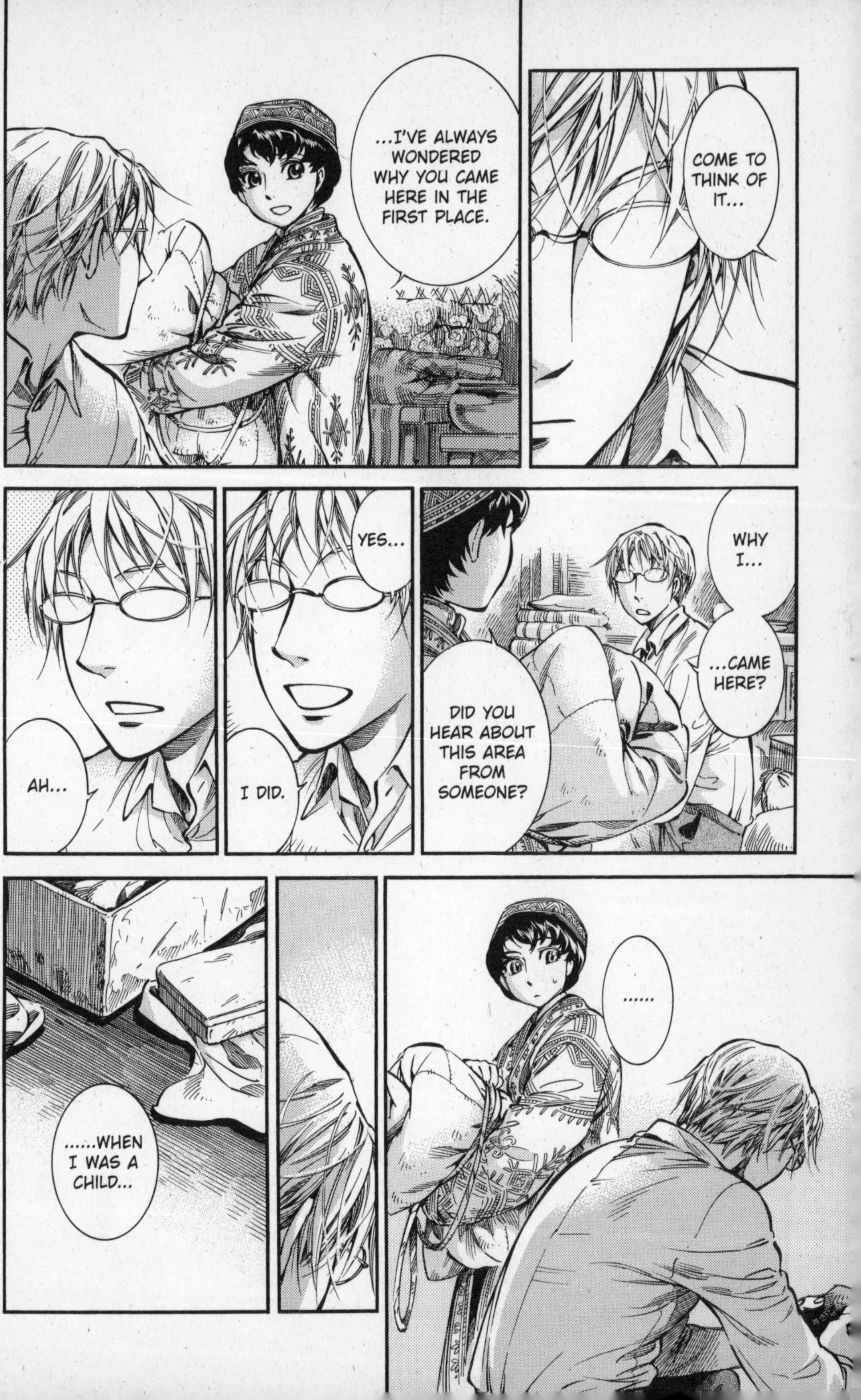
COME TO THINK OF IT...
...I'VE ALWAYS WONDERED WHY YOU CAME HERE IN THE FIRST PLACE.
WHY I...
...CAME HERE?
DID YOU HEAR ABOUT THIS AREA FROM SOMEONE?
YES...
I DID.
AH...
......
......WHEN I WAS A CHILD...

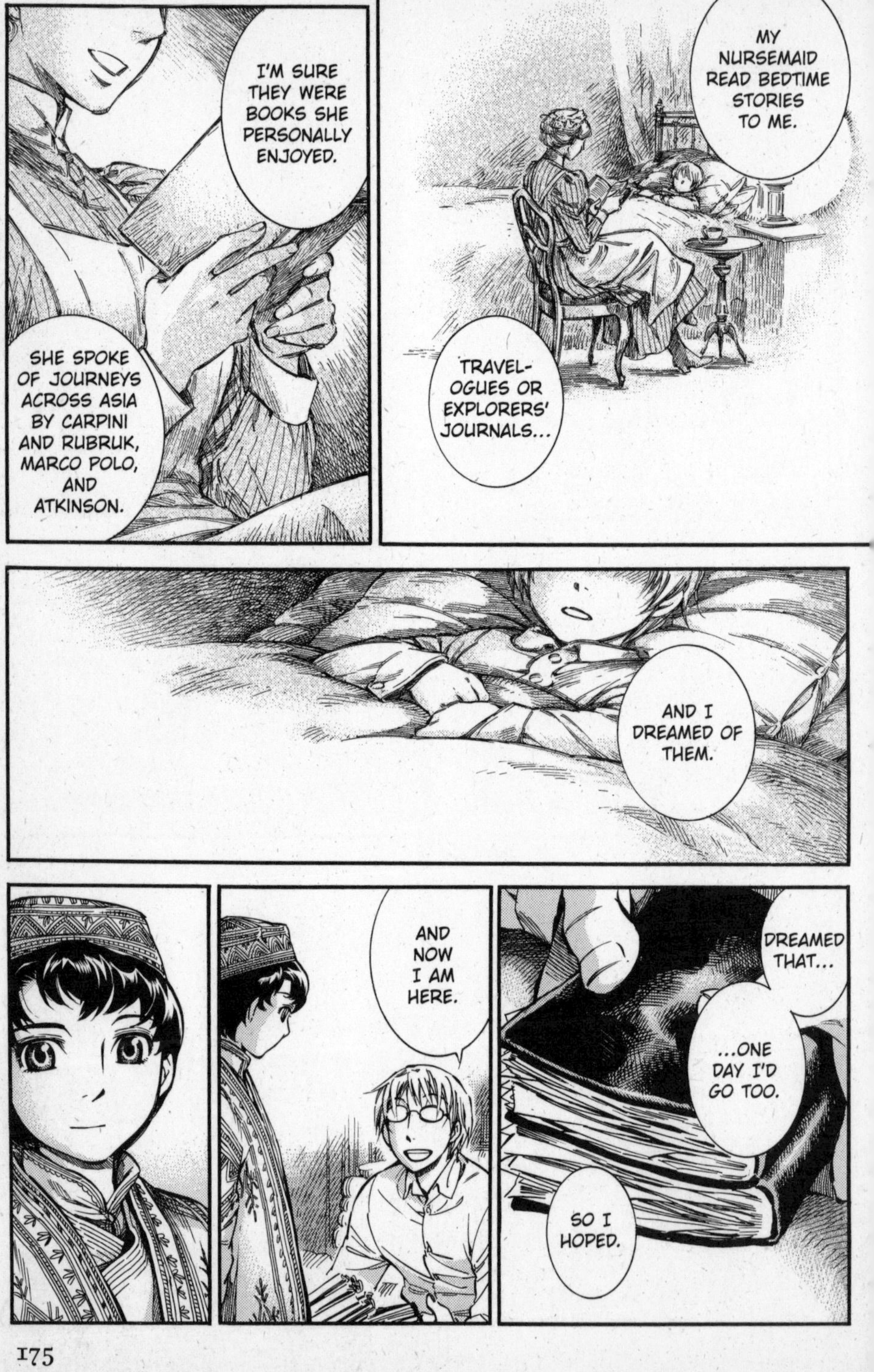
MY NURSEMAID READ BEDTIME STORIES TO ME.
TRAVEL-OGUES OR EXPLORERS' JOURNALS...
I'M SURE THEY WERE BOOKS SHE PERSONALLY ENJOYED.
SHE SPOKE OF JOURNEYS ACROSS ASIA BY CARPINI AND RUBRUK, MARCO POLO, AND ATKINSON.
AND I DREAMED OF THEM.
DREAMED THAT...
...ONE DAY I'D GO TOO.
SO I HOPED.
AND NOW I AM HERE.

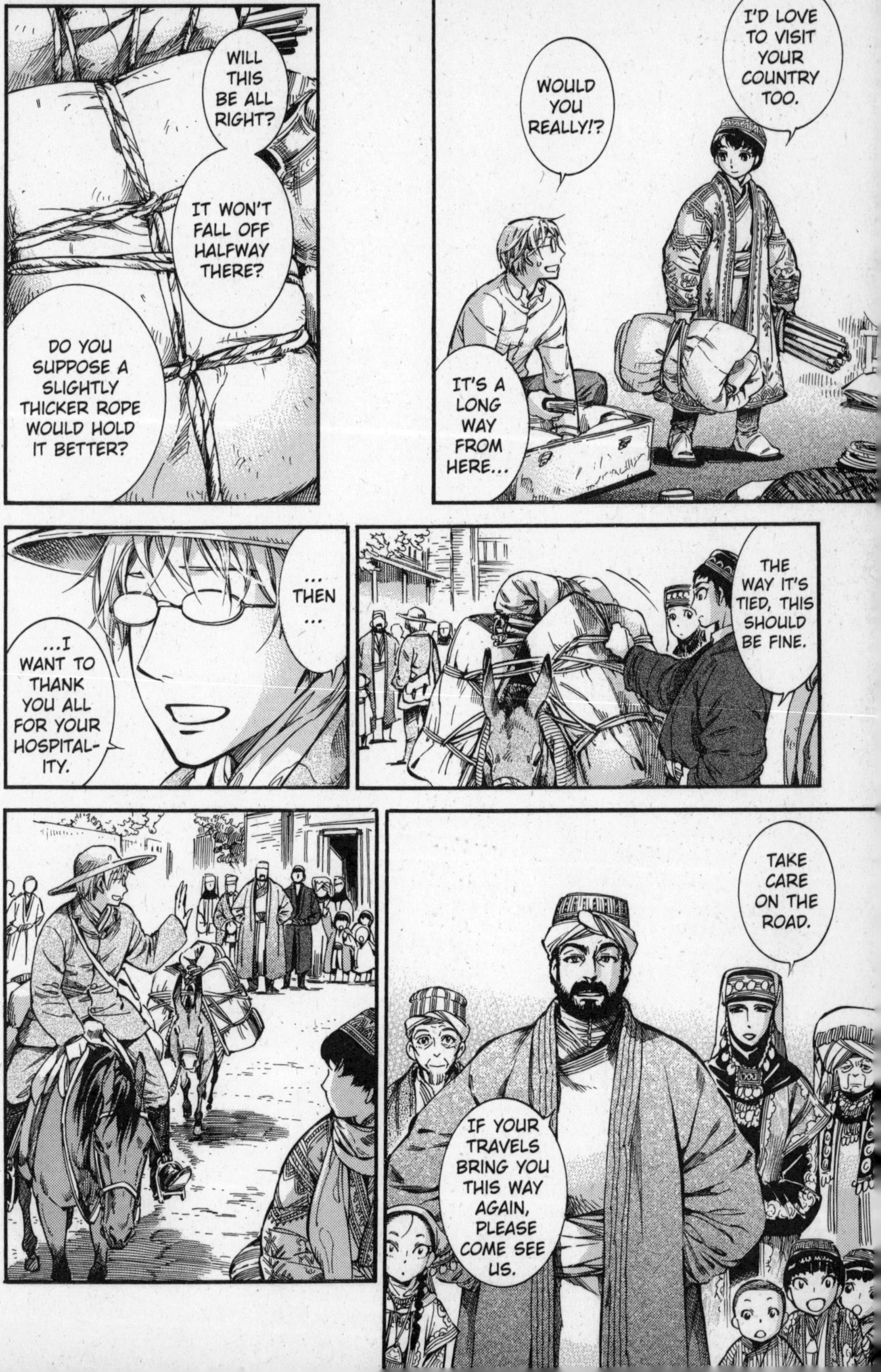
I'D LOVE TO VISIT YOUR COUNTRY TOO.
WOULD YOU REALLY!?
IT'S A LONG WAY FROM HERE...
WILL THIS BE ALL RIGHT?
IT WON'T FALL OFF HALFWAY THERE?
DO YOU SUPPOSE A SLIGHTLY THICKER ROPE WOULD HOLD IT BETTER?
THE WAY IT'S TIED, THIS SHOULD BE FINE.
...THEN...
...I WANT TO THANK YOU ALL FOR YOUR HOSPITAL-ITY.
TAKE CARE ON THE ROAD.
IF YOUR TRAVELS BRING YOU THIS WAY AGAIN, PLEASE COME SEE US.

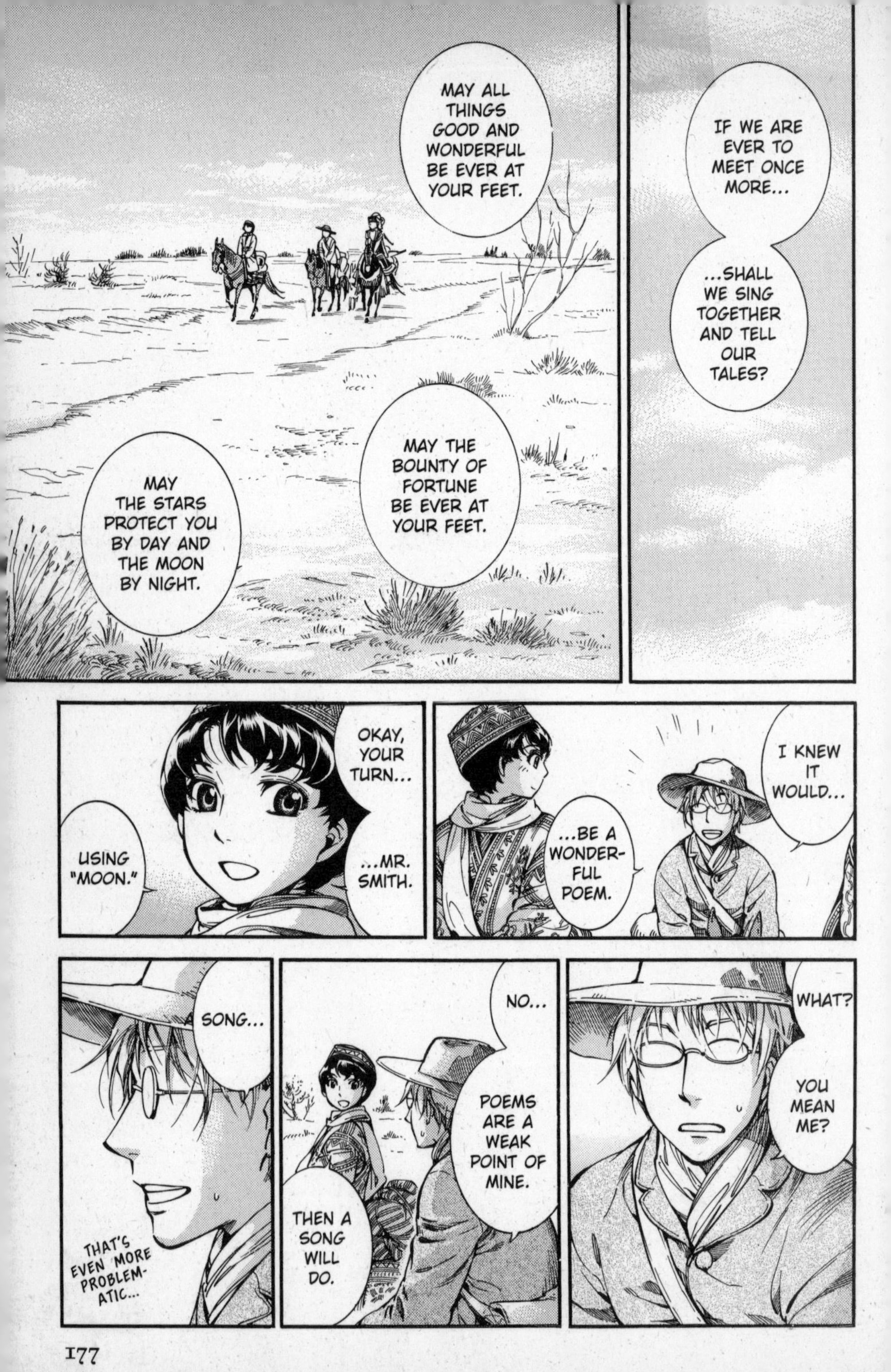
IF WE ARE EVER TO MEET ONCE MORE...
...SHALL WE SING TOGETHER AND TELL OUR TALES?
MAY ALL THINGS GOOD AND WONDERFUL BE EVER AT YOUR FEET.
MAY THE BOUNTY OF FORTUNE BE EVER AT YOUR FEET.
MAY THE STARS PROTECT YOU BY DAY AND THE MOON BY NIGHT.
I KNEW IT WOULD...
...BE A WONDERFUL POEM.
OKAY, YOUR TURN...
...MR. SMITH.
USING "MOON."
WHAT?
YOU MEAN ME?
NO...
POEMS ARE A WEAK POINT OF MINE.
THEN A SONG WILL DO.
A SONG...
THAT'S EVEN MORE PROBLEMATIC...

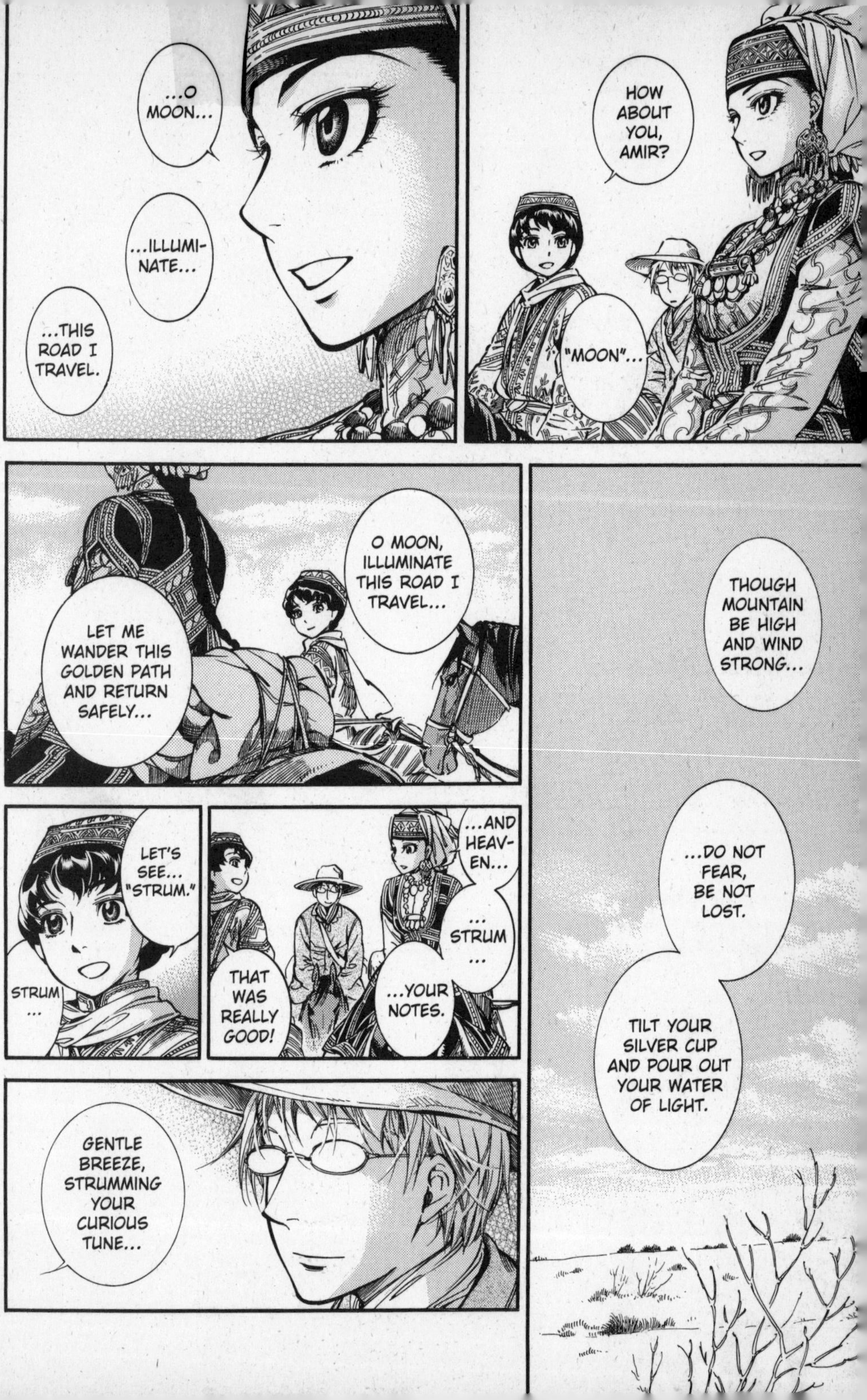
HOW ABOUT YOU, AMIR?
"MOON"...
...O MOON...
...ILLUMINATE...
...THIS ROAD I TRAVEL.
THOUGH MOUNTAIN BE HIGH AND WIND STRONG...
...DO NOT FEAR, BE NOT LOST.
TILT YOUR SILVER CUP AND POUR OUT YOUR WATER OF LIGHT.
O MOON, ILLUMINATE THIS ROAD I TRAVEL...
LET ME WANDER THIS GOLDEN PATH AND RETURN SAFELY...
...AND HEAVEN...
...STRUM...
...YOUR NOTES.
THAT WAS REALLY GOOD!
LET'S SEE... "STRUM."
STRUM...
GENTLE BREEZE, STRUMMING YOUR CURIOUS TUNE...

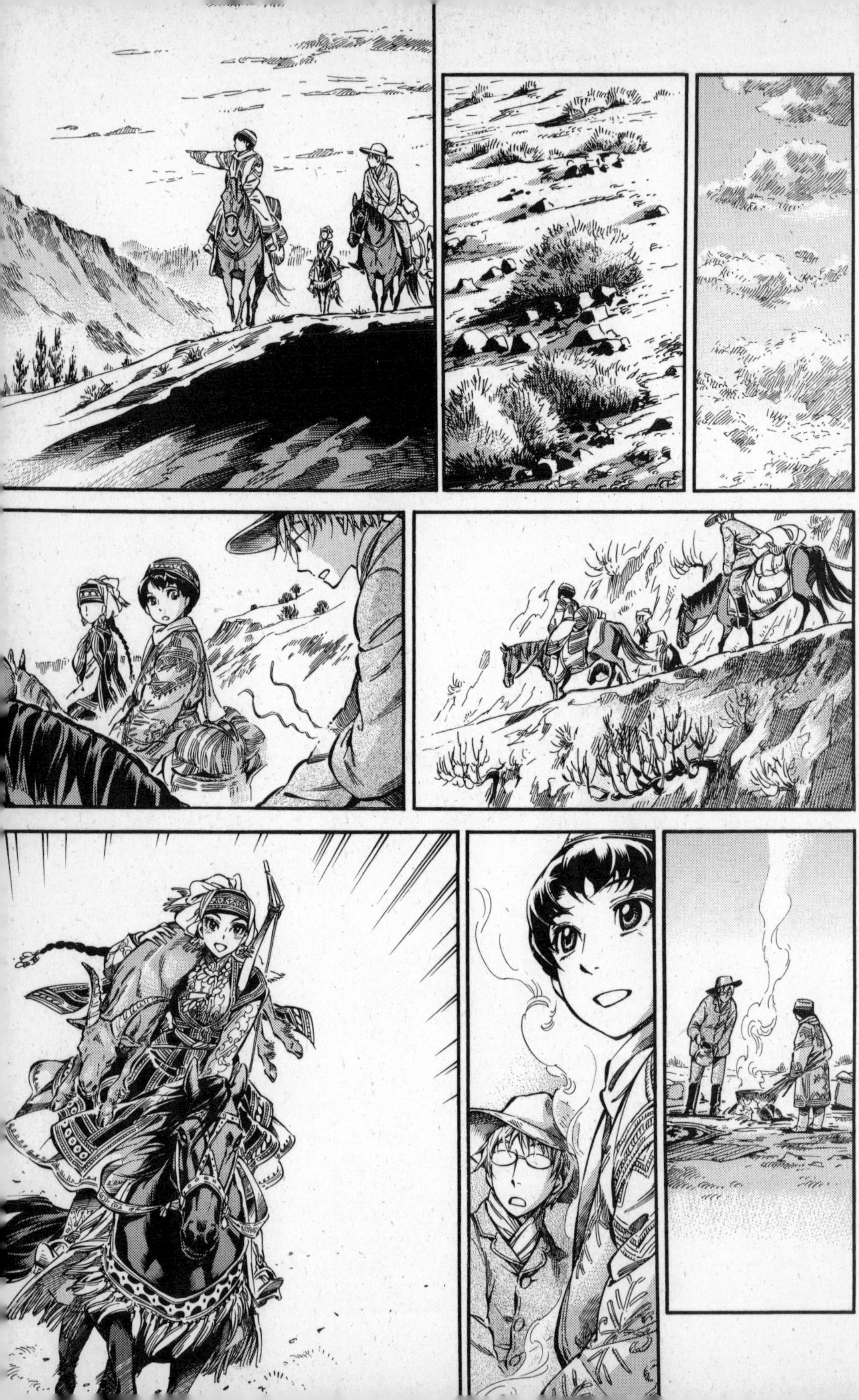

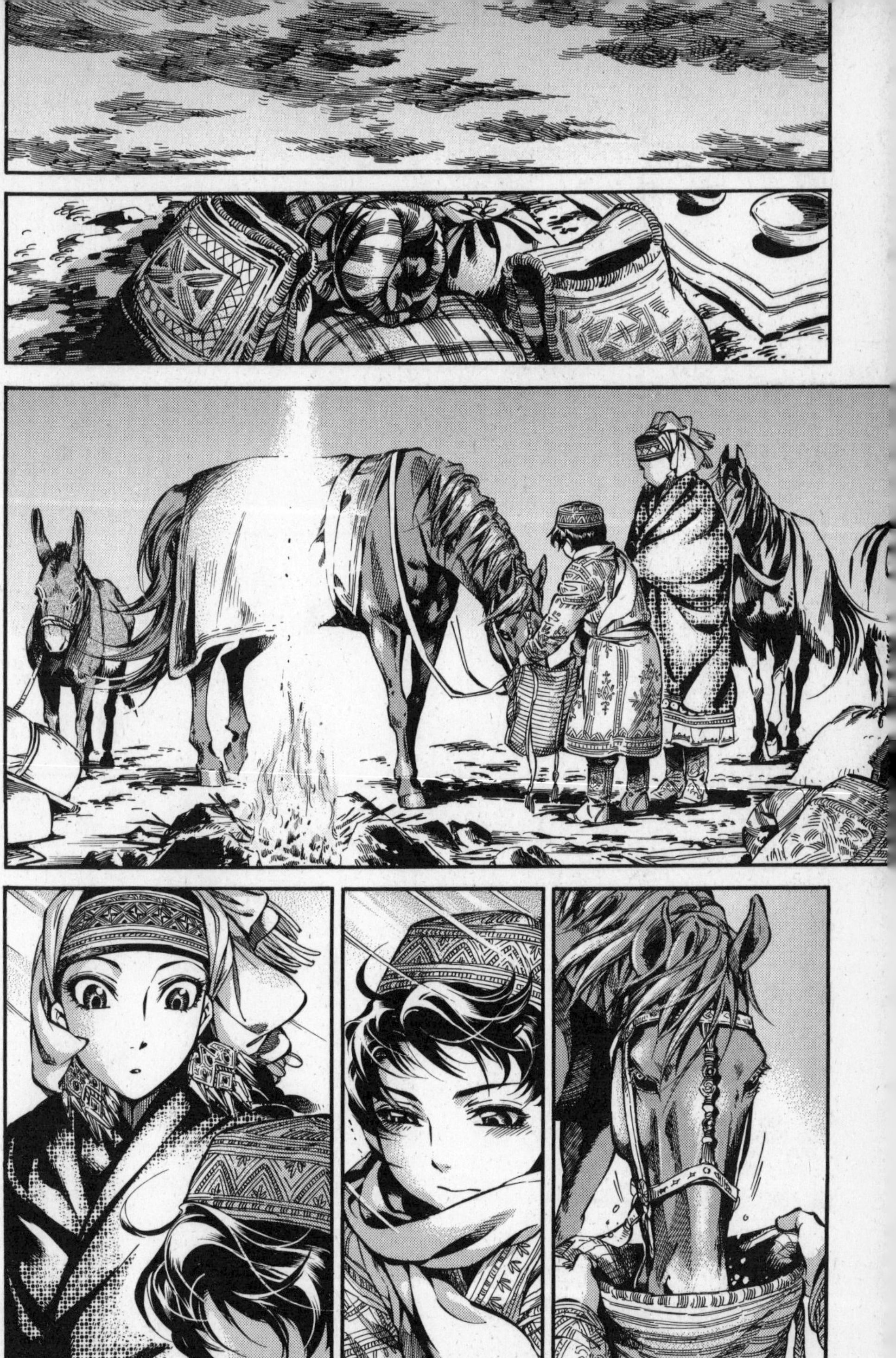

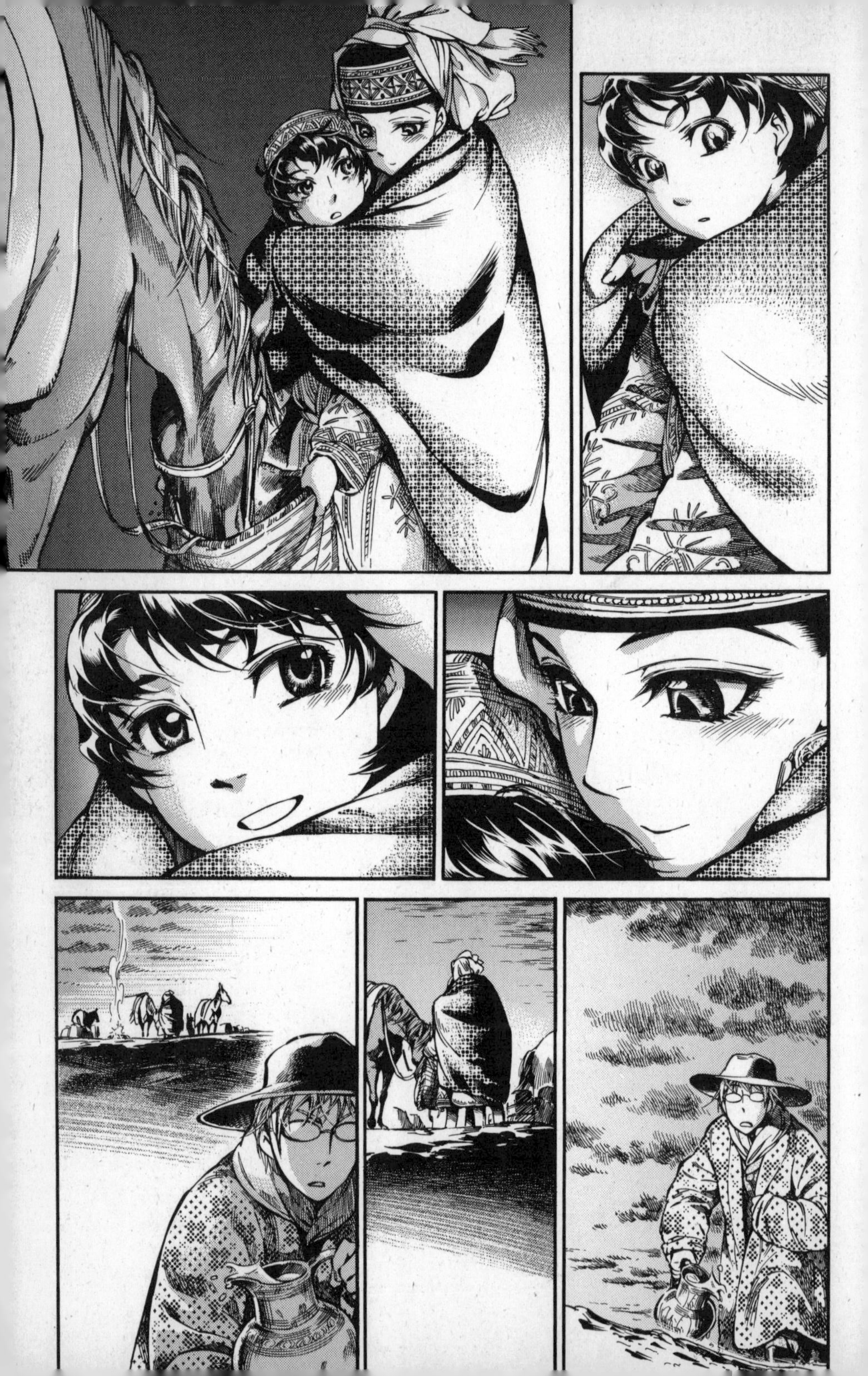

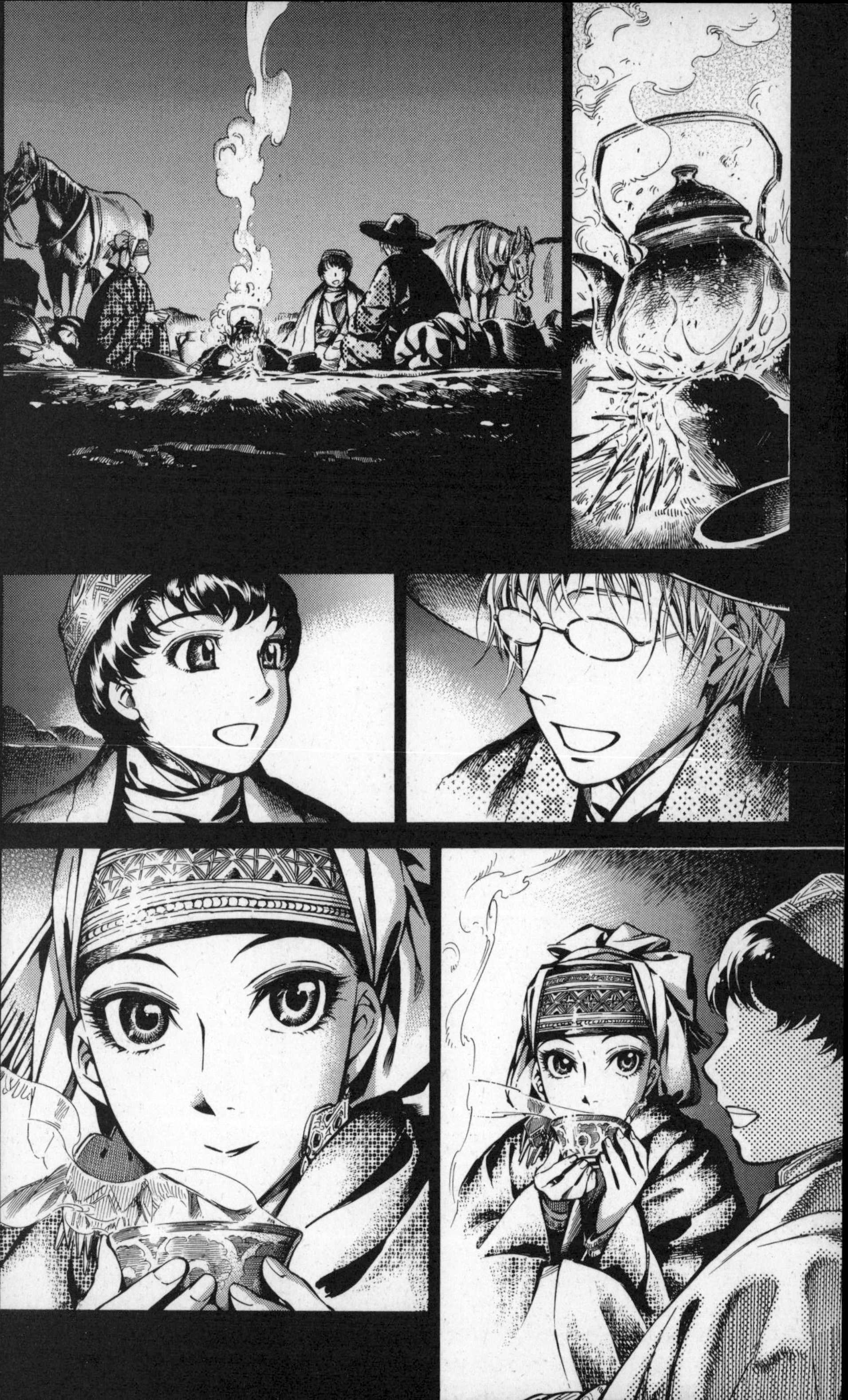

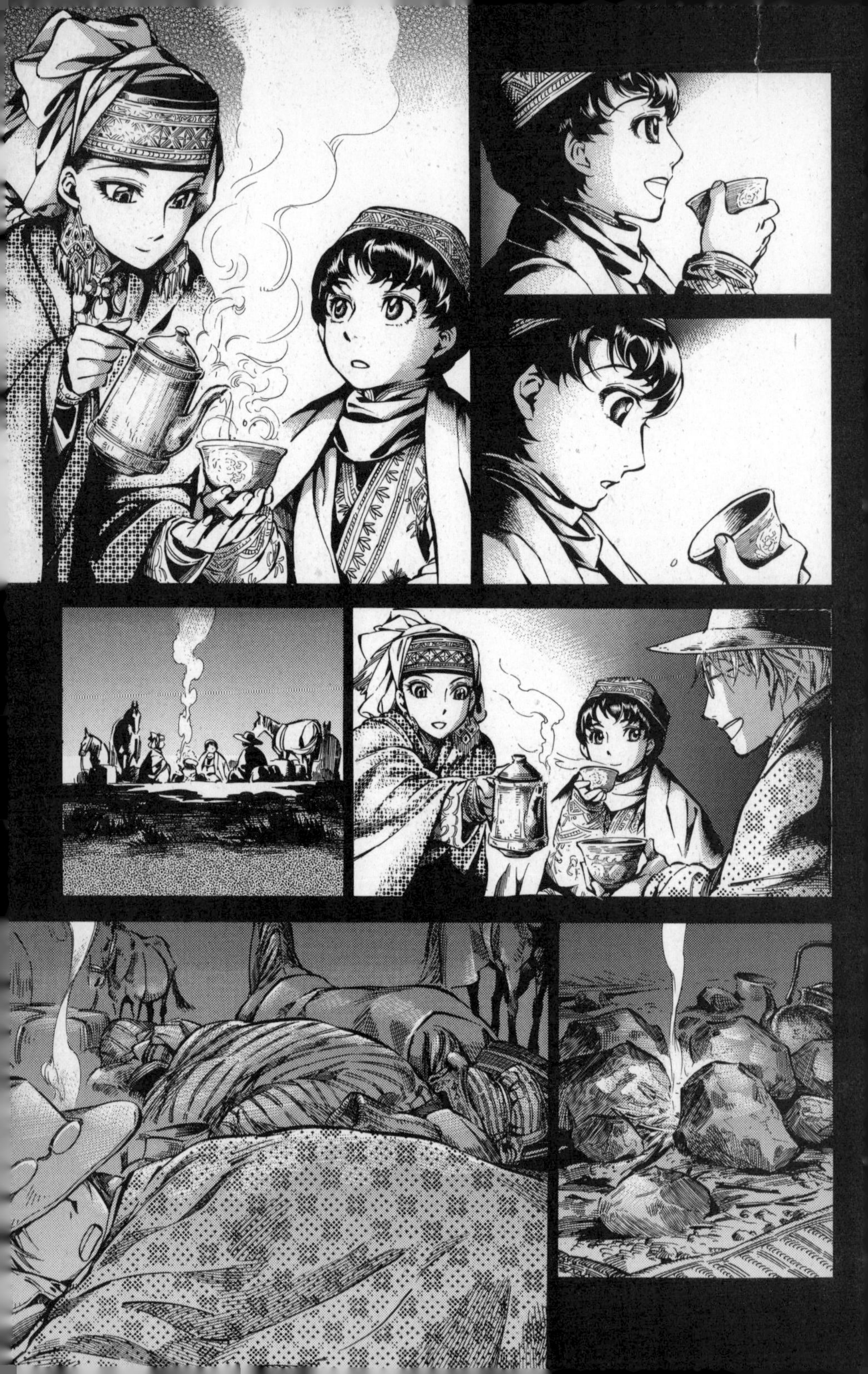

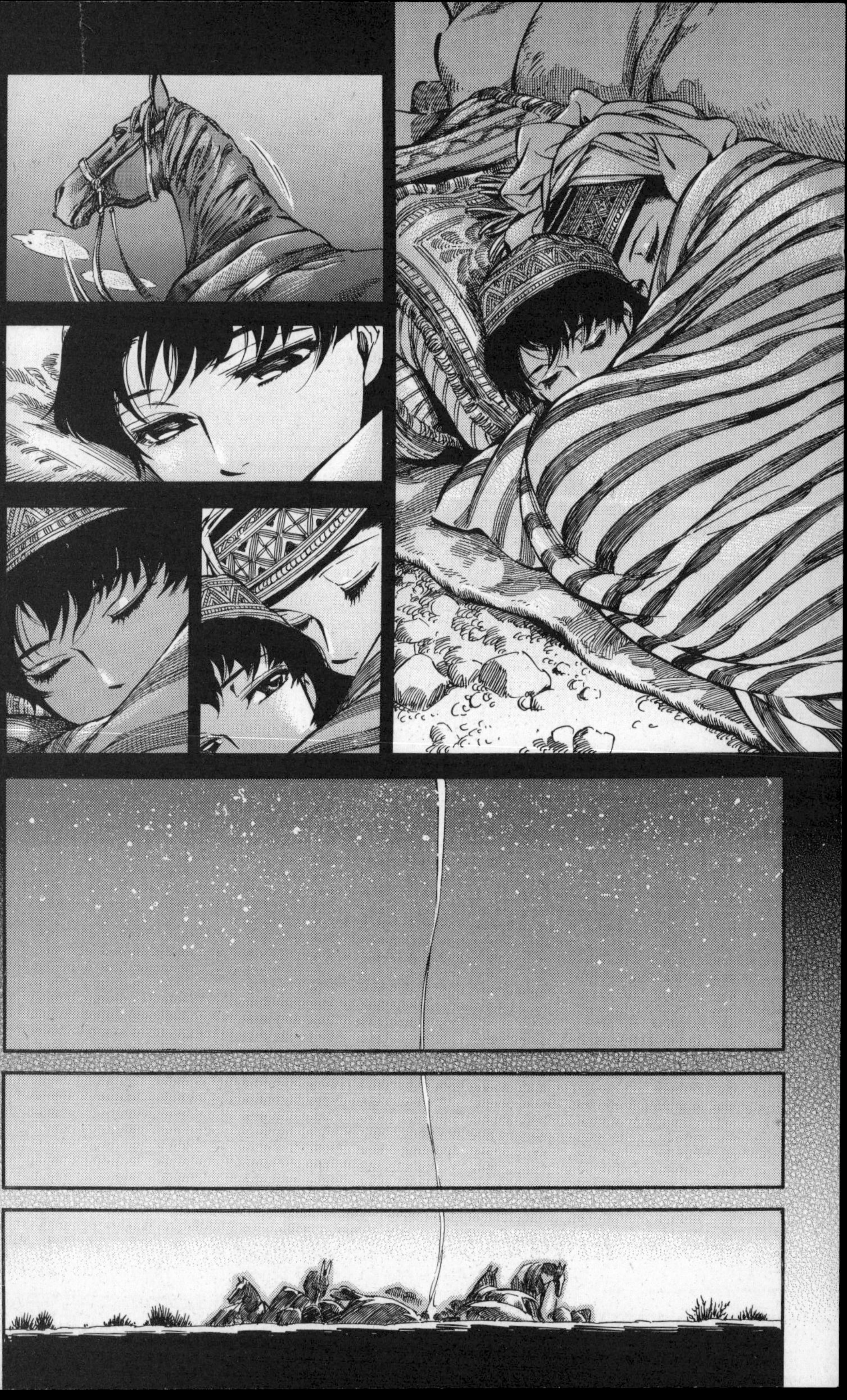

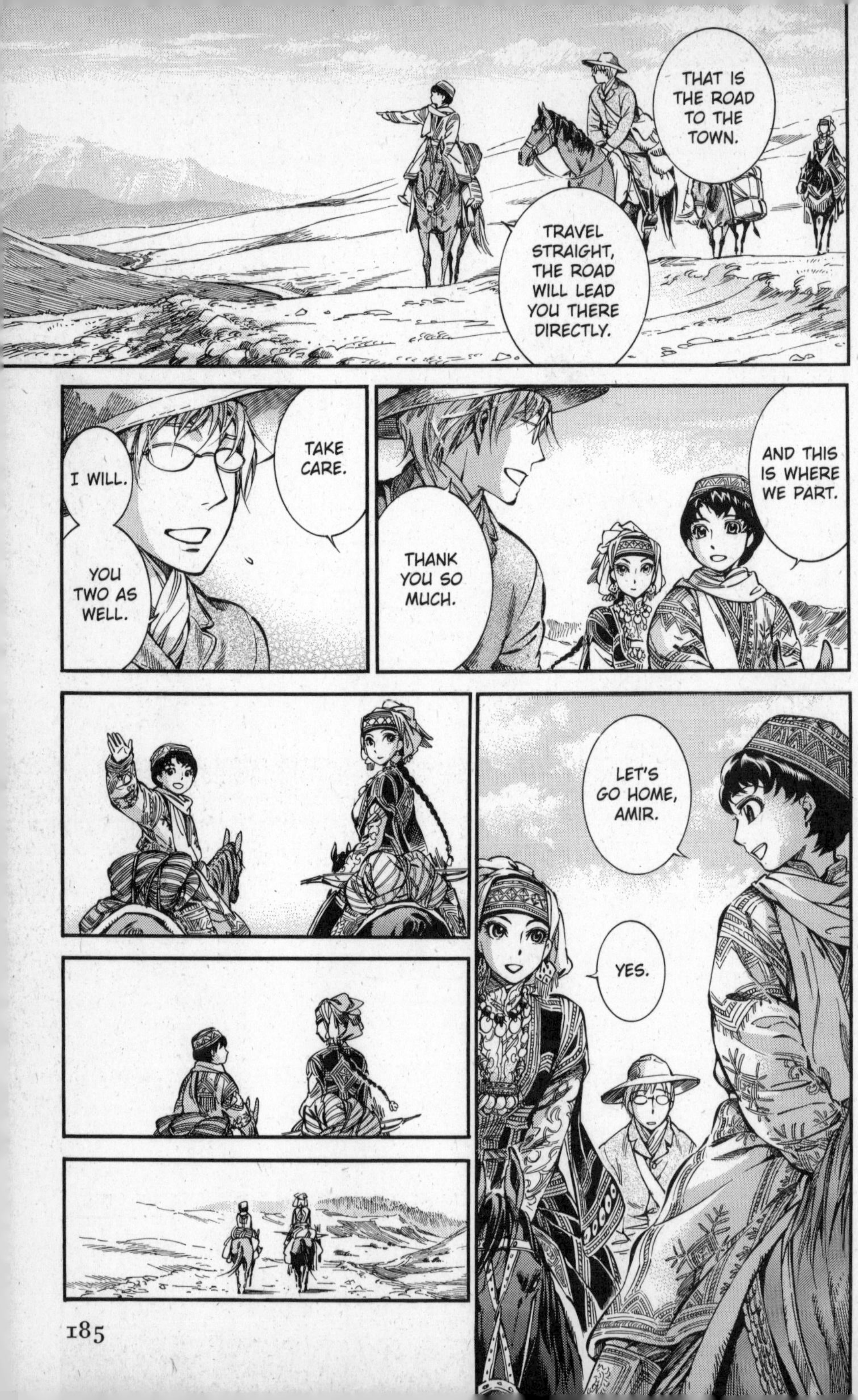
THAT IS THE ROAD TO THE TOWN.
TRAVEL STRAIGHT, THE ROAD WILL LEAD YOU THERE DIRECTLY.
AND THIS IS WHERE WE PART.
THANK YOU SO MUCH.
TAKE CARE.
I WILL.
YOU TWO AS WELL.
LET'S GO HOME, AMIR.
YES.

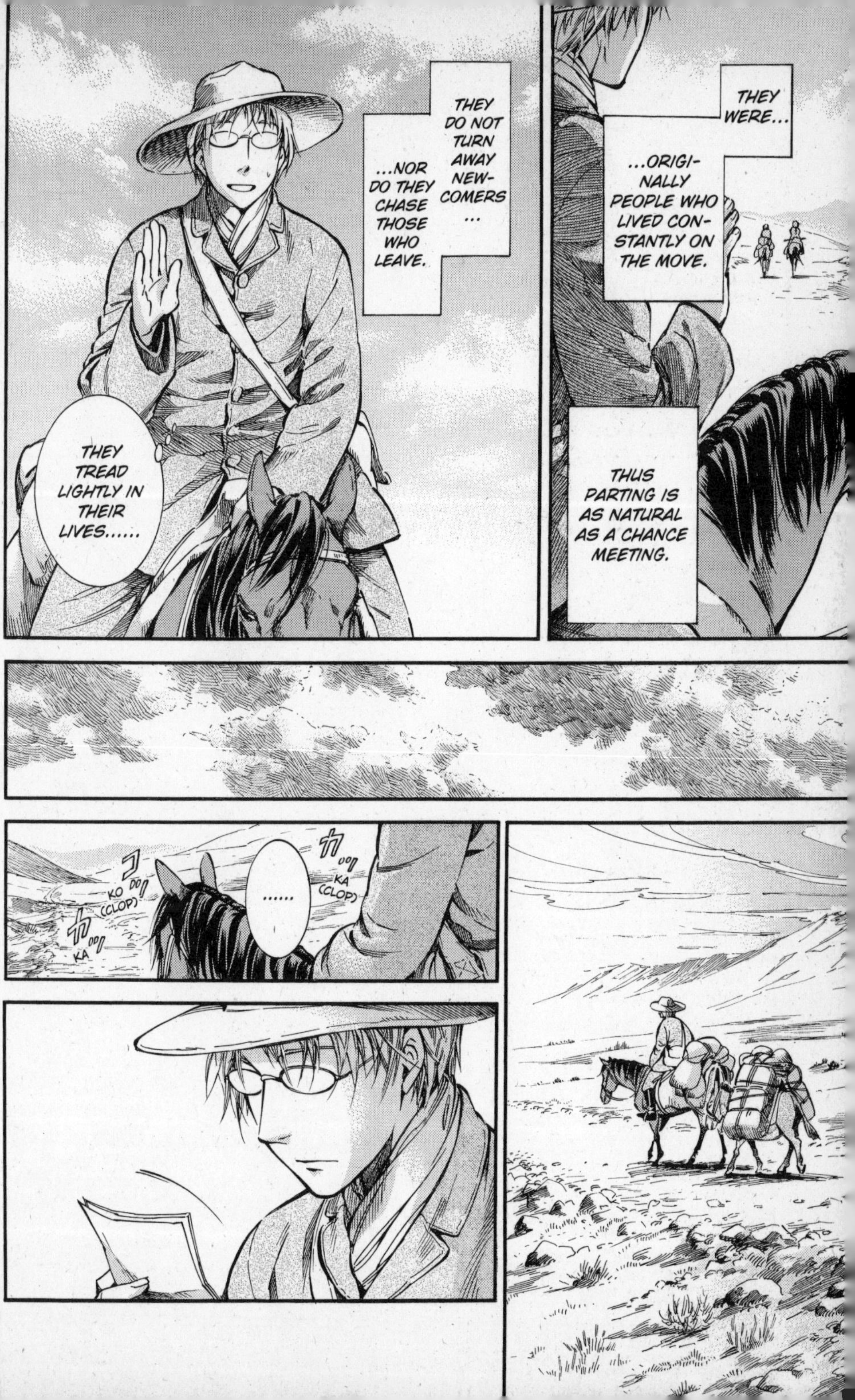
THEY WERE...
...ORIGINALLY PEOPLE WHO LIVED CONSTANTLY ON THE MOVE.
THUS PARTING IS AS NATURAL AS A CHANCE MEETING.
THEY DO NOT TURN AWAY NEWCOMERS...
...NOR DO THEY CHASE THOSE WHO LEAVE.
THEY TREAD LIGHTLY IN THEIR LIVES......
KA (CLOP)
......
KO (CLOP)
KA

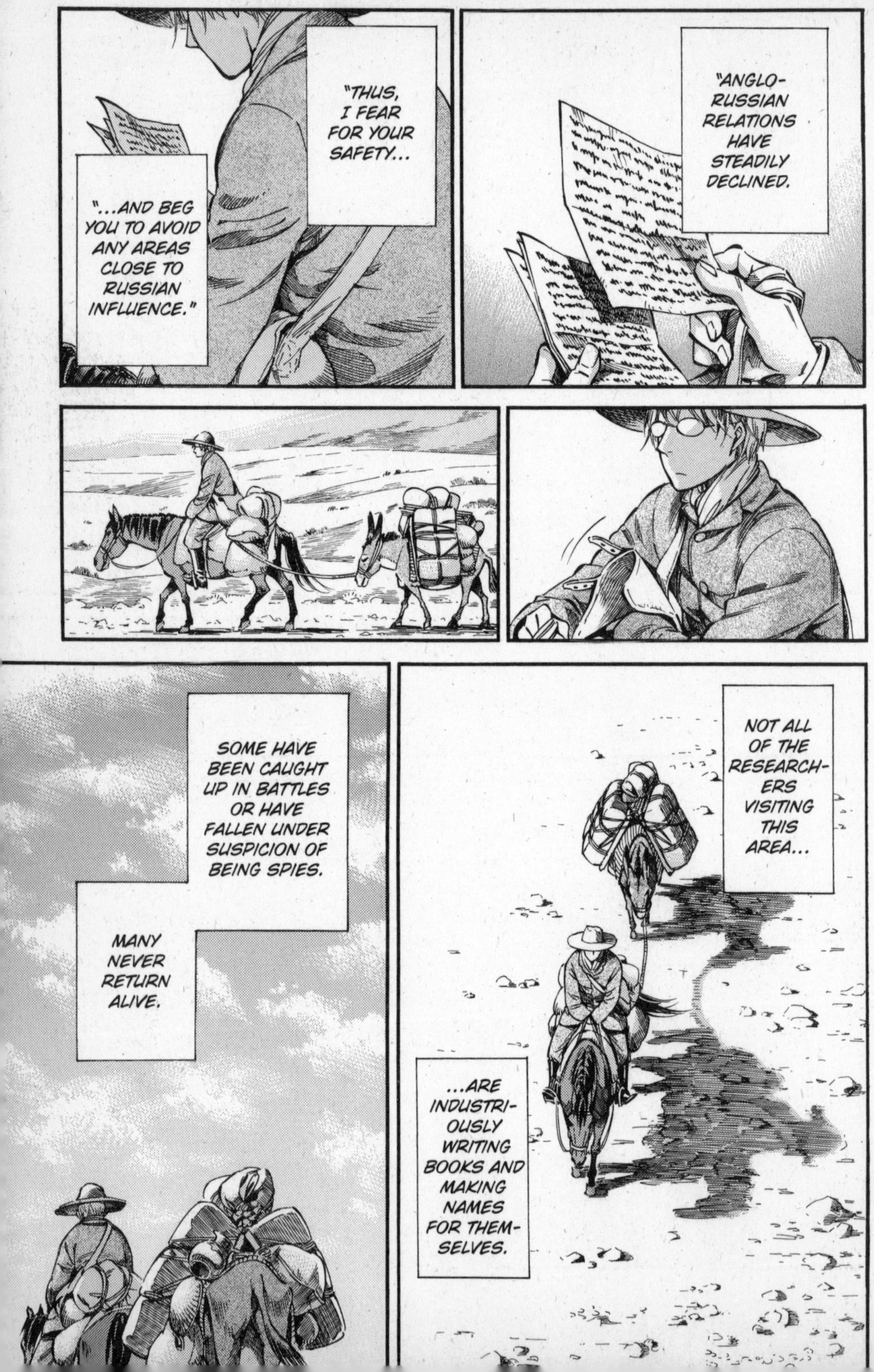
"ANGLO-RUSSIAN RELATIONS HAVE STEADILY DECLINED.
"THUS, I FEAR FOR YOUR SAFETY...
"...AND BEG YOU TO AVOID ANY AREAS CLOSE TO RUSSIAN INFLUENCE."
NOT ALL OF THE RESEARCHERS VISITING THIS AREA...
...ARE INDUSTRIOUSLY WRITING BOOKS AND MAKING NAMES FOR THEMSELVES.
SOME HAVE BEEN CAUGHT UP IN BATTLES OR HAVE FALLEN UNDER SUSPICION OF BEING SPIES.
MANY NEVER RETURN ALIVE.

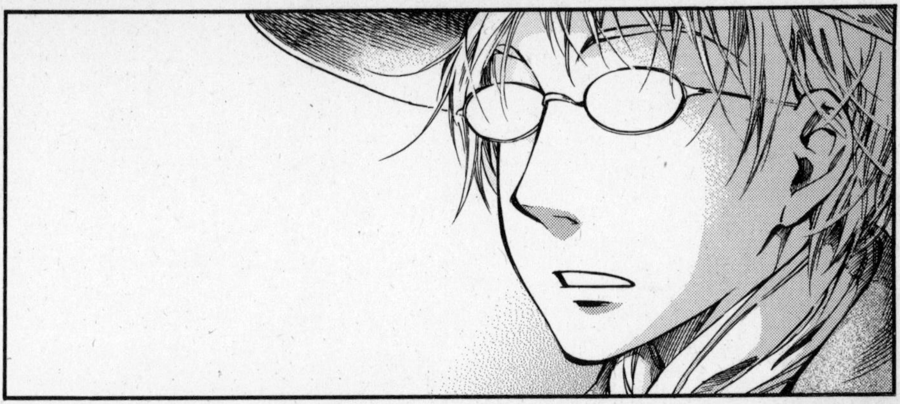

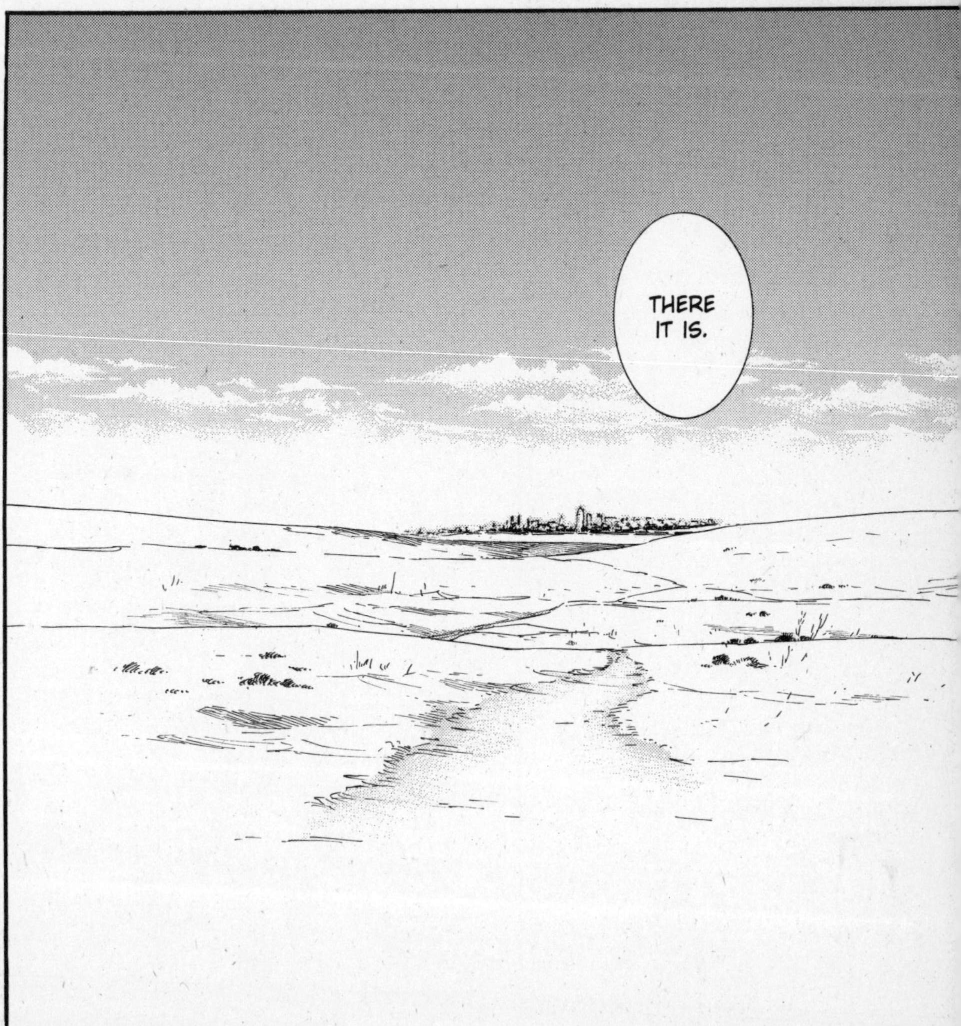
THERE IT IS.

✦ Chapter Eleven: End ✦

AFTERWORD

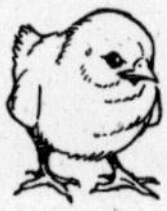
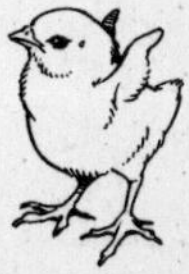

AFTERWORD TAN-TA-DAAH MANGA

"THE MOUNTAIN WHERE I ONCE CHASED RABBITS"

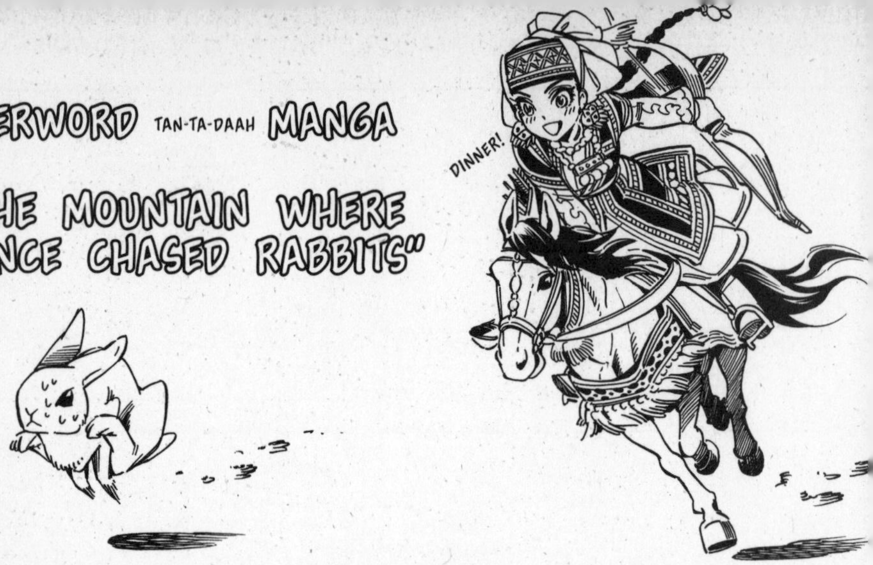
DINNER!

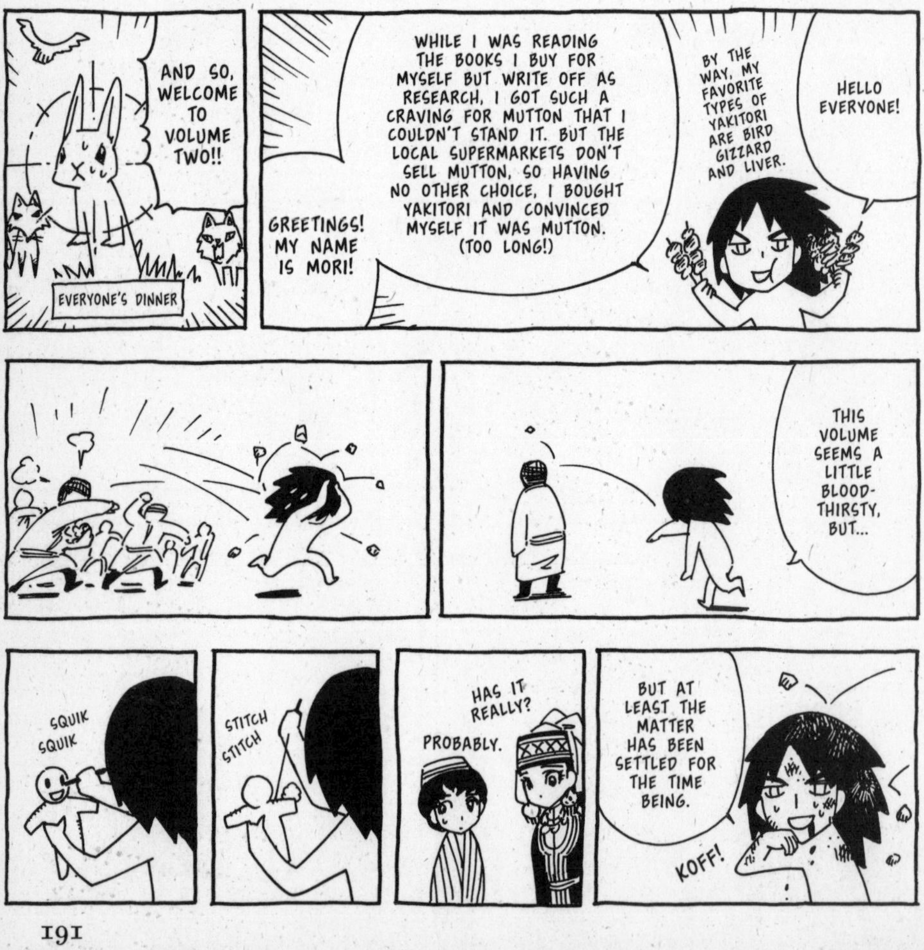
HELLO EVERYONE!
BY THE WAY, MY FAVORITE TYPES OF YAKITORI ARE BIRD GIZZARD AND LIVER.
WHILE I WAS READING THE BOOKS I BUY FOR MYSELF BUT WRITE OFF AS RESEARCH, I GOT SUCH A CRAVING FOR MUTTON THAT I COULDN'T STAND IT. BUT THE LOCAL SUPERMARKETS DON'T SELL MUTTON, SO HAVING NO OTHER CHOICE, I BOUGHT YAKITORI AND CONVINCED MYSELF IT WAS MUTTON. (TOO LONG!)
GREETINGS! MY NAME IS MORI!
AND SO, WELCOME TO VOLUME TWO!!
EVERYONE'S DINNER
THIS VOLUME SEEMS A LITTLE BLOOD-THIRSTY, BUT...
BUT AT LEAST THE MATTER HAS BEEN SETTLED FOR THE TIME BEING.
KOFF!
HAS IT REALLY?
PROBABLY.
STITCH STITCH
SQUIK SQUIK

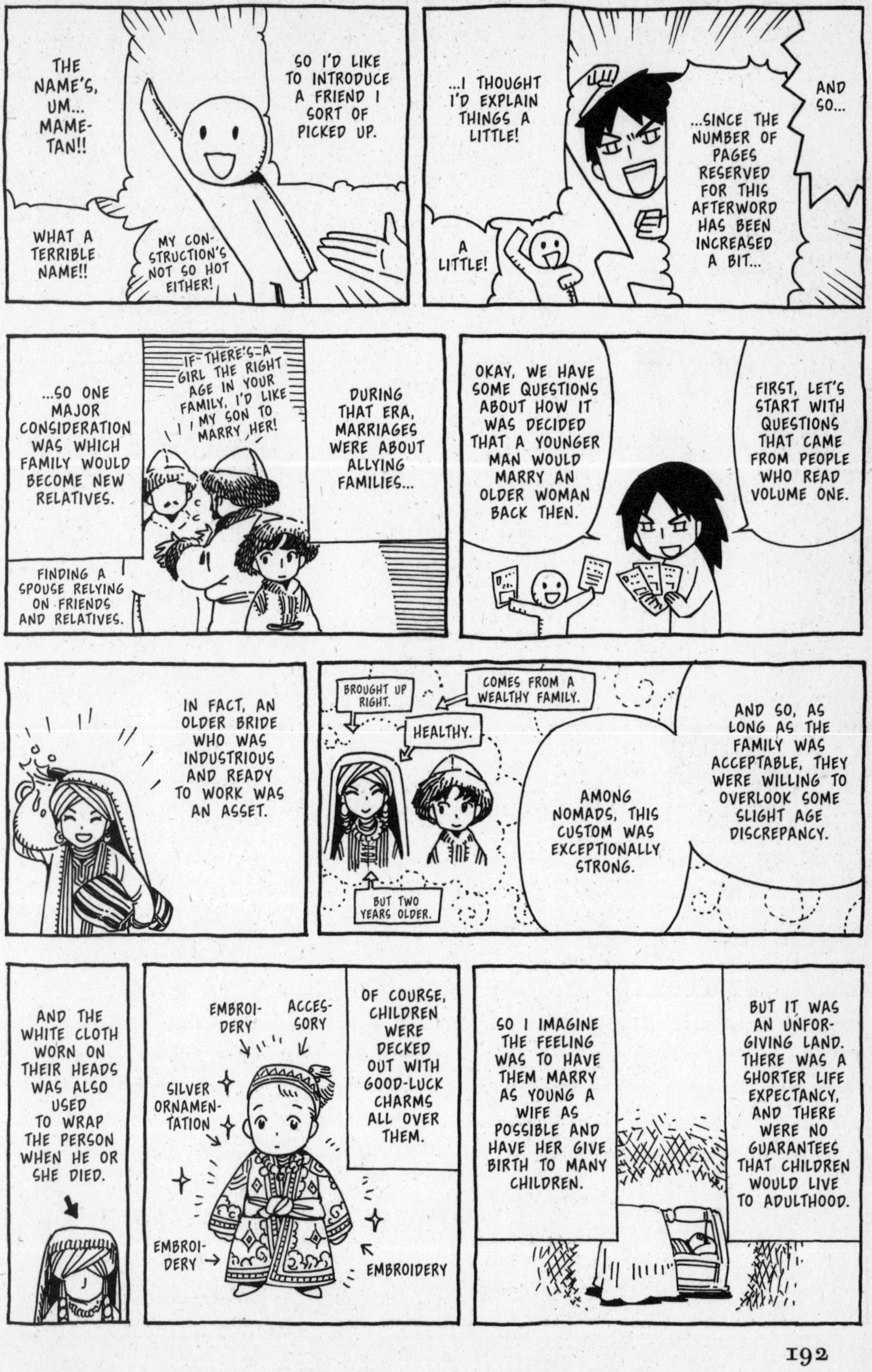
AND SO...
...SINCE THE NUMBER OF PAGES RESERVED FOR THIS AFTERWORD HAS BEEN INCREASED A BIT...
...I THOUGHT I'D EXPLAIN THINGS A LITTLE!
A LITTLE!
SO I'D LIKE TO INTRODUCE A FRIEND I SORT OF PICKED UP.
THE NAME'S, UM... MAME-TAN!!
MY CONSTRUCTION'S NOT SO HOT EITHER!
WHAT A TERRIBLE NAME!!
FIRST, LET'S START WITH QUESTIONS THAT CAME FROM PEOPLE WHO READ VOLUME ONE.
OKAY, WE HAVE SOME QUESTIONS ABOUT HOW IT WAS DECIDED THAT A YOUNGER MAN WOULD MARRY AN OLDER WOMAN BACK THEN.
DURING THAT ERA, MARRIAGES WERE ABOUT ALLYING FAMILIES...
IF THERE'S A GIRL THE RIGHT AGE IN YOUR FAMILY, I'D LIKE MY SON TO MARRY HER!
...SO ONE MAJOR CONSIDERATION WAS WHICH FAMILY WOULD BECOME NEW RELATIVES.
FINDING A SPOUSE RELYING ON FRIENDS AND RELATIVES.
AND SO, AS LONG AS THE FAMILY WAS ACCEPTABLE, THEY WERE WILLING TO OVERLOOK SOME SLIGHT AGE DISCREPANCY.
AMONG NOMADS, THIS CUSTOM WAS EXCEPTIONALLY STRONG.
COMES FROM A WEALTHY FAMILY.
BROUGHT UP RIGHT.
HEALTHY.
BUT TWO YEARS OLDER.
IN FACT, AN OLDER BRIDE WHO WAS INDUSTRIOUS AND READY TO WORK WAS AN ASSET.
BUT IT WAS AN UNFORGIVING LAND. THERE WAS A SHORTER LIFE EXPECTANCY, AND THERE WERE NO GUARANTEES THAT CHILDREN WOULD LIVE TO ADULTHOOD.
SO I IMAGINE THE FEELING WAS TO HAVE THEM MARRY AS YOUNG A WIFE AS POSSIBLE AND HAVE HER GIVE BIRTH TO MANY CHILDREN.
OF COURSE, CHILDREN WERE DECKED OUT WITH GOOD-LUCK CHARMS ALL OVER THEM.
ACCESSORY
EMBROIDERY
SILVER ORNAMENTATION
EMBROIDERY
EMBROIDERY
AND THE WHITE CLOTH WORN ON THEIR HEADS WAS ALSO USED TO WRAP THE PERSON WHEN HE OR SHE DIED.

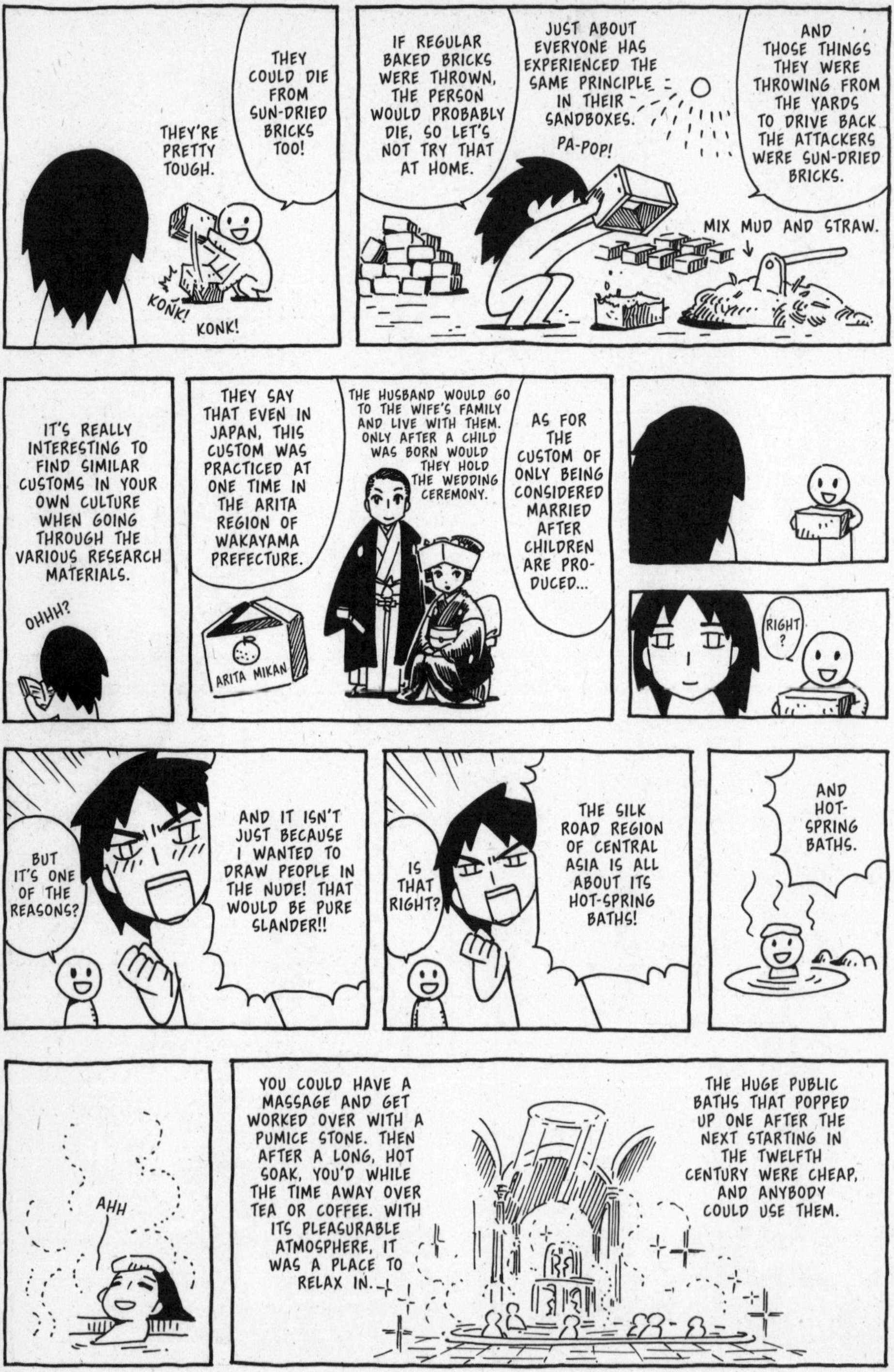
AND THOSE THINGS THEY WERE THROWING FROM THE YARDS TO DRIVE BACK THE ATTACKERS WERE SUN-DRIED BRICKS.
JUST ABOUT EVERYONE HAS EXPERIENCED THE SAME PRINCIPLE IN THEIR SANDBOXES.
IF REGULAR BAKED BRICKS WERE THROWN, THE PERSON WOULD PROBABLY DIE, SO LET'S NOT TRY THAT AT HOME.
PA-POP!
MIX MUD AND STRAW.
THEY COULD DIE FROM SUN-DRIED BRICKS TOO!
THEY'RE PRETTY TOUGH.
KONK!
KONK!
RIGHT?
AS FOR THE CUSTOM OF ONLY BEING CONSIDERED MARRIED AFTER CHILDREN ARE PRO-DUCED...
THE HUSBAND WOULD GO TO THE WIFE'S FAMILY AND LIVE WITH THEM. ONLY AFTER A CHILD WAS BORN WOULD THEY HOLD THE WEDDING CEREMONY.
THEY SAY THAT EVEN IN JAPAN, THIS CUSTOM WAS PRACTICED AT ONE TIME IN THE ARITA REGION OF WAKAYAMA PREFECTURE.
ARITA MIKAN
IT'S REALLY INTERESTING TO FIND SIMILAR CUSTOMS IN YOUR OWN CULTURE WHEN GOING THROUGH THE VARIOUS RESEARCH MATERIALS.
OHHH?
AND HOT-SPRING BATHS.
THE SILK ROAD REGION OF CENTRAL ASIA IS ALL ABOUT ITS HOT-SPRING BATHS!
IS THAT RIGHT?
AND IT ISN'T JUST BECAUSE I WANTED TO DRAW PEOPLE IN THE NUDE! THAT WOULD BE PURE SLANDER!!
BUT IT'S ONE OF THE REASONS?
THE HUGE PUBLIC BATHS THAT POPPED UP ONE AFTER THE NEXT STARTING IN THE TWELFTH CENTURY WERE CHEAP, AND ANYBODY COULD USE THEM.
YOU COULD HAVE A MASSAGE AND GET WORKED OVER WITH A PUMICE STONE. THEN AFTER A LONG, HOT SOAK, YOU'D WHILE THE TIME AWAY OVER TEA OR COFFEE. WITH ITS PLEASURABLE ATMOSPHERE, IT WAS A PLACE TO RELAX IN.
AHH

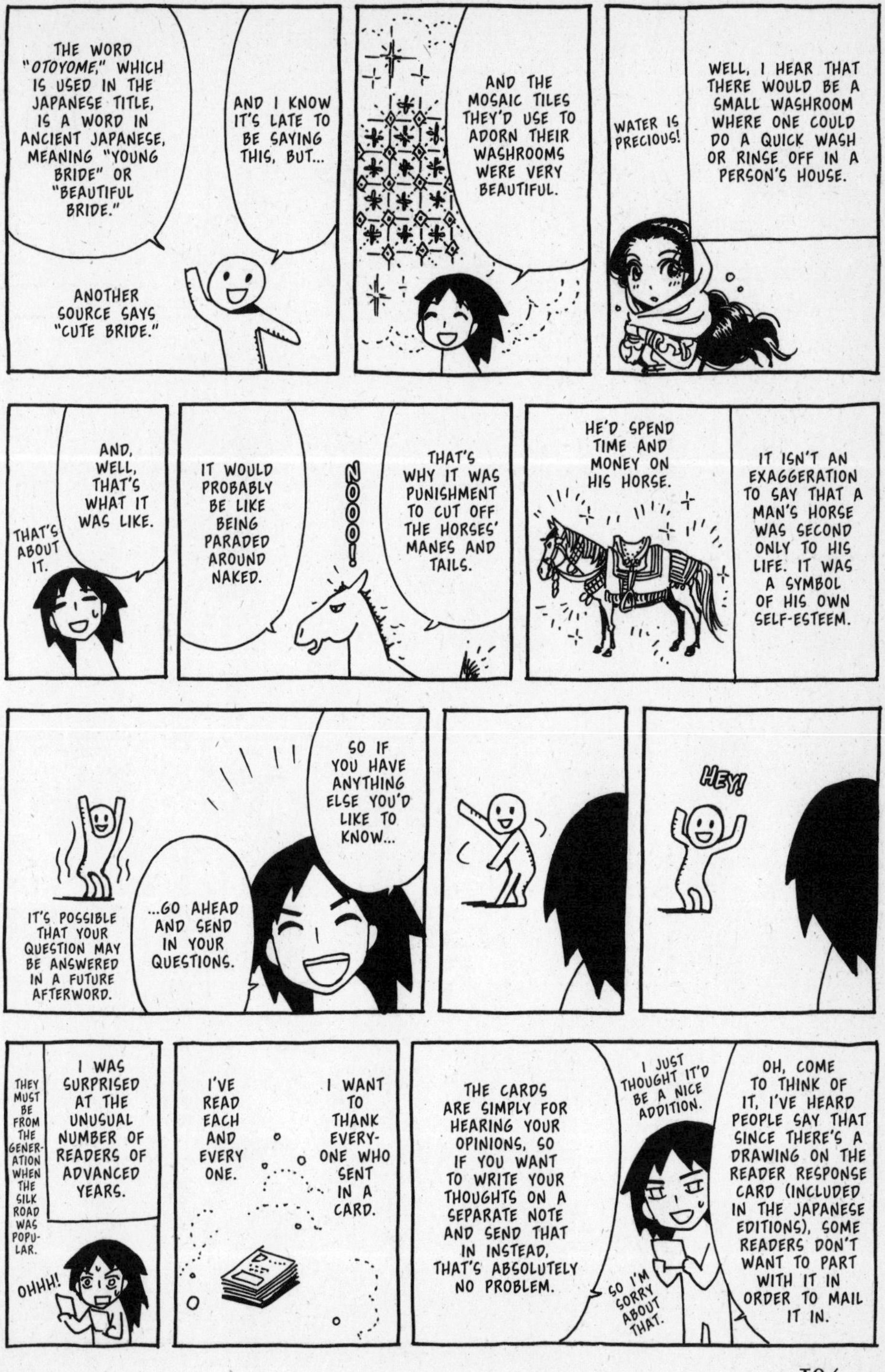
WELL, I HEAR THAT THERE WOULD BE A SMALL WASHROOM WHERE ONE COULD DO A QUICK WASH OR RINSE OFF IN A PERSON'S HOUSE.
WATER IS PRECIOUS!
AND THE MOSAIC TILES THEY'D USE TO ADORN THEIR WASHROOMS WERE VERY BEAUTIFUL.
AND I KNOW IT'S LATE TO BE SAYING THIS, BUT...
THE WORD "OTOYOME," WHICH IS USED IN THE JAPANESE TITLE, IS A WORD IN ANCIENT JAPANESE, MEANING "YOUNG BRIDE" OR "BEAUTIFUL BRIDE."
ANOTHER SOURCE SAYS "CUTE BRIDE."
IT ISN'T AN EXAGGERATION TO SAY THAT A MAN'S HORSE WAS SECOND ONLY TO HIS LIFE. IT WAS A SYMBOL OF HIS OWN SELF-ESTEEM.
HE'D SPEND TIME AND MONEY ON HIS HORSE.
THAT'S WHY IT WAS PUNISHMENT TO CUT OFF THE HORSES' MANES AND TAILS.
NOOOO!
IT WOULD PROBABLY BE LIKE BEING PARADED AROUND NAKED.
AND, WELL, THAT'S WHAT IT WAS LIKE.
THAT'S ABOUT IT.
HEY!
SO IF YOU HAVE ANYTHING ELSE YOU'D LIKE TO KNOW...
...GO AHEAD AND SEND IN YOUR QUESTIONS.
IT'S POSSIBLE THAT YOUR QUESTION MAY BE ANSWERED IN A FUTURE AFTERWORD.
OH, COME TO THINK OF IT, I'VE HEARD PEOPLE SAY THAT SINCE THERE'S A DRAWING ON THE READER RESPONSE CARD (INCLUDED IN THE JAPANESE EDITIONS), SOME READERS DON'T WANT TO PART WITH IT IN ORDER TO MAIL IT IN.
I JUST THOUGHT IT'D BE A NICE ADDITION.
SO I'M SORRY ABOUT THAT.
THE CARDS ARE SIMPLY FOR HEARING YOUR OPINIONS, SO IF YOU WANT TO WRITE YOUR THOUGHTS ON A SEPARATE NOTE AND SEND THAT IN INSTEAD, THAT'S ABSOLUTELY NO PROBLEM.
I WANT TO THANK EVERYONE WHO SENT IN A CARD.
I'VE READ EACH AND EVERY ONE.
I WAS SURPRISED AT THE UNUSUAL NUMBER OF READERS OF ADVANCED YEARS.
THEY MUST BE FROM THE GENERATION WHEN THE SILK ROAD WAS POPULAR.
OHHH!

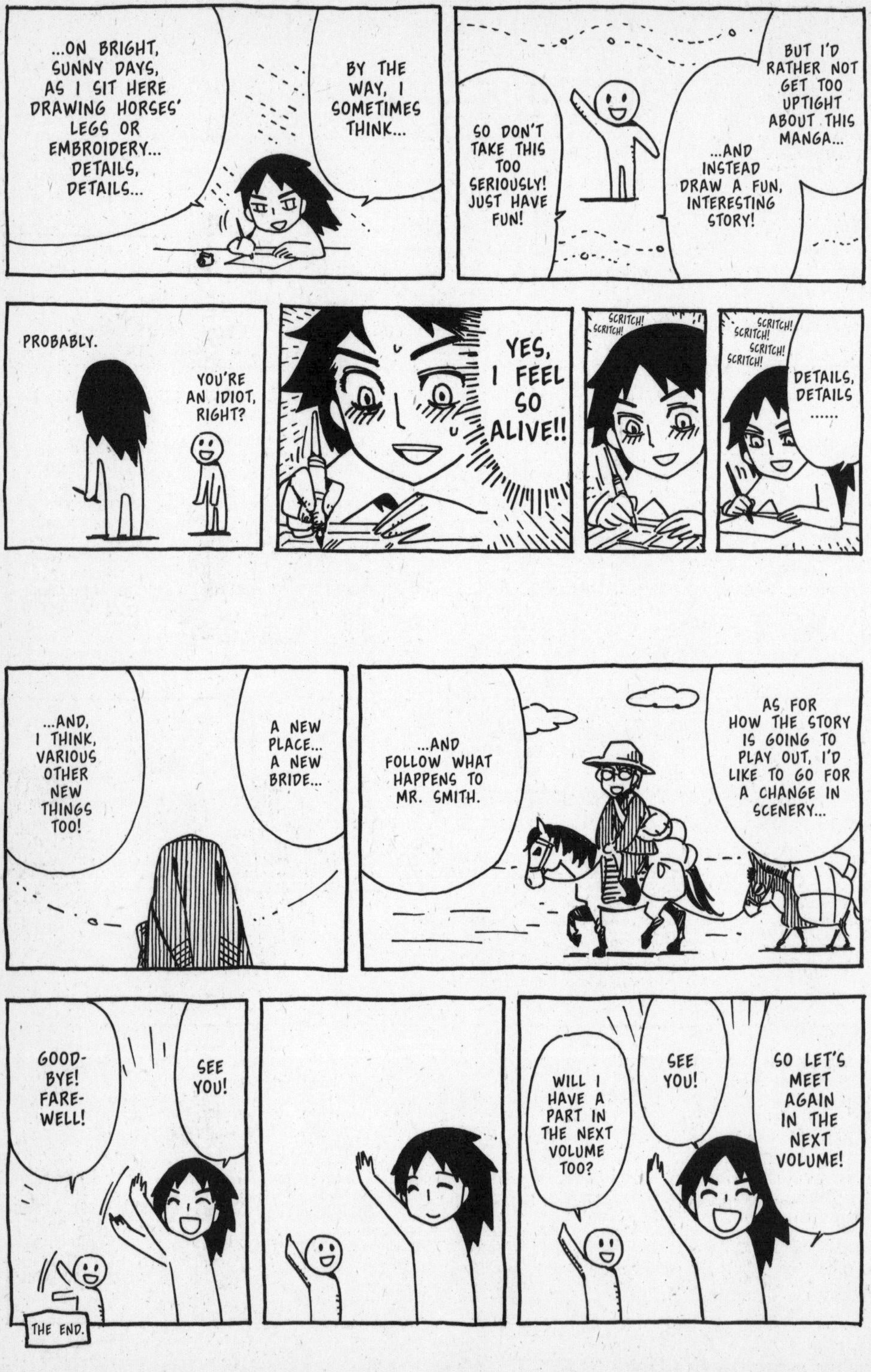
BUT I'D RATHER NOT GET TOO UPTIGHT ABOUT THIS MANGA...
...AND INSTEAD DRAW A FUN, INTERESTING STORY!
SO DON'T TAKE THIS TOO SERIOUSLY! JUST HAVE FUN!
BY THE WAY, I SOMETIMES THINK...
...ON BRIGHT, SUNNY DAYS, AS I SIT HERE DRAWING HORSES' LEGS OR EMBROIDERY... DETAILS, DETAILS...
SCRITCH! SCRITCH! SCRITCH! SCRITCH!
DETAILS, DETAILS ......
SCRITCH! SCRITCH!
YES, I FEEL SO ALIVE!!
YOU'RE AN IDIOT, RIGHT?
PROBABLY.
AS FOR HOW THE STORY IS GOING TO PLAY OUT, I'D LIKE TO GO FOR A CHANGE IN SCENERY...
...AND FOLLOW WHAT HAPPENS TO MR. SMITH.
A NEW PLACE... A NEW BRIDE...
...AND, I THINK, VARIOUS OTHER NEW THINGS TOO!
SO LET'S MEET AGAIN IN THE NEXT VOLUME!
SEE YOU!
WILL I HAVE A PART IN THE NEXT VOLUME TOO?
SEE YOU!
GOOD-BYE! FARE-WELL!
THE END.

A BRIDE'S STORY ②

KAORU MORI

TRANSLATION: WILLIAM FLANAGAN

LETTERING: ABIGAIL BLACKMAN

A BRIDE'S STORY Volume 2 © 2010 Kaoru Mori All rights reserved.
First published in Japan in 2010 by ENTERBRAIN, INC., Tokyo.
English translation rights arranged with ENTERBRAIN, INC.
through Tuttle-Mori Agency, Inc., Tokyo.

Translation © 2011 by Hachette Book Group

Yen Press
Hachette Book Group
237 Park Avenue, New York, NY 10017

www.HachetteBookGroup.com
www.YenPress.com

Yen Press is an imprint of Hachette Book Group, Inc. The Yen Press
name and logo are trademarks of Hachette Book Group, Inc.

First Yen Press Edition: October 2011

ISBN: 978-0-316-19446-4

10 9 8 7 6 5 4 3 2 1

BVG

Printed in the United States of America